Fang Mu
—Eastern Crime Series

Profiler

Author: Lei Mi
Translator: Gabriel Ascher

He who fights with monsters should be careful, lest he thereby become a monster. And if thou gaze long into an abyss, the abyss will also gaze into thee. ——Friedrich Nietzsche

CONTENTS

PREFACE

Freak

They came for me again last night.

As before, they quietly surrounded my bed, not saying a word. As before, I lay frozen in place, staring wide-eyed at their scorched and headless bodies. And as before, he leaned in close and whispered into my ear: "Actually, you and I are the same."

By then I was used to meeting them in the night. And yet, I was still dripping with sweat.

At last they left without a word, and I could once more hear the sound of Du Yu breathing peacefully on the bed across the room.

A cold shaft of moonlight streamed through the window. The flames had disappeared. The air was a little cool.

I heaved myself onto my stomach and reached for the military dagger hidden beneath my pillow. As I grasped its scarred handle, my breathing grew calm.

Soon I was once more fast asleep.

Occasionally I still visit the old teacher's college. I sit amid the flowerbeds on a bench that faces the door to Men's Dormitory 2. An ancient scholar tree once stood there, but now there are flowers of all colors and sizes, their names unknown to me. They wave coquettishly in the faint breeze without a care in the world. Often I will stare at the building before me, a modern, seven-story student apartment block, and do my best to remember how it used to look: faded red brick, tottering wooden window frames, paint peeling from the iron outer door.

And I will see the faces of the young students who once lived here.

Without warning, my heart will seize with pain, as if struck by a sudden sadness. And in this moment of distraction, the floodgates to my memory will quietly slide open, unleashing an endless torrent.

If you knew me, you'd probably think I was a loner. Most of the time, I make an effort to keep to myself. I eat alone, I walk alone. Even when I'm in class, I avoid sitting with anyone else.

Stay away. That's what the look in my eyes says to anyone who tries to understand me. But while people keep their distance, I still know all about them; their behavior, their temperaments, their daily habits. So if you're in class, in the cafeteria, or walking around campus, and you see a pale, carelessly-dressed young man who's sizing-up everyone around him, that's me.

I live in Room 313, Building B of Dormitory 5 at Jiangbin City University. My roommate is named Du Yu, a post-grad studying for his Master's in Jurisprudence. Seeing as we live together and are both at the law school, he's one of the few people I talk to on a regular basis. He's a sweet-natured guy, and is always trying to get me to hang out so I won't "seem so lonely all the time"—not that I care, of course. Still, I don't mind chatting with him from time to time, nor with Zhang Yao, his slightly over-the-top-delicate girlfriend.

"Hey, let's eat together."

I was eating a bowl of hand-cut noodles slathered in chili paste and focusing intently on my computer screen, which was displaying several photographs and their accompanying descriptions. I hadn't noticed Du Yu and his girlfriend came in.

They were barbecued lamb skewers that seemed to have just gotten out of the fire. The meat was sprinkled with chili and cumin powder and dripped with yellow grease. Du Yu held one out for me. A scorched odor flooded my nostrils.

In an instant my face must have turned whiter than the wall behind me. I stared blankly at the outstretched kabob. Then my stomach burbled, I retched, and vomited a mouthful of half-chewed noodles back into my bowl.

Covering my mouth, I grabbed the bowl—now filled to the brim with the still-steaming contents of my stomach—and rushed out of the room. Behind me I could hear Zhang Yao cry out in surprise, "What's wrong with him?"

Drained, I leaned over the bathroom sink and scrubbed my face with water. When I looked up, the dirty mirror on the wall reflected a pale face, dripping with water and cold sweat. A dull look was in its eyes and traces of vomit stuck to the corners of its mouth.

Again I bent over and retched, but I could feel my stomach was empty. There was nothing left to expel. So I climbed shakily to my feet, put my face under the tap, and gulped several mouthfuls of cold water. I swished it around in my mouth and then spat it back out.

Tossing the bowl in the trash, I stumbled back to my room.

The place was a mess. Zhang Yao was sitting on Du Yu's bed, her head between her knees. A big pool of vomit covered the floor before her and an acidic odor filled the room. Holding his nose, Du Yu tossed a washbasin in front of his girlfriend.

Seeing me enter, Zhang Yao looked up. Her face was soaked with tears and sweat. Pointing at me, she tried to say something, but was racked by another fierce bout of vomiting.

Du Yu gave me an awkward look. "Yaoyao was curious what was up with you just now, so she went to look at your computer screen. She only glanced at it for a second before..."

I ignored him and walked straight to my computer. The monitor still showed the web page I had been browsing. On it were several photographs. One was of a rotted skull, the skin of its face and neck already peeled away. The other three were of the victim's limbless torso and of her left and right hands. These pictures were from the scene of a murder committed in Wisconsin in the year 2000. After downloading them to my hard drive, I saved them in a folder titled: "Excessive Damage".

When I was done, I stood up and walked over to Zhang Yao. I bent down beside her. "You all right?" I asked.

Zhang Yao was so weak from throwing up that she was practically limp. When she saw me, she looked terrified and tried to back away. "Don't come near me!" she cried.

Trembling, she raised one arm, pointed at the computer, and then pointed at me. For a moment, her lips quivered. At last, through clenched teeth, she spat out a single word: "Freak!"

"Yaoyao!" yelled Du Yu, giving me an uneasy look.

I grinned at him to show I didn't mind.

After all, I really didn't. I am a freak. I know.

My name is Fang Mu. Two years ago, something terrible happened, and I was the only survivor.

1 RAPING THE CITY

Jiangbin City had been having an unusually muggy spring. The trees were still bare, without a single green bud in sight, but the temperature was already over 65 degrees. It was on one such hot day that Tai Wei came flying down the road in his jeep, impatiently buttoning his shirt as he drove.

He was on edge, but it wasn't just because of the weather. In his ten years on the police force, Tai Wei had never faced a case as thorny as this one.

On March 14, 2002, in Building 32 of the Brilliant Pearl Residential Area at 83 Taipei Street in the Hongyuan District of Jiangbin City, Ms Chen – female, Han Chinese, 31-year-old – was murdered in her home, Apartment 402. According to the autopsy, the victim died sometime between the hours of two and three in the afternoon, due to mechanical asphyxiation. There were deep bruises on the victim's neck, making strangulation the clear cause of death. An investigation of the crime scene did not find any sign that the apartment had been ransacked, nor that any valuables were taken. As a result, it was deemed unlikely that the murder had happened during the course of a robbery. The victim was discovered naked from the waist up, however from the waist down she was clothed normally, and there was no sign of sexual assault. All in all, it did not have the makings of an ordinary burglary, rape and murder case. But the strangest part was that after the victim was dead, the killer had disemboweled her with a knife, which was then left at the crime scene. The victim's husband later identified this as one of their kitchen knives. The scene itself was horrifying, covered in the victim's blood and viscera. In the kitchen, police located a cup containing trace amounts of an unknown liquid. Tests later determined this to be a mixture of milk and the victim's blood.

This couldn't help but cause those involved to think of a certain mythical monster—the vampire.

Over the following month and a half, two more victims were murdered in their homes. Both were women, between the ages of 25 and 35, and both were found disemboweled. A container, holding remnants of a mixture of blood and other matter, was also found at each scene.

In this mid-sized city of two million residents, homicides were common enough to be almost trivial; however these murders were so savage and strange that they raised a storm of suspicion. All across Jiangbin City, rumors were soon flying back and forth. Had an ancient vampire been revived from its thousand-year slumber? Had the biological weapons left behind by the Japanese invaders during World War II caused some terrible genetic mutation? And these were just the beginning. City Hall started paying attention, too, and they ordered the Public Security Bureau to crack the case as soon as possible.

A special investigation team was quickly established, but one week had passed since then with no progress whatsoever. Just as things were beginning to look bad, Ding Shucheng, a Changhong City Criminal Police officer visiting Jiangbin City on police business, made a startling suggestion: they should talk to a certain Criminology post-grad studying at Jiangbin City University.

Tai Wei was one of the leaders of the special team, and at first he thought Ding Shucheng was joking. But the visiting officer swore he was not, and told Tai Wei the following story.

In the summer of 2001, four successive acts of rape and murder were committed in Changhong City. The four victims were all female, white-collar workers between the ages of 25 and 30, and after being raped, all four were strangled to death with a rope. The murders took place on the top floor balcony of four different high-rises that were then still under construction. At the time, Xing Zhisen, Ding Shucheng's direct superior and the leader of Changhong City's Criminal Police Unit, had just been promoted to Deputy Director of the entire Public Security Bureau, and he wasted no time in making his presence felt. After revealing the case to the local media, he appeared on television and promised that it would be cracked within two weeks. Two days later, a letter appeared on the desk of the special investigation team. Its writer had watched Deputy Director Xing's recent TV appearance, and in the letter he asserted that the killer was a sexual psychopath unable to have normal relationships with women, which caused him to exercise his desires through rape and murder. The writer even went so far as to conclude that the killer was less than 30-year-old.

At first, the policemen who read the letter assumed it was no more than the amateur effort of some detective fiction fanatic, and they ignored it. But when Deputy Director Xing heard about it, he was intrigued, and he assigned someone to investigate the letter writer's background. Once it was determined that the writer was one Fang Mu, a senior at Changhong City Teacher's College, Deputy Director Xing became very excited, and had Fang Mu brought to the station at once. After the two of them spoke privately in Xing's office for half an hour, the Deputy Director personally drove Fang Mu to each of the four crime scenes. When they returned, all the data from all four murders was brought to Deputy Director Xing's office, where Fang Mu pored over it in detail. Later that night (as according to the autopsies, the murders had each taken place between 10 and 11 pm), Fang Mu was driven back to the crime scenes. This time, Ding Shucheng came along as well. While on the exposed top floor of one of the buildings (which, at the time, happened to be the tallest of the four), the kid stood in silence for a very long time.

Finally, he said something that Ding Shucheng would never forget.

"He's not raping those women, he's raping the city!"

When they returned to the station, Fang Mu made the following suggestions to the special investigation team: First, search every seedy video playhouse in the city, especially those located near construction sites, for a right-handed, short-haired, fairly thin man between 20- and 25-years-old, standing 5'3" to 5'5", wearing glasses, a watch on his left hand and with a scratch on his left wrist, and possessing no more than a high school education. Second, conduct a citywide search of every construction team with projects underway for a man with the above-mentioned characteristics. Third, investigate the towns and villages near Changhong City for evidence of a former resident with said characteristics who failed the College Entrance Exam and then moved to the city to work—with an emphasis on only children with no female elders, or boys with older brothers but no sisters. He even went so far as to say that at the time of the killer's arrest, he would likely be wearing a white-collared dress shirt.

Hearing this seemingly wild-eyed speculation, the members of the special investigation team remained somewhat unconvinced; however Deputy Director Xing ordered that they begin searching for a suspect according to Fang Mu's advice. Two days later, the boss of a small video playhouse by the train station said that she knew a man who fit those characteristics; he worked at a nearby construction site. The workers from that site would often arrive in groups to watch movies, however this man always came alone, and only in the hours after midnight when pornographic films were shown. One time, while he was at the theater watching such a film, another worker from his site arrived, and at once the man blushed red from embarrassment and sneaked out. This event left a deep impression on the theater boss, and as a result she remembered the man well.

The police then traveled to the construction site in question, and with the theater boss in tow, they located the man in one of the on-site work sheds. His name was Huang Yongxiao, and he was the project's surveyor. As soon as the police produced identification and asked to see Huang Yongxiao's left wrist, the man leaped to his feet and attempted to flee, however he was quickly apprehended. After being brought back to the station for interrogation, Huang Yongxiao admitted that he had raped and killed the four women, and confessed to everything.

Huang Yongxiao was 21-year-old, a high school graduate, and a former resident of the town of Batai, near Changhong City. After flunking the College Entrance Exam in 2000, he decided to redo his final year of high school and retake the test; however, he failed again. Afterwards, he followed his paternal uncle and moved to Changhong City. There he worked on numerous construction projects, but never on any for long. Later, with the help of his uncle, he was recommended to this most recent project, and because he had a high school education, was made a surveyor. Huang Yongxiao had always impressed people as a nice, quiet young man, so it was shocking to learn that he had committed these horrifying crimes.

It also did not pass unnoticed that at the time of his arrest, Huang Yongxiao was wearing a white-collared dress shirt—which, although very old, had been washed exceedingly clean.

Fang Mu's description of the killer's appearance, family background, work environment, and lifestyle were startling close to those of Huang Yongxiao. The only discrepancies were that Huang's parents had divorced several years ago and he had no brothers, only an older sister who had gone to live with their mother and her new husband, and with whom he had long-since lost contact. But despite these errors, the officers of the special investigation team had already begun treating Fang Mu, this unremarkable-looking young man, with newfound respect. They even went so far as to wonder whether he'd actually been present during Huang Yongxiao's crimes—for how else could his judgments have been so accurate?

Fang Mu explained himself as follows: Based on his analysis of the crime scenes and the data, he had learned that all four victims had had their pants pulled down just below their knees, and their knees themselves scratched up. Also, traces of skin had been discovered on the balcony railings of each building and that skin perfectly matched the respective scrapes found on the breasts of the four women. This suggested that the killer had chosen to rape his victims from behind.

This was a most significant position.

First of all, if a man either holds down a woman's torso or grabs her arms while he is entering her from behind, her ability to struggle will be extremely diminished. And because the women's pants were down around their knees, their leg movements would have been restricted as well. Consequently, this position is the least likely to encounter any effective resistance on the part of the victim.

Second, from a psychosexual standpoint, doggy-style is the most primitive sexual position; as a result, it gives the man the most intense feelings of "conquering" and satisfaction. Therefore, for the man, it is far more psychologically arousing than any other position.

When Fang Mu had stood atop those buildings under the dark sky, he had been given a panoramic view of the whole nighttime cityscape: the immense buildings ablaze with lights in the distance ahead, the flickering river of cars rushing far below his feet.

Savagely thrusting back and forth. The woman beneath him: high class, well-dressed, struggling in vain. The city arrayed before his eyes, filling his heart with delight.

Fang Mu closed his eyes.

Somewhere out there, in some luxury apartment, there's a man anxiously waiting for his wife to come home. Whoever you are, I bet you'd never guess that right now I'm raping your woman—straddling her like a dog!

In his eyes, the whole city was probably nothing more than a gigantic cunt.

And in that moment, he must have felt the delight of conquering it—of conquering the entire city.

Which meant that, in reality, this guy had to be a loser.

Since the killer was raping and murdering his victims as a way of venting his hatred for society, sexual behavior had to possess a special significance for him. The mystery of it must have made him far more curious and excited than the average person. But at the same time, these feelings must have caused him deep shame. When boys are able to form normal relationships with girls from a young age, these sorts of excessively strong feelings toward sex will lessen as their socialization increases. Therefore, the killer was very likely a man unable to form such relationships. And as is often the case with such individuals, he probably grew up in an environment that lacked female affection. Additionally, given his psychological makeup, he was certain to be quite young—for as he grew older, this aberrant sexual fixation would likely be eliminated through normal social experience. And because these problems generally arise during adolescence, an older man still suffering from them would long since have committed a similar crime—however, nothing of the sort had been seen in the city in years.

Thus, the murderer: Male, 25 or younger, from a home with either no female elders or only brothers, and with a history of failure.

As for the location of the crimes, the top floor of an unfinished building clearly satisfied the killer's psychological need to conquer the city. At the same time, it showed that he was familiar with this sort of environment. Therefore, the killer was likely to have had experience working at a construction site.

And given his low wages and psychosexual aberrance, it was probable that he used pornography. Prostitutes? Unlikely, though even if he had visited them, it couldn't have been too many times. His economic situation simply wouldn't allow for it.

Those seedy video playhouses, which often showed pornographic films after midnight, were much more fitting.

According to the autopsy reports, one of the victims had lost a fingernail from her left hand, which was found near her supine corpse. Notably, her body had the fewest cuts and bruises of all the women, meaning that during the rape she must have struggled less violently than the others. The fingernail had probably been torn off afterwards, once the killer had begun to strangle the woman, causing her to fight for her life. Traces of skin tissue (Blood Type A) not belonging to the victim were also found on her broken fingernail. This meant that it probably ripped while the woman was digging her nails into the body of her killer. Because he was strangling her from behind, she would not have been able to reach much of his body, making it highly likely that she had scratched him around the hands and wrists.

Fang Mu also paid particular attention to the fact that the fingernail had torn rather than snapped. This suggested that while the victim was raking her nails across the killer's skin, some object had gotten in the way and ripped one of them off. What kind of thing, worn on the hand or wrist, could do something like that? Fang Mu immediately thought of a watch, and likely a metallic one at that. For a construction worker to wear a metallic watch was rather outside the norm. This man definitely wanted to demonstrate that he was different than those around him.

In that case, he was probably someone who possessed a certain amount of education.

So then, someone no older than 25, with a decent education, a history of failure, and experience working at construction sites.

The likely culprit: a young man from the countryside who failed the College Entrance Exam.

If that's who he was, then there would also be other ways for him to show he was different than the peasant workers laboring at the construction site.

For example, he could keep his hair short and perfectly clean, rather than long and greasy like theirs. Glasses would proclaim his status as an "intellectual", and a white dress shirt would look very different than their cement-stained work clothes.

In sum, he should be rather thin with short hair, wearing a white dress shirt and a metallic watch on his left wrist; there should also be scratches on the skin nearby. And, the fact that he wore his watch on his left wrist meant that he was likely right-handed.

Once Fang Mu had finished relating the grounds for his conclusions, the members of the special investigation team were silent. Each man's face wore a complex expression. Indeed, now that every step of his reasoning process had been explained in painstaking detail, cracking the case seemed perfectly natural—the simplest thing in the world. Yet, how many people could have even taken the correct first step?

At last, it was Xing Zhisen who broke the silence. "Man, you should have just told us Huang Yongxiao's name from the start and saved us all this trouble."

Everyone roared with laughter.

Everyone but Fang Mu, that is. The whole time he remained staring at the floorboards beneath his feet, lost in thought.

After that everything went smoothly, and Huang Yongxiao's trial date was soon scheduled. By this point the people of Changhong City were all praising the incredible speed with which the police had cracked the case. Xing Zhisen wanted to give Fang Mu some kind of reward (he had already explained to him, tactfully, that the police could never publicly announce that the case had been solved with the assistance of a 22-year-old university student, and Fang Mu had indicated that he understood). However, Fang Mu refused to accept anything. So Xing Zhisen asked Fang Mu if he had any requests. Fang Mu's answer was simple: He wanted to speak alone and in person with Huang Yongxiao before he went to trial.

Many people were filled with curiosity about this face-to-face chat; however Fang Mu persisted, and in the end the bureau arranged it so that he could speak one time with Huang Yongxiao, by himself and uninterrupted. The conversation lasted more than two hours. Fang Mu jotted notes the whole time. When it was over he had filled half a notebook and recorded two tapes. Ding Shucheng once listened to a segment of the recording, and based on what he heard, it seemed that the talk barely involved the case itself. Fang Mu seemed to be much more interested in Huang Yongxiao's life experiences, from as far back as he could remember up until he was 21.

When Huang Yongxiao was five, his parents divorced. His mother then remarried, taking his big sister, who was one year older than he, to live with her new husband in another town; from then on Huang Yongxiao lived with his father. Although he was an introverted child not given to speaking with others, Huang Yongxiao was extremely studious, and everyone believed that he was the likeliest of the village students to test into the university. When he was eight, Huang Yongxiao accidentally discovered his father secretly having sex with a local married woman, and was given a harsh beating because of it. Then, when he was 14 and attending middle school, Huang Yongxiao was led by an older girl into the nearby mountains. When the girl took Huang Yongxiao's hand and placed it on her naked breast, he was terribly frightened and ran as fast as he could back down the mountain. But two years later, when the 16-year-old Huang Yongxiao was out working in the fields, he suddenly forced the girl laboring beside him—his classmate and someone with whom he'd always gotten along well—to the ground, where he began to wildly kiss and grope her all over. The girl was so scared she began to scream at the top of her lungs, alerting the other villagers who ran over and saved her.

Later, through Huang Yongxiao's father's compensatory gift of a donkey and the mediation of the village elders, the event blew over, but from then on his academic achievements suffered a disastrous decline. At last, after twice failing the College Entrance Exam, he followed his uncle into the city to find employment. Within a year he had worked at a total of five construction sites, moving from one to the next, and had experienced more than his share of rejection and supercilious looks from the city's populace. Because of his introverted and rather proud and aloof personality, he did not remain at any site for long. In his free time, Huang Yongxiao would go to a nearby video playhouse to watch kung fu movies. It was here that he saw his first pornographic film. Afterwards, things quickly got out of hand. All day long his head would be filled with images of the porn actress' overpoweringly seductive bodies, until finally, late one night, he followed a white-collar woman on her way home…

After that, Fang Mu more or less became the Changhong City Public Security Bureau's "special consultant", and with his assistance, two more murders were solved, as well as a kidnapping case and another involving extortion. In each, Fang Mu's description of the suspect's characteristics proved a huge help in cracking the case.

2 MARKED MAN

Hearing this almost absurdly bizarre story about Fang Mu's exploits, Tai Wei remained skeptical.

"This student, Fang Mu," Tai Wei paused, considering his words carefully, "he profiles the suspects?"

Ding Shucheng nodded.

"Is he really that good?"

Ding Shucheng laughed and leaned in close, a mysterious look on his face. "You know why Ronaldo's the best striker in the world?"

Tai Wei was baffled. "Huh? What are you talking about?"

"Why can't Hao Haidong become the world's number one striker?" *(Translator's note: Hao Haidong is a former international football player widely regarded as the best Chinese striker ever)*

Totally lost, Tai Wei just stared at Ding Shucheng.

"Genius. This kid is a genius at understanding crime."

After checking the graduate student rolls at Jiangbin City University, Tai Wei discovered that Fang Mu lived in Building B of Dormitory 5, Room 313. However when he went to speak to him, he found that Fang Mu was out—off playing to play basketball, according to his roommate.

When Tai Wei asked what Fang Mu looked like, the roommate laughed.

"Don't worry about that. Just look for someone practicing free-throws all by himself—that's Fang Mu."

The weather was beautiful. A warm breeze blew softly across the campus, and the pleasant smell of pollen filled the air. Most of the students had ditched their thick winter clothes and were bustling about in lightweight attire. Too impatient to wait any longer, some of the girls were even wearing short skirts. Tai Wei's black windbreaker was clearly quite unseasonal, and before long he began to sweat. Pulling aside a short young man with a basketball under his arm, Tai Wei asked where the courts were, and the young man enthusiastically led the way.

The courts were located at the southwestern corner of campus, all of them full-sized and lined up next to each other. There were eight in total, made of cement and surrounded by a chain-link fence. Tai Wei passed court after court of students playing high-spirited games, his eyes peeled for a young man practicing foul shouts all by himself.

He wasn't hard to find.

Standing at the free-throw line of the farthest court was a young man, basketball in hand. He raised his arms to shoot and released the ball, which arced through the air and dropped perfectly into the hoop.

Tai Wei stood beside the court and watched the young man repeat the same actions over and over: shooting the ball, watching it drop through the net, fetching it, shooting the ball, watching it drop through the net...

His movements were graceful and precise, and he almost never missed.

Suddenly, without turning his head, the young man coldly spat out a single sentence: "What do you want?"

"Huh?" Tai Wei was somewhat taken by surprise. He awkwardly cleared his throat. "Ahem, are you Fang Mu?"

The young man's outstretched arms paused for an instant, then he flicked his fingers and the basketball rocketed towards the hoop, ricocheted off the backboard, and dropped back into his hands.

Holding the ball, he turned around.

His face was flushed. Fine beads of sweat rested on the end of his nose. His cheeks were sunken, his chin sharp, his thick eyebrows knitted together. And the look in his eyes—

—It was cold, weary, and yet incomparably penetrating, seeming to pierce the bright rays of afternoon sunlight and bore into the body of the policeman.

Tai Wei couldn't help but shiver. Averting his eyes, he was about to say something, when he realized that he hadn't prepared anything appropriate to break the ice.

"You...you know Ding Shucheng, right?" Tai Wei stuttered.

Fang Mu's frown deepened. Staring at Tai Wei, he said, "You're a policeman?"

The moment the words left his mouth, he turned and, without waiting for a response, walked over to the bleachers beside the basketball court.

Tai Wei hesitated for a moment, then followed behind him and sat down.

On the bleacher lay a very old backpack. Retrieving a pack of tissues from within, Fang Mu removed a few and wiped his face. Then he fished out his glasses and put them on.

"What do you need me to help you with?" His face remained totally inexpressive.

Tai Wei felt a twinge of discomfort; however he had come here for a reason, so he withdrew a sheaf of papers from his leather briefcase and handed them to Fang Mu.

"I work for the Jiangbin City Vice Squad. My name's Tai Wei. Since March of this year we've had three linked forced entry-and-murder cases. These are the materials from those cases. From what I've heard..." At this point, however, Tai Wei realized that Fang Mu wasn't paying any attention to what he was saying, and had begun reading through the pile of documents in his hands, utterly absorbed. Annoyed, Tai Wei shut his mouth and quietly stuffed his police badge, which he had been about to show Fang Mu, back in his pocket.

As it turned out, nothing could be more aggravating than spending an afternoon with this kid.

From start to finish, Fang Mu sat in silence, reading through the materials. At first, Tai Wei patiently assumed a posture of being ready to listen attentively at any time. However, as time dragged on, his shoulders grew painfully sore, and he became antsy. Stretching out his limbs, he leaned comfortably against the bleachers and gazed around, bored out of his mind.

The court where Fang Mu had just been shooting hoops was now occupied by several other young men. They looked not much older than twenty, 20 and spared nothing as they sprinted up and down the court, fighting for the ball, yelling with excitement, and occasionally arguing loudly about whether a foul had been committed or a point counted. Watching their energetic play, Tai Wei couldn't help but think back to his days studying at the police academy, and gradually the corners of his mouth curled into a faint smile.

Suddenly he realized that the person sitting beside him was also a young student, just like the carefree boys now running the court, and yet how dissimilar they were! It was as if there was some mark on him that made him totally different from all the people around him. Once more, Tai Wei couldn't help but turn and look at Fang Mu.

He was reading very slowly. His head bent over, his eyes focused nonstop on the photographs, crime scene reports, and autopsy reports in his hands. Every now and then he glanced up, and Tai Wei, thinking he was about to say something, would look at him hopefully. But Fang Mu just stared at the distant scenery, not saying a word, and then a moment later would drop his head and continue poring over the data. Tai Wei noticed that he was paying particular attention to a few of the crime scene photographs.

Finally, Fang Mu stood up and let out a deep breath. He removed his glasses, rubbed his eyes, and handed the sheaf of papers back to Tai Wei, who was staring at him.

"The person you're looking for is male, between twenty-five- and thirty-five-years-old, under five-feet nine-inches, and probably rather thin."

Tai Wei stared at him. Several seconds passed before he couldn't bear it any longer: "That's it?"

"That's it."

Tai Wei felt greatly disappointed. He had originally thought that Fang Mu's analysis would be just as Ding Shucheng claimed—a specific, detailed description of the killer's appearance, living circumstances, and family background, but the verdict Fang Mu had just given was brief and entirely ambiguous. And to be honest, it really didn't offer any valuable new clues; given the brutality of the crimes, the perpetrator was almost certain to be male, and the vast majority of serial killers are less than 40-year-old. As for the suspect's height and weight, both could be determined by footprints found at the crime scenes. And since there was also evidence of a struggle between the killer and his victims, he probably wasn't all that strong.

"Based on the reports and photographs, that's all I can see," said Fang Mu, seemingly aware of what Tai Wei was thinking. However, a moment later he added, "I also feel like this guy has some kind of mental problem, but as for what this problem is, I can't say for certain."

Humph, thought Tai Wei, even an idiot could see this killer's a psycho!

"Being a psycho and having a psychological disorder are not the same."

Tai Wei's mouth nearly dropped open—it was clear that in less than a minute Fang Mu had already seen through him twice. To conceal his surprise, he stood up and extended his hand toward the young man.

"All right, then. Thanks for the help. If we need your assistance on something else, we'll contact you. See you later."

Fang Mu grasped Tai Wei's hand. The young man's hand was cold—Tai

Wei couldn't even feel a hint of warmth.

"It would be best if we don't see each other again."

"Oh?" Tai Wei's eyebrows rose.

"If we see each other again, it means someone else has died."

Tai Wei opened his mouth to respond, however nothing came out. At last, unable to do anything else, he simply nodded, turned and walked away.

As he left the basketball courts, Tai Wei couldn't resist looking back. Fang Mu was no longer beside the bleachers. Instead he was on one of the distant courts, his back to Tai Wei, shooting by himself. Dusk had fallen, and only a few players remained on the courts. As the darkness deepened, Fang Mu's silhouette became increasingly faint, until all that could be seen was the continuous rising motion of his arms and the ball as it flew through the air towards the hoop.

3 THE MEANING OF FEAR

Today was the first day of Criminal Procedure class. Its professor, Song Yaoyang, had only just returned from an exchange trip to Japan, delaying the start of the class.

As usual, Fang Mu was sitting in the last row. Although class was supposed to begin over a month ago, Professor Song was hardly anxious to begin teaching; instead he kept going on and on about Japan's high level of economic development and comfortable lifestyle. Then he launched into several stories he "just had to tell" about his exploits with some Japanese criminal procedure specialists. As he continued to boast enthusiastically, a student knocked on the half-open classroom door. With a self-satisfied look on his face, Professor Yang beckoned the student inside with a magnanimous sweep of his arm.

The student walked briskly to the back row, sat heavily beside Fang Mu, and gave him a friendly nod.

Fang Mu recognized him. He was Meng Fanzhe, a Civil Law graduate student.

Arriving late to class was as common as could be, ,and professors were generally quick to forgive the offending students. What gave Fang Mu pause was the expression on Meng Fanzhe's face: he looked far more relieved than he should be, as if—

As if he had just escaped some terrible trial.

Once Professor Song finally finished what seemed to be his"Reflections on Traveling in Japan" lecture, he grabbed the attendance sheet and, with a feigned show of affection, gave a wink and said, "Before beginning class, why don't we first get to know one another?"

All the students who, a moment before, were about to fall asleep immediately perked up. This was a required course and nobody wanted to lose credit points. As Professor Song went down the list, reading name after name, the word "Here" sounded again and again from every corner of the classroom. Inadvertently, Fang Mu's eyes fell on Meng Fanzhe. What he saw took him completely by surprise.

Only moments before Meng Fanzhe had appeared exceptionally relaxed; now he looked as nervous as if he were confronting a mortal enemy. His hands tightly gripped the corners of his desk, knuckles white, and his eyes were wide and fixed on Professor Song. He gnawed tensely on his upper lip. It was as if Professor Song, rather than speaking students' names, was actually shooting bullets from his open mouth.

What was up with him? Fang Mu wondered.

"Meng Fanzhe."

Big drops of sweat streamed down Meng Fanzhe's face; his lips fluttered open and closed. But he made not the slightest sound. Professor Song scanned the classroom. Then he read the name once more: "Meng Fanzhe."

Several of Meng Fanzhe's acquaintances called softly to him, but he seemed not to hear. He continued to stare rigidly at Professor Song, leaning forward, his mouth half open, as if he were anxious to speak but powerless to actually do so.

"Absent? Cutting class on the first day?" An angry look on his face, Professor Song withdrew a fountain pen and prepared to make a note on the attendance sheet.

At that moment, Meng Fanzhe leaped to his feet. Although still unable to speak, he raised his arm high in the air.

"Oh, are you Meng Fanzhe?"

At last two words tumbled out of the student's mouth: "I am."

"Then please sit down. Next time try to pay a little bit more attention."

Meng Fanzhe flopped exhaustedly into his seat, as if speaking those two words had used up every ounce of his strength. Several students covered their mouths and stole a laugh. Even more shot looks of astonishment in Meng Fanzhe's direction.

For the rest of class Meng Fanzhe seemed to hide from his classmates' eyes—head down, diligently taking notes. However, he was clearly no longer as anxious as before.

But what exactly was he afraid of?

Professor Song turned out to be a merely average lecturer. During the break, several students sneaked off while the professor was out smoking a cigarette (of course, none of his own graduate students dared move an inch). When Professor Song returned to find that the class had shrunk by several students, he grew enraged, grabbed the attendance sheet, and once more began to take roll.

Fang Mu noticed that Meng Fanzhe, who moments before had been calm, now seemed to drop once more into an abyss. A mixture of despair, nervousness, and hatred played across his face. And as his name drew closer and closer, Meng Fanzhe actually began to shake.

Fang Mu continued to quietly observe Meng Fanzhe, all the while taking note of the names being read.

"Wang Degang."

"Here."

"Chen Liang."

"Here."

"Chu Xiaoxu."

"Here."

Fang Mu knew who was next.

"Meng Fanzhe."

Just as the word "Meng" left Professor Song's mouth, Fang Mu suddenly clapped Meng Fanzhe on the back.

"Hey!"

Surprised, Meng Fanzhe involuntarily turned toward Fang Mu; just then, the word "Fanzhe" filled the air.

Without thinking, Meng Fanzhe said, "Here."

This time Professor Song did not pause, but continued down the list.

Meng Fanzhe was stunned for an instant, but then his expression quickly returned to normal. After wiping the sweat from his forehead, he turned to Fang Mu and, somewhat awkwardly, asked, "What's the matter?"

Fang Mu thought for a moment. "What time is it?"

Meng Fanzhe glanced at his watch. "It's nine-o-five. Oh," he hastened to add, "nine-o-five and thirty-eight seconds."

Fang Mu laughed, and for a split second Meng Fanzhe's face went red, as if someone had just seen right through him.

Fang Mu stuffed himself at lunch, to the point where he felt a bit drowsy. Checking his watch, he saw that there was less than an hour before his afternoon class, so he hustled upstairs to the rooftop balcony, hoping to catch a breeze.

By the time he reached it, Fang Mu found someone already there.

It was Meng Fanzhe.

He was sitting on the low cement barrier at the edge of the roof, his legs dangling casually over the side. His eyes were fixed on something in the distance and he seemed to be deep in thought.

Not wanting to be seen, Fang Mu was about to quietly leave when Meng Fanzhe suddenly stood up.

The barrier was no more than eight inches wide. Meng Fanzhe stood carefully atop it, his heels and toes hanging off either side. Teetering, he spread his arms wide, took a deep breath, and, using what seemed to be all of his determination, looked down.

Fang Mu held his breath. It was a seven-story building! What could he see down there?

Button-sized people milling about? Cars like a child's toys? Or the earth that he seemed prepared to fling himself toward at any moment?

But no—Fang Mu could not call out to him. The sound of his voice would surely surprise Meng Fanzhe, who could easily fall as a result.

Fang Mu carefully stepped forward. In that moment, the sound of his shoe sole rubbing against the sandy roof seemed as loud as thunder.

Meng Fanzhe's body began to sway even more violently. He was about to lose his balance!

There was no time to think. Fang Mu rushed forward, grabbed Meng Fanzhe around the waist as tight as he could and hauled him backwards.

Meng Fanzhe gave a short cry of surprise, and then he and Fang Mu fell back onto the balcony.

"What are you doing? You wanna die?" Fang Mu yelled, looking angrily at where the skin had scraped off his elbow from the impact.

"I—I'm sorry," Meng Fanzhe mumbled as he sat on the ground. He was still badly shaken.

Seeing Meng Fanzhe's ashen face, Fang Mu extended his arm and helped him up.

Meng Fanzhe's legs remained fairly limp, and it was only with effort that, shaking, he managed to stand upright and wipe the dust off his clothing. Still, his body continued to tremble, as if at any time he might topple to the ground.

Fang Mu sighed and then helped him over to a nearby stone bench. There Fang Mu withdrew his thermos from his backpack and handed it over.

Meng Fanzhe took several deep gulps of water. Gradually his breathing became calm.

"Thank you," said Meng Fanzhe. Then he took out a tissue, carefully cleaned the rim of the thermos, and handed it back to Fang Mu.

Sitting down beside him, Fang Mu grabbed a pack of cigarettes, removed one and put it in his mouth and lit it. Then, after thinking about it, he took a second, lit it, and offered it to Meng Fanzhe. Following a moment's hesitation, Meng Fanzhe accepted, though when he took a puff he immediately began to cough.

"You don't smoke?"

"No."

"Waste of tobacco." he said with a chuckle.

How familiar their words sounded, reminding Fang Mu of something that had happened long ago.

For some reason, his spirits suddenly fell.

The two of them sat in silence, Fang Mu taking drag after deep drag of smoke, Meng Fanzhe staring at his gradually shortening cigarette as if in a daze.

After a long time, Meng Fanzhe finally spoke. "You must think I'm crazy."

"Beg your pardon?"

Meng Fanzhe flung his cigarette away. "You must think something's wrong with me."

"Why would you think that?"

"Why else would you not ask me what I was just doing?"

"Um, all right then. What were you just doing?" Fang Mu found this mildly ridiculous.

"Man!" Meng Fanzhe laughed. "I really wasn't doing anything. I guess I just wanted to experience the feeling of fear for a moment." He looked over at Fang Mu, feigning a laid-back smile, as if he hoped Fang Mu would think he was cool.

Fang Mu laughed and lit another cigarette.

Meng Fanzhe continued to look expectantly at Fang Mu for a while, as if waiting for him to say something like, "So that's what was going on?" or "Man, you really must have been bored." But after sitting in silence for a time, Fang Mu suddenly looked up and asked:

"What are you afraid of?"

Meng Fanzhe's eyes went wide as he stared at Fang Mu. The look on his face seemed to say, 'How did you know?'

Of course I know, thought Fang Mu. Why else would I have pushed you while the professor was taking roll?

If a person is terrified of something, and when confronted with this thing, displays extraordinary fixation and sensitivity towards it, a sudden disruption of his attention will cause his fear to be instantly eliminated. But of course, this lasts only for the instant.

Meng Fanzhe was probably afraid of roll call, so when it was taken, his fear would manifest as total absorption. The more afraid he became, the less capable he was of responding. So when Fang Mu pushed him just as his name was being read, his attention was diverted from the roll call to Fang Mu, and naturally he was able to answer.

Meng Fanzhe's expression changed from surprise to dejection. Hanging his head, he said nothing.

"What are you afraid of?" Fang Mu asked.

When Meng Fanzhe looked up, Fang Mu could see the weakness in his eyes. He stared at Fang Mu for a long while. Smiling softly, Fang Mu casually returned his gaze.

Slowly, the look in Meng Fanzhe's eyes became friendlier, more trusting.

"I'm..." he began, scratching his head, "a little afraid of the roll call." He laughed. "It's pretty weird."

"You know where it comes from?"

"Not a clue." Meng Fanzhe gazed off into the distance. "I also don't know when it started—only that it scares me. As soon as someone begins taking roll, I get nervous, and the more nervous I become, the less I'm able to say 'Here'. Often I'll jump to my feet, flush with agitation, but unable to say a word, while the whole class stares at me." He dropped his head and his voice abruptly fell. "A lot of people make fun of me."

"Do you stutter?"

"No. Does it sound like I have trouble speaking?"

"No."

"I can't understand it either. Why should the word 'Here' be so impossible for me to say? Sometimes I secretly practice by myself. I read my name and say 'Here' and I never have a problem. But when I get to class, I still can't say a thing." His voice fell. "Pass me a cigarette."

Fang Mu handed him one and helped him light it. Meng Fanzhe inhaled carefully.

"Four years of college. How'd you make it?" Fang Mu asked.

"...I've got my methods." Meng Fanzhe smiled thinly. "Teachers usually take attendance at the beginning of class, so I'd wait until they'd finished and come in late, pretending it was an accident. When class was over, I'd go up and give some excuse. Back then people called me the Tardy King. A lot of teachers had a bad impression of me, but luckily my grades were always pretty good."

Laughing, Fang Mu made it clear he understood.

"There was one class I had, International Economic Law. The professor was awful; he had to rely on roll call to make sure anyone showed up. Twice he took attendance four times in a single class. Four times. You know what that was like for me?" Shaking, Meng Fanzhe placed the cigarette in the side of his mouth and took a deep, vicious drag. Almost immediately he began hacking like he'd torn his lungs in half.

Fang Mu clapped him on the back, and then when his breathing returned to normal, asked, "You ever thought of seeing a psychologist?"

He hesitated for a moment. "I guess you could say I've seen one. Why? You think there's something wrong with me?"

"No, you've just got a slight disorder, that's all. Nearly everyone has something like that—it's the degree that differs. You're scared of roll call. Tons of other people are scared of heights, elevators, or sharp objects. It's not a big deal."

"Really?" Meng Fanzhe still seemed a little skeptical. However, his expression was much more relaxed. "In that case," he said, looking at Fang Mu with curiosity, "what are you scared of?"

Fang Mu didn't respond, just finished smoking his cigarette in silence. Then he looked at his watch. "I should get to class. We can talk about this later." Saying this,, he got up and left the balcony, leaving Meng Fanzhe a little disappointed.

Fear. You don't even know the meaning of the word.

4 BLOODSUCKER

Carrying two grass carp, Uncle Qin walked the corridor at an even pace. He was getting on in years, and by the time he climbed to the fourth floor he was already panting.

He leaned against the banister, hoping to rest a spell before continuing to climb. Glancing around, he happened to notice that the door to Apartment 401 was open a crack. Feeling curious, he walked over and glanced inside. At once he stumbled backwards and fell heavily to the floor.

The two grass carp, their stomachs cut open and cheeks slit, dropped to the floor. Unwilling to give up, they struggled fiercely; one even made it inside Apartment 401. Eyes wide and mouth hanging open, it flopped around a pool of thick, sticky, dark red liquid, totally ignorant of the silent, similarly gutted figure lying at the other end of the room.

Two policemen patrolling nearby soon hurried to the scene. The moment the first stepped through the doorway and glanced around, he told his partner to radio headquarters.

"It's the vampire. He's back."

Speeding towards the crime scene, Tai Wei abruptly changed his mind. Telling his fellow officers to continue on ahead of him, he headed to Jiangbin City University.

Even though his previous conversation with Fang Mu had offered no new leads or ideas for cracking the case, Tai Wei decided to hear him out one more time. When it came to understanding a crime, nothing could beat observing the scene in person.

At that moment, Fang Mu was in Japanese class.

Since Japanese class was an elective jointly attended by 700 of Jiangbin City University's graduate students, it was held in the school's largest, multi-level lecture theater. The class had only just begun when a tall, strapping young man burst into the classroom. It was Tai Wei, and he walked straight to the Japanese professor, withdrew a card from his pocket, waved it in the professor's face, and then whispered something in his ear. At once, the professor grabbed the microphone and said:

"Fang Mu, where is Fang Mu?"

"I'm here." From one of the corners of the theater, a bespectacled student rose to his feet.

"Our comrade from the Public Security Bureau would like a word with you."

In an instant the theater went silent. All eyes left the PSB agent, swept the room with an audible whoosh, and fell on Fang Mu.

Fang Mu stood in place, seeming to ignore all the curious, astonished, suspicious looks shot in his direction. He just stared at Tai Wei, eyebrows knitted together.

Tai Wei waved at him, as if to say "Let's go "

Fang Mu put his belongings into his backpack, and then in front of all the gazing eyes, descended the steps one at a time and followed Tai Wei out of the room.

Tai Wei said nothing as they drove to the crime scene. Fang Mu remained silent as well.

Sure enough, they were seeing each other again because another life had been lost. This made it very difficult for Tai Wei to think of something appropriate to say. And strangest of all was the kid sitting beside him. Tai Wei expected "What happened? Where are we going?", but Fang Wu didn't ask these or any other questions, for that matter. He just stared out the window, not saying a word.

Suddenly, the strange kid opened his mouth. "Isn't this the Brilliant Pearl Residential Area?"

Tai Wei looked around. "Yeah, you're right." All of a sudden he realized that this was where the first murder had taken place.

A few minutes later, he parked his jeep outside Bright Gardens, the worker dorms for the Jiangbin City Machine Plant.

Bright Gardens was built during the eighties. At the time, the Jiangbin City Machine Plant was a large-scale, nationally famous, state-owned company with excellent pay and benefits for its workers. During the days of government-allotted housing, the apartments of Bright Gardens were some of the few seven-story buildings around. But circumstances change with the passage of time. All across the city, huge, modern buildings were springing up one after another, each taller than the last, and today these towering, 20-year-old apartment blocks looked terribly rundown.

The crime had taken place in Unit 3 of Building 2, Apartment 401. The scene was already sealed off when Tai Wei and Fang Mu arrived. After stepping over the police cordon, they hurried up to the fourth floor. All around them police rushed upstairs and down; many shot puzzled looks at the backpack-wearing, bespectacled kid accompanying Tai Wei.

Tai Wei walked inside 401. It was an old-fashioned, one-bedroom apartment, roughly 120-square feet. Several medical examiners and technical personnel were busy inspecting the body, snapping pictures and scouring the crime scene. The place was crowded to capacity. A policeman who had arrived earlier told Tai Wei that the victim, a single woman, had only just rented the apartment. The owner was hurrying to the scene.

The dead woman didn't appear older than 35. She was lying on her back, naked from the waist up, her head pointing south and her feet north. She had been torn open from throat to abdomen with a sharp object. Her ribs and organs were visible.

"How's it looking?" Tai Wei asked, patting one of the medical examiners on the shoulder.

"Cause of death was mechanical asphyxiation. The murder weapon was a nylon cord; some of the investigators already located it. Time of death was no more than two hours ago."

Tai Wei looked at his watch. "In other words, she probably died sometime between two and two-thirty?"

"Correct."

Killing someone in broad daylight—this guy was too savage. Muttering to himself, Tai Wei looked around for Fang Mu, only to discover that he was still standing in the doorway, ashen-faced and staring at the corpse.

"Over here," Tai Wei called out to him.

Fang Mu was trembling like he'd had some terrible fright. He nodded, but still didn't move.

"You scared?" Tai Wei frowned.

Fang Mu looked at Tai Wei, and then he took a deep breath and walked inside.

The medical examiners were closely inspecting the victim's abdominal wound, carefully lifting open her sliced skin and muscle tissue. Fang Mu stared at the wound for a moment and then swept his eyes across the congealed pool of blood on the floor. Suddenly he turned and fled back to the hallway, nearly knocking over a policeman carrying a bag of material evidence. The man angrily swore at him as Fang Mu passed.

Tai Wei hurried after him. He found him in a corner of the hallway, bent over, one arm on the wall for support. He was retching.

Useless, thought Tai Wei, swearing beneath his breath. He told a nearby officer to fetch Fang Mu some water. Then he returned to the crime scene and got back to work.

Although Fang Mu had always known that, sooner or later, he'd be brought to one of the bloodsucker's crime scenes, he never expected to embarrass himself like this. Normally he could look at revolting crime scene photographs while eating lunch and not bat an eye, but walking through this building—with its dark and dirty hallways, stone-faced policemen rushing past, bright yellow security tape, medical examiners with their ice cold tools, the corpse lying in its dark red pool, and the thin scent of blood that filled the air—he couldn't help but tremble with fear. After all, pictures were just pictures. They could never communicate, through sight, touch, and smell, the message: A life has just been lost here. Thinking about this made him shiver, as if some deep part of his memory, which he dared not touch, had just been struck open.

Get a hold of yourself, he thought between retches. Don't let it affect your judgment.

"You all right?" Tai Wei's voice sounded impatiently in his ear.

Fang Mu gasped for breath, one arm braced weakly against the wall. Lifting the half-full water bottle that the officer had just given him, he emptied it in one gulp. Then he wiped his mouth on his sleeve and, with difficulty, managed to say: "There's probably someone else."

"What?" Tai Wei's eyes went wide in surprise.

Ignoring him, Fang Mu walked unsteadily over to Apartment 402 and knelt beside the door. On the floor was a tiny button printed with the image of Mickey Mouse's face. Just now, when Fang Mu had run out into the hallway to throw up, he happened to spot it. He picked up the button and handed it to Tai Wei. Then he walked into 401, bypassed the corpse, and entered the bedroom.

The furnishings were very simple. There was only a bed, a chair, a desk, and an old-fashioned wooden armoire in the corner against the wall. A pile of clothes lay messily on the floor, and on the bed, four large duffel bags—in red, blue, green, and orange checkered, respectively—were filled to bursting. One of them was already open; several blouses were folded neatly beside it. Fang Mu looked at the mess of clothes on the floor, then at the bags on the bed. He turned to face a policeman who was photographing the scene.

"You finished?" Fang Mu asked.

When the man responded that he was, Fang Mu immediately opened the other three bags. Camera dangling from his neck, the policeman hurriedly tried to stop him, but Tai Wei held him back. After quickly rifling through the clothing folded inside the bag, Fang Mu stood up and sped into the kitchen.

In the kitchen, the wooden knife rack beside the gas stove held a fruit knife, a large kitchen knife, and a boning knife—however one space was empty. From the look of things, the missing knife was probably around six inches long, with a fine blade and wooden handle. A midsized kitchen knife. Nearby, a policeman was busy collecting fingerprints from the kitchen.

"Have you found the knife yet?" Fang Mu asked him.

The policeman was momentarily taken aback. He looked Fang Mu over.

"Have you found it or not?" Fang Mu asked impatiently.

The policeman hesitated. "Not yet," he said.

At this point Tai Wei rushed in. He was holding the button. "You said there was someone else. What was that supposed to mean?"

Fang Mu didn't answer, just continued questioning the policeman.

"Have you found a cup or some other container filled with a mixture of blood and another liquid?"

The policeman looked at Tai Wei. "No."

Fang Mu shut his eyes tight and swore beneath his breath. Then he turned to Tai Wei. "There's another victim, probably a child."

"There's someone else, and it's a child?" Tai Wei frowned. "What are you basing this off?"

But by then Fang Mu was already headed for the hallway. "You want me to explain it to you now? This kid's probably still alive! Tell your men to follow me!"

Tai Wei, Fang Mu, and several policemen had already jumped into Tai Wei's jeep and sped to the edge of the residential area when Tai Wei slammed on the brakes.

"Where are we going?" he asked.

"Taking this area as our center," said Fang Mu, "we make wider and wider circles, looking for a fairly thin, dull-eyed man between twenty-five and thirty, about five-foot seven-inches, with long, greasy hair and holding a large checkered duffel bag." He paused for a moment. "He'll probably also be wearing rather heavy clothing."

The policemen stared at each other in disbelief.

Tai Wei considered this for a moment. Then he turned to the men in the back. "You hear that? Keep your eyes peeled for this guy!"

After twice circling Bright Gardens, Tai Wei found himself approaching a crossroad that extended in all directions. Slowing down, he turned to Fang Mu.

"Which way?" he asked.

Fang Mu stared at one of the cross-streets for several seconds before decisively pointing in a direction. "There!"

At that moment the sky suddenly darkened, and big black clouds like blocks of lead rolled in from the horizon, layer upon layer of them, and the faint rumble of thunder could be heard.

It was a newly-built road heading towards the outskirts of the city. Both sides were lined with little fruit stands and low, flat-roofed homes. There were very few pedestrians.

The wind grew stronger and stronger, battering the jeep windshield with sand and stones from the road. Everyone left outside was rushing for shelter, by bike or on foot. A big storm was about to arrive.

The men in the jeep pressed against the windows, closely scanning their surroundings. Tai Wei's palms were slick with sweat; several times they nearly slipped off the steering wheel. Frequently he would glance at his watch. Three hours had already passed since the crime was committed. It begged the question: could the child still be alive?

Tai Wei hadn't noticed that Fang Mu's face was growing increasingly somber.

Minutes later, huge raindrops finally began to fall, and at once countless little potholes opened in the road, spewing white dust. The scene outside the window became a blur. By then no one was even looking anymore; visibility was too low to make out a thing.

No one said a word as the jeep flew down the endless road, the sky so low it seemed about ready to collapse. Angry bolts of lightning frequently tore across the lead-black heavens, and after each dazzling flash, there followed a blast like something had been ripped apart.

"Stop the car!" Fang Mu suddenly yelled.

Tai Wei slammed on the brakes, causing the jeep to slide shakily across the surface of the road. Finally it came to a stop.

Before the jeep had even stopped swaying, Fang Mu had jumped outside and was running back the way they'd come.

The remnants of an old, seemingly long-abandoned factory stood beside the road, its crumbling walls covered in broken tile. Perhaps many people once worked there to the roar of machinery, but now everything was swallowed by waist-high weeds.

Fang Mu's whole body was soon drenched from the heavy rain as he walked to where the drops pattered against the tall grass. He was trembling.

Holding his coat overhead, Tai Wei ran to catch up with Fang Mu. But before he could say anything, he heard Fang Mu call out through clenched teeth: "Here. Search over here!"

Without hesitation, everyone immediately split up and began scouring the thick weeds.

Minutes later, one of the men searching to the west cried out in surprise. Then he yelled, "Over here!"

Everyone looked up. Simultaneously, several pairs of eyes swung in his direction.

He knew what this meant. Swallowing, he spoke with difficulty

"We're too late."

It was a little girl. Her corpse had been stuffed into a cement pipe, her chest and abdomen torn open. An empty bottle of mineral water lay beside the body. Inside were traces of a thick, sticky, red-colored substance. It looked like blood. A large, yellow-checkered cloth duffel bag was soon discovered in the grass nearby, as was a sharp, wood-handled knife.

Telling his men to seal the area, Tai Wei radioed headquarters for backup. By the time everything was set, he felt profoundly exhausted. Opening his jeep door, he saw Fang Mu sitting in the passenger seat. He was soaked from head to toe, water dripping from his hair. His eyes were fixed on the rain-blurred windshield in front of him, the cigarette in his hands burned to a stub.

Tai Wei didn't say a word. Even though he had a bellyful of questions to ask Fang Mu, he just lit a cigarette and slowly organized his thoughts.

"Male," said Fang Mu suddenly, his voice hoarse. "Under thirty, very thin, slovenly, lives nearby. His parents probably worked for a state-owned company, but now they're either dead or don't live with him. He has a serious psychological disorder. For him, blood possesses an extremely special significance."

He took a ferocious puff from his cigarette and then rolled down the window and threw it outside.

"I have two recommendations: First, search the entire city for people who have sought hospital treatment for blood diseases in the past five years. Then within this group, look for someone with the characteristics I just mentioned. Second, search hospital records citywide for people who have received blood transfusions in the past three years, especially those who didn't need it but demanded the transfusion anyway."

Tai Wei jotted this down in his notebook. Then after thinking for a moment, he carefully asked, "How did you know there was a second victim?"

"The button. The woman at the crime scene was around thirty-year-old; she'd never wear a button with a cartoon character printed on it. Also, I couldn't find any clothing that matched the button at the scene."

"That button could easily have been dropped by a previous tenant."

"Impossible," replied Fang Mu, gazing out the window. "There wasn't a speck of dust on it. Not to mention that the victim had just moved in, hadn't even opened her bags, and yet somehow there was a pile of clothes on the floor and no bag to go with them. The kitchen was also missing a knife—most likely the one used by the killer. And even though the victim was cut open, nothing at the crime scene indicated that the killer drank her blood. This showed that he must have found an even more attractive blood source—a second victim—whom he stuffed into a duffel bag and brought with him." He turned toward Tai Wei. "Younger blood." He paused. "What do you think that means?"

Tai Wei was taken aback by the question. "I—I don't know."

Fang Mu did not seem to expect an answer. Lost in thought, he turned to stare at the darkening sky.

Tai Wei thought for a moment before speaking again. "In that case, how'd you know the killer murdered the child here?"

Fang Mu did not immediately reply. At last, word by word, he said, "For him, this was the most suitable place."

5 THERAPY

One week earlier.

It was lunch break and the library corridors were very quiet. A young student carefully ascended the stairs, hand on the railing. He made an effort to calm his breathing.

The corridor appeared endless. The student adjusted his backpack, and then with what seemed a sense of determination, walked quickly over to one of the doors. He glanced both ways. No one was there. He looked up at the placard above the door:

Psychological Consultation Room.

Taking a deep breath, he knocked.

In the vast, empty corridor, the sound was extremely jarring, and the student couldn't help but shiver. There was no response. He knocked twice more—still nothing. He placed his ear to the door; inside was absolutely silent. The student let out a deep breath, his expression somewhere between relief and disappointment. When he turned to go, the door across the hall suddenly opened and a man stuck his head out.

"Who are you looking for?"

The student was clearly startled. He pointed at the tightly locked door behind him, but couldn't manage a word.

The man walked over and looked at the door. "Looking for Professor Qiao? He's not here." He looked at the student. "Was there something you wanted to discuss with him?"

"N-no."

The man smiled.

"When you have problems you should say them out loud. Keeping them trapped inside will make you sick."

The student looked up at him. His hair was neatly parted and his eyes were kind and friendly. When he smiled, the corners of his mouth curled slightly upwards, showing his glistening white teeth.

"I—I sometimes feel afraid."

The man laughed softly. "Everyone feels afraid sometimes. Can you tell me what it is you're afraid of?"

The student looked down, his jaw clenched.

He clearly did not want to speak, and was not about to force himself.

"You can conquer this sort of feeling," said the man. He lightly placed his hand on the young man's shoulder. "For example, imagine every dangerous scenario possible, starting with the worst. Do this over and over, and you'll gradually feel at ease in any situation, and will no longer be afraid of what you once feared."

As the student looked up, the man gave him a friendly wink, as if to say, Trust me.

Suddenly the sound of the class bell rang out in the corridor. Startling in surprise, the student said a hurried word of thanks, turned and left.

The case analysis meeting, led by the Director of the Public Security Bureau, had just concluded. At it, Tai Wei had given a detailed report on the state of their preliminary investigations into the most recent forced entry-and-murder case.

In total there were two dead. The first was Yao Xiaoyang, female, 32-year-old, divorced, a teacher at Jiangbin City Teacher's College. When the crime was committed two days prior, she had only recently rented Apartment 401 in Unit 2, Building 3 of the Bright Gardens Residential Area. Based on the state of the crime scene, it seemed that Yao Xiaoyang had just moved in on the day of the murder and was in the process of unpacking her things when she was attacked. Because the lock on her door showed no signs of tampering, the special investigation team briefly considered whether the perpetrator was friendly with the victim. However, a comparison of the fingerprints found at the scene with those of the victim's closest friends eliminated this possibility.

Preliminary analysis: After entering the apartment, the killer struggled with Yao Xiaoyang, finally using a nylon cord left on the living room table (likely used by the victim to tie up her belongings) to strangle her to death. Afterwards, the killer sliced open the victim's chest and abdomen with a knife from the kitchen, his method fundamentally the same as those of the previous murders. What was different, however, was that this time the killer did not drink the victim's blood. The reason for this, police believed, was that it was at this point that the killer discovered the second victim.

The second victim was a six-year-old girl named Tong Hui. She lived next door with her family in Apartment 402. On the day of the crime, Tong Hui's mother and father were at work in the factory, leaving only Yu Huifen, her 70-year-old maternal grandmother, to look after her. According to Yu Huifen, she and Tong Hui had just laid down for an after-lunch nap when, half-asleep, she realized that the girl had jumped out of bed to go play. "Don't go too far," she had said before falling back asleep. Only when the police began examining the crime scene next door did she wake up. It was then that she realized Tong Hui was gone. As for any sounds of movement she might have heard from Apartment 401 earlier that day, the elderly Mrs. Yu had no idea.

The police deduced that Tong Hui had most likely run into the killer while either heading out to play or returning home, and that he immediately changed his plans and decided to drink her blood instead of Yao's. Based on the state of the first crime scene (Apartment 401 of Unit 2, Building 3 in Bright Gardens), the second crime scene (the old site of the original DaMing Fiberglass Factory), and an examination of the victim's corpse, the killer probably strangled her with a rope until she was comatose, tied her up (at which point a button on her dress fell off and landed in the doorway), returned to the bedroom and emptied a duffel bag (large with yellow check), then stuffed her inside and carried her away from the scene. Then the killer traveled roughly 40 minutes southeast on foot before coming across the abandoned Yuanda Ming factory on the side of the road. There he killed Tong Hui, cut open her chest and abdomen, and drank approximately seven ounces of her blood.

Interviews with those living nearby turned up nothing of value, because when the crime was committed, the vast majority of Bright Garden residents were at work in the factory; so even though the killer openly kidnapped Tong Hui in the middle of the day, not a single person noticed. However, an interview on the road between the first and second crime scenes provided an important clue. According to the proprietor of a small Hongyuan Road food stand (located a mile and a half from the second crime scene), he had sold a bottle of mineral water to a familiar-sounding man on the day of the crime. The man had been about 5' 7", very thin, with long, greasy hair, with nervous, bloodshot eyes, and a swath of blisters around the corners of his mouth. He was carrying a large, cloth duffel bag. When the proprietor asked him what was inside, the man responded that it was a dog. Based on the proprietor's description, the police had already made a sketch of the man and begun circulating it with orders for his arrest.

After the meeting ended, Tai Wei was about to leave when the director called after him. "Wait a moment, Little Tai."

The director was a very fat man, and he strained as he changed position in his leather swivel chair. Seeing that Tai Wei was still standing up, he waved for him to have a seat. Then, rotating a tea cup in his hand, the director paused to think for a moment before saying, "From what I've heard, you've been having a Jiangbin City University student help crack the case."

"That's correct. Ding Shucheng of the Changhong City PSB recommended him. He's supposed to be quite gifted."

"And as for your opinion?"

Tai Wei considered his words carefully. "This person is rather interesting. It was under his guidance that we discovered the second victim. Also, his description of the suspect was essentially identical to the one given by the food stand proprietor. He said he would contact me in the next few days. I'm looking forward to hearing his opinion on the case."

"No!" The director held up his index finger and waved it back and forth. His tone was firm. "You will not allow this so-called genius to participate any further. And not just on this case—I do not want to see you using any such methods again."

"Why?" Tai Wei was stunned.

"Have we not suffered enough for that incident already?" The director was nearly shouting. His face was contorted with urgency.

Now Tai Wei was even more at a loss. He stared blankly at the director.

Suddenly the director clapped his hand to his forehead, as if something had just occurred to him. "How long ago were you transferred here?" he asked.

"Four years."

"No wonder." The director's face relaxed slightly. "You can't be blamed for not knowing. Still, you must remember what I told you. That's an order." Saying this, he waved Tai Wei out of the room.

Baffled, Tai Wei returned to his office. He was about to go ask a senior colleague what the director was talking about when his phone rang. It was Fang Mu.

The heavy rain on the night of the murder had caused Fang Mu to catch a bad cold, and the next day he lay in bed from morning 'til night. Once his spirits had lifted a bit, he climbed to his feet and went to the library.

From the materials he had seen during his initial meeting with Tai Wei, as well as his first-hand experience at the most recent crime scenes, Fang Mu had already begun forming some ideas about these murder-and-bloodsucking cases. If most serial killers left a symbol at the scene of their crimes, then what was the symbol of the bloodsucker?

Well, that was obvious. The reason he was even called the bloodsucker was because his symbolic behavior was to cut open his victims after he killed them and drink their blood. Clearly, this excessive damage to the corpse was not done to vent anger or conceal the victim's identity—it came from a special need.

So then, what was this need?

Drinking the blood of the victim could be understood as a kind of "supplement" to the killer's own blood, suggesting that he was regularly filled with fear and anxiety that his was somehow lacking. While the source of this belief was currently unknown, it was certain that the killer's agitation had already reached very serious levels—otherwise he would never have resorted to murdering people and drinking their blood to ease his worries.

The circumstances of the murders bore out this verdict.

The first victim was killed right after she got off the night shift. Her key was still in the door when police arrived at the scene. The killer probably followed her into the building corridor, and then as she opened the door, he seized the opportunity to strike, shoving her inside and strangling her to death. Afterwards, he cut her open, mixed her blood with milk and drank it down.

The second victim was a female doctoral student. On the day of the murder she should have been in class. While taking out the trash, her neighbor noticed that her door was open. She had been killed in the living room, the weapon a flower vase taken from atop the shoe cabinet.

The third victim was a merchant just returned from the morning market after finishing her sales early. She was killed in her own home, a flat-roofed, one-story house. Grabbing her hair, the killer had slammed her head into the kitchen stove and then strangled her to death with a lamp cord. Finally, he mixed her blood with some soybean milk she hadn't sold at market and drank it.

The fourth victim was a divorced female teacher who had just moved into an apartment. The killer strangled her to death with the cord she had used to tie her belongings. Just as he was preparing to drink the victim's blood, he happened to spot a little girl out in the hallway. As a result, she was killed as well.

Without this symbolic bloodsucking behavior, it would be very difficult to imagine these four cases as having been committed by the same person. The age and social status of the victims were all different, the crimes were committed in large buildings and one-story homes, and the causes of death included strangulation by rope, by hand, and being bludgeoned with a flower vase. However, the victims themselves were all cut open in the same way: with a sharp object that the killer had found at the scene and then casually left behind. He also seemed to have paid almost no mind to getting rid of the evidence. His fingerprints covered every crime scene, and when he left, he did not even close the door.

Regarding crimes like these, Fang Mu could think of only one thing: total chaos.

The attacker did not carefully choose his victims. He did not bring the murder weapon with him, and he did not even clean up the crime scene once it was over.

And yet this sort of killer was not actually some ultra careless scatterbrain; rather, he was merely someone who frequently devolved into one.

So the question was: what exactly did the mental disorder that caused this behavior to happen have to do with blood?

At the library, Fang Mu typed the keywords "blood" and "psychological disorder" into the computer, which then responded that the library's third floor reading room had several books on these topics. After copying down their titles, he went directly there.

Because Fang Mu often borrowed books from the library, the librarians working in the third floor reading room were quite familiar with him. After no more than a brief hello, Fang Mu handed Sun, one of the librarians, his book list, and asked where he could find the titles.

"Oh?" Librarian Sun looked at the book list. "Aren't you at the law school? These are all medical titles. What are you doing researching this stuff?"

"Nothing. Just curious, really."

From behind his glasses, Librarian Sun looked closely at Fang Mu. Then he smiled. "They're over in that corner, shelves Z1 and Z3."

Fang Mu followed where Librarian Sun was pointing and found the books. Heading back to check them out, he grabbed a newspaper off one of the tables. One page held an article about the two most recent murders. Above it was a sketch of the killer.

"What do you think?" asked one of the librarians, seeing what Fang Mu was reading. "An article in the paper and an order for the suspect's arrest—won't the vampire be getting out of here as soon as he can?" He sighed and gave the paper a disdainful flick.

"No way," said Fang Mu, not even looking up. "This kind of person generally doesn't pay attention to the news."

"Oh, is that so?" Librarian Sun suddenly became interested. "Where'd you learn that? In class?"

Fang Mu laughed. "It's just a wild guess." But he didn't say anything more. After taking the books from Librarian Sun, he quickly left the library.

After shutting himself in the dorm for an entire day, Fang Mu called Tai Wei. First he asked him what had come of the hospital investigations; however Tai Wei replied that, given how many there were, it would require some time. At this point they had yet to turn up anything of value. As for their interviews with those living near the crime scenes, those were still underway. Fang Mu then told Tai Wei that he had just read several books on blood diseases and psychological disorders. He now felt that the killer had probably been treated at a mental institution—or at least had gone in for a consultation.

"So when we have time," said Fang Mu, "you and I should go to some psychiatric hospitals and check things out." He paused. "However, the sooner the better, because a guy like this is going to strike again—and soon."

"You're back."

"Are you busy? I'm not bothering you, am I?"

There was a laugh. "Not a problem. Come in."

"Were you reading?"

"Aimlessly. Something to drink? Coffee or tea?

"Coffee sounds good."

"I only have instant. That okay?"

"Yeah."

"Oh, my mistake. I'd better give you water instead. You're already not sleeping well."

Another laugh." That's fine too."

"Hey, careful. It's a little hot."

"Thank you. Whoa, the books you're reading look so complex. Blood Disease and Psychological Disorders, Psychogenic Disorders, and this one, A Study of..."

"A Study of Agoraphobia."

"Agoraphobia? What's that?"

"Putting it simply, agoraphobia is one of those things where a person fears a situation that he knows will cause him to feel helpless and terrified. "

"Oh, so it's just another phobia?"

A chuckle. "More or less."

"You're really something, knowing all that stuff."

"Oh, it's no big deal. I just like to read a bit in my spare time. Now, about that method I taught you last time—how was it? Effective?"

"Um, not bad."

"In that case, can you tell me what it is you're afraid of?"

"There...really isn't anything."

"Relax." A short laugh. "With many things, so long as you change your perspective, your view of the thing will change as well. For example..."

A mouse is clicked.

"Which of these animals are you afraid of?"

"Um, the rat."

"Okay then, the rat. Look, here's a photograph of a rat ." A small chuckle, but not condescending. "No need to be nervous. Look at the screen. Are you afraid?"

"Of—of course."

"That's fine, don't be nervous. Were you bitten by a rat when you were young?"

"No."

"In that case, who among your family is scared of rats?"

"My mom."

When you were young, your mother would often take you out to play, correct?"

"Yes."

"When you and your mother were together, did you ever see a rat?"

"Yes."

"What happened?"

"One time my mom was carrying me to preschool. We were passing through a park when a rat sprinted across the road in front of her. My mom screamed at the top of her lungs and ran, nearly dropping me. Another time when we were returning home there was a dead rat outside our door. My mom was too scared to get close. She just held my hand tight and we stood there for a very long time. We didn't go back inside until our neighbor finally picked it up and took it away."

A chuckle, and then: "I understand. Do you love your mother?"

"Of course."

"If your mother were in danger, would you be willing to protect her?"

"Of course."

"How old is your mother?"

"Um, fifty-one."

"All right, imagine this scene: Your gray-haired mother—wait, is your mother's hair gray?"

"Yes, on her temples."

"Okay, let's continue. It's wintertime, a strong wind is blowing outside, and your gray-haired mother is standing in the wind, shaking. Crouched before her is a rat, blocking her path. The rat is huge, with black fur and red eyes. And it's staring right at your mother. Don't tremble now, you must be brave."

"O—Okay."

"Your mother tries to go left, she tries to go right, but no matter what, she can't get past. Her fear and worry increase. Tears drip down her face. She mumbles to herself, 'What do I do, what do I do?' Will you help your mother?"

"Yes!"

"Sit down. Now look. It's less than a foot long; with one stomp you could turn it into a pulp and make sure it never frightened your mother again."

"That's true."

"All right then; protect your mother! Come over here, stomp the thing to death."

A chair is suddenly knocked over. There follows the bang-bang-bang of someone stomping on the floor.

"Good, good. Calm down. Want some water?"

"No, no. I'm okay. Thank you."

"Deep breaths. Very good, very good. Now, take another look at this picture. Is the fear still there?"

"It's a little better."

"This is just a hateful little thing, unworthy of your fear. For your mother, you can be brave."

"Yeah, yeah, that's much better."

"Wipe your sweat with this."

"Thanks. You should be a psychologist."

"A psychologist? No, I merely enjoy investigating peoples' minds."

"Man, when I'm with you I feel so relaxed, so happy."

"That's good. I'm more than willing to help."

"You know, you remind me a lot of one of my friends."

6 BLOODLUST

It was already the second time Tai Wei was pulling Fang Mu out of class.

This time it was Criminal Procedure. Fang Mu and Meng Fanzhe were sitting in the last row. Meng Fanzhe looked relaxed and self-satisfied. The reason for this was that he and Fang Mu had developed a plan; whenever attendance was called, Fang Mu would answer for him, saying Meng Fanzhe's name out of the corner of his mouth. Although Fang Mu didn't mind helping out, this did mean that he and Meng Fanzhe would have to attend every class together. Having gotten used to being alone all the time, Fang Mu found this rather difficult. And he also knew that it was doing nothing to solve the problem itself.

As Fang Mu followed Tai Wei out of the room, he sensed that Meng Fanzhe was again becoming anxious and upset. Fang Mu wished he could reassure Meng Fanzhe that Professor Song was highly unlikely to take attendance a second time that day, but he didn't have time. The look in Tai Wei's eyes made him too nervous to think about anything else.

When they reached the hallway, Fang Mu asked Tai Wei in a whisper: "What is it?

Did something else happen?"

"Yes. No deaths, but another girl has gone missing."

The words slipped out of Fang Mu's mouth. "She's young, isn't she?"

There was no need to respond. The look in Tai Wei's eyes made the answer obvious.

At around 10 p.m.. the night before, Police Substation Eight in the Hongyuan District received a report that a female first-year student at Number Eight Middle School had gone missing. According to those who gave the report (the student's parents), she was a 13-year-old named Xu Jie. Normally Xu Jie would head straight home after school, arriving around 5 p.m., but by 10 p.m. there was still no sign of her. Filled with worry, the parents searched for her every way they could, all without success. Finally, they notified the police.

During the subsequent investigation, an important piece of information was provided by the owner of a street-side barbecue stand. At around 4:40 p.m. on the day of the disappearance, the owner had seen a girl fitting Xu Jie's description speaking to a very thin, slovenly-dressed young man. Feeling that this man's physical characteristics were very similar to those described in the so-called "vampire's" arrest warrant, the officers of the local substation immediately contacted the city bureau's special investigation team.

Fang Mu and Tai Wei soon arrived at the address where the witness had seen Xu Jie and the young man. As Fang Mu surveyed the area, Tai Wei asked him, "You think this is our guy?"

Fang Mu didn't respond. Instead he asked: "You have a map of this area?"

"One step ahead of you," said Tai Wei, as he reached into his car and grabbed one.

Realizing they had been thinking the same thing, Fang Mu smiled.

After all this time the kid finally smiles, thought Tai Wei as he opened the map.

"Seems you've also noticed how geographically concentrated the murders have been," said Tai Wei. He pointed at a section of the map. "Here, here, and here—they all took place in this same area. And the little girl disappeared somewhere around here as well." He looked up at Fang Mu. "Normally, when a suspect commits multiple crimes in roughly the same place, we assume he's unfamiliar with the area, and most likely is not from around here. So then why do you think he lives nearby?"

"This guy's an exception," said Fang Mu, shaking his head. "His crimes are highly random—and he puts essentially no thought into choosing his victims. However, this time is a little different." He raised his head to look at Tai Wei. "He's begun picking children."

Tai Wei thought for a moment. "In that case, you think this little girl is still alive?"

"It's possible." Fang Mu checked the calendar on his watch, and then thought in silence for a moment. "The killer normally commits a murder every twenty days, more or less; however, this time it's been only a week since his last crime. He's probably hoping to store-up some blood reserves, so that when he needs them, they'll be easy to get."

It was a bright and sunny morning, but hearing this, Tai Wei couldn't help but shiver. "Storing" a living human being until the time you should need her. Then slaughtering her like a pig and drinking her blood. What kind of person would do that?

"Let's head to the psychiatric hospitals," said Fang Mu, hopping into the car. "If I'm right then we still have some time. We'll catch him for sure before he feels the need for blood."

Most hospitals in Jiangbin City contained a psychiatric ward, but when it came to stand-alone psychiatric hospitals, there were only two in the whole city. Tai Wei told his subordinates to visit the regular hospitals (emphasizing that they were not to let the PSB director know), while he and Fang Mu would investigate the psychiatric ones.

They were looking for someone who had either sought consultation or been admitted to the hospital for paranoia in the last five years—particularly blood-related paranoia. The staff at the first hospital was actually quite cooperative; unfortunately, they had no record of such an individual. At the second hospital, however, the moment Tai Wei explained their reason for coming, the hospital director immediately thought of someone.

The person in question was a man named Feng Kai. Two years ago, when Feng Kai was 26, his father and older brother died within months of one another, and he became severely depressed. After being admitted to the hospital, Feng Kai responded well to treatment, and his depression appeared to be going away. But then one time, while a nurse was walking the grounds outside the hospital, she saw Feng Kai catch a small bird and drink its blood while it was still alive. After that, he began demanding that the hospital give him a blood transfusion, believing that he was afflicted with a serious case of anemia. But when the hospital gave him a detailed physical examination, they found his hemoglobin count to be perfectly normal. Feng Kai refused to accept this result, however, and continued to believe he was dangerously anemic. It was because of this that the hospital discovered he was also suffering from paranoia. After receiving treatment for paranoia for a period of time, Feng Kai suddenly left without a word.

According to the doctors and nurses, Feng Kai was about 5'8", very thin, and a slob. His room was always a total mess. Feng Kai did not enjoy socializing with others, and no one ever came to visit him. The hospital did try to locate him after his disappearance, but they learned that the address he had registered with was a fake.

This discovery made Fang Mu and Tai Wei unbelievably excited. Thinking that Feng Kai was probably a fake name as well, Fang Mu advised Tai Wei to investigate city records for a father and son who, in the last two years, died one after the other from a blood disease. He also told him to search the whole city—and Hongyuan District especially—for a man fitting the description of this "Feng Kai."

It took two days for the search to finally bear fruit. Jiangbin City had over 1,244 people named Feng Kai, and not one fit the description. There were also no cases within the last two years of a father and son surnamed Feng each dying of a blood disease. However, in 1988 and 1999 respectively, a father and son surnamed Ma had died of aplastic anemia. The father, Ma Xiangwen, was a widower with two sons. Within a year of his father's death, Ma Tao, the elder son, contracted acute aplastic anemia and died soon after. The younger son, Ma Kai, inherited the father's home, where he lived now, at 83-4 North Evergreen Street in Hongyuan. The address was no more than three miles from the locations of the five crimes.

"That's him!"

They were in the housing registry room of the Hongyuan Police Substation, and Fang Mu had just been shown a picture of Ma Kai. There wasn't a trace of doubt in his voice.

In the picture, Ma Kai's hair was neat and clean, his expression composed. But in his slightly dull-looking eyes, Fang Mu could see a reservoir of anxiety and despair.

At this point, Tai Wei was still very cautious. He had the witnesses from the fourth murder case (victims: Yao Xiaoyang and Tong Hui) and the kidnapping case (victim: Xu Jie) brought to the station. The witness to the kidnapping could not be certain that Ma Kai was the man he had seen that day. The food stand proprietor, however, was absolutely certain that Ma Kai was the man who had bought a bottle of mineral water from him on the day of the double murder.

"I'd bet anything!" he said. "He was a little thinner than in the picture, but it has to be him!"

They couldn't hesitate any longer. Tai Wei immediately asked the department to assemble a squad to arrest Ma Kai. When they were ready to leave the substation, Tai Wei asked Fang Mu whether he would rather wait there or return to school.

Fang Mu quickly replied that he would wait at the substation for news of what happened. After telling his colleagues at the station to look after the kid, Tai Wei turned and was about to go when Fang Mu grabbed his arm.

"Be careful," he said. "This guy is extremely dangerous."

8:22 p.m. that night.

It was an old building, built more than 20 years ago at least. According to their investigation, it served as family housing for workers from the Red Light Tractor Factory. Tai Wei looked up at the window of Ma Kai's third floor apartment. Deep blue curtains covered it completely, but a faint orange light could be seen from within.

Accompanying Tai Wei were nine policemen. He had divided them into three groups: attack, rescue and support. The attack group was responsible for subduing the suspect after the room was breached, the rescue group was responsible for saving the girl (if she was still alive), and the support group was responsible for sealing off the corridor and window, so the suspect couldn't escape.

To ensure the operation was successful, that afternoon Tai Wei and another officer had disguised themselves as workers from the gas company and inspected one of the first floor apartments. It was a two-bedroom residence, the layout identical to Ma Kai's. Tai Wei concluded that the girl was most likely being held in the small northern bedroom. He told the rescue team that the moment they entered the apartment, they needed to get inside that northern bedroom as soon as possible and save the little girl. The others would worry about grabbing the suspect.

At 8:25 p.m., the rescue mission began on schedule.

Tai Wei led the attack and rescue teams as they crept up to the third floor. At last they stopped right outside Ma Kai's apartment. There was no peephole. Once the attack team was in position on either side of the door, Tai Wei knocked.

No response. Tai Wei heard soft footsteps from within. Then the light leaking from under the door went out.

Tai Wei knocked three more times. Still no response.

"No one's home," said Tai Wei in a loud voice. "Let's go to the apartment across the hall."

After walking to the apartment opposite, Tai Wei knocked on the door. Almost immediately, a woman's voice sounded from inside. "Who's there?"

Still speaking in a loud voice, Tai Wei said, "We're from Pharmaceutical Plant Three. Recently we've been developing a new product called Happy

Blood Enrichment Pills. They're specially made to cure various kinds of blood deficiencies and anemia. To reward our many customers, we're holding a special Million Pill Giveaway. We've come to your house today to present you with some pills, and I assure you that they're completely free."

"Really? Wait one moment." The door opened and a middle-aged woman with a big puff of hair stuck her head out and asked, "They're really free?"

At almost the same time, the door across the hall suddenly opened.

The attack team charged through the doorway and leapt on the man standing there. With no time to react, he was knocked to the ground.

Leaving the woman staring wide-eyed in fear, Tai Wei crossed the hall and rushed into Apartment 302.

Inside, the man was being pinned tightly to the floor by several policemen. Grabbing his hair, one of them yanked it back and ordered, "Speak. What's your name?"

At a glance Tai Wei knew it was Ma Kai. Without stopping, he followed the rescue team heading to the northern bedroom.

The door was locked. Immediately a member of the rescue team kicked it open. Raising his gun, Tai Wei stepped inside.

The lights were all off. They could see the shape of a large bed, and on it the shape of a person could be dimly made out. While the rest of the men began examining the room, Tai Wei walked to the bed and shined it with his flashlight. Lying on it was a young girl, her arms and legs tied to the four bedposts in a spread-eagle position. Her hair was a mess and her eyes were tightly closed. Tape covered her mouth. Tai Wei could tell she was Xu Jie, the missing girl.

Was she still alive?

Tai Wei placed his hand under her nose. She was breathing. The weight that had been pressing on his heart now vanished in relief.

They soon determined there was no one else in the room. Tai Wei had his men untie the comatose girl, and he notified the support team to radio the ambulance.

The ambulance that had been waiting nearby since the start of the mission now rushed to the scene. In no time they had taken the girl to the hospital to begin her examination.

By then the suspect was already handcuffed and lying face down on his living room floor. Two members of the rescue team had their guns aimed at his head.

Tai Wei grabbed the man's hair and lifted his head. It had a disgustingly greasy feel. He looked at Ma Kai's emaciated face. His skin was pale white, the sides of his mouth were covered in yellow scabs, and gunk surrounded his eyes. His nose appeared to have been broken when he was knocked to the floor and it dripped with blood. Ma Kai twisted like a worm on the ground, mumbling to himself, "The blood...make it stop..."

"Are you Ma Kai?" Tai Wei asked in a loud voice.

Ma Kai opened his eyes slightly and looked at Tai Wei. Then he closed them and continued to mumble. "The blood...the blood... You have to stop it."

Tai Wei suddenly wanted nothing more than to smash the man across the face with the butt of his gun, but he quickly restrained himself. With a disgusted look on his face, he rose to his feet and motioned to the other officers. "Take him away!"

The on-duty officer at the North Evergreen Street substation kept glancing over at the strange young man.

He never said a word or smoked a single cigarette the whole night. He just sat there looking straight ahead, like he was in a trance. He didn't even touch his carton of takeout food.

When the phone rang, the on-duty officer picked it up and said a few words. Then he turned to the visitor: "Are you Fang Mu?"

The kid spun toward him at once, a strange light burning from his eyes.

"They asked for you."

Fang Mu jumped to his feet. His legs were stiff from having sat so long. As he ran over to grab the phone, he smacked into the desk with a loud bang. "Hello?"

A wall of noise met his ear. He heard yelling and the scream of the police siren, and above it all Tai Wei's voice. He sounded rushed, but also very excited. "We got him, it was our man!"

"What about the girl?"

"She's alive and well, at the hospital now. I just called and the doctor told me that, aside from being scared and a little malnourished, the girl is completely fine."

Fang Mu shut his eyes and hung up the phone. Only then did he feel the piercing pain in his leg from where it smacked into the desk. Returning to his chair, he sat in silence for a moment. Then he opened the carton of takeout. "Excuse me."

The on-duty officer looked over to see a weak but hugely relieved smile on Fang Mu's face.

"Can you grab me a cup of water?"

7 SYMPATHY FOR THE DEVIL

It was after 11 o'clock when Tai Wei remembered to bring Fang Mu home. In the car, he told Fang Mu that the crime scene technicians had already determined that Ma Kai's fingerprints matched those from the other murders, so even though he hadn't yet confessed, charging him would be a cinch.

Fang Mu didn't say a word. He just stared at the darkness outside the window.

"You take it easy when you get back," said Tai Wei, noticing Fang Mu's exhausted expression. "I'll stop by in a few days."

At the school gate Fang Mu got out of the car and said goodbye to Tai Wei. He had turned to go when Tai Wei called out for him to wait.

Fang Mu looked back.

Tai Wei had stuck his head out of the passenger side window, his shoulder resting on the frame. He stared at Fang Mu for several seconds, and then his face broke into a wide smile.

"Kid," he said, "you're incredible."

Fang Mu laughed, waved goodbye, and then turned and left.

By now it was already close to midnight, and most of the dorms were dark. Streetlights lit the campus roads, so that ahead of Fang Mu the darkness was occasionally broken by pale yellow pools of light, in which could be seen the mad fluttering of unknown insects. Fang Mu walked slowly, silent as a ghost traveling through the night.

Looking up, he saw an endless array of stars glittering in the dark canopy overhead. The air was fresh and he could feel a slight coolness as he breathed it in.

There's a sentimental notion that, when people die, they become stars in the night sky, shining down on friends and enemies alike.

Rest in peace, all of you.

The light in Room 313 was off. Fang Mu took out his key and placed it in the keyhole, only to find that the door had been locked from within.

A burst of startled noise sounded from inside. Then in a faltering voice, someone asked, "Who is it?"

"It's me, Fang Mu."

"Oh," Du Yu audibly sighed with relief. "Wait one second."

A girl's voice grumbled softly that she couldn't find her underwear.

Laughing, Fang Mu leaned against the wall opposite and lit a cigarette.

The hallway was dark as a cave. The only light was from a little 15-watt bulb in the stairwell. The light in the bathroom seemed to have gone out again. Standing in the doorway, everything looked pitch black, like an enormous, wide-open mouth.

Low noises filled the hallway.

People talking softly in their sleep.

People grinding their teeth.

The drip of the bathroom faucet.

Someone walking lightly in slippers on the floor above.

Fang Mu felt his forehead suddenly cover in thin beads of sweat. His lips trembled as he smoked his cigarette.

All of a sudden he was terrified. He glanced back and forth.

On either side of the corridor, the doors were shut tight, silent, and seemingly full of malice.

Unable to help himself, Fang Mu looked down the other end of the corridor.

The doors on either side gradually receded. Fang Mu stared rigidly at the darkness before him. What was hidden inside?

He didn't dare look away. These doors, normally so unremarkable, now seemed to come alive in the dark hallway. Laughing secretly, they watched him, this trembling loner, as he proceeded step by step toward his unknown fate. They all seemed about to fly open at any second and lead him down some alluring path, a path that would lead to his own death.

Suddenly a scorched odor filled his nose.

Fang Mu almost cried out. On either side of the hallway, the doors were now in flames. And in the smoke nearby, the outline of a person was barely visible, flickering in and out of sight.

Stepping backwards, Fang Mu reached into his backpack and groped wildly for the dagger.

By the time he finally gripped its scarred handle, he was nearly overcome with terror.

The figure slowly approached through the smoke.

Suddenly Fang Mu realized who it was.

No. Don't do it.

It was then that the door behind Fang Mu creaked open.

Rubbing his eyes, a tall, well-built young man walked out of his room. He looked at Fang Mu. At once his formerly sleepy-looking eyes opened wide.

"What are you doing out here?"

Fang Mu recognized him. He was Liu Jianjun, a Criminal Law graduate student.

Fang Mu was about to yell, "Get out of here now!" But the words caught in his throat.

The smoke and the flames instantly disappeared. As before, there was only darkness. Nothing could be seen within.

"N-nothing really," Fang Mu answered. He slowly withdrew his hand from his backpack.

Frowning, Liu Jianjun looked at him for a moment. Then he snorted, turned, and strolled over to the bathroom, his feet clapping against the floor.

Once his silhouette disappeared into the darkness of the bathroom, the door to Room 313 slid soundlessly open. Sticking his head out, Du Yu glanced toward the bathroom. Then he turned and whispered something, and a moment later Zhang Yao ran out of the room, her hair a total mess. She shot Fang Mu a vicious glare as she passed.

That's when Du Yu noticed Fang Mu was still standing awkwardly across the hall. He waved for him to come inside.

Once inside, Fang Mu sat on his bed and took a very deep breath, and then he looked up at Du Yu. "I'm sorry."

"You bastard!" muttered Du Yu, clutching his head. "I figured you weren't coming back tonight, so when I heard you knocking I thought it was campus security. Scared me so bad I almost went soft."

Fang Mu gave an exhausted laugh.

"You okay?" asked Du Yu. "You're not looking too good."

"I'm fine," said Fang Mu, shaking his head. "You should get to sleep. I know I interrupted you just now, and for that I really feel sorry."

Embarrassed, Du Yu just nodded in response. Then he climbed into bed, pulled up the covers, and before long was snoring away.

Fang Mu switched off the light and sat for a long time in the darkness. When his breathing was completely calm, he took off his clothes and slid under the covers.

You've returned.

The figures silently surround my bed. Someone standing behind me places a pair of hands on my shoulders.

"Actually, you and I are the same."

There's no need to look back. I already know it's Wu Han, his face distorted beyond all recognition.

No, you and I are not the same!

Four days after his arrest, Ma Kai finally started to talk. But even though he openly admitted to having killed the four women, he insisted that it was done out of necessity, since he was afflicted with the same serious case of anemia that killed his father and older brother. A doctor was then brought in to give Ma Kai a full physical examination. The results showed his blood levels were perfectly normal. Their evidence assembled, the city bureau decided to bring his case to trial as soon as possible.

When Tai Wei called Fang Mu to give him a summary of the recent developments in the case, Fang Mu asked if he could speak alone and in person with Ma Kai prior to the trial. At first Tai Wei was hesitant, but at last he relented.

The conversation was arranged to take place in one of the reception rooms at the lockup where Ma Kai was awaiting trial. Although Tai Wei suggested that he be in the room as well, Fang Mu insisted on being alone with Ma Kai. Unable to dissuade him, Tai Wei had no choice but to agree.

At last, the big day arrived. As Tai Wei led Fang Mu into the reception room, he repeatedly warned him to be extremely careful. "This guy's been placed in solitary confinement. You know why? Because on the night he arrived, he attacked another prisoner, bit his neck and wouldn't let go. Keep that in mind while you're in here."

The reception room was empty except for a table and two chairs, all of them fixed to the floor. There were no windows and only a single iron door. Tai Wei pointed to a red button on the wall beside the door.

"We're going to be right outside. When you're done talking, just press this button and we'll come get you." He paused. "And if anything bad happens, you be sure to press it then as well. Understand?"

Fang Mu nodded.

Tai Wei looked him over. "You didn't bring any kind of weapon, did you?"

Fang Mu hesitated for a moment. Then he reached into his backpack, grabbed his dagger and handed it to Tai Wei.

"What did you bring this thing for?" Taking the dagger, Tai Wei looked at it and frowned. "I'm going to have to confiscate it for now; afterwards I'll give it back." Raising his index finger, he feigned a threatening expression. "Ordinarily, it's illegal to own a blade like this. You follow me?"

Fang Mu laughed but said nothing.

Tai Wei placed the dagger in his pocket. "Have a seat. I'll go get the prisoner."

A few minutes, Fang Mu heard shackles dragging along the floor.

Hobbling, Ma Kai was led into the room by Tai Wei and two guards. He kept his eyes on the floor the whole time. Bruises were visible on his newly shaved head. The guards placed him in the seat opposite Fang Mu. They were about shackle him to the chair when Fang Mu stopped them.

"Take off his shackles," he said.

"Absolutely not," said Tai Wei, his tone firm.

Fang Mu took Tai Wei aside. "He has to be completely relaxed for me to get what I need," he said in a low voice.

According to the available data, despite having lost his mother as a child, Ma Kai was a normal young man until the age of 26. After graduating high school he went straight to college, where the only blemish on his record was a single failed exam. Following his college graduation, he became a business manager at a small company, and although he rarely socialized, he displayed no sign of mental illness. He was even in a serious relationship, which ended for the normal reasons. In other words, if Ma Kai's ordinary, unexceptional life was really proceeding on the proper course until he turned 26, then something must have happened to him afterwards, something that changed him completely and ended the lives of four innocent people.

What Fang Mu wanted to know was also the chief question of the entire case: what happened to Ma Kai's mind in the past two years?

"Not a chance," said Tai Wei. "This guy is extremely dangerous, and I'm responsible for your safety."

"Nothing's going to happen. But on the outside chance something does, I'll just press the button."

Tai Wei gave Fang Mu a long look. Then he signaled to the guards that they could remove the prisoner's shackles. A moment later Tai Wei walked over to Ma Kai and stood directly in front of him.

"Behave yourself!" he snapped fiercely. "You hear me?"

Once Tai Wei and the two guards exited through the iron door, Fang Mu returned to his seat at the table. He opened his notebook and switched on his tape recorder.

"Your name is Ma Kai, yes? Hi, I'm from the behavioral science department at the city bureau." Fang Mu had been about to say he was from the local TV station, but at the last second decided to switch identities.

Ma Kai made no response; just continued to hang his head.

"Are you able to hear me?" asked Fang Mu, raising his voice. At the same time, he made sure his tone remained calm. "Ma Kai, please lift your head."

Very slowly, Ma Kai looked up.

Fang Mu held his breath.

My God, what kind of eyes are these? Under the too-bright incandescent lights overhead, Ma Kai's eyes looked ashen, as if there were no pupils, as if they were just a pair of tombs set in his face. They held not a shred of life.

A graveyard, deathly still and cloaked in mist. Bare branches swaying in the wind. Crumbling structures, vaguely discernible in the distance. In a flash, Fang Mu felt himself transported into a waking dream, one from which he could not escape. Faint sounds filled his ears: the mournful squawk of crows, the peal of the funeral bells.

Fang Mu and Ma Kai faced each other for several seconds. When at last Ma Kai dropped his head once more, Fang Mu let out a deep breath.

"The reason I've come today," said Fang Mu, doing his best to keep his voice calm, "is because I'm very interested in you. If you don't mind, I would like to speak with you about yourself and the things you've done."

Still Ma Kai said nothing. His hands were clasped between his legs and Fang Mu noticed that he was swaying back and forth—slightly, though with a definite rhythm.

He was trying to divert Fang Mu's attention.

An instinctive defense mechanism.

"You've been to college," said Fang Mu, "so perhaps you're aware that my opinion will not affect the verdict of your case." He now spoke very slowly. "But I can sense that inside you there is terrible pain. If you do not want this pain to torment you until the end of your life, if you want those who have misunderstood you to know the truth, then please, trust me. Tell me what happened."

Ma Kai seemed unmoved. But then several seconds later he again raised his head. "Many people believe I'm a homicidal monster, don't they?"

Fang Mu nodded.

Ma Kai smiled wanly and shook his head. "None of you understand. I didn't want to kill anyone."

"What do you mean by that?"

Ma Kai didn't respond. He just stared at the blank wall behind Fang Mu. Again his body began to rock.

Fang Mu thought for a moment. Then he grabbed a pack of cigarettes and offered one to Ma Kai. "Would you like to smoke?"

Ma Kai looked up. He stared at the cigarettes on the table before him. Then he slowly shook his head, a look of scorn flashing through his eyes.

Seemingly indifferent, Fang Mu lit one for himself and took several deep drags. A cloud of smoke soon filled the air between him and Ma Kai. He sensed that Ma Kai's eyes were following the rising smoke. At last they came to rest on the cigarette in Fang Mu's mouth.

Suddenly he blurted out: "Smoking is bad for your health."

Fang Mu immediately seized on this topic: "Oh, well, in that case, how do you feel about your health right now?"

Ma Kai stared at Fang Mu for several seconds. Finally he shook his head. "It's not good."

"In what way is it not good?"

The muscles in Ma Kai's face twitched. Then he looked away and his voice grew soft. "I have severe anemia."

"But the doctor already examined you and said your blood is completely normal."

"What do they know?" said Ma Kai, his voice rising abruptly. At once his body straightened up and he whipped his hands out from between his legs. "I know my own illness the best! My father died from blood sickness, my older brother, too, and as for me, sooner or later all the blood in my body will dry up, and I'll die like a crumbling, old mummy. I know it's true."

"You don't trust the doctor's diagnosis?"

"You're all liars. You all want me to die. You'd never help me. I pay you money, you give me blood! But suddenly they say it's not okay. What kind of logic is that? Why is it not okay? My father was lying on the hospital bed, his face growing paler and paler. I knew his blood was slowly drying up. Then they gave him a transfusion and he could walk, he could eat, he could talk with me. Why won't they give me a transfusion? They want me to die. That's why. I know it."

"So what did you do?"

"I won't die, not like my father and my brother, lying on the hospital bed, withered to nothing. I won't do it," he said heatedly. "I will save myself!"

Fang Mu sat there in a daze, as if he had just received an electric shock. All of a sudden, the words in his ears seemed to grow farther and farther away....

One library card. Eleven trembling students. Chen Xi, her long hair fluttering. A devil's banquet: the twisted bodies of Fourth Brother and Wang Jian, burned black as charcoal.

And him.

A scorched odor filled the air. The person before him blurred. He looked close. A smiling mouth, wriggling slowly open:

Actually, you and I are the same.

Click. The tape recorder abruptly stopped.

With a start, Fang Mu snapped back to reality. Ma Kai's nervous chatter continued to sound in his ears:

"…she was such an ample woman. Her cheeks were so flushed. I followed her all the way back to her building corridor…When I forced my way inside she still thought I was going to rob her…" He chuckled to himself.

"Why always women?" asked Fang Mu as he changed the tape.

"Because their blood is clean and soft and easy to absorb. Male blood is too thick, too coarse."

"Really? How do you know?"

"It's just what I think."

"In that case, why this woman?"

Ma Kai was silent for a moment. He seemed not to have considered this question. After thinking about it for a while, he scratched his head and said, "No reason, really. I was walking along, I saw her, so I followed."

"You never considered whether there might be someone waiting for her at home?"

"If there was, I'd get out of there. It happened once; this woman's husband was already there. Good thing I'm a fast runner!" Ma Kai opened his mouth and laughed aloud.

"Sucking blood," said Fang Mu, staring into Ma Kai's eyes, "does it work?"

At once Ma Kai's expression became serious. "Of course it does. I'm still alive, aren't I? Without it I'd already be dead."

"Then why do you mix the blood with other liquids? Couldn't you drink a lot more of it by itself?"

"Look, I'm not some crazed killer; I just need it to survive. Also," Ma Kai shook his head, "the stuff tastes terrible."

"Well if you want to suck blood, why not just suck it? Why do you need to cut open their stomachs? Wouldn't it just be easier to slit their wrists?"

Ma Kai shook his head, a faint smile on his face. "You don't understand. I like the feeling, all of it rushing out at once. Like a flood. I would do anything to make my blood rush like that."

Ma Kai closed his eyes, his expression that of a man savoring a delicious memory.

What was he imagining? Fang Mu wondered. Was he swimming through a boundless lake of blood, one that was all his, that beckoned him to the endless horizon? Here he could stop to drink his fill whenever he wanted—never needing to wipe his mouth, or worry that it would ever dry up. How wonderful to live forever, even if he was cursed to become a vampire.

"Tell me about the little girl."

"Which one?" asked Ma Kai, sounding puzzled.

"The one you killed." Fang Mu suddenly wanted to vomit.

"Oh, her." Ma Kai leaned back as if it was nothing. "What do you want to know?"

"You already killed the woman, why didn't you suck her blood? Why'd you take the little girl instead?"

"Ah, yes, the little one." Ma Kai smacked his lips. "Oh, she was very pretty. Plump little arms, such delicate skin. She seemed ready to burst if you pinched her. And her neck was so thin. After only the slightest effort she was unconscious."

"Why did you need to kill her? At that point you already had blood ready to drink."

Ma Kai laughed quietly. "Little brother, if I offered you a potato or a cherry, which would you eat?"

Fang Mu's clenched his fists. Potatoes? Cherries? These were two living human beings!" He thought of Tong Hui's big lifeless eyes, still wide open when they found her. Struggling to keep his cool, he forced himself to speak as flatly as possible. "Why did you bring the little girl with you? You could have just killed her and drank her blood right there. Why take that big of a risk?"

"Are you crazy?" Ma Kai frowned at Fang Mu, the look in his eyes like he was sitting across the table from a madman. "How could I let a child see something like that? She was far too young."

Fang Mu's blood, which had only just now settled down, began to boil once more. He looked at Ma Kai in disbelief. The other man stared back at him, a scolding look on his face, as if he were lecturing an ignorant young man.

You need to calm down. He's beginning to trust you. Don't blow it.

"Do I take you to mean that..." Fang Mu forced his voice to remain relaxed, "You still very much respected...those women?"

"Of course." Ma Kai's voice was very serious. "As I said, I killed them purely out of necessity. There was no reason to make them suffer any further." Ma Kai then dropped his head and thought for a few moments. When he looked up, his voice was sincere. "Couldn't my behavior be considered a case of dire necessity? I remember one of my college professors taught us about a legal case in which the British Crown sued two men, Dudley and Stephenson. They were being charged with cannibalism. My situation was the same as theirs; we were each just trying to save ourselves. If you have a chance, do me a favor and talk to the judge. Tell him it was dire necessity."

"Yeah, sure," said Fang Mu, not wanting to continue on the topic. "Now back to the little girl. How did you feel when you drank her blood?"

"Excellent. Pure, clear-headed, full of energy. She was a child, after all." Ma Kai paused for a moment, remembering the sensation. The look on his face was one of great satisfaction. "That night I slept very well, and for many days after, my spirits were high. It's just different when they're young."

"That's why you decided to begin selecting young girls?"

"Correct," said Ma Kai, without a hint of shame. "Their blood is much more ideal."

Fang Mu stared into Ma Kai's eyes. He imagined Xu Jie convulsed with terror, trapped in Ma Kai's apartment. What had this man felt when he strapped her to his bed? Joy? Excitement? Or was it satisfaction?

Noticing the expression on Fang Mu's face, Ma Kai quickly added: "You think I was only considering myself? This way I could last a lot longer." Again he dropped his head. "And I could also hurt fewer people."

"You'll never hurt anyone again!" As soon as the words left his mouth, Fang Mu felt a burst of vengeful delight. There was nothing else he needed to ask. They could send this guy straight to hell. He began organizing his things, his arms shaking. It took a lot of effort to remove the tape from the recorder.

He put on his backpack and glanced over at Ma Kai, and then he walked to the door and pressed the red button.

There was no response.

The whole time Fang Mu was interviewing Ma Kai, Tai Wei was next door in the control room, observing everything on the security camera screen. Next to him stood a prison guard, holding an electric baton. Although he was also staring at the screen, his mind was actually tuning into the on-duty room across the hall where the voices of his coworkers could frequently be heard cheering wildly and swearing in disgust.

It was a World Cup warm-up match: France versus South Korea. The score was tied 2-2. Zidane had been hurt and was sitting out.

Suddenly Tai Wei's cell phone rang. He picked it up.

"Hello, Officer Tai?" said the voice on the end. "It's Little Chen from the Hongyuan substation."

Tai Wei was about to ask which Little Chen when he heard a sudden beep from the phone, indicating another call.

"Officer Tai? It's Xu Liansheng."

Now Tai Wei was even more confused. Who the heck was Xu Liansheng?

"Thank you, thank you," continued Xu Liansheng, his voice choked with sobs. "You saved my daughter, you saved my whole family! Thank you, Officer Tai!"

Now Tai Wei remembered. Xu Liansheng was the father of Xu Jie, the little girl they had rescued.

Over the course of the next 10 minutes, Tai Wei used all his skill to convince Xu Liansheng not to immediately come to the city bureau and give him a silk banner as a reward. And because cell phone reception in the control room was spotty, he had no choice but to go out into the hallway to begrudgingly finish the conversation.

"That guy was too much," muttered Tai Wei as he walked quickly back down the hallway. Passing the on-duty room, he noticed the electric baton-wielding guard standing outside the door with his mouth open and eyes fixed on the TV screen, just as Park Ji-Sung dribbled beautifully past Christophe Dugarry.

Tai Wei just shook his head and walked into the control room. He glanced at the screen. Suddenly he was yelling: "Get in here now! Someone get this door open!"

Fang Mu held his breath and pressed the red button a second time. Again nothing happened.

His forehead immediately broke out in a sweat.

Should he turn around? Behind him was the most dangerous bloodsucking son of a bitch he'd ever faced.

He turned anyway. He mustn't let his distress show; otherwise he'd be at a serious disadvantage.

"The guard is in the bathroom," said Fang Mu, affecting an expression of total casualness as he returned to his seat. He made a show of coolly glancing over at Ma Kai.

What he saw shocked him.

The trust and sincerity that had been in Ma Kai's eyes only a moment before was now gone, replaced by a look of the deepest hatred.

"You'll never hurt anyone again!" was what he'd last said to the convict.

Idiot! He thought. Why did I have to say that?

It was essential to divert his attention.

"The bruises on your head—how'd you get them?" he asked, plucking a cigarette from the pack and placing it in his mouth. He fumbled several times with the lighter before getting it lit.

Ma Kai didn't make a sound. He just continued to stare fixedly at Fang Mu.

Suddenly Fang Mu remembered. Ma Kai's first night in lockup; he had attacked another prisoner. The bruises must come from the guards and other prisoners.

"Did you attack someone?"

Although Ma Kai still said nothing, his breathing grew heavier.

Noticing this change, Fang Mu's nervousness reached its peak. However, he continued to speak.

"What happened? You suck his blood? I thought you said that male blood was too thick, too difficult to absorb." Damn! Why did I just say that?

Ma Kai's mouth twisted into a strange smile.

"I can make do if I have to. Such as with you, for example." A look of hunger flashed through his eyes, like a bat in sight of its prey.

Fang Mu's mind went blank. He laughed dryly. "You really think I didn't bring anything to protect myself?"

"Oh?" Ma Kai had been about to stand up, but now he hesitated. A moment later, however, he was once more at ease. "Impossible. They'd never let you bring a weapon in here."

"You think not?" said Fang Mu, forcing himself to keep a thin smile on his face. The smile was there, but he couldn't keep from trembling.

Suddenly, Ma Kai rose to his feet, rushed in on Fang Mu and reached his emaciated arms toward Fang Mu' neck.

Already stretched to their limits, Fang Mu's nerves snapped. With a yell, he rolled out of his chair and scrambled to the other side of the table, keeping it between him and Ma Kai.

The two of them began circling the table like they were playing a game of tag. Ma Kai's eyes were wide and bloodshot and he was breathing deeply, as if in anticipation. Froth bubbled from the corners of his mouth. Several times Ma Kai tried to jump onto the table, but Fang Mu always beat him back with a swing of his book bag, the contents inside sent flying all over the room.

He wanted to yell for help, but the words caught in his throat.

Finally, Ma Kai lost his patience and leapt successfully onto the table. In desperation, Fang Mu swung his book bag as hard as he could, but since nearly all his things had already flown out, the hit landed soft as a feather and did nothing. Protecting his face, Ma Kai dove forward. Fang Mu dodged back, slipped on a ballpoint pen that had rolled out, and fell face up on the floor.

Seeing his advantage, Ma Kai leapt on him, hands groping for Fang Mu's neck. Fang Mu blocked the grabbing hands and got his foot under him, then he kicked as hard as he could, launching Ma Kai across the room.

As Ma Kai writhed on the floor, groaning in pain, Fang Mu climbed to his feet and ran to the door. He banged on it in desperation, yelling for help. Seconds later he felt Ma Kai's hands on his shirt from behind, pulling him down.

Their previous struggle had nearly exhausted Fang Mu, and he was increasingly incapable of fighting back. Ma Kai, on the other hand, despite his thin, sickly appearance, had become crazed and tireless in his thirst for blood.

I can't keep this up, thought Fang Mu, watching Ma Kai's gaping mouth draw closer and closer. Instinctively, he turned his head away, but in doing so offered his carotid artery up to his opponent.

Ma Kai's heavy breath sounded in Fang Mu's ear, his saliva dripping onto his open neck. Fang Mu could practically imagine the pain of those sharp teeth tearing into his flesh.

Help me...

With eyes closed, Fang Mu heard the iron door slam open and someone rush inside. At once Ma Kai's grip on his shoulders relaxed, and then his body softly rolled off of him.

He opened his eyes to see Tai Wei's worried face hovering over him. The electric baton was in his hand.

"Are you okay?"

Tai Wei reached out and helped Fang Mu to his feet. Stumbling, Fang Mu quickly grabbed onto the table to steady himself. After taking several ragged breaths, he felt his neck. Suddenly a wave of nausea washed over him, and he bent over and retched.

Several guards had Ma Kai pinned to the floor, and were replacing his shackles and handcuffs.

Fang Mu waited until he was no longer shaking so badly. Then he crouched down and, with difficulty, picked up his belongings scattered on the floor and put them in his bag.

Although Ma Kai's head was pressed against the floor, he watched Fang Mu the whole time, a calm, almost serene expression in his eyes. Not daring to meet his gaze, Fang Mu did his best to look away as he organized the things in his backpack and then haltingly made his way to the door. Tai Wei hurried over to help him, but Fang Mu shoved away his hand.

"Get off me!" he yelled. Then he left the room without looking back.

One hour later, at a small restaurant outside the Jiangbin City University gate, Tai Wei was looking across the table at Fang Mu, who was drinking cup after cup of water, his head down.

"All right, all right," said Tai Wei, passing Fang Mu a cigarette. "You still pissed at me?"

Fang Mu didn't want to take it, but when he saw that it was a super-expensive Zhonghua brand cigarette, he accepted.

Tai Wei hurried to light it for him. "That's the right idea," he said. "Don't be angry with me."

Cigarette hanging from his mouth, Fang Mu mumbled something that sounded like, "I wasn't angry."

"I've already yelled at that guard," retorted Tai Wei in a fierce voice, keeping one eye on Fang Mu's expression as he spoke. "It's a good thing you weren't hurt, otherwise I wouldn't have been so merciful!"

Fang Mu's face seemed to relax a little. Actually, he had been partly responsible for what had happened that afternoon. If he hadn't enraged Ma Kai by saying, "You'll never hurt anyone again!" he could have kept the situation under control. Still, he couldn't help but take it personally that he was nearly killed while Tai Wei was absent from his post.

"You should really eat something, too. My treat," said Tai Wei effusively, mostly because inside he was filled with guilt and fear over what could have happened. He ordered a heap of food and several bottles of beer.

After emptying several glasses of beer, the two of them began talking more freely, as if they had forgotten the terrifying events of earlier that day.

"You know," said Tai Wei, his face flushed, "I really admire you, little brother. If it weren't for you, who knows when we would have cracked this case."

Shaking his head, Fang Mu just smiled and took a sip of beer.

"Still, there's something I don't get," Tai Wei continued.

"Oh," said Fang Mu, "what's that?"

"Well, for one thing, how'd you determine Ma Kai's appearance? Or where he lived and what his family was like?"

Fang Mu placed his glass of beer on the table. "The first time we met, you gave me a bunch of crime scene photographs and reports to look at. Later, we went to one of the scenes together—the one where Yao Xiaoyang and Tong Hui were killed. Taken together, all this information gave me a distinct impression: total chaos. The victims were chosen without rhyme or reason, no forethought was put into any of the crimes, and the scenes themselves weren't straightened up at all. He was even taking the knives used to cut open his victims from their own homes, and then leaving them there afterwards. This led me to believe the culprit was what criminologists call a Disorganized Serial Killer."

"A disorganized serial killer?"

"That's right, as opposed to an Organized Serial Killer. This classification was created by the American F.B.I. in the 1980s. So-called disorganized serial killers usually suffer from serious mental disorders. Additionally, they have often lost much of their intelligence and social awareness—or never had much to begin with—and are either partly or fully disconnected from reality. This results in certain commonly recognizable aspects to their crimes; i.e., they are often impulsive and commit the crimes in areas well-known to the killer. And the scenes themselves are generally messy—carelessly so—and full of evidence. In the case of the bloodsucker, all of these characteristics were obvious."

"Is that so?" Tai Wei was listening intently. "Regardless, it still doesn't seem possible to determine the killer's appearance, family background, and living situation from this information alone."

"Of course it's not. But first let me ask you a question. Have you ever felt a certain way about someone, good or bad, the moment you saw them, and then after meeting them found that your intuition was exactly right?"

After thinking for a moment, Tai Wei nodded. "Yeah, I have."

"Any idea why this happens?"

"Not a clue," said Tai Wei honestly.

Fang Mu smiled. "It's because this person closely reminded you of someone you met in the past, someone who definitely left a deep impression on you. So when you encountered this new individual, you subconsciously replaced his personality with that of the old person, and as a result immediately liked or disliked him. And as we have discovered, there are times when this seemingly improbable kind of intuition is totally correct, which goes a long way to solving the problem."

"What problem?"

"Sometimes, people who look alike are alike."

Tai Wei frowned. "Are you talking about Cesare Lombroso? Born criminals?"

"Yes, very good. In his book, Criminal Man, Cesare Lombroso set forth his theories about so-called born criminals. He also boldly detailed the physical appearances of various kinds of criminals. For example, murderers often have cold, detached eyes, aquiline noses, strong jaw lines, and large ears; while thieves have short hair, narrow foreheads, and thick, closely-spaced eyebrows. Many people have criticized these theories as being unrealistic, but they forget that that Lombroso was a classic empiricist. He made sure that all of his theories were based on concrete evidence. So although a lot of modern empiricists doubt it, I believe his theories about born criminals are entirely scientific. For example, environment, upbringing, culture, and diet all have clear effects on criminality."

"In what way?"

"Let me give you a simple example. You ever hear how husbands and wives look alike?"

"Of course."

"One man, one woman, different in appearance before marriage, increasingly similar afterwards. Why is that? It's because when people live together, their diets become more or less the same—their work and leisure habits, too—and as a result their complexions follow suit. For this reason they will seem to be growing more and more alike."

"Huh." Tai Wei nodded, seemingly lost in thought.

"Now let's look at Ma Kai. I deduced he was very thin for two reasons. The first was that I knew the killer struggled violently with some of his victims. The second was that I sensed an extreme anxiety in his crimes, which I felt was connected to his perceived lack of blood or some other negative physical condition. Think about it: if a person were to live with this kind of anxiety over the long term, his diet would definitely be affected, and he would display signs of malnourishment. In other words, he would look thin and weak. A person like this, who couldn't even attend to his most basic needs, would obviously not be doing squat for his appearance. Among other things, this would lead most notably to him having long, dirty hair. He was also almost certain to live alone, because if he shared a house with relatives or friends their guidance would have calmed him down and prevented his anxiety from devolving into paranoia. His sickness must have only come on in the past few years, otherwise he would have killed sooner, and there have been no crimes like these in the city for some time."

Fang Mu took a sip of water and then lit another cigarette.

"The disorganized serial killer has a few classic characteristics," he said. "These include poor social skills, a tendency toward anxiety, and the inability to hold skilled jobs, among other things. They are also often the youngest son, pay little attention to the news, and live alone, generally near the scenes of their crimes. This is why I felt the killer probably lived nearby. And since Hongyuan District is in the old part of the city, it has very little commercial housing. This is significant. Because the killer would have been unable to hold a high-paying job due to his mental disorder, he also would have been unable to afford an apartment at market price. Therefore, he most likely lived in a house inherited from his parents. This meant that they must have worked for some state-owned company, because back then only state employees received discounted housing."

Fang Mu tapped the ash from his cigarette. "So, to sum things up, the killer was under thirty, emaciated, unkempt, with an apartment near the crime scenes, parents who once worked for a state-owned company, and with a very serious mental disorder."

Tai Wei stared at Fang Mu. He was dumbstruck, and it took him a while to snap out of it.

"My god," he said. "You were right about everything."

Fang Mu smiled faintly. "Not quite. I was initially wrong about the connection between blood and his crimes. I thought his anxiety about blood had something to do with the weather."

"Really?" Tai Wei thought for a moment. "Oh yeah, now I remember. When Tong Hui was taken, you said the killer would probably be wearing thick clothing."

"That's right. Since his first murder was committed just after the end of winter, I had thought he was afraid of his blood freezing, or something along those lines, and was taking various measures to keep warm—like wearing thick clothing, for example. But after seeing where Tong Hui was murdered, I decided he was actually paranoid about his blood being somehow deficient."

Seeing the reverent look on Tai Wei's face, Fang Mu laughed. "Look, I'm not that good. There were still a bunch of things I was unclear about; for example, how he chose his victims, why he cut them open, why he mixed their blood with other liquids, why he carried Tong Hui away from the scene—a ton of stuff."

"Oh…" said Tai Wei, as if he had suddenly realized something. "So that's what you asked Ma Kai during your interview?"

"Exactly."

"You're so interested and have studied a bunch of cases." Tai Wei gave him a meaningful glance. "Want to be a criminologist in the future?"

Fang Mu was taken aback. "I don't think so," he said after a moment. "Actually, I've never really thought that far ahead."

"So then why are you so interested in this stuff," asked Tai Wei, finally voicing the question that had been puzzling him for so long.

Fang Mu's face fell, and for a while he was silent. At last he spoke: "I don't know."

Tai Wei was a little drunk when they left the restaurant and went to his car. "Little brother," he said, clapping Fang Mu on the shoulder, "you've helped me a hell of a lot. Any reward you want—it's yours!"

Fang Mu smiled and shook his head. "You don't need to do that."

"Yes, I do!" cried Tai Wei gruffly. "You want some kind of material reward? Or should I write a commendatory letter to your school? Oh, right…" Suddenly remembering something, he shook his head. "Oh yeah, perhaps it had better not be me who writes it." He chuckled to himself.

Fang Mu was about to ask him what he was talking about when Tai Wei slapped him heavily on the back and said, "Well if the damn bureau won't reward you, I will! What do you students need these days?" He scratched his head, racking his brain for an answer.

"Don't worry about it," said Fang Mu, waving his hand. "Seriously, I don't need anything." When he saw Tai Wei take out his wallet, his expression dropped. "Tai Wei, would you consider us friends?"

Tai Wei nodded forcefully.

"Well, if that's really the case, don't do this."

Scratching his head, Tai Wei thought for a long moment. Finally, in what seemed an act of great determination, he withdrew his Type-64 pistol from its holster and ejected the clip. Then he removed a single bullet and grasped Fang Mu's hand.

"What are you doing?" asked Fang Mu in surprise.

"For us cops, our gun is our best friend." Tai Wei's face was very serious as he placed the bullet in Fang Mu's palm, and then closed his hand around it. "I can't give you my gun, so this bullet will have to do. Keep it as a souvenir."

Damn, brother, thought Fang Mu, isn't this is a little unlucky? Handing over bullet as if it were no more than a piece of candy and saying, 'Here, try it!'

Nonetheless, Fang Mu carefully placed the bullet in his pants pocket. Then he waved goodbye to Tai Wei. "I should head back now," he said. "Be careful driving home."

Fang Mu turned to go, but after only a few steps Tai Wei called for him to wait. Fang Mu looked back.

Tai Wei stared at him for several moments, as if examining a specimen. "Fang Mu," he said at last, his voice gravely serious, "have you considered being a policeman in the future?"

"Not once!" Fang Mu said with finality, and then turned and walked away without looking back.

Embarrassed, Tai Wei angrily yanked open the car door, climbed inside, and started the engine. Glancing at the "Policeman's Five Prohibitions" sign hanging from his rear view mirror, Tai Wei prayed that he wouldn't get stopped, and then he pulled out. *(Translator's note: "Policeman's Five Prohibitions": Gambling, Carrying guns while drunk, Carrying guns off duty, Drinking on duty, and, Drunk driving.)*

Instead of returning to his dorm, Fang Mu walked to the bus stop just outside the campus gate. Hiding behind the covered bench, he watched Tai Wei's car fade smaller into the distance, then he hopped on Local Bus

315.

When the bus reached Eternal Life Road, Fang Mu got off. After walking up the street for a short way, he reached Prolonging Life Road, the site of Jiangbin City's main market for funeral products. Eternal life, prolonging life—in fact, the windows of every store here were filled with wreathes and papier-mâché burial figures. It was common knowledge that too many things on this earth failed to live up to their names.

Twenty minutes later, Fang Mu boarded the bus heading back to school, a bulging black plastic bag in his hands.

1 o'clock a.m.

The plastic bag kept crinkling in Fang Mu's hands as he tiptoed up to the seventh floor. The sound was terribly annoying. This was an all-girls floor, and should some unlucky lady choose this moment to walk to the bathroom, she'd almost certainly faint from fear.

After carefully opening the window that led to the rooftop, Fang Mu tossed the bag out. Then he climbed through without a sound, grabbed the bag, and walked directly to the northeast corner.

It was a pleasant night, silent but for the faint rustle of the wind, which sounded like a group of people quietly chatting. A pile of sand sat in the northeast corner, countless pieces of ash mixed in. Crouching down, Fang Mu reached into his bag and withdrew several bundles of paper burial money. He undid the bundles, took out his lighter and set them aflame. Soon a small bonfire was softly illuminating the midnight rooftop.

With nearly all its students wandering through sweet dreams or vivid nightmares, the darkened campus was unusually tranquil. But should any humans or ghosts have been passing in the night, none would have noticed the strange memorial taking place on the roof of Dorm 5, Unit B—though it was far from the first.

Fang Mu lit a cigarette and took a drag, and then he placed it on a brick beside him. Lighting a second cigarette, he inhaled deeply and slowly exhaled, the smoke curling upwards in the firelight like a veil. For a moment it fluttered gently, and then it disappeared into the night air.

Wang Jian, Fourth Brother, how have the two of you been?

And you, Chen Xi.

Tears fell from Fang Mu's eyes.

I caught another demon. Are you happy for me? What number was this? Six, I think. He was ruthless, killing women and then sucking their blood. And I did really well: we caught him before he could kill the final girl, and now he'll never kill again. He's going straight to hell.

I'll never be too late again. That nightmare was enough for a lifetime.

And if it really was all just a dream? How wonderful that would be.

Fang Mu whispered softly as he stirred the fire. The flames lit his pale face. His expression was surreal, as if he were in a dream. Large tears rolled down his face. He didn't wipe them away, allowing them to fall to the rooftop.

A burst of wind whirled the paper ash. Some of it stuck lightly to Fang Mu's face. When he tried to brush it away, his hand was streaked with black. He knew his face couldn't look much better.

He laughed softly.

Was that you, Chen Xi?

All right, I won't cry.

Fang Mu stood and tossed more burial money on the fire. He turned to look at the cigarette. It was almost out.

He lit Wang Jian another one. Then one more for himself.

The fire slowly burned down, until the only thing left was a pile of ash. Fang Mu covered the ashes with sand, and then took another bundle of burial money from his bag and set it aflame.

And with that, his corner of the darkened rooftop was illuminated once more. By now Fang Mu's eyes had long since dried, his mouth was pinched at the corners and his brows were knit. His expression was inscrutable.

Sun Mei, I've come to see you.

Even though he was never particularly fond of Sun Mei, he couldn't deny that she had saved him twice. Her fate had been horrible beyond imagining.

No matter one's luck, life always comes to an end, like the ash from the fire. Whirling through the air, only to be broken to pieces and forgotten.

Love will be there in the next world, too. Just remember to be happy.

Fang Mu held the final bundle of money for a long time. It wasn't until the fire had almost died that he tossed it in.

I hope you too can find some happiness there, Wu Han.

When he returned to his dorm room, Fang Mu felt unspeakably exhausted. However, his mind was at peace.

He felt this way every time he memorialized the dead, as if the burden he carried was somehow lightened.

Fang Mu slumped carelessly onto his desk chair. Moonlight shined through the open window. Softly, gently, it blanketed Fang Mu, seeming almost tangible. A light wind brushed his face, the air cool and refreshing. It felt wonderful, as if it were passing right through him, leaving him translucent and pure. He rested his head against the windowpane. His eyelids grew heavier and heavier...

Several minutes later, Fang Mu woke with a start.

Du Yu was talking in his sleep. "Actually, B Cafeteria's spare ribs are the best!"

Rubbing his temples, Fang Mu leaned over and switched on his computer.

The machine buzzed to life. Half a minute later, he opened a folder on his hard drive titled "Ma Kai".

Fang Mu's face was tinted blue in the light of the screen, his eyes once more cold, weary, and incomparably sharp.

8 HAPPINESS

"Oh, it's you. Come in."

"I'm not disturbing you?"

"Not at all. Some water?"

"Yes, thank you."

"Did you finish those books?"

"Yeah, I actually came by today to return them."

"How were they? Could you understand them?"

"Only some parts. A lot of it I didn't understand at all."

"No problem. That's perfectly normal. Those books really were a little deep for you. How have you been recently?"

"Pretty good."

"Still your complexion's not looking so great. Is it the same thing as before? The thing you're afraid of?"

"Um…yeah, it is."

"Then can you tell me what it is exactly that you're afraid of?"

No response.

"Look at me. I hope that you trust me. I might be able to help."

The student sighed.

"All right. I'm…afraid of roll call."

"Roll call?"

"It's really strange, isn't it?"

"No, I actually don't find it strange in the least. I once knew someone who was afraid to cross bridges by himself."

"Really? Afraid to cross bridges?"

"That's right. Eventually he wouldn't even walk down fairly narrow streets alone. His wife had to go with him."

"But why? Was it another phobia?"

"Correct. In fact, it's another manifestation of agoraphobia. This man had been pampered since he was young. Everything was done for him, and after marrying he relied entirely on his wife to take care of things. Therefore, he developed a subconscious need to be near her, like a child. But on the surface he refused to admit this puerile need, so his agoraphobia functioned as a way of forcing his wife to stay by his side."

"Did he get better?"

"Of course. Thanks to a combination of medicinal treatment and behavioral therapy, he was soon completely cured."

"Oh. So he needed to use medication to recover?"

"Of course. So how about it? Will you tell me why you're afraid of roll call?"

"To be honest, I don't really know myself."

"Indeed? Well in that case, when did you first became afraid of it?"

"Hmm. I—don't remember that either. I'm sorry."

"Don't worry about it. Here, come lie down on this couch. How is it?

Comfortable?"

"Yeah, really comfortable."

"Would you like to listen to some music?"

"Okay."

"Let's listen to this one first."

The sound of Mozart's Cradle Song filled the room. Next was Mendelssohn's A Midsummer Night's Dream. Then Tsai Chin's Lost Time.

"Which was the most relaxing?"

"The last one. I couldn't understand the first two."

"Okay. How many classes did you attend this afternoon?"

"What? Oh, um, two classes."

"Then what did you do?"

"Played some basketball."

" That's a pretty packed day. Do you feel tired?"

"A little."

"That's good. I want you to imagine that you're just relaxing. Now please follow what I say. First, get as comfortable as possible. Then relax your body and begin taking deep breaths."

"...Like this?"

"Yes, very good. Breathe out slowly, just like that. Excellent. Now one more time. Take a deep breath, and then exhale. Good. What sort of environment do you like?"

"Um, how about the beach?"

"All right, then imagine that you're lying on the beach right now. The sea breeze is cool and refreshing. Very pleasant. The waves crash rhythmically against the shore. Whoosh, whoosh, like that, one after another. Can you sense your inner mind? Very good. Use it to feel every part of your body. When you feel your head, your head will relax. When you feel your chest and back, your body will relax. As you relax your torso, your breathing will become smoother and smoother. When you feel your arms, your arms will relax. When you feel your legs, your legs will relax. Your body is becoming more and more relaxed, more and more relaxed... Good. How do you feel now?"

"Very...comfortable. My mind feels so... so at ease. My body—it's like there's a...white light."

His voice was low, as if every word required a huge effort.

"Very good. Quietly enjoy it."

Five minutes passed.

"Okay. I will now count slowly from one to ten. When I reach ten, your subconscious will return you to a time in the past, and you will witness an event that has had an enormous impact on you. When I reach ten, no matter what you see or feel, you will speak it aloud. Afterwards, if it is a happy memory you will remember it, and if it's not a happy memory, you will let it go. All right?"

The student slowly nodded.

"Okay, then let's begin. 1...2...3...4...5...6...7...8...9...10."

Suddenly, the student's eyeballs began moving rapidly beneath his eyelids. The man smiled. Very good. This meant his subconscious was already giving him information.

"We're in the courtyard... I can smell roasted grasshoppers... Dad took me home on his bike... I have to finish my homework before I can go play... Wooden gun... Much better than Big Meng's."

He must not be older than ten in this memory, the man thought.

"I'm in a sandpit, playing machine gun war with my friends." His voice was now more childish, livelier. "...Little Fatty is such a cheater; he never lies down when he dies... I can see PLA soldiers drilling over there." His voice was full of admiration and longing. "They're so awesome... Left, right, left; left, right, left... Roll call.... Wang Libo, here. Meng Fanzhe, here... Huh, what's wrong with him? Why won't he answer when they say his name? Oh, no, now the officer is angry." His voice became fearful. "They're calling his name again... Why can't he say it? They're calling him again... Come on, you can do it... Is he stuttering? No, don't hurt him. His body began to shake. "...So much blood... They punished him; he's running alone around the field..."

 Suddenly his breathing became fast and his body began to convulse.

"What do you see?"

"I've fallen." He began to cry. "... My forehead... The blood won't stop... Gym teacher... Roll call... He hits me... Please no..."

"That's enough; this memory is over. Now then, the things you saw just now are imprinted deep in your consciousness, and at all times are never far from your mind, correct?"

"Yes... yes, that's right."

"Can you still feel the white light?"

"...I can."

"Very good. The white light will now gradually disappear, and you will gradually regain consciousness. I am going to count backwards from ten. When I reach one, you will wake up. Do you understand?"

"...I do."

"Good. Now then. Ten, the white light is becoming fainter and fainter, your body and mind are very relaxed. Nine, you're becoming more and more awake. Eight, your body is gradually regaining normal sensations. Seven, feeling is returning to your fingers. Six, your heart is tranquil and serene, you feel very happy. Five, more and more awake now. Four, your neck gradually begins to move. Three, you feel an enormous energy throughout your body. Two, wake up, the way out is in front of you. One, you're now fully awake; open your eyes!"

The sound of a deep breathing commenced.

"My god, was I just…hypnotized?"

"More or less."

"I remembered all of it. When I was nine, I saw them beat a stuttering soldier."

"Yes, that's what it sounded like."

"But then why couldn't I think of it before?"

"This is called Psychogenic Memory Loss. This kind of memory loss comes from a sort of choice. In other words, you have chosen to forget these painful experiences. To be perfectly honest, it's an escape."

"Is it good for me to remember this stuff?"

"Of course. To solve any problem you must locate its source, especially psychological problems. Once we find the cause, it's easy to fix."

"Will you help me?"

"Do you trust me?"

"Of course, but will you?"

"Haven't I been helping you all along?"

"Yes, you're right. Thank you."

"No need to be so polite. However, I do have one request. Will you keep our sessions a secret?"

"Yes."

Sleep. Read. Class. Basketball occasionally.

No worrying about who might be killed. No coming face to face with a bloodsucking madman. Even the old nightmares were few and far between.

This was happiness.

Fang Mu passed that week like a normal student, his days filled with study and leisure. Life was peaceful. When the weekend came, he used the time to visit home, where he filled up on his mother's cooking and gained four pounds.

The weather grew hotter. And though he did not know why, his spirits improved.

Riding the bus back to school, he felt the wind brush softly against his face. His skin tingled delightfully. The sun was blazing down outside, and the smell of green grass filled the air. He felt the bottles and jars stuffed inside his bag, filled with meat sauce and pickled vegetables that his mom had prepared for him. Leaning lazily against the seat back, he closed his eyes and dozed off.

How long had it been since he'd last felt this way?

When Fang Mu walked into the dorm room, Du Yu was playing Counter-Strike.

"You're back?" he asked when he heard the door open, though he didn't take his eyes off the screen.

"Why aren't you out with Zhang Yao? The weather's perfect today."

Du Yu laughed. "She's at her private tutoring job. Anyway, it's nice having some time to myself."

Fang Mu took out a jar of meat sauce and placed it on Du Yu's desk. "Here, this is for you. My mom made it. You should try some."

"Huh?" Taken off guard, Du Yu turned to look at it. "Oh, thanks."

"Watch out!" Fang Mu yelled, pointing at the screen.

"Wha—?" Du Yu spun around and grabbed for the mouse and keyboard. But he was too late. With a bang, his character's head exploded.

"Shit. That's it, I'm done." Du Yu exited the game. Then he withdrew a pair of chopsticks from his desk drawer and opened the jar of meat sauce. Sticking his chopsticks in, he stirred the sauce around, and then grabbed a few chunks of meat and ate them.

"Oh, man!" he cried, chewing. "This stuff is good! Your mom is a serious cook."

"Then eat up. I've got a bunch more over here."

"All right, tonight I'll eat noodles for dinner. Mixed with some of this sauce, it'll be delicious." Du Yu grabbed another big piece and ate it.

"Guess you like salty things, too." Fang Mu smiled.

"You know, brother," said Du Yu, chewing as he spoke, "recently you've seemed pretty happy."

"Yeah?" said Fang Mu, only half paying attention as he put away his things.

"I think it's good for you, being around other people more. No reason to be so standoffish all the time."

Fang Mu laughed. "Everyone thinks I'm pretty weird, don't they?"

"Um…" Du Yu hesitated for a moment. "I wouldn't put it that way. Really they just think you're too introverted."

Fang Mu laughed. "Yeah, I understand."

"Over the past little while it always seemed like something was troubling you. Liu Jianjun told me he once saw you walking alone in the hallway in the middle of the night. You know if there's ever anything on your mind you can talk to me. We're good friends, aren't we?"

Fang Mu studied Du Yu thoughtfully. The guy's expression was totally sincere.

Man, thought Fang Mu, first time I ever give him something and he's touched this deeply?

He smiled. "That's right. We're good friends."

After eating lunch, Fang Mu and Du Yu sat at their desks, each using their computer. Du Yu was once more massacring players in Counter-Strike like he didn't know the meaning of exhaustion. As for Fang Mu, he had originally intended to organize his records from the Ma Kai case, but now he found that he had no desire to let that dark and bloody affair occupy his mind that afternoon. So having nothing much else to do, he went online and browsed aimlessly.

The door opened. Holding a basketball, Liu Jianjun burst into the room along with several other students, all of them talking and laughing it up. When they saw Fang Mu their voices suddenly fell.

"Still at it?" asked Liu Jianjun, tossing the ball on the floor. "How many times have you been headshot so far?" He pulled off Du Yu's mic and headphones. "Come on, let's go play."

"Stop, let me just finish this game," said Du Yu distractedly, his eyes on the screen

The basketball rolled over to Fang Mu and rubbed against his pants, leaving a mark.

Fang Mu kicked it away.

Seeing Fang Mu's dirty pant leg, Liu Jianjun looked a little embarrassed.

"Sorry about that," he said.

"No problem," said Fang Mu, waving his hand. Then he turned back to his computer and continued surfing the net.

"Aw, man, this guy is frickin' deadly," said Du Yu, leaning back in his chair in

annoyance. "I'm done. This just isn't my day. Let's go play some ball."

Bending over, he grabbed his basketball shoes from under the bed and pulled them on. Then he turned to Fang Mu. "Hey, let's both go."

"What? Oh, no thanks."

"What? Since you're such a superstar, are we gonna have to give you an appearance fee to play with us?" said Du Yu, laughing.

"Aw, don't listen to him," said Liu Jianjun, politely joining in. "You should just come."

Fang Mu hesitated for a moment, and then grabbed a pair of athletic shorts from his dresser, put them on, and followed the others out.

When it came time choose teams at the court, Du Yu made sure Fang Mu was on his side.

"You all had better watch out," he said, pointing at Fang Mu with a half-serious look on his face. "This guy's a beast."

The game began. It was four on four, half-court, and before long eight people were competing fiercely; cutting to the hoop, leaping for rebounds, and scrambling for the ball. Actually, that wasn't quite correct; in fact, during the first several minutes of play, only seven people were doing those things, while Fang Mu remained practically rooted in place, unsure what to do.

He couldn't even remember the last time he'd played in a game like the one he now found himself in. For who knows how long, all he'd done was practice free throws by himself, and he now found it extremely difficult to adapt.

Suddenly, Du Yu burst through the crowd towards the hoop, dribbling fast. Leaping into the air, he saw Liu Jianjun's enormous frame come flying at him, arms up and ready to block the ball into the stratosphere. At the last second, he spotted Fang Mu out of the corner of his eye, still standing by the foul line, and with a flick of the wrist he passed the ball.

Stunned, Fang Mu instinctively caught the ball. At that moment, one of his teammates cut under the hoop. No one was nearby. Without thinking, Fang Mu immediately passed him the ball, and the teammate unhurriedly laid it in.

"Beautiful!" cried several players in admiration.

The player who just scored ran excitedly over to Fang Mu with his hand raised. At a loss, Fang Mu lifted his own hand.

Smack! The two of them high-fived.

This sound sent sparks shooting through Fang Mu's brain, and all of a sudden he was filled with a strange yet familiar feeling.

Sweat-soaked backs and blazing-hot afternoons. Friendly cheers and shouted taunts.

The bygone days of his youth, when he had lived without worry or sadness.

Again someone passed the ball to him. This time he caught it smoothly, dribbled between his legs, and then faked left and crossed hard to the right...

Yes, that's how I used to do it.

Is that Eldest Brother jumping to block me?

Stopping on a dime, he leapt into the air and extended his arm. That old familiar feeling.

Swish. The ball dropped through the net.

"Nice one!" cheered Liu Jianjun.

"What did I say," said Du Yu proudly. "He's untouchable."

"I'll guard him," said Liu Jianjun. He ran over and stuck close to Fang Mu.

As the pace quickened, the game grew more and more intense. Bodies slammed into one another. The ball flew through the air. Pass, catch, shoot, rebound. High-five.

"Jeez, he doesn't miss."

"Man, looking at him you'd never know."

"New teams, new teams. We want Fang Mu!"

Sweat dripped from Fang Mu's forehead. He closed his eyes.

Yes, that's right. Back then, this is how happy I was.

They played until it got so dark they could barely see the ball. At last they gave up, albeit reluctantly. On the way back to the dorm they stopped at a store on campus, where Fang Mu bought a watermelon that had been sitting in a tub of icy water.

The watermelon was still coated with bits of ice when they got back to the dorm room. After slicing it open, everyone grabbed a piece and began to eat. Every now and then someone would cough from choking on one of the seeds, provoking a round of good-natured derision from the others.

"I'm saying, Fang Mu," said Liu Jianjun, wiping watermelon juice from his mouth, "you should join the law school basketball team. Next Grad School Cup, you'll play shooting guard."

"Me?" said Fang Mu, throwing away his rind. Suddenly he smiled: "I'll need an appearance fee."

Everyone roared with laughter. Liu Jianjun grabbed a watermelon rind and pretended to chuck it at Fang Mu, who laughed and fell back as if it were a direct hit.

Everyone was still carrying on when Meng Fanzhe pushed open the door.

As soon as he stepped inside he nearly slipped to the floor on a watermelon rind.

"Jeez, what are you guys up to in here?" he asked.

"Oh, hey," said Du Yu. "Want a piece of watermelon?"

"No thanks," said Du Yu, waving his hand. "I'm just looking for Tom."

"Tom? Who's Tom?" asked Fang Mu, confused.

Liu Jianjun laughed. "Guess you haven't heard. A few days ago this guy got a cat and decided to name it Tom. Which is why," he paused to wink at Fang Mu, "we're all calling Meng Fanzhe 'Jerry'."

As the room once more exploded with laughter, Meng Fanzhe leapt on Liu Jianjun.

"All right, all right," said Du Yu, his voice suddenly serious. "I know where your cat is."

"Where?" said Meng Fanzhe, releasing his hands from Liu Jianjun's throat.

"Here," said Du Yu, lifting his half-finished bowl of meat sauce and noodles. "I saved the tail. Want a taste?"

Meng Fanzhe's face fell. "No way," he said.

"It's so delicious," said Du Yu, licking his lips like he could barely keep from eating it.

"It's okay," Fang Mu quickly butted in, "they're just messing with you." From the look in Meng Fanzhe's eyes, Fang Mu could see he was about to cry.

"You're such a jerk," Meng Fanzhe bit out to Du Yu. He had regained his composure, but his tone was still angry.

"And you're so naive. How could you have believed me?" Du Yu laughed loudly.

Just then a voice shouted angrily from down the hall. "Meng Fanzhe!" it called. "Get over here now! Your stupid cat just shit on my bed!"

"I'm coming, I'm coming," said Meng Fanzhe as he whipped around and ran out of the room.

Laughing, several of the others followed him: "Man, this idiot's way too unlucky," they said almost in unison.

"All right, I should be going, too," said Liu Jianjun, climbing to his feet. "Fang Mu, you and I need to play one-on-one sometime."

Fang Mu smiled. "It's a deal."

"As for these watermelon rinds..." Liu Jianjun paused, pretending to be deep in thought, "you guys take care of them!" Then with a laugh he opened the door and slipped out.

Du Yu grabbed a sandal and threw it after him, but it was too late. The sandal merely smacked against the door.

"That jerk," he said, laughing.

Before going to bed, Fang Mu went to the showers to cool down. There, standing beneath the showerhead, his body drenched with ice-cold water, he felt an indescribable happiness well up inside him. Tilting his head back, he let the water wash over him.

Two math students were showering nearby, all the while discussing the "ridiculous body" they'd seen on some girl at the library that day.

Through the frosted glass of the window beside him, Fang Mu could faintly make out the lights of the dormitory opposite. Although blurry, the view seemed somehow warm and cozy.

Actually, life really is full of happiness—it's just that I never felt myself worthy of enjoying it.

Du Yu was already snoring when Fang Mu returned to the dorm, but he'd still been thoughtful enough to leave the desk light on for him.

Fang Mu was exhausted. He hadn't exercised in forever, and his legs and shoulders were already painfully sore. Without waiting for his hair to dry, he climbed immediately into bed.

Feeling something hard beneath his head, he reached under the pillow. It was the dagger.

Lying there, Fang Mu turned the dagger in his hands, inspecting it. The handle was dark green and rough and partly scarred from where it had been burned in the fire. He took the blade from its sheath. It shone cold as death in the light of the desk lamp.

Rolling out of bed, Fang Mu sheathed the knife and stuffed it underneath some clothes in his dresser.

He then lay down once more, switched off the light, and went to sleep.

Later that night, Du Yu woke to the sound of his roommate tossing and turning in his sleep.

"This guy's not having a nightmare again, is he?" he mumbled softly, before once more falling fast asleep.

At 1 o'clock in the morning, Fang Mu suddenly woke with a start, got out of bed and grabbed the knife from the dresser.

Expressionlessly, he slid it underneath his pillow, and then lay back down and pulled the covers overhead.

At last, drowsiness swept over him like a heavy black curtain, and he fell asleep.

9 EXPOSED

It was Wednesday afternoon, and Jiangbin City University was holding a school-wide assembly.

The topic at hand was how to implement the State Education Commission's new principle: "Study for the Purpose of Application, and Use Technology to Promote Great Enterprises." In addition to the students, all of the school's teachers and administrative staff were there, too, filling the auditorium to the limit.

The university president spoke. The school's party secretary spoke. Now it was the provost of research and Education's turn.

Provost Qi had only just been promoted from his former position as head of the Department of Scientific Research, so this was probably his first time addressing the whole school. He seemed both very nervous and very excited. While the two previous speakers had talked for less than 30 minutes combined, this guy had already been at the mic for nearly an hour when he finally began discussing "the second aspect of the second issue."

In the audience, Fang Mu was drifting in and out of sleep. The auditorium was extremely hot. He could feel the sweat dripping down his neck and sticking uncomfortably to the back of his shirt. Forcing himself to open his eyes, he fanned himself with his collar and looked around.

Du Yu was sleeping soundly in the seat to his right, head tilted to the side and saliva dripping on his shoulder. Fang Mu smiled. The poor guy had no idea. The person sitting to his left was actually still awake, though his head kept slowly nodding. He seemed unable to last much longer.

"Comrade Deng Xiaoping once said that 'Science and technology are our primary forces of production.' This demonstrates the importance of science and technology in a modernizing socialist economy, but it also raises a question for those of us engaged in scientific research. That is: Why do we research?" Provost Qi paused for a moment, but the sleepers in the audience before him kept right on sleeping, while those still awake were barely even paying attention. Since this pause was doing nothing to elicit the moment of deep thought that Provost Qi had intended, he had no choice but to answer his own question: "To serve society."

To cover up his embarrassment, he lifted his cup of tea, took a sip, and then spit out the tea leaves. Newly invigorated, he continued. "In this we are not doing nearly enough. In search of personal and professional gain, our professors diligently research the most abstract issues, but very rarely do they consider whether their work will offer anything of significance to society at large. This has caused scientific research to become seriously out of touch with practical reality. If no one makes use of your discoveries, then they are useless. And if your discoveries are useless, then what is the point of all the hard work you have put into them?"

Provost Qi withdrew an envelope from his coat pocket and waved it back and forth in an exaggerated manner. "I have here a commendatory letter, and while it was written on behalf of a student, I believe that this student can nonetheless serve as a model for all those present!"

At once the auditorium became silent. Many of those who had been dozing off opened their eyes.

Provost Qi was obviously pleased with this result. He opened the envelope and took out the letter. "As I'm sure everyone is aware, over the past few months a series of brutal murders were committed here in Jiangbin City. For a long time the police were stumped and the killer remained at large. But then one of our students, armed with knowledge he had learned at our school, put it to practical use by helping the public security bureau crack the case."

Fang Mu's mouth fell open.

"One of the victims, a little girl, was successfully rescued by the police and our student, and her father wrote this letter in thanks. Reading it, I was deeply moved. To think that one of our students could boldly act in the face of danger and hardship, merging the theoretical and the actual into a most effective tool—this sort of spirit deserves our most vigorous encouragement and praise!"

Whispering excitedly, the crowd began looking around at one another, scanning the auditorium.

"Settle down, please!" Practically glowing, Provost Qi extended his arms in a motion meant to pacify the murmuring crowd. "Now, we would like to invite Fang Mu, Class of 2004 at the law school's criminology department, to come to the stage and say a few words." He leaned in close to the microphone and intoned, "Fang Mu, Fang Mu, where are you in attendance today?"

Fang Mu's mind had gone completely blank, and it wasn't until Du Yu gave him several sharp nudges that he snapped out of it and dazedly raised his hand.

Click. A spotlight was immediately shined on him, illuminating Fang Mu and all those nearby.

"All right then, come on up here," said Provost Qi, brimming with enthusiasm as he beckoned Fang Mu.

The light was painfully bright. At a loss, Fang Mu looked back and forth. The students in his row were already standing to give him room to get out. Seeing that he had no other choice, he struggled past them and then walked down the aisle toward the stage. The spotlight followed him the whole time. Cameras flashed on either side.

How long is this aisle? How have I not yet reached the stage? He found himself wondering. White light filled his eyes; he could barely see a thing. He felt dizzy and astonished and certain that he might fall over at any moment.

Run away—just go for it. Turn and disappear like a cloud of smoke.

Anxious to begin, Provost Qi was already standing at the corner of the stage. As soon as Fang Mu arrived, the provost reached out, grabbed Fang Mu's hand, and pulled him up. Then with one arm on Fang Mu's shoulder, he half-pulled, half-pushed him over to the microphone.

"Very good, very good," he said. "Now please, Fang Mu, tell us your thoughts."

Fang Mu froze. He looked helplessly at the crowd sitting before him. They were all staring at him, everyone's face expressing something different: curiosity, surprise, scorn, admiration—and jealousy.

This has to be a nightmare. Make it all go away and let me disappear.

After more than 30 seconds, Fang Mu forced open his mouth, and a single word tumbled out: "I…"

Standing beside him, Provost Qi couldn't wait any longer. "Tell everyone how you helped the Public Security Bureau crack the case."

Fang Mu's face looked white as paper in the spotlight. A river of sweat dripped down his forehead. His teeth were clenched tightly together as if he were having a spasm.

Holding its collective breath, the audience quietly watched him. He didn't say another word.

"All right then," said Provost Qi, finally losing his patience. He walked over to the microphone and forced a smile. "Right now it would seem that silence is superior to speech. While I am certain that Fang Mu has many things he would like to tell us, at the moment he appears to be a little too nervous. Okay, Fang Mu, please return to your seat."

In an instant, energy seemed to return to Fang Mu's body, and he stepped stiffly away from the microphone and left the stage. But rather than return to his seat, he continued down the aisle, past all the whispered comments and prying eyes, and walked straight out of the auditorium.

"Hello?" Tai Wei's voice was cold and detached. There was silence on the other end of the phone line. "Hello? Who is this?"

"Was it you who gave my name to the little girl's father?"

"So it's you." Tai Wei laughed and his voice became cheerful despite Fang Mu's frustrated tone. "Well, how was it? Did you get the thank you letter?"

"You—!"

Tai Wei laughed. "So did the school commend you?"

"What were you thinking?" Not wanting to swear, Fang Mu forced himself to keep his cool.

"What do you mean, what was I thinking?" asked Tai Wei, a little shocked. "I just wanted to give you a nice surprise is all. What's wrong? You afraid someone will try and get revenge? Well, rest easy, because there's no way. Ma Kai's family is long gone and he doesn't have a friend in the world."

Fang Mu angrily hung up the phone.

Tai Wei was baffled. "What's wrong with this kid?" he mused, looking at his cell phone. His good intentions had been taken for malice, and now he felt more than a little angry himself.

Fang Mu kept his head down on the way to his dorm. Doing his best to remain inconspicuous, he took the long way back, walking along the campus wall.

The assembly had ended by now. All around him packs of students were rushing to the dining hall or back to their dorms. They shot him curious looks when they recognized him. Staring at his shoes, Fang Mu hurried back to Room 313.

It seemed like an inordinately long walk, but he finally reached his dorm room. Taking a deep breath, he opened the door, only to be confronted by a room full of people.

They seemed to have been in the midst of an intense discussion, but as soon as they saw him, they went silent. Seconds later, however, they all crowded around him and began asking a million questions at once.

"Fang Mu, was what the provost said true?"

"What did the guy look like?"

"I heard he even sucked their blood; is that true?"

"Did the public security bureau give you a cash reward?"

Pushing them forcefully aside, Fang Mu walked over to his desk. Then he turned back, his gaze sweeping across the hopeful faces of the crowd. When he spoke, his voice was suddenly cold. "Get out."

When some of them still seemed about to say something, he roared, "Get out!"

Everyone leaped in surprise. Dissatisfied, some of them began to grumble.

"What's the big deal?" one mumbled. "All you did was crack the case, right?"

Fang Mu turned away from them and sat at his desk. He did not look back.

The crowd stood there awkwardly until Du Yu quietly ushered them out. "He's not feeling so well today," he said. "You guys had better go."

At last Fang Mu and Du Yu were the only people left in the room. Fang Mu took out a cigarette, lit it shakily, and took several deep drags. He leaned back in his chair and looked up at the ceiling, exhausted.

Du Yu cautiously watched Fang Mu's expression. After a thoughtful moment, he spoke. "That provost is too much, making you go onstage like that and say something. No matter what, he should have at least given you time to prepare. Doing it cold is just too awkward."

"Thanks," said Fang Mu listlessly, "but please shut up or else I'll have to leave, too."

Taken aback, Du Yu seemed about to respond. Thinking again, he said nothing more.

The phone rang. Seeing that his roommate wasn't about to move, Du Yu walked over and picked it up. After asking who was calling, he handed the phone to Fang Mu.

"It's Professor Qiao. He wants to speak to you."

Rousing himself, Fang Mu took the phone. "Hello, Professor. How are you?"

"Hi, Fang Mu. Are you busy now?" Professor Qiao's voice was as deep as ever, but today it was also very stern, with none of the warmth Fang Mu had come to expect.

"No, I'm not busy."

"Good. Then please come over to my house." Before Fang Mu could respond, Professor Qiao had already hung up the phone.

Professor Qiao Yunping sat in his living room smoking one cigarette after another. Before long he began feeling a tightness in his chest, so he stood up, walked over to his French window, and looked off into the distance. Dark clouds filled the gray sky. It was not a sight to make one feel at ease. Looking down, he saw Fang Mu haggling with the boss of the fruit stand just outside his building.

The youth's face was dripping with sweat. It looked like he had run the whole way. After bargaining a little longer, he bought a bunch of bananas, two pineapples, as well as several peaches and mangosteens.

Seeing the anxious look on Fang Mu's face, Qiao Yunping's anger began to subside.

Of all of his students, Fang Mu was his favorite. Qiao Yunping still remembered how Fang Mu's scores on the general Graduate Entrance Exam had been mediocre, but when he came in for the oral examination at the beginning of school, his performance had been genius. When Qiao Yunping asked him several questions about Western criminal history, Fang Mu responded without a hitch. Not only did his answers demonstrate a sturdy grasp of the fundamentals, but his personal opinions were unique and incisive. Qiao Yunping decided at once to be his graduate advisor. As he later found out, Fang Mu was much more hardworking than the majority of graduate students, many of whom simply idled away their time after getting into school. In addition to his required homework, Fang Mu would often comb through old cases in the judicial archives. Qiao Yunping wholeheartedly approved of this style of work, for he had always believed that when it came to criminological research, it was best to let the facts speak for themselves. Today, however, his most adored pupil had made him incredibly angry.

When the doorbell rang, Mrs. Qiao was sitting on the couch watching TV. Seeing the somber expression on her husband's face, she sighed, stood up, and answered the door.

"Oh, hello, Fang Mu. Please come in."

"Hello, Mrs. Qiao," he said politely.

"Oh my, what's all this?" she said, seeing the bags he carried. "You shouldn't have. Fang Mu, you're just too much!"

"It's nothing. Anyway, I barely paid a thing for it."

Mrs. Qiao took the two bags of fruit from Fang Mu. Then turning toward the living room, she called, "Old Qiao, Fang Mu is here to see you."

Professor Qiao continued to stare out the window, saying nothing, a cigarette in his hand. There was a hard look in his eyes.

Feeling a little awkward, Fang Mu forced himself to smile as he exchanged his shoes for slippers. Pulling lightly on Fang Mu's sleeve, Mrs. Qiao leaned in and whispered, "My husband is in a bit of a mood again today, so just humor him a little. No matter what he says to you, don't argue."

Fang Mu nodded, and then walked into the living room.

Looking away from the window, Professor Qiao glanced at Fang Mu only long enough to note his presence, and then rose and walked into the study. Fang Mu had no choice but to follow him. Once they were inside he paused for a moment, and then turned and shut the door.

Professor Qiao took a seat in a swivel chair and puffed on his cigarette. He didn't say a word. Fang Mu didn't dare take a seat, so he just stood there with his arms hanging at his sides. When Professor Qiao finished his cigarette he motioned to the chair in front of him, then he lifted his cigarette pack and offered one to Fang Mu. After cautiously sitting down, Fang Mu hesitated for a moment, but then he removed a cigarette from the pack and lit it.

As the two of them smoked in silence, the air seemed to grow heavy. At last it was Professor Qiao who was first to speak.

"Is what Provost Qi said this afternoon true?"

Fang Mu felt his heart skip a beat, although he had already guessed on his way over that this was why Professor Qiao wanted to speak to him. Of course, the events of the day had made Fang Mu plenty angry himself; Tai Wei giving his name to Xu Jie's family without permission, Provost Qi calling him onstage to speak in front of the whole school. In all fairness, he realized that helping the Public Security Bureau solve a case was nothing to be ashamed of; still, he didn't want to become famous for it. In other words, the real reason Fang Mu was so furious had everything to do with his own personality. But as to why Professor Qiao should be so upset about it, Fang Mu had no idea.

"Um, so, about that…" Fang Mu didn't quite know how to respond.

"Just be straight with me!" said Professor Qiao, his voice rattling the apartment. "Is it true or not?"

"It's true."

"So then tell me, what exactly happened?"

Having no other option, Fang Mu related the details of the Ma Kai case to Professor Qiao, from beginning to end.

After he had finished, Professor Qiao was silent for a moment. At last he asked,

"Was this your first time doing something like this?"

Fang Mu hesitated. Then he shook his head. "No."

Professor Qiao snorted but said nothing. Then he took another cigarette from the pack, lit it, and began puffing away, a frown on his face.

Although Fang Mu wanted to ask him what he was so upset about, he didn't dare open his mouth. All he could do was sitting there, at a total loss.

"Fang Mu," said Professor Qiao all of a sudden, "what is the essence of criminal profiling?"

"Um," Fang Mu was momentarily taken aback, but he quickly recovered. "Criminal profiling is a way of making certain inferences about a crime that requires special training." He paused. "Its conclusions cannot be considered scientific fact."

"In that case, do you believe you are a well-trained criminal profiler?"

"…No," said Fang Mu quietly. He hung his head.

Suddenly Professor Qiao was irate. "Then what were you doing giving your so-called 'conclusions' to the police, influencing their case," he yelled, "and profiling their suspect?"

Fang Mu said nothing, but by now he had a pretty good idea why Professor Qiao was so angry.

"A good criminologist reveres his discipline and object of study," said Professor Qiao, his expression heatedly animated. "This is especially true when he is using his knowledge to direct the police in solving real-life crimes. First, he must have a deep understanding of the fundamentals of theory, and second, he must take a careful, serious-minded approach. As you are surely aware, our opinions can affect people's rights, their freedom—even their very lives." Professor Qiao rapped his finger against the desk to emphasize his words. "This is not child's play. The measure of a criminologist is not found in the number of papers he has published, or the abstract problems he has solved, but by looking at whether he has taken his years of learning, ironclad grasp of theory, and rich experience and used these to serve the public." His glare met Fang Mu's stare head-on. "All of which has absolutely nothing to do with having read a few books, thinking oneself a so-called genius, and going out and trying one's luck!"

Blushing bright red, Fang Mu still said nothing.

"It might seem like you scored a huge victory with the Ma Kai case, but I can see it was all luck!"

Fang Mu looked up.

"Oh, so you disagree?" asked Professor Qiao, his eyes flashing with anger. "Well, first, Ma Kai was one of the most obvious cases of a Disorganized Serial Killer that I've ever seen, and I'll be amazed if he doesn't become a textbook example in the future. Second, what method did you use to determine where Tong Hui had been taken? Intuition? You were lucky enough to come across her eventually, but do you realize that the wrong judgment in a situation like that can lead to the victim's death? When you left the apartment to go searching for her, Tong Hui was probably still alive! And third, since you obviously realized that the kidnapping of Xu Jie was not the killer's style, why, instead of considering whether this might be a copycat crime, did you insistently believe that he was stockpiling blood reserves?"

Cold sweat ran down Fang Mu's forehead as the details of the Ma Kai case raced through his mind.

He's right, he thought. *I was far too lucky.*

And too self-confident as well. If any of my guesses had been wrong, things could easily have turned out very differently.

Tired from all the talking, Professor Qiao lifted his cup of Dragon Well tea and took a sip. It had long since gone cold. When he looked up and saw Fang Mu was still frozen in place, big drops of sweat rolling down his face, his heart softened and his tone became much less harsh.

"Your dedication to empirical research is worthy of approval," he said. "But, young man, you're a little impatient. If you really want to work effectively with the police to solve crimes, you'll need to study hard for another twenty-plus years."

Fang Mu forced himself to nod.

Just then Mrs. Qiao opened the door. "I made some dumplings," she said. "Fang Mu, why don't you stay for dinner?"

When he tried to decline, Professor Qiao gave him a look. "What's wrong?" he asked. "Can't take a little criticism?" Then he stood and pushed his student into the dining room.

When Fang Mu was about to leave later, Professor Qiao slipped him a pack of expensive Hibiscus King cigarettes. Then he stood on the balcony and watched him disappear into the night.

Professor Qiao sighed. What a good student, he thought. Although he had nitpicked the young man's work, he had to admit that what he felt most of all was admiration.

He just hoped the same mistake wouldn't be made twice.

By the time Fang Mu reached campus he still didn't want to go back to his dorm. All those curious eyes staring at him—even the thought of it was uncomfortable. He hesitated for a moment, and then took the long way to the track and field stadium.

After baking in the sun all day, the bleachers surrounding the track were still warm. Fang Mu sat down and enjoyed the feeling.

Amid the darkness, he could see groups of people strolling leisurely around the track. Frequently the sound of cheerful laughter broke the night air, and Fang Mu couldn't help but smile.

Suddenly he wanted to smoke. Taking the Hibiscus King cigarettes from his pocket, he lit one and inhaled.

Actually, for a long time now Fang Mu had no idea what he was doing. It was as if he had been continuously chasing a particular kind of life, but when asked to describe what sort of life that was, he felt frequently at a loss. Ceaseless pondering. Snap judgments. Blood-soaked crime scenes. Terrifying pictures on the computer. And never-ending nightmares. All of this had followed him like a shadow for the past two years. And right now, it made him feel exhausted beyond reckoning.

What exactly do I want?

He looked up at the stars flickering in the night sky. It felt almost as if someone were winking down at him from the heavens.

All of you up there…what should I do?

Fang Mu made it back to the dorm just before it was locked for curfew. The moment he entered his room, Du Yu told him his mom had been calling all night.

Fang Mu called her back. She picked it up on the first ring.

She had probably been sitting beside the phone the whole time.

"What are you doing getting back so late?"

"Oh, I had to go out." Fang Mu didn't want to get into it. "Is something wrong?"

"No, no, nothing's wrong. It's just that the last time you were home you were much too thin. Your father and I were both worried, and we wanted to talk to you about it, but then you left before we had a chance."

"Oh, well, I'm fine. You don't need to worry about me. How are you and Dad?"

"We're both doing very well." She paused. "Little Mu, can you tell me what exactly you've been doing lately?"

"Nothing really. Going to class, reading."

"Have you also been helping the police to catch criminals?"

"No." Nothing was harder than lying to one's family. Fang Mu could feel the difference in his voice as he said it.

His mother was silent for a moment, and then she sighed. "Fang Mu, I'm not so young anymore. Do you know how worried I get thinking of you doing these kinds of things all day, dealing with these kinds of people? Please don't make me worry like that again."

He said nothing.

"The last few days I've been having the same nightmare. In it that boy Wu Han murders you, and every time it scares me awake. Your father has asked me what's wrong, but I won't tell him."

"Mom, you don't need to worry about that stuff anymore. It's history."

"I know, but I can't help it." She sounded as if she were holding back tears. "Little Mu, promise me that you'll never do anything dangerous like that again, that you'll just be an ordinary person leading an ordinary life, okay?"

"…Okay."

"Do you promise?"

"I promise."

After hanging up the phone, Fang Mu remained seated for a moment, staring at nothing in particular. Then he grabbed his toiletries and went to the bathroom to wash up.

Once there, the bathroom mirror reflected a young man's skinny frame. He wasn't wearing a shirt, and his skin was pale white and his chest sunken.

He moved closer to the mirror and looked at himself; short, spiky hair, broad forehead, pale, gaunt cheeks, blood-flecked eyes, black stubble on his chin, arched eyebrows, and deep crow's feet.

Was this face really only 24-year-old?

Fang Mu turned his head left and right, closely inspecting himself.

At the sink beside him, a commercial law grad student named Zou Tuanjie was thoroughly washing his face. He looked over at Fang Mu, his face white with acne cleanser.

"Are you breaking out?" he asked, squinting at Fang Mu, who was still gazing absently into the mirror. Offering his bottle of face wash, he asked, "Want to try using this?"

"What? Oh, no. I'm fine."

Zou Tuanjie continued scrubbing his face a little longer, and then used fresh water to wash away all the cleanser. Afterwards he dried off his face and looked in the mirror for a long time. At last he smiled at his reflection, and then walked away, satisfied.

After watching this detailed face-washing process, Fang Mu thought for a moment, and then smiled into the mirror like Zou Tuanjie had just done.

Jeez, he thought, I'd look less ugly if I cried.

Still, it was better to smile.

He filled his washbasin with cold water and then dunked his head.

After all, there's more to life than just serial killers.

10 THE FIVE-POINTED STAR

It was the night of June 30th, 2002, and in Yokohama, Japan, Brazil was playing Germany in the World Cup finals.

From the start of the World Cup, all of the little restaurants outside the Jiangbin City University campus gate had been showing the games. Since tonight was the finals, every single one was now overflowing with people.

Fang Mu and several of his classmates were eating at a Sichuan-style restaurant called Guang Yuan. On the table in front of them were a number of beer bottles, piles of peanut shells and edamame skins, and several plates of cheap fried food that had already been picked clean. This state of affairs was roughly replicated on all the other tables in the restaurant. Now all the customers were staring up at the 21-inch color TV hanging on the wall, while the owner stood behind the bar, obviously elated, his fingers flying over the calculator and punching the buttons like fireworks going off. The smug look on his face told everyone he wished there was a world Cup every month.

Du Yu, Zou Tuanjie, and Liu Jianjun had dragged Fang Mu along. Initially Fang Mu hadn't wanted to go, but after thinking about it he realized he didn't have anything else to do, and anyway it might be fun. However, he had one condition: no barbecue.

Naturally, the people at the restaurant were split into two groups. One supported Brazil, the other Germany. Fang Mu didn't really follow soccer, so aside from Ronaldo, he didn't know any of the other player's names. But seeing that Du Yu and the others were all rooting for Brazil, he decided that for the time being he might as well do the same.

Neither team was able to get much going on the field during the first half. On the face of things, Brazil had seemed a little passive, but Germany hadn't been able to score either, despite several good chances. At halftime, everyone in the bar began enthusiastically discussing the play up until then and loudly arguing over who would come out on top. A number of bets were made, with late-night snacks at stake, and it wasn't until the second half began that peoples' attention returned to the TV.

At first, Fang Mu had been rather bored. His first night as a soccer fan, and his team wasn't even playing well. But the crowd's excitement was contagious, and before long he found himself yelling along with everyone else.

After stealing the ball near Germany's goal, Ronaldo passed to Number 10 – "That's Rivaldo," said Du Yu – who then dribbled to the edge of the penalty box and took a long shot at goal. It was not a very powerful kick, and as Oliver Kahn, the German goalkeeper, grabbed the ball, he hardly looked concerned. Little did he expect, however, that a moment later the ball would pop out of his hands and back onto the field.

"You can't relax like that!" cried a tall, well-built young man at the next table. But before the words had even left his mouth, Ronaldo was on the ball like lightning, and without breaking stride he kicked it into the lower right-hand corner—goal!

Brazil had taken the lead!

At once everyone cried out in surprise. Then a second later the restaurant erupted in a flurry of cheers and curses.

"Kahn was way too relaxed," said the tall guy at the next table, shaking his head. "When the ball is kicked low like that, you should use your body to press it to the ground. Otherwise it can easily slip out of your hands. He's being overconfident."

"What a professional analysis," said Zou Tuanjie with a smile.

"Come on, man, you're my hero; don't let me down." The tall guy was staring at the screen, his expression as upset as Kahn's.

"That's Qu Weiqiang from the physics department," whispered Liu Jianjun to Fang Mu. "He's the goalie for the school soccer team."

"Oh, no wonder."

Germany now began going all out trying to score, but despite several near misses, they were unable to get the ball into the net. Then in minute 79, Rivaldo threaded a long, beautiful pass to Ronaldo at the top of the penalty box. Before anyone could stop him, Ronaldo turned and kicked it low and fast into the bottom right corner of the goal, making the score 2-0. Brazil's victory was now assured.

Germany's fans swore ceaselessly.

Heaving a deep sigh, Qu Weiqiang said, "Brazil definitely analyzed Kahn's technique before the game. Those kinds of low shots are his biggest weakness."

Before long the World Cup was over and Brazil was the champion. As confetti rained from above, Rivaldo sprinted around the field, holding his country's flag aloft.

As the game ended, the assembled students were either raising their arms in the air and shouting happily or hanging their heads, paying and leaving.

In a loud voice, Qu Weiqiang called out: "Hey, boss, give me four more beers. I want them to go."

At this, the lovely, petite young woman who had been watching the game with him whispered, "Don't drink anymore. You've already had a lot tonight."

Qu Weiqiang's eyes went wide. "You're going to tell me what to do?" he yelled. "After a game this depressing I'm not allowed to have a little bit to drink?"

Pouting, the young woman said nothing.

For his part, Fang Mu hadn't really cared about who won. His only thought was getting to a bathroom. Having drunk way too much beer during the game, he felt as if he were about to burst.

So, after paying, he rushed out of the restaurant and back to the dorm, where he went straight into the bathroom and relieved himself.

Feeling much better, Fang Mu walked cheerfully back to his room. He was surprised to find Du Yu standing in the hallway and using a rag to vigorously wipe something off the door.

"What's the matter?" asked Fang Mu, shaking his hands dry. "What are you wiping off?"

"I don't know who drew this," said Du Yu, pointing at the door, "but it seems we have a practical joker around here."

Fang Mu looked up. Several marks still remained on the door, seemingly drawn with a big felt-tip marker. It was a total mess.

"What was it?"

"It looked like a five-pointed star," said Du Yu, frowning. "Jeez, who could be that bored?"

"A five-pointed star?" Fang Mu looked down either end of the corridor. None of the other doors had anything written on them.

"You haven't erased it yet?" asked Liu Jianjun, sticking his head out of the doorway opposite.

"Almost." Du Yu redoubled his efforts, and at last the marks disappeared.

"Man, that was some freaky stuff," said Liu Jianjun, grimacing. "Sort of like Ali Baba and the Forty Thieves."

Fang Mu laughed. "In that case I'll go draw a five-pointed star on every door in the corridor!"

In the middle of that night, Fang Mu suddenly awoke.

Something was rustling in the dorm room. He forced his eyes open and scanned the small area by the light of the moon.

His breath caught in his throat.

Someone was standing in front of his closed door.

Fang Mu wanted to reach under his pillow and grab the knife, but his body felt frozen and he couldn't move an inch. He wanted to open his mouth and yell for Du Yu to wake up, but the words seemed trapped inside his throat and he couldn't make a sound.

Cold sweat dripped down his forehead. He stared at the intruder, struggling with all his strength to react.

The person stood with his back to Fang Mu, seemingly unaware that he was awake. He was drawing something on the inside of the door.

Flames burst from its surface following the movements of his hand.

No.

Fang Mu felt himself begin to shake. A scorched odor filled his nostrils.

A five-pointed star burned on the door.

The intruder slowly turned. In the light of the flames, Fang Mu could see Wu Han's ruined face.

No...!

Suddenly a blinding white light shined in Fang Mu's eyes. Du Yu's voice sounded in his ears: "Fang Mu, Fang Mu. Are you okay?"

Fang Mu opened his eyes. He could vaguely see Du Yu standing over him, a worried look on his face.

"What happened? Did you have another nightmare?"

Fang Mu struggled to sit up. He pushed Du Yu away from him and looked at the door.

Besides their class schedules, it was bare.

He had been dreaming.

Drained, Fang Mu lay back on the bed. The sheet beneath him was damp with perspiration. He reached down and felt it. Cold sweat soaked the bed.

"You okay?" Du Yu asked, handing Fang Mu a towel.

"Thanks," said Fang Mu. "I'm fine. You should get back to sleep." He took the towel and wiped his face and neck.

Du Yu pulled the cord on the lamp and the room returned to quiet darkness.

But Fang Mu couldn't sleep.

It was obvious that this nightmare was completely different than the one he was used to.

A five-pointed star? What did it mean?

The five-pointed star was one of the earliest symbols of nature worship in the world. It was also one of the purest, most perfect geometric shapes. At first it represented the female sex; later it became a mark of paganism, and more recently it indicated warfare.

Does this mean someone's offering me a challenge? Fang Mu thought about this and found it ridiculous. Don't worry about it, he told himself. Didn't you just promise yourself that you'd be an ordinary person?

After that Fang Mu slept very deeply. If Du Yu hadn't woken him up for breakfast, he might have slept all day.

The two roommates walked leisurely to the dining hall, chatting all the while. Frequently, however, people would rush past them, and though at first Fang Mu took little notice of this, he soon realized that something was amiss. Everyone on campus seemed to be hurrying toward the same place: the track and field stadium.

"What's going on?" asked Du Yu, pulling aside a foreign language student.

"I'm not totally sure," the student said. "But I heard there's a dead body on the soccer field."

The track and field stadium was located at the northwest corner of campus. At its center was a regulation-size soccer field covered with artificial turf, a rarity at the time, surrounded by a synthetic track. When Fang Mu and Du Yu reached the stadium, over a dozen police cars were already parked outside, lights flashing. Walking inside, they saw at least a couple hundred people crowded around the northern goal. Frightened yet excited students packed the surrounding stands.

Before they had reached the front, Fang Mu spotted Liu Jianjun's tall frame squeezed into the crowd. He was up on his tiptoes and doing his best to see what was happening. Fang Mu walked over and, putting a hand on his shoulder, asked: "What's going on here?"

Liu Jianjun almost jumped with surprise. When he turned around and saw it was Fang Mu, he laughed and said, "Ah, so the master sleuth has arrived."

Ignoring him, Fang Mu stood on his tiptoes and looked toward the center of the crowd. "I heard someone died. Is that true?"

"Yeah, but I don't know who it was. There are too many people."

As those at the back jostled to see, several of the students in front of Fang Mu were almost knocked over. Turning around, they were about to complain when they saw Fang Mu. Much to his surprise, they spontaneously opened a path for him to get by, looks of awe on their faces.

Feeling a little embarrassed, Fang Mu was about to turn and leave when Du Yu and Liu Jianjun seized the opportunity and pushed him deeper into the crowd.

The scene was already sealed off with a police cordon. Compared to the crush outside, the area within the cordon looked almost empty. Lying face down beneath the goalpost was a corpse. Based on its build, it appeared to be a man. His face was pressed against the turf and couldn't be made out, but there was something extremely strange about the length of his arms extending to either side.

As several medical examiners in white lab coats bustled about the body, one carefully lifted a pale object from beside the left goalpost and examined it closely.

The surrounding students gasped in terror. It was a hand.

Several policemen who appeared to be part of the evidence unit combed the area surrounding the goal, while nearby an officer holding a notebook was interviewing a male student dressed in gym clothes. The student's face was deathly pale, as if he might faint at any time.

Not long after, the medical examiners turned the dead man onto his back, revealing his frozen face. Several of the students nearby cried out in alarm.

"Who is it?" asked Liu Jianjun, craning his neck to see. "Why does he look so familiar?"

Fang Mu also felt the dead man's clothing looked very familiar, but he couldn't remember where he'd seen him before.

"I'm going over there to take a look," said Liu Jianjun. He began squeezing his way through the pack toward the area just opposite the corpse. A few minutes later, he looked back at Fang Mu and Du Yu. His face was pale.

"It's Qu Weiqiang," he said to them. "His hands have both been cut off. It's horrible."

That day, every corner of campus was buzzing with discussion about the murder on the soccer field. Frequently people would come and ask Fang Mu for news on the case. The subtext was clear: If you don't take care of this, who will?

Fang Mu was soon fed up. After turning a contemptuous look on the nth visitor, he couldn't take it any longer and left the dorm to find somewhere to hide out.

It was already 8:30 p.m., but still the campus was busy with students hurrying to and fro. Wanting to avoid the crowds, Fang Mu made sure to stick to the darkest corners. Before long, he had inadvertently arrived at the track and field stadium.

This was normally the top spot for couples wanting to meet up after dark, but tonight it was completely empty. Everyone was scared away by that morning's tragedy. Evidently, now that this arena of romance had been transformed into a crime scene, wandering the track and whispering in a sweetheart's ear no longer seemed so pleasant.

Fang Mu climbed down the stadium steps to the edge of the soccer field. Then stepped onto the soft turf and walked slowly toward the north goal.

The turf around the goal had been trampled out of shape. Before it, the chalk outline of a figure lay in silence, its two shortened arms pointed at either post. Fang Mu stood and looked at the outline for a long time before walking slowly over to the left goalpost. That morning, one of Qu Weiqiang's hands had been found here. The killer had left the other by the right post.

Fang Mu knelt and looked at the grass. It was too dark to tell how much blood there had been, but he doubted it was a lot.

Most likely, Qu Weiqiang's hands were cut off after he was already dead.

He walked back to where the body had lain. Copying its position, he spread his arms wide. In a flash, he felt himself go so lightheaded that he nearly fell over. Steadying himself, he quickly stepped back.

The goal stood in silence beneath the night sky, Qu Weiqiang's chalk silhouette prostrated beneath it. The combination somehow made this normally unremarkable goal seem incredibly dangerous, as if it was death's gate itself, and this empty outline the last thing the victim had left of himself before leaving this world.

Fang Mu took a careful step forward, and then another and another. Holding his breath, he stepped over the police cordon and inside the goal.

Nothing happened. Rather than being met by the raging flames of hell,

Fang Mu saw only the dark and empty stadium. Flickering stars still filled the night sky above him. He took a deep breath. There was no hint of blood in the dry air.

Then he turned and hurried out of the stadium, thinking, Fang Mu, you are goddamned crazy.

On July 1, 2002, a dead body was discovered on the Jiangbin City University soccer field. A male student who had gotten to the field early to run spotted the body lying face down beneath one of the goals. As soon as the crime was reported, the PSB's State Enterprise and Nonprofit Institution Investigative Division rushed to the scene and got to work.

The victim was found to be one Qu Weiqiang, a 19-year-old physics major from Linjiang City in Jilin province. Cause of death was a blow to the head, most likely from a hammer or similar weapon. The body was found placed beneath the soccer field's northern goal, with the head pointing south and the feet north. Both the victim's hands were chopped off and left beside either goalpost. Based on a preliminary examination of the body and the scene, it was determined that the victim was most likely killed at another location and then transported to the soccer field.

According to their initial interviews, the police discovered that the victim had been assigned to Dormitory 4, Room 611, but that he had been living off-campus with his girlfriend in a rented apartment since the beginning of the semester. With the help of the victim's former roommate, the police found the apartment. They knocked on the door for a long time but received no response. After locating the landlord, they were let inside. The scene was unimaginable, but it was also exactly what they had expected.

Wang Qian, Qu Weiqiang's girlfriend, had been killed as well, and the apartment was thick with the smell of blood. After entering the bedroom, the police found her naked corpse lying on the floor. Her head pointed north (toward the bedroom door) and her feet south (toward the open window), and her limbs were spread-eagled on the floor. After taking a closer look, the police discovered that the body had been hacked into six pieces (head, torso, legs and arms) and then pieced back together as if still whole. Even though a medical syringe was found inserted in the victim's chest on the underside of her left breast, the medical examiners determined that the actual cause of death was mechanical asphyxiation— seemingly by hand, based on the marks on the victim's neck. According to the autopsy, the victim had long since lost her virginity. There were also signs that she had been violently raped prior to her death, but there was no trace of semen in her vagina, meaning that the killer must have used a condom.

The murder scene was located in a residential area near Jiangbin City University. The couple's apartment was on the left-hand side of the second floor of a small, three-story building. Their bedroom window had its screen torn open and overlooked a bicycle shed. Because of the hot weather, all the windows in the apartment had been open on the night of the murder, which had allowed the killer to climb onto the bicycle shed, break through the screen and then sneak into the apartment. On the bed were found a large amount of blood, hair, and skull fragments. These were brought in for testing, and identified as belonging to Qu Weiqiang. As a result, it was believed likely that this had been the scene of his murder. But even though two people had been killed here and one of them hacked apart, the apartment hardly resembled a slaughterhouse, and not a single fingerprint or footprint was found. Someone had cleaned the place well.

Because the murder was committed on the anniversary of the Communist Party, the director of the PSB initially took great interest in it. However, once it was clearly established that the crime had no political undertones, it was handed off to the State Enterprise and Nonprofit Institution Investigative Division.

A double homicide. Immediately the case raised an uproar at Jiangbin City University, and the school began actively cooperating with the police to help solve it. Campus security was also greatly strengthened, as was supervision of the dormitories. A direct result of this was that all the young couples who had been covertly living off-campus were forced to return to their respective dorm rooms. A less direct result was that all those students who liked studying in lonely corners of campus after dark were now often treated to live shows of a most intimate variety.

Uniformed police could often be seen on campus interviewing students, especially the victims' friends and classmates. More than once the school's soccer coach suggested that the police should investigate Jiangbin City's other university soccer teams. When they ignored him, he decided to hold a retirement ceremony for Qu Weiqiang's jersey on his own.

Even though everyone had finals, the jersey retirement ceremony still attracted a lot of people, Fang Mu among them.

It was held on the soccer field. Qu Weiqiang's teammates had formed two lines, and in front of them were the team captain, co-captain and two others, each holding the corner of a soccer jersey and walking slowly and solemnly toward the north goal, while everyone else followed. There a table had been set up, and on it stood a very large, framed picture of the deceased, a soccer ball, and Qu Weiqiang's old cleats. When the team members reached the table they lined up on either side, standing tall with their hands behind their backs. The team captain bowed three times before Qu Weiqiang's picture, and then withdrew a slip of paper from his pocket and began to read aloud.

The speech was mainly a retelling of how Qu Weiqiang had first joined the team and the "outstanding contribution" he had made. The wording was ornate and the content rousing, but it all did seem rather suspiciously over the top. For example, saying that the deceased was an "impregnable god of the goal" and "the future hope of China's soccer world" might have made onlookers think that Wang Dalei had died rather than Qu Weiqiang. Still, the speech was well-received, and by the end tears were rolling down the faces of all the straight-backed players. *(Translator's note: Wang Dalei is a young hotshot Chinese goalie.)* Most of those in the audience were also drying their eyes.

When the speech was over, the team captain sprinkled some liquid over the jersey and then used his lighter to set it on fire. In an instant the "1" on the back was engulfed by flames. Before the team captain could react, the jersey had been reduced to a ball of fire, burning his hand and causing him to drop it on the turf. The smell of burning fabric and plastic filled the air. A moment later, the stadium manager cried out and came running over.

When he reached the still-burning jersey, he stamped wildly on it until the fire was out. This upset the members of the soccer team, who immediately surrounded the manager and began shouting at him.

But the manager was just as angry himself. "You can have whatever ceremony you want, but don't start any fires!" he yelled. "If the turf is ruined, are you guys going to pay for it?"

Both sides continued to jostle and shout at each other until they had left the stadium, each saying they would be speaking with the university president to get the matter straightened out. Thus the ceremony ended, leaving only Qu Weiqiang's half-burned jersey smoking sadly on a patch of scorched turf. Glancing back at the ceremonial table, where Qu Weiqiang's picture had been knocked over in the confusion, Fang Mu laughed bitterly, and then followed the crowd out of the stadium.

Returning to his dorm, he was surprised to find Tai Wei sitting on his bed reading a book. At this point Fang Mu still bore a bit of a grudge against Tai Wei from last time, so he just ignored him.

But Tai Wei didn't seem to care. Grinning at him, he said, "Where have you been? I've been waiting for you all day."

"Is there something you wanted to say to me?" Fang Mu asked coldly. Still, in the back of his mind he felt a shiver of fear. What had happened now?

"Oh, nothing in particular. The bureau just sent us down here to investigate a case, so I figured I'd stop by and say hi."

"What are they doing sending you here?" Fang Mu paused to think for a moment. "Not for that double homicide? A case like that wouldn't normally belong to the vice squad."

"You really know a lot kid," Tai Wei said, chuckling. "Actually, that case belongs to the State Enterprise and Nonprofit Institution Investigative Division. When I heard some of them were heading down here to look things over, I decided to tag along. So how's it going? You doing all right?"

"I'm fine; thanks for asking," said Fang Mu brusquely, as he sat down in his desk chair.

Tai Wei laughed. "You're still mad at me, huh?" He asked, not seeming to mind at all. "I admit that what I did was perhaps a little bit less than ideal, but I figured that if I couldn't give you an award, then at least you should get some commendation from your school. I was taking a risk, too, you know. If the director finds out he's going to hit the roof."

"For a moron like you, getting yelled at is a good thing." As soon as the words left Fang Mu's mouth, he couldn't help but laugh.

Tai Wei laughed as well, and then said, "It's actually not what you think. For some reason, the bureau director doesn't want you to participate in our investigations."

Fang Mu was about to ask why when Tai Wei pulled an envelope out of his bag.

"As for the reason I came, this letter's for you." He handed Fang Mu the envelope. Then his eyes narrowed and his expression grew serious. "It's from Ma Kai."

Fang Mu had been about to take the letter when he heard Ma Kai's name. Without meaning to, he drew his hand back and hesitated for a moment. At last he reached out and took it.

It was a white envelope of the most common variety. Nothing was written on the outside; no recipient, no sender. The letter inside didn't seem particularly thick, and when Fang Mu held the envelope in his fingers it felt light enough to float away. Turning it over, he saw the envelope wasn't sealed.

"I swear on Chairman Mao I never read it," said Tai Wei. Then seeing the look in Fang Mu's eyes, he continued, "Ma Kai gave it to me and now I'm giving it to you; that's all."

He watched Fang Mu stare blankly at the envelope in his hands. "Well," he said, "you're not going to read it?"

Fang Mu didn't respond. He just kept staring at the envelope, not moving a muscle. *Ma Kai, what did you want to tell me?*

Seeing that Fang Mu wasn't going to say anything, Tai Wei lost interest, stood up and said goodbye. Fang Mu still said nothing. When Tai Wei reached the door, he suddenly turned around.

"Ma Kai has already been sentenced to immediate execution," said Tai Wei. "He didn't try to appeal. Barring anything unexpected, he'll be executed this Thursday at dawn." Then he nodded at Fang Mu, opened the door and left.

The late-night rooftop was bathed in mist. There was no moon or stars above, only the dark canopy of heaven. The wind was strong, blowing the rooftop sand in all directions with a sound like soft footsteps.

Fang Mu stood at the edge of the roof, silently gazing at the pitch-black campus. It felt as if he were standing before an endless abyss. He glanced at his watch. It was already 2:30 in the morning. Ma Kai, he thought, has your execution already begun?

He looked as far as he could into the distance, his ears straining to catch any sound. Somewhere in the darkness ahead, Ma Kai was being led out of a police car. Maybe there was another prisoner with him, maybe he was alone. But either way, this was the end of the road.

…Ahead of him was a shallow sandpit. He knelt in it, feeling sharp bits of gravel press painfully against his knees. Three judicial policemen stood behind him, leveling fully-automatic Type 81 rifles at the back of his head, while 600 feet back, members of the People's Armed Police gripped Type 54 pistols, safeties off, and waited silently for the execution team to fire. In an instant his world would disappear, the good and the bad, things owed and things lent. All debts would be settled…

Fang Mu knew he would never hear the gunshot, but still he waited for the sound, his whole body taut.

And yet he himself wasn't even sure that's what he really wanted.

Suddenly, Fang Mu no longer knew how he felt about Ma Kai. Was he a homicidal maniac who deserved to be hacked to pieces, or just a poor sick man?

Without a doubt, Ma Kai had a very serious mental illness, but according to Chinese penal code, this had not affected his judgment or self-control in the least. Therefore, he bore full responsibility for his crimes and needed to accept the legal consequences.

Fang Mu saw Ma Kai's face. There was no trace of anger in his eyes, only fear and despair. He looked like some pitiful animal caught in a maze: smashing into walls, crying, bleeding from the head, trying desperately to get out. But there was no exit, and no one was coming to save him. Blood was the sweetest curse. Drinking it, he'd felt as if he'd gained something, though in fact he'd lost it forever. Fang Mu imagined Ma Kai waking exhaustedly from some unknown dream in that small room on North Evergreen Street, where the shades were drawn day and night. Opening his eyes, would he rejoice at being alive to see another day, or merely remind himself that his own death was soon at hand?

Wait a second; am I sympathizing with this guy?

Shaking his head, Fang Mu forced these thoughts from his mind.

Listen, that man was a crazed killer and you're a normal guy. You should be cursing him to hell!

But then, why am I standing here?

It was already 3:30 in the morning when, sighing, Fang Mu picked up a black plastic bag and then, as usual, walked over to the small sand pile on the northeast corner of the roof.

Once the fire had begun to burn, black pieces of ash floated into the air, fell, and then struggled aloft once more. Finally they spun out in all directions, settling softly and soundlessly on every dark corner of the rooftop.

Fang Mu took the still unread letter out of his pocket. He had originally wanted to say something, but when he opened his mouth nothing came out, so he simply tossed it on the fire and watched it twist in the flames. Soon the paper was ashes, no different than all the rest, and then picked up by the wind, they floated away.

Everything you had is gone now. You will never leave another trace on this world.

At 7:35 that morning, Fang Mu was awakened by a phone call. It was Tai Wei. He said that Ma Kai had been executed at 2:50 a.m. One shot to the head. He did not suffer.

11 MEMORY CITY

Teacher's College felt deserted during summer break. Walking through campus with the hot sun overhead, Fang Mu passed familiar sights on either side; dormitories, dining halls, academic buildings and the track and field stadium. But there were unfamiliar ones, too, like brand new dorms where old ones had once stood. He found himself looking around as if it was his first time there, though it wasn't warm nostalgia he felt. It was loss.

Fang Mu had already been on break for three weeks. After returning home to Changhong City, he had done his best to be an obedient son. His mom was delighted to have him around, and cooked a different, delicious meal for him every day. There never seemed to be much to do. If he wasn't online then he was watching DVDs with his dad or biking aimlessly through the streets. Changhong City had changed enormously. Many of the places that he remembered so vividly now looked completely different, and he often ended up lost in areas that he used to know well. When some of his old high school classmates invited him to a reunion, he found an excuse not to go.

One day, while helping his mom to clean the house, Fang Mu found a bunch of old clothes and toys from when he was young. After much time and effort spent writhing about on the ground, he finally managed to squeeze into one of his old elementary school uniforms. His mom burst out laughing when he showed her. Then, when he was almost done straightening up, he happened upon the cane he had used two years ago. After thinking about it for a moment, he decided to take the bus to Teacher's College.

It had already been four months since he'd last visited. In that time, the school had built a number of new facilities. The old student club was now a four-story recreation center. Although it wasn't finished yet, it still looked very impressive. After standing outside for a while and looking up, Fang Mu decided to head in and check it out, but he was stopped at the entrance by several men wearing hardhats. Feeling a mix of disappointment and relief, he didn't stop to argue. Instead, he turned around and went straight to Dormitory 2.

Dormitory 2 was now a modern, seven-story student apartment building. As usual, Fang Mu sat amid the flower beds on a bench facing the front door and stared up at the huge structure. The faint fragrance of fresh, unknown flowers surrounded him. Occasionally a dragonfly would flit by, the bravest pausing to land on his body. The sun was blindingly bright, forcing him to squint as it flashed off the building's tiled exterior. On the left side of the third floor there had once been two ratty, wood-framed windows. Now these were made of steel and plastic and shut tight like all the rest since the students were away on break. Fang Mu took all this in for a moment, and then stood up and walked over to the building's main door.

The old iron doorway covered in peeling paint had been replaced by double doors of toughened glass. Walking inside, Fang Mu felt cool air wash over him. The floor was marble, shiny enough to reflect his face. Hearing his footsteps, a roughly 40-year-old woman holding a half-knit sweater stuck her head out of the on-duty room. Fang Mu nodded at her like a long-time resident and walked straight for the stairs. She watched him go for a moment, skeptical, but then shrunk back into her room.

He climbed to the third floor. The hallway he arrived at was completely unfamiliar to him. Where Room 352 had once been there was now a stairwell, and all the dorm rooms on either side of the hall were hidden behind heavy antitheft doors. Fang Mu stood for a moment in the hallway, feeling rather at a loss. Suddenly, a door opened behind him and out scurried a shirtless young man wearing shorts and sandals and holding a washbasin. Seeing Fang Mu, he nearly jumped in surprise. Then he frowned and said, "Hey, who you are looking for?"

Fang Mu looked at the room the student had just left: 349.

"Where is Room Three-Fifty-Two?" he asked.

"Three-fifty-two?" said the student with surprise. "There is no Room Three-Fifty-Two on this floor. Look for yourself." He pointed at the rooms on either side of the corridor. "Three-forty-nine, three-fifty, three-fifty-one, three-fifty-three. There's no three-fifty-two."

"Why not?"

"I can't say for sure, but I did hear one of the older students say that in the old Dormitory Two, a bunch of people died in Room Three-Fifty-Two, so after the building was rebuilt they decided to get rid of it." He studied Fang Mu, his expression curious. "Are you looking for someone from that room?"

Fang Mu didn't answer, just turned and walked back downstairs.

One room, one number, four people. All lost to oblivion in the cold solidity of this new building.

They had knocked it down and built it back up, hoping to seal away those memories forever.

If only it were that easy.

Walking back through campus, Fang Mu happened to brush shoulders with a middle-aged woman who looked to be in a hurry. She glanced at him as she passed. Then a moment later she stopped in her tracks and called out: "Fang Mu, is that you?"

Fang Mu looked back. He recognized her. It was Librarian Zhao.

She smiled. "It really is you," she said, looking him over. "You're a little thin, but otherwise you look the same."

Librarian Zhao was the first familiar face Fang Mu had seen that whole afternoon. He too couldn't help but smile.

"How are you, Librarian Zhao?" he asked.

"Oh, I'm fine, I'm fine." She placed a hand on his shoulder. "I've heard you're attending graduate school at Jiangbin City University. How do you like it? Must be pretty exciting."

"It's all right."

As she gave his thin face a longer scrutiny, her tone softened. "I haven't seen you since you graduated," she said, sighing. "Though after what happened I can't really blame you."

Fang Mu looked down and said nothing. He could feel the warmth of her hand on his shoulder.

"By now that whole thing is almost a legend here. People are always asking about it, even over the past few days. Someone even wanted to know about you specifically." Taking no notice of his expression at this point, she continued. "I know it all sounds a little ridiculous, but college students are so superstitious these days; none of them would ever checkout that book anymore…"

Fang Mu frowned. "Someone was asking about me?"

"That's right. It was a man, a little over thirty. He seemed very professional. He even borrowed that book everyone is so scared of and read it for several hours."

Probably Tai Wei. What a snoop.

Seeing the look on his face, Librarian Zhao realized that it would be best not to bring all this up. Suddenly her voice became cheerful. "How about I treat you to lunch? As I recall, I still owe you a meal."

Fang Mu was about to decline when the cell phone in his pocket suddenly rang.

The phone, a gift from his mom, was a newer model Motorola and not cheap. Although this meant she could get in touch with him at all times, he knew that he was still young and she was obviously concerned about him, so he had gone along with it. After all, the thing was pretty cool.

Answering the phone, he heard his mom's voice on the other end. "Fang Mu, where'd you run off to now?"

"Oh, I just went to buy some computer games," he lied. "I'll be back soon."

"Was that your girlfriend?" asked Librarian Zhao with a smile once Fang Mu had hung up the phone.

"No, just my mom. She wants me to head home." The topic made Fang Mu even more uncomfortable.

She laughed. "Then you'd better hurry. Remember to look me up next time you stop by."

After spending another week at home, Fang Mu headed back to school early.

When he arrived at his dorm, he was surprised to find that the majority of students were already back. Du Yu had been the earliest. He had only stayed at home for a week before rushing back to school; though in his case it was because Zhang Yao was spending her summer break on campus, temping for a translation agency.

When Fang Mu opened the door, he again saw Du Yu and Zhang Yao hurriedly roll off one another.

Jeez, he thought, it's the middle of the day.

Acting as if he hadn't seen anything, Fang Mu sat on his bed, took a bottle of meat sauce out of his bag and handed it to Du Yu. "Here," he said. "My mom made this especially for you."

But before Du Yu had a chance to take it, Zhang Yao grabbed it out of Fang Mu's hands.

"I'll hold onto this," she said, and then glanced to Fang Mu. "Your mom's meat sauce is so delicious."

Helplessly, Du Yu just looked at Fang Mu and smiled.

Fang Mu laughed. "You should have said something. I would have told my mom to make some more."

"Then the next time you go home you better not forget," she said.

"Deal." Fang Mu smiled.

Zhang Yao laughed. "You know, you're actually quite handsome when you smile. When I have time I'm going to find you a girlfriend."

Fang Mu just laughed and waved away the idea.

When Fang Mu went to the bathroom to wash his face, he ran into Liu Jianjun, who was hand washing a pair of pants in a big basin, with a rolled-up basketball magazine in his mouth.

"You're back?" he said, words garbled behind the magazine.

"Yep," said Fang Mu, splashing cold water on his face.

"Has the case been solved?"

"What case?"

"Qu Weiqiang and his girlfriend. The double homicide."

"How would I know?"

"Man, I don't know when they're going to crack that thing. Goddamn tragedy." With that, Liu Jianjun stumbled out, taking all of his things with him.

Back in his room, Fang Mu really wanted to give Tai Wei a call, but after hesitating for a long time, he abandoned the idea.

In fact, the case was far from solved. While Fang Mu was sitting around at home, dying of boredom, the officers of the Jiangbin City State Enterprise and Nonprofit Institution Investigative Division had been working day and night with little success.

Over a month had passed since the murders, and in that time police had already traveled several times to both Linjiang City in Jilin province, the registered permanent residence of victim Qu Weiqiang, and Hegang City in Heilongjiang province, the registered permanent residence of victim Wang Qian. There they had investigated nearly a thousand people, and still the crime was no closer to being solved than on the day it was committed. Above all, the police were puzzled by a single question: what was the motive?

It was clear from the crime scene that nothing had been stolen. The several hundred renminbi lying in one of the drawers hadn't been touched, nor had the victims' cell phones, jewelry or other valuable objects. As a result, the possibility that this was a case of burglary ending in murder could essentially be eliminated.

Based on the brutality of the killings, revenge initially seemed a probable motive, but after repeated investigations, police could find no evidence that the victims had any enemies to speak of. Qu Weiqiang's parents were both laborers, while Wang Qian's father was a doctor and her mother a teacher. The possibility that some enmity from the parents' generation had led to the deaths of their children appeared unlikely.

If this was simply a forced entry, rape and murder case, then there were even more questions to answer. First, why dismember Wang Qian? If the reason was to conceal the body, why piece her back together and leave her lying on the floor? And what about the syringe in her left breast? Where did it come from and what did it mean?

Second, why bring Qu Weiqiang's body to the soccer field, cut off his hands, and then leave him there? The field was over a mile away from the scene of the crime and transporting him could not have been easy, so why go to all that trouble? If this was meant as a kind of challenge to the police, why not take the far lighter Wang Qian instead?

Although many questions remained unanswered, the police did feel certain about one thing: this was an exceedingly calm and intelligent killer. After breaking through the screen window, he had first killed the dead-drunk Qu

Weiqiang (toxicology reports later showed the victim's blood-alcohol level to be extremely high) by striking him with a blunt object. Then he raped Wang Qian, strangled her to death, hacked her apart and pieced her back together, cleaned the apartment, carried Qu Weiqiang's corpse to the soccer field, and cut off his hands. From the state of the crime scene it was clear that the killer had been methodical in everything—even the bathroom where he dismembered Wang Qian had been scrubbed so clean that the police could not find the smallest clue.

Analyzing the crime through the lens of criminal psychology, the killer's murder methods had been extremely rigorous—and this rigor seemed to please him greatly. This meant he was highly likely to kill again.

To the police, this was a terrifying prediction.

12 DEADLY HOSPITAL

Catching a cold during the hottest days of summer is notoriously unpleasant.

So early one morning, Tang Yu'e walked into the Jiangbin City University Hospital, wiping her nose every few steps. She felt good enough about the place; it was near her home, well-maintained, and, most importantly, cheap.

The problem was that the doctors' attitudes were not quite as caring as the plaque on the wall of the outpatient services entry hall promised. After speaking with a Dr. Cao, who asked her a few hurried questions and then wrote out several prescriptions, Tang Yu'e was sent to the nurses' station and told to ask for an IV.

The young nurse who intubated her was brusquely mechanical in her methods. It hurt a lot. Minutes later, Tang Yu'e was holding up her own IV bag and wandering the halls with a look of irritation, searching for the observation room. She hadn't gone ten steps before her arm was sore. Just as she was struggling to continue, a white-coated male doctor wearing a surgical mask appeared. With one hand he retrieved the IV bag from her outstretched arm, while with the other he helped her along, saying, "This way, ma'am." His voice was warm and friendly and lovely to hear.

The doctor led Tang Yu'e to Observation Room 2. No one else was inside. After helping hang her IV bag on the hook beside the chair, he placed a soft cushion beneath her.

"Thank you, young man," she said.

The doctor waved his hand to say she needn't be so polite. His eyes twinkled behind his glasses—he was obviously smiling. After helping Tang Yu'e get comfortable, he opened the door and left.

When the doctor returned he was carrying a cup of water. He placed it in Tang Yu'e's hand. It was ice-cold.

"You should drink this water, ma'am. It's so hot out today and there's no air conditioning in here. This will help you cool off."

"Thank you so much, young man. What's your name? I'd like to tell the hospital director how good you've been to me." Having never received this kind of treatment there before, Tang Yu'e felt a little overwhelmed.

But the doctor just waved his hand again, his eyes as lively as before, and then he turned and left.

Tang Yu'e was already planning on telling her husband how nice this man had been when she got home. She sipped the water. Ah, she could feel its chill run all the way down to her stomach. Truly pleasant—though it did have a faintly medicinal taste. But perhaps all hospital water tasted like that. Regardless, she didn't think about the matter any further. To be well over 40 and have a young man treat her like that—how delightful.

Fifteen minutes later, when the doctor quietly pushed open the observation room door, Tang Yu'e was already leaning back in the chair, fast asleep. The doctor took the empty paper cup from her hand and placed it in the pocket of his white coat. Then, from another pocket, he produced a syringe and injected its contents into the IV tube. Finally, he placed a thin book in Tang Yu'e's bag, and then departed just as he had come, swiftly and soundlessly.

After nine, the number of sick people coming to the Jiangbin City University Hospital gradually increased. One after another, various IV bag-toting patients sat in Observation Room 2, but no one took any notice of the middle-aged woman napping in the chair. At last, a young woman who was there accompanying her boyfriend while he got an IV pointed at Tang Yu'e.

"Hey, look at that woman over there. She hasn't moved an inch this whole time."

"She's probably just sleeping," her boyfriend said, holding his stomach.

Pushing the glasses up off the bridge of her nose, the girl stared at the motionless woman.

"No way..." she said, her face growing pale. "I don't think she's even breathing!"

Plucking up her courage, the girl took a few steps forward, cautiously leaned into the woman's ear and shouted, "Miss!"

No response.

After hesitating for a moment, the girl reached out and pushed her.

It was like pushing a block of wood.

Before the girl could react, Tang Yu'e fell rigidly off the side of the chair and onto the floor.

When Tai Wei walked out of Observation Room 2, a frown on his face, the director of the outpatient clinic was screaming his head off at the nurse who had given Tang Yu'e the IV.

The young nurse was backed against a table, sobbing and sniffling and saying that 30 minutes after she'd injected the IV, she'd gone to Observation Room 1 to check on Tang Yu'e. When she didn't see her, she assumed that once the IV was empty, the lady had removed it herself and left. After that, she hadn't thought about the matter again.

Seeing Tai Wei appear, the director quickly motioned for the nurse to shut her mouth. Then, before Tai Wei could speak, he abruptly stated their position: "We don't know a thing, so all this will have to wait until the higher-ups tell us what to do."

Tai Wei laughed, and then told one of his fellow officers to go to the hospital pharmacy and get the medicine Tang Yu'e had been prescribed so they could take it back to the lab for testing. Then he told the director to summon Dr. Cao, who had been in charge of the woman's case.

Minutes later, as Dr. Cao was rushing over, he was stopped on the way by members of the dead woman's family. One of them, a man in his early 40s, asked the doctor if he was Dr. Cao. When he said yes, the man slugged him in the face without another word. If the police hadn't heard all the commotion and hurried to see what was going on, Dr. Cao may well have joined his patient in the afterlife.

Sighing, Tai Wei looked at Dr. Cao's battered face, at the sobbing young nurse, and at the dead woman's family who were still trying to break free of the policemen so they could rush at the doctor.

"All right," he said, waving his hand, "we'd better just take them back to the station and figure things out there."

Dr. Cao and the young nurse both shot looks at the outpatient director, but he had intentionally turned away.

The young nurse gave the outpatient director a hostile look. It certainly wasn't the way he'd acted two days ago when he was grabbing her butt.

While trying to get the witnesses into the cop cars, the police ran into some more trouble. The middle-aged, self-proclaimed husband of the deceased simply refused to let them leave with Dr. Cao, saying that he needed to kill him to avenge his wife's death. For a while Tai Wei just held him back, but eventually he got fed up and let him go.

"Well, go on then," Tai Wei relented. "Kill him! This will be the easiest murder case we ever solve!"

Hearing this, the man stopped in his tracks and just stared at Dr. Cao, panting heavily.

As Tai Wei was about to get into the car, the man again stopped him and asked, "This has to be a case of medical negligence, right?"

"Who knows!" yelled Tai Wei, slamming the door in his face. "We haven't even started our investigation."

Then as he started the car, Tai Wei clearly heard the man ask the person standing next to him: "So how much does the hospital have to pay if someone dies?"

Man, what a world, thought Tai Wei. Smiling grimly, he shook his head and drove off.

Any hope the husband had of compensation was eliminated by the test results. There was no problem in the least with Dr. Cao's prescription, the medication dispensed by the pharmacy, or the compound concocted by the young nurse and then fed into the IV. Although traces of sedative were found in the victim's blood, the actual cause of death was brain swelling and respiratory exhaustion resulting from heroin poisoning. This finding shocked the police, who then closely reexamined the evidence taken from the scene. At last they discovered a tiny, needle-sized hole in the IV tube, leading them to suspect that someone had injected liquid heroin into the victim's IV, poisoning her to death.

But that wasn't even the strangest part, for while going through the victim's bag, police discovered a pornographic Japanese manga, which contained shockingly graphic drawings of gay sex and BDSM. Taking for granted that a middle-aged married woman like the deceased really did have a special fondness for such stuff, it was clearly best enjoyed secretly, in the privacy of her own home; so what was she doing bringing it to the hospital? And if it wasn't hers, then whose was it?

After interviewing members of the victim's family and other related parties, the police learned the following information: The victim was a 43-year-old woman named Tang Yu'e who had been unemployed since 1999 after being laid-off at a state-owned company located in Jiangbin City. Her husband, Pang Guangcai, was an electrician who worked for the maintenance department at Jiangbin City University. Together they had one daughter, then in high school.

Tang Yu'e had been an honest and hardworking woman never known to have bad blood with anyone. She also lived a highly moral life, and was so strict with her daughter that if there was so much as a kiss on TV, she would immediately change the channel. At one point, the police wondered whether the manga might have belonged to the husband Pang Guangcai, but not only did he flatly deny this charge, he also had only a sixth-grade education, so the difficulty of reading a Japanese comic would have been quite high. Aside from that, every big street in the city was full of shops selling pornography. If he had wanted to read something like this in Chinese it would have been easy; no reason to spend all that effort deciphering a foreign language.

A significant discovery was soon made while interviewing the staff at the Jiangbin City University Hospital. According to one of the nurses, she had been leaving work the morning of the murder when she saw Tang Yu'e being led by a roughly 5'9", white-coated doctor into Observation Room 2. Unfortunately, she had only glanced at him from behind, and for no more than a moment. Feeling almost certain that this man was the killer, police ordered all the doctors from the hospital to wear white coats and line up facing away from the nurse, so that she could identify whom she had seen. Although she indicated several of them as potential suspects, each man was soon cleared of suspicion. Thus it could be more or less concluded that the killer was someone from outside the hospital.

This meant that he had most likely disguised himself as a doctor, brought Tang Yu'e to Observation Room 2, found some opportunity to give her a sedative, and then injected enough heroin into the IV to kill her.

Still, two questions remained. First, why use something as expensive as heroin to kill her? Far cheaper poisons were easily available and just as deadly.

Second, where had that pornographic manga come from? And what did it mean?

Tai Wei had the nagging feeling that the manga was not only the most curious part of the case—it was also a way to split it wide open. After considering the matter over and over, he jumped in his car and drove to Jiangbin City University.

Again he found him on the basketball courts, but instead of shooting alone, Fang Mu was now playing in a fiercely competitive game of three-on-three. Tai Wei had to basically pull him aside to get him to talk. He could tell Fang Mu was a little reluctant.

Tai Wei hadn't brought the case files, so he just told Fang Mu a summarized version of what happened. Fang Mu kept his head down the whole time and wiped the sweat from his face. But even though he didn't look too pleased, it was clear that he was playing very close attention.

When he was finished speaking, Tai Wei turned to Fang Mu and asked him frankly: "What do you think of all this?"

Fang Mu didn't immediately answer, just frowned and stared off into the distance. After a long time, and with a seemingly great amount of determination, he finally said: "What does this have to do with me?"

"Huh?" For a moment Tai Wei was stunned, and he didn't know what to say.

"Officer Tai, I'm not a cop, I'm just an ordinary person. This stuff has already caused me a great deal of trouble. I don't think I can help you." Fang Mu's eyes were on the ground as he spoke, his voice almost a whisper.

Tai Wei stared at him for a long time before saying: "You're not still mad at me because of that other thing, are you?"

"No," said Fang Mu, looking up. "I just feel exhausted, and want to be a normal student like everyone else."

Tai Wei opened his mouth to say something, but no words came out. The two of them sat there in awkward silence for a moment. At last, forcing a smile, Tai Wei patted Fang Mu on the shoulder. "I can understand," he said. "After all, you're still too young to be spending all your time dealing with this kind of stuff." He sighed, and then shrugged his shoulders. "It's funny, this whole time I never thought of you as a student, but as a fellow officer." He smiled and patted Fang Mu's shoulder again. "Take good care of yourself." Then he stood up and got ready to leave.

"You know…" said Fang Mu, suddenly opening his mouth.

"What?" Tai Wei immediately sat back down and focused all his attention on him.

"It's probable that the pornographic comic was put there to dishonor the victim," said Fang Mu, his head down, seemingly speaking to himself. "Especially given that she was this nice, upstanding woman. Yeah, leaving something that obscene beside the body, I'd say he wanted to humiliate her."

"So what was the motive? Why would he want to do that to her?"

"I'm not sure. But I'd say it has something to do with sex."

"Are you saying…this was a crime of passion?"

"I'm merely saying it's a possibility. As for the heroin, I have no idea why he used that to kill her. Using a murder weapon like that takes preparation, therefore I believe it has something to do with whatever special need the killer is trying to fulfill. But as for the need itself, I also have no idea."

Seemingly deep in thought, Tai Wei nodded and said, "That's it?"

"That's it," said Fang Mu, before quickly adding, "but this is just my personal opinion, so take it with a grain of salt. Also," and now his face fell, "don't go looking into my past, and don't try convincing me to become a cop. I won't do it."

Then before Tai Wei could respond, Fang Mu stood up and walked away. He didn't look back once.

The police once more investigated the victim and her husband, this time focusing on their relationships with people of the opposite sex. As for the victim, they found that she had almost no male friends whatsoever, and according to her relatives and former coworkers, she had strongly disdained any sort of immoral male-female relations. But while investigating the husband, police made a significant discovery: a number of people they interviewed said that Pang Guangcai had been involved with a

30-something cleaning lady from the Jiangbin City University maintenance department. Police then focused all their energy on this lead, but found themselves greatly disappointed. As it turned out, Pang Guangcai and the cleaning lady did indeed have illicit relations: she had only just gotten divorced at the time, and in her loneliness had seduced him. But three months prior to the murder, she had gotten remarried to the boss of a snack food wholesaler, and her home life could be considered happy once more. She had absolutely no reason to want to kill Tang Yu'e and take her place.

Once more the investigation ground to a halt.

For the first time ever, it seemed to Fang Mu, Du Yu was not eating lunch with his arm draped over Zhang Yao. Instead, he had dragged Fang Mu to the dining hall by himself and had seated them in a very conspicuous spot.

"What's going on?" asked Fang Mu, obviously surprised as he ladled winter melon sparerib soup into his bowl. "Are you and Zhang Yao fighting?"

"No, no, no." Du Yu was clearly not in any hurry to chat. Spooning food into his mouth, he craned his neck and looked all around. After a moment, he spotted Zhang Yao amid the crowd of people lined up to get their food. He waved at her. Beaming, she waved back.

Third wheel again. Irritated, Fang Mu grabbed his tray and stood up. "You guys eat together; I'll go sit over there."

"Hey, don't leave," said Du Yu, waving him back to the table. "She's not going to sit here. It'll just be you and me."

Carrying their trays, Zhang Yao and another girl walked over to a nearby table and sat down. She winked at Du Yu, and then began eating.

"The hell's going on?" muttered Fang Mu, as he hunched over the table and continued to eat.

Du Yu barely paid attention to his food. He and Zhang Yao kept looking over at one other and gesturing back and forth. After a little while, he grinned at Fang Mu and said, "Well, what do you think?"

"What do I think about what?" asked Fang Mu, confused.

"That girl, the one sitting with Zhang Yao." He nodded in her direction.

Fang Mu glanced over. "She's all right."

At that very moment the girl happened to be looking in his direction, but as soon as their eyes met she looked away.

"Look at that dirty smile on your face," said Fang Mu, shaking his head at Du Yu. "You're crazy trying to check out some girl with Zhang Yao sitting right there. Don't come crying to me after she catches you."

"Man, what are you talking about? I was asking what you thought of her."

"Me?" Suddenly Fang Mu understood. When Zhang Yao said she was going to find Fang Mu a girlfriend, she had apparently been very serious.

Zhang Yao motioned for them to come over and join them. Clearly able to take a hint, Du Yu stood up at once. "Come on," he said, "let's all eat together."

"Stop making trouble," said Fang Mu, his face red.

The girl in question, however, looked totally at ease. She moved her tray out of the way so Du Yu and Fang Mu would have room to eat with them.

Seeing that Fang Mu still hadn't moved, Du Yu tried to provoke him, whispering, "Come on, man, you don't even have the nerve to do this?"

After hesitating for a moment, Fang Mu steeled himself, and then walked over with Du Yu and sat down.

"Fang Mu," said Du Yu, motioning at the girl, "this is Deng Linyue, Zhang Yao's classmate. Deng Linyue, this is my roommate, Fang Mu."

"Hello, master sleuth," said Deng Linyue, smiling at Fang Mu. Her voice was a little husky, sensuous.

Hearing the words "master sleuth", Fang Mu felt even more at a loss.

Without looking up from his meal, he mumbled a brief "Hi" and then nearly buried his face in his food and continued to eat.

The table immediately fell silent. After a few seconds, Fang Mu felt Du Yu step roughly on his foot beneath the table.

"What are you doing?" said Fang Mu sharply, but when he looked up he saw Deng Linyue's outstretched hand hanging in the air over the table. The look on her face was extremely awkward.

Fang Mu hurriedly reached out and shook her hand, forgetting that he was still holding his spoon. In the process he smeared her whole hand with soup.

"Sorry," he said, obviously flustered. He dug through all his pockets, searching wildly for a pack of tissues, but by the time he finally found some, Deng Linyue had already wiped her hand clean with a pack from her bag.

Now it was Fang Mu's turn to feel awkward. After sitting stiffly for several seconds, he decided that he might as well not say anything else, so he grabbed his tray and began eating as fast as he could.

For the rest of lunch, Du Yu and Zhang Yao tried to enliven the atmosphere by keeping up a constant, cheerful chatter, while the two individuals whom the lunch was actually about remained silent, focused on their food.

Fang Mu was first to finish. Although he wanted to get out of there immediately, he now realized this wouldn't be particularly polite, so he took out a cigarette and began to slowly puff away. As soon as the smoke drifted across the table, Deng Linyue, who up until then had been eating and drinking with gentle refinement, frowned slightly and batted it away.

Rather than put out his cigarette, Fang Mu used this opportunity to check her out while she was looking down to avoid the smoke.

She was about 5'5", her long hair tied in a loose bun, and several dyed-blonde strands hung across her oval-shaped face. Her skin was quite fair, her eyebrows painstakingly plucked, and the mascara and lipstick she wore were obviously not cheap. In her ears she wore diamond studs that matched her necklace perfectly, and she had on a light yellow spaghetti-strap top that revealed a swimsuit tan on her shoulders. However, her skin looked soft and smooth, not like that of someone who lived by the ocean; she had probably just vacationed there over summer break. Her legs were long and slender and she was wearing a short, white skirt and colorful sandals. Lavender polish glistened on her toenails.

This petite young woman was clearly quite well-off, and from her bearing it was clear that if her parents weren't high-ranking intellectuals, then they had to be government officials.

Seeming to realize that Fang Mu was observing her, Deng Linyue blushed slightly. When she finished eating, she lightly dabbed the corners of her mouth with a tissue, stood up, and bid a polite goodbye.

"I've got some things to take care of," she said. "See you guys soon." Then she nodded at everyone, picked up her tray, and walked gracefully away.

Once she was gone, Zhang Yao muttered in disappointment, "What the heck were you doing, Fang Mu?"

Cigarette hanging from his mouth, Fang Mu stared at the ceiling and ignored her.

"You colossal fool!" said Du Yu once they were back in the dorm. He was still upset over what had happened at lunch.

"She's beautiful, from a good family, and her dad is the director of the local Bureau of Industry and Commerce. You know how many guys are after her? It took a whole lot of work on Zhang Yao's part before she'd even agree to chat with you."

"Why don't you go for her if you like her so much?" said Fang Mu. He was shirtless and wearing only a pair of shorts, and he climbed into bed and pulled the top sheet over him. "Tell Zhang Yao that while I'm very grateful, she shouldn't waste so much energy on me in the future."

"Jeez, let no good deed go unpunished," said Du Yu, also getting ready for an afternoon nap. After undressing, he stared off into space for a moment. Then he smiled.

"She really does have some long legs, though." He laughed and smacked his lips in delight.

"Manwhore!" yelled Fang Mu, although he couldn't help but smile.

While the sound of Du Yu's snoring soon filled the room, Fang Mu tossed and turned, but couldn't get to sleep.

A girlfriend?Do I really need a girlfriend?

Even though Fang Mu had long remained aloof on campus, rarely socializing with anyone else, he had noticed at various points that a few girls seemed to regard him with interest. But because he was so accustomed to avoiding other people, those girls had gradually shifted their attentions to more open, enthusiastic boys.

Chen Xi.

The name alone caused Fang Mu's spirits to plummet. Rolling over, he buried his face in the cool side of the bed.

Never mind a kiss, never mind the feel of her hand in his, Fang Mu had never even spoken those three simple words to Chen Xi before it was too late. With some things, make one mistake and you can never take it back. With some people, make one and they never come back.

In the movie A Chinese Odyssey II, when a sword was held to Glorious Bao's throat, he spoke a heartfelt lie: "If God were to give me another chance, I would tell her I love her. And if He said that one day our love must end, I would wish for ten thousand years."

If God gave me another chance, I would wish that none of this ever happened, that I had never even met Chen Xi.

Don't think about it anymore, he told himself, blinking his already moist eyes. Since he was choosing to say goodbye to the past, that meant choosing to forget every part of it.

Half asleep, Fang Mu was surprised to find himself thinking about Deng Linyue. Although that afternoon he had scrutinized her from head to toe, he now couldn't remember what she looked like at all.

All he remembered was that she used Soulmate brand tissues, the pack printed with drawings from the Jimmy Liao graphic novel Turn Left, Turn Right.

---

13 INSTINCT

Before getting off work, Tai Wei ran into Zhao Yonggui, deputy chief of the State Enterprise and Nonprofit Institution Investigative Division. Old Zhao was leaning against the hallway window, smoking sullenly. A number of butts already littered the floor around his feet. When Tai Wei walked over and said hello, Old Zhao glanced up at him with cavernous, bloodshot eyes.

"How's your case going?" asked Tai Wei, offering him a cigarette.

Old Zhao tossed the spent cigarette in his hand to the ground and accepted the one from Tai Wei. He lit it and took a deep drag.

"No progress whatsoever," he said, digging his fingers into his temples. "We've interviewed nearly six hundred people and still haven't learned a thing. How about yours?"

"The same," said Tai Wei, his voice sounding a little disheartened.

The two men smiled bitterly at each other, and then smoked together in silence.

At some point it began to rain, blurring the view from the window. As Tai Wei watched the drops run endlessly down the glass, he suddenly remembered how he and Fang Mu had searched through a storm for Tong Hui. Unable to help himself, he smiled.

That pale, quiet, somewhat nervous kid had actually seemed a lot better the last time they'd met. His complexion had improved, and there was a more youthful look in his eyes.

160

It was true; making a kid his age confront blood-drenched murder scenes day after day was a little cruel. He should get to be like his fellow students, happy and carefree, idling his time away. And then later: graduating, getting a job, marrying, having children—enjoying the common pleasures of an ordinary life.

Ding Shucheng had said Fang Mu had a gift for understanding crime. But as Tai Wei saw it, this gift didn't seem to give him any pleasure at all. When Tai Wei tried to ask him why he was so interested in this stuff, he had said he didn't know. But that was obviously not the truth. Instead, it seemed to Tai Wei that the kid was constantly struggling with some memory he was powerless to shake. What terrifying experience was haunting him from the past?

If a person like Fang Mu wanted to choose an ordinary life, Tai Wei didn't know whether he should be happy for him or disappointed that he was wasting his talents. Take the case he was currently working on: if Fang Mu were there, Tai Wei was certain he'd never feel so stuck. But the way that Fang Mu had acted last time made him feel a little apprehensive about asking for his help. So although his advice about looking for a sexual dimension to the crime hadn't panned out, Tai Wei did not plan on consulting him again.

"If we see each other again, it means someone else has died."

Tai Wei just shook his head. That kid was a real piece of work. He truly hoped that one day the two of them could meet up for drinks when there was nothing else to worry about, and then get dead drunk together.

"Tai Wei," said Old Zhao suddenly.

"Huh?" grunted Tai Wei, quickly coming back to reality.

"You guys did a good job on that Ma Kai case," said Old Zhao, roughly smoothing his hair. "From the start, I've felt that our killer from the seven-one case is also abnormal, with some kind of mental disorder most likely, but I've been unable to figure a thing out on my own. Will you help me out with the psychological analysis?"

"Me?" asked Tai Wei, pointing at himself. "Stop kidding around. Since when have I had those kinds of skills?"

Still, Old Zhao's words made Tai Wei's heart skip a beat, because he was absolutely right. Constructing a criminal profile of Ma Kai had been hugely beneficial in cracking his case, so why not use a tactic like that again? The 7/1 double murder and the hospital heroin killing were both unusual crimes with seemingly unexplainable aspects. If psychological profiles could be made of their perpetrators, Tai Wei was confident this would greatly help to push both cases along.

"We should find an expert on psychology to help us out," said Tai Wei.

For an instant Old Zhao hesitated, clearly ill at ease. Then he tossed his half-smoked cigarette on the ground and crushed it roughly with his foot. "We'll see," he said. He glanced at his watch. "Shit, look how late it is. I'm not working overtime today. I need to head home and get some rest." He nodded to Tai Wei. Then turned and left.

Tai Wei watched Old Zhao's slightly hunched form disappear into the darkness at the end of the hallway. The guy was over 50 and had only just been promoted to deputy division chief. During this mess, the pressure had to be unimaginable.

At that moment, Fang Mu was sitting in class and spacing out, watching the same raindrops patter against the windowpane.

Rain always caused people to daydream—or at the very least, seemed to make it impossible to pay attention to what was going on in front of them.

It was Professor Song's class again. Because the professor worked as a lawyer during the day, he had no choice but to teach his graduate lessons outside of normal class hours. Dinnertime had already passed, but the professor showed no sign of finishing. Instead he just told everyone to take a short break.

Grumbling, some students braved the rain and sprinted to a nearby market to buy bread and other snacks to stave off hunger. The gutsier ones, on the other hand, covertly packed up their belongings and slipped out. After drinking some tea and smoking a cigarette in his office, Professor Song returned to class in great spirits, but when he saw how many students had left, his face went red and he pulled the attendance sheet from his briefcase.

The sound of students responding "Here" from every corner of the classroom brought Fang Mu back to reality, and he involuntarily glanced over at Meng Fanzhe. This was the first time the professor had taken attendance in a long time, and it had also been a long time since Fang Mu and Meng Fanzhe had sat next to each other. Meng Fanzhe was now too far away to help, and Fang Mu felt both worried for him and unwilling to watch another of those incredibly awkward scenes.

It was clear Meng Fanzhe was nervous himself. He sat stiffly, his back straight and his eyes focused unblinkingly on the attendance sheet in Professor Song's hands.

"Wang Degang."

"Here."

"Chen Liang."

"Here."

"Chu Xiaoxu."

"Here."

Unable to do anything, Fang Mu forced himself to look away.

It was good breeding not to knock over one's tableware at dinner. But when someone else knocked over their tableware, it was even better breeding to pretend not to see.

Next time, man. Right now there's nothing I can do.

"Meng Fanzhe."

Meng Fanzhe hesitated for about a second. Then he stood halfway up and spoke very clearly: "Here."

Astounded, Fang Mu looked back over, only to meet Meng Fanzhe's eyes. Meng Fanzhe smiled brightly at him, and gave a cheerful, victorious wink.

Before going to bed, Fang Mu ran into Meng Fanzhe in the bathroom. Meng Fanzhe was carrying two large kettles that he had just filled with boiling water.

"What are you doing with those?" Fang Mu asked, pointing at the kettles as he scrubbed his face at a sink.

"I'm giving Tom a bath," said Meng Fanzhe with a smile.

"Then you really don't need that much. It's a waste."

"You don't understand. Tom is so naughty. He always gets himself filthy from head to toe." Hearing Meng Fanzhe cheerfully complain about Tom, Fang Mu remembered how Liu Jianjun had called Meng Fanzhe Jerry, and he couldn't help but smile. Looking to either side, he made sure no one else was in the bathroom.

He turned to Meng Fanzhe and said quietly, "It seems like you're no longer afraid of roll call."

"Yep!" Meng Fanzhe nodded vigorously. "That seems to be the case." He placed the kettles on the floor and reached out to shake Fang Mu's hand, a serious look on his face. "Fang Mu, I want to thank you so much for the help you gave me."

Fang Mu smiled and shook his hand. "Don't mention it."

"When you're free, you'll have to come visit me in my room," said Meng Fanzhe. Then he waved goodbye, picked up his kettles and left.

Seeing Meng Fanzhe so relaxed made Fang Mu deeply happy. As he looked in the mirror, a slight smile gradually climbed his face.

That's right, he thought. Nothing is impossible.

It rained for two days straight, and as September began there was an unexpected chill in the air.

Umbrella overhead, Fang Mu carefully climbed the rain-slick library steps. He glanced at a piece of paper on the wall. It looked like a missing person notice. Momentarily distracted, he nearly slipped on some fallen leaves. He looked up. It seemed like only yesterday that the big tree had been covered in green. Now the leaves were all golden yellow, and as another gust of wind blew, several more floated down.

Five minutes earlier, he had received a call from Professor Qiao telling him to meet in the Psychological Consultation Room. He had not said what was going on, only that Fang Mu should hurry.

The Psychological Consultation Room was on the second floor of the library. It was the first of its kind to be located in any of the city's universities, and Professor Qiao was the man in charge. In 2000, the members of the Provincial Education Commission had held a meeting concerning university students' mental health, at which they called for all schools of higher education to establish mental health services for the benefit of their students. Jiangbin City University administrators had then tapped several professors from the schools of law and education to form the staff of a psychological consultation room located at the university. Being the eldest staff member, Professor Qiao Yunping had been chosen to be the project's director. But in the two years since its founding, very few people had come in for a consultation. Of course, this did not in the least mean that no one at Jiangbin City University had psychological issues; just that most would rather not confront them head-on. And since Professor Qiao usually had many things to attend to, he began showing up at the center less and less, until he was rarely there. So Fang Mu found it very puzzling that this was where the professor wanted to meet that day.

After Fang Mu knocked on the door, he heard Professor Qiao's distinctly calm voice. "Come in."

Fang Mu opened the door and walked inside, only to find that Professor Qiao was not alone.

On the sofa against the wall sat two visitors wearing police uniforms. One of them wore the stripes of a top-ranked officer. Both men turned to look at Fang Mu as he entered, obviously sizing him up.

Professor Qiao sat behind his desk. Several thick folders were stacked in front of him. He held one open in his hands. Glancing at Fang Mu from over the top of his presbyopic glasses, he motioned for him to sit in a nearby chair, and then handed him one of the folders.

The two policemen glanced at one another.

Without looking up, Professor Qiao said, "My student."

This didn't seem to ease their doubts in the least.

Feeling a little awkward, Fang Mu had no choice but to take a seat and open the folder.

Once he saw the first page, he knew exactly what they were: the files from the Qu Weiqiang and Wang Qian murder case.

Preliminary case notes. Autopsy reports. Crime scene investigation details and photographs. Interview transcriptions. Almost casually, Fang Mu flipped through it all.

Qu Weiqiang face down on the turf, arms extended, severed bones sticking out of either wrist.

His hands beside the goalposts, pale white and bloodless, like they had been chopped off a plastic mannequin.

Beneath his caved-in skull, his face wore a serene expression.

In a flash, Fang Mu's mind returned to that night he had stood alone in front of the goal. Everything around him became quiet. The overflowing bookshelves, Professor Qiao and the two policemen sitting up straight on the sofa, the large oil painting of Sigmund Freud on the wall—all of it now seemed very far away.

A single person now slowly took shape before Fang Mu, as if raised from the pit of his stomach. The person extended his vine-like arms farther and farther until they were wrapped tightly around Fang Mu, and then they burrowed under his skin, without leaving a mark or making a sound. Then a moment later a piercing pain spread throughout his body, and with it a calm, clear sort of feeling gradually emerged from within.

Green turf. Goalposts. Both hands. Sharp blade.

Three stiff, hard knocks echoed through the room.

Someone was pounding loudly on the door. In an instant Fang Mu came back to reality.

"Come in," said Professor Qiao.

In walked Librarian Sun, a stack of books held in his arms. "Professor Qiao, these are the books you wanted."

"Put them over here," said Professor Qiao, pointing at his desk expressionlessly.

Librarian Sun carefully placed the books on the only open spot on the desk. Then he smiled at Fang Mu, turned and left.

After looking through the folder again, Professor Qiao took a few books from the stack and glanced at them. He lit a cigarette and leaned back in the chair, deep in thought.

The two policemen sat respectfully on the sofa, not daring to say a word.

After some time, Professor Qiao suddenly sat up straight and said, "What do you make of this?"

Fang Mu was taken aback. It took him a moment to realize that Professor Qiao was talking to him. "Me?"

"Correct."

"I'm still sort of figuring it out; perhaps you should go first prof—"

"If I ask for your opinion then I want to hear it. Since when were you so timid?" Professor Qiao pointed at the top-ranked officer. "This is Bian Ping, director of the Criminal Psychology Research Division at the province-level Department of Public Security. He is also my former

student, and therefore your shixiong. What do you have to be afraid of?"
*(Translator's note: Shixiong means "elder apprentice to the same master," or in this
case, graduate advisor. By the same token, Fang Mu is Bian Ping's shidi, or "younger
apprentice to the same master.")*

Bian Ping nodded at Fang Mu.

"After looking through that folder, what caught your attention?" asked
Professor Qiao, staring straight at Fang Mu.

Fang Mu hesitated for an instant, and then said simply: "The hands."

Without betraying a hint of emotion, Professor Qiao said, "After
murdering the victim, the killer chopped off both his hands and left them
on the soccer field. What does that suggest to you?"

This time Fang Mu took a little longer to think through his response.
"Deprivation."

"Oh?" said Professor Qiao, raising his eyebrows. "What do you mean by
that?'

"When he was alive the deceased loved soccer and was the goalie for the
school team. I don't know much about the sport, but I do know that the
only player on a soccer field who can touch the ball with his hands is the
goalkeeper. For him, hands are the weapons with which he defends the
goal. So when you cut off a goalie's hands, you are implicitly depriving him
of his most valuable objects. And behind this act of deprivation, I sense a
kind of…" Fang Mu paused for a moment, and then said: "Jealousy."

Still expressionless, Professor Qiao pushed the pack of cigarettes toward
Fang Mu. Then without looking at him further, he turned to the policemen
on the couch.

"After the killer raped Wang Qian, the second victim, he strangled her to
death and then dismembered her. Then, however, he pieced her back
together. This is the most curious part of the case. If the symbols left by
the killer at the crime scenes represent the fulfillment of a special need,
and if, as Fang Mu said, the symbols left on the body of the first victim—
the severing of the hands—represent jealousy, then what is meant by the
fact that he dismembered the second victim and then pieced her back

together?"

Fang Mu and the two policemen stared with bated breath at Professor Qiao, just as if they were back in class.

"I sense that the killer desired to construct Wang Qian anew. He seems to have simultaneously lusted after her flesh and despised it, and it was this inner contradiction that caused him, after he raped her, to strangle and dismember her. Then deep within him, the feeling that he needed to possess an 'all-new' Wang Qian led him to piece her severed limbs back together. I believe that while the killer was in the process of reconstructing the deceased, he must have felt extremely conflicted. The fervor of revenge and the delight of having conquered, yes, but also an irredeemable sadness and regret at everything he had done."

Pointing at the folder, Professor Qiao continued. "I've noticed that the Public Security Bureau has barely investigated whether Wang Qian's personal history might have something to do with the case. I believe this could be a breakthrough point. My idea is that one of Wang Qian's former suitors watched helplessly as the girl he was in love with went everywhere with another man—even to the point of living together. And when he imagined how the pure, well-bred young goddess of his heart—for I have noticed that Wang Qian was a notably attractive and innocent-looking girl—was having crazed-sex with this muscled, simple-minded young man in the couple's own apartment, his emotions must have erupted like a volcano. Thus he went mad, and did what he did. However," he paused for a moment, "these are merely a few of my thoughts on the matter, for there are still several questions I am unable to answer. The syringe, for example. Maybe it belonged to the victim, but wherever it came from, why did the killer plunge it into her chest?"

"Perhaps as a way of venting his conflicted feelings for the victim's body; the killer spontaneously grabbed the syringe and stuck it in her," interjected Bian Ping.

"Right now it's still unclear," said Professor Qiao, shaking his head. "But if you think there's some merit to my idea, then you should begin investigating this possibility. And you had better start with people who knew Wang Qian as far back as middle school. Such intensity of feeling does not simply emerge after a day or two—it takes many unfulfilled years."

The two policemen rose to their feet and said their goodbyes. But when they were about to leave, the one who had been silent throughout turned back to Professor Qiao and, pointing at Fang Mu, said: "So this one's your student, too?"

Professor Qiao raised his eyebrows. "That's right," he said, a hint of arrogance in his tone.

The policeman said nothing further, just glanced at Fang Mu one more time, and then turned and followed Bian Ping out of the room.

After returning to his room, Fang Mu sat at his desk for a long time, staring at nothing. Other than smoke cigarette after cigarette, he didn't move an inch.

Then the door opened and Du Yu appeared, a grin on his face. As soon as he entered the room he began to cough.

"Jeez, keep smoking like this and you'll get cancer if you're not careful," he said, opening the door to aerate the room. "Brother, if you're trying to kill yourself, you've picked an awfully slow method."

Fang Mu said nothing, just smiled bitterly, his brows knitted together.

Du Yu's appearance made him realize that this whole time he had been reflecting on the case files he had seen that afternoon. Even now his mental state was much as it had been while in Professor Qiao's office. It was as if a second Fang Mu had quietly emerged within him while he wasn't paying attention, and then had taken over his whole being. This feeling had changed the very nature of his thoughts, and just as any addictive habit that had taken a stronghold, it was difficult to break.

This lack of control was terrifying.

Du Yu walked over and cautiously looked down at Fang Mu.

"What's up with you?" he asked.

"With me? Nothing, I'm fine."

"Then why are you wearing that same gloomy look as before? If something's on your mind you should let it out."

Fang Mu shut his eyes, but then a moment later he opened them and smiled. "It's really nothing. Let's go get something to eat."

14 THE GRAYSON PERRY VASE

The Jin family household was already in a panic.

Holding a cordless phone in his hand, Jin Bingshan anxiously paced back and forth in his living room. On the sofa behind him sat his wife, Yang Qin, her eyes red from crying, along with several female coworkers who were supporting her limp frame and babbling all sorts of worthless words of consolation.

Jin Bingshan looked at the clock on the wall. It was already almost 10 p.m. He turned his attention back to the phone and dialed forcefully. Seeing this, Yang Qin stopped crying and struggled upright, looking expectantly at the phone in her husband's hand.

The call went through. After speaking briefly to the person on the other end, Jin Bingshan hung up. He turned toward his wife, but unable to meet her eyes, just shook his head.

With the piercing wail of an injured animal, Yang Qin collapsed back on the couch. As the sobs reached her throat, she began to choke and her face went bright red.

Jin Bingshan hurried over and began hitting his wife soundly on the back. A moment later she coughed violently, and then burst out crying once more.

"I don't care what you have to do, Jin Bingshan," she said, pointing a finger as skinny as a chicken's talon at her husband, "you are finding our daughter and bringing her home! What kind of father are you, ignoring your child for the sake of some goddamned clients?" Grabbing a pillow, she hurled it at him.

Jin Bingshan let the pillow bounce off of him and drop to the floor. At that moment, his normally dignified, understanding wife, an assistant professor at the university, had become little more than a screaming shrew. Looking at her, he felt his heart fill with immense grief.

Turning away, he glanced quickly around the room and then yelled, "Little Chen!"

Little Chen, his driver, immediately scurried out of the kitchen. Wiping instant noodle soup from his mouth, he said, "I'm here, Boss Jin."

"Do we still have more missing person notices?"

"A few."

"Then let's go. We're going to make one hundred more copies and then paste them up."

Saying this, he grabbed his jacket and headed for the door. While putting on his shoes, he looked back at his wife. She was crying soundlessly on the shoulder of one of her coworkers. Taking a deep breath, he opened the door and stepped out.

By the time he returned, it was already two in the morning. Jin Bingshan quietly opened the door to his apartment. The light in the living room was still on, but the room was empty. He tiptoed to his bedroom door and quietly pushed it open. His wife was already asleep on the bed, her face streaked with tears. In one hand she clutched a piece of their daughter's clothing.

Jin Bingshan's heart was seized with pain. After a moment, he carefully shut the door and returned to the living room. He stood there dazed for a moment, and then took off his ripped jacket and lay down on the couch.

While posting the notices, he had gotten into an argument with several security guards, and one of them, a young punk, grabbed one of his daughter's missing person photos and ripped it to pieces. Enraged, Jin

Bingshan struck the kid, and as a result he and his driver Little Chen were beaten up. Later, after they were dragged into the local police substation and questioned, the officers on duty decided not to give Jin Bingshan any more trouble, and let him off with only a warning.

After sleeping restlessly on the sofa for a few hours, Jin Bingshan got up and decided to post the remaining notices in a more distant location. Rubbing his eyes, he tried to open the door, only to discover that something was blocking it from the other side. Then with a strong push he opened it. In the hallway sat a large cardboard box.

Jin Bingshan froze for an instant, and then, instinctively, began tearing off the tape sealing it closed. As soon as he peeled back the lid, a putrid scent shot forth.

His daughter, Jin Qiao, was curled inside, her body stark naked and covered with wounds.

In the courtyard of the Public Security Bureau, Tai Wei and his fellow officers had just switched on their sirens and were about to leave when Tai Wei saw Zhao Yonggui rush out of the building and into another police car. Hurriedly rolling down the window, Tai Wei called out. "Where are you off to, Old Zhao?"

"Hegang City," he said, and then without another word stepped on the gas and peeled out.

Seeing the smug look on Old Zhao's face, Tai Wei figured the guy must have finally gotten a lead.

Tai Wei thought about the still-unsolved hospital murder case, and then about his destination that night. At last he gave a tired wave of his arm and said, "Let's head out."

Once more they were driving to Jiangbin City University. Tai Wei didn't know what in the world was wrong with this school, but in the last three months, two students and the wife of a staff member had already been killed. And from what he had heard, this time the deceased was a professor's daughter.

It can't be a curse, thought Tai Wei. That kind of thing just doesn't happen.

The squad cars flew through the city and before long they had reached the Jiangbin City University campus. Tall buildings stood on either side as far as the eye could see, giving the campus a very modern, impressive air. But to Tai Wei, these peaceful ivory towers now appeared enshrouded by a dense and gloomy haze, which, although it was a sunny morning, seemed to be spreading a somber chill through the air.

Tai Wei knew that because of the nature of their work, many of his fellow officers carried some sort of protective talisman on them, and in the past he had always been quick to laugh at their superstitious nature. But now, speeding toward Jiangbin City University, he felt a nameless terror come over him, and deeply wished he had some good luck type of object to hold and calm his fears.

Several officers from the local substation were waiting at the entrance to the Jiangbin City University residential area when Tai Wei arrived, although he hardly needed to be told where to go, for as he drove into the courtyard he saw a large crowd had already formed outside of one of the buildings.

Feeling for the gun on his waist, Tai Wei roused himself and called out, "All right, let's get to work!"

Zou Tuanjie told them the news at dinner. While playing soccer that afternoon, a philosophy student had told him that Assistant Professor Yang Qin's daughter had been murdered.

"What the hell?" said Du Yu, smacking the table. "This is happening way too often."

"I heard the girl was only seven-year-old," said Zou Tuanjie, shaking his head. "How could anyone be so goddamn cruel?"

Just as Du Yu was about to say something else, he suddenly turned and prodded Fang Mu.

"Look over there," he said.

Holding a tray of food, Deng Linyue was looking all around for an empty seat.

"Come on, Tuanjie, let's go sit somewhere else," said Du Yu, hurriedly grabbing his tray and standing up. "Once we're gone," he said to Fang Mu, "you've got to quickly call her over."

"Stop acting crazy," said Fang Mu, blushing. "Sit down and eat your food."

"Damn, too late," said Du Yu regretfully, as he craned his neck for a better view.

Fang Mu looked back to find that Deng Linyue had already found an empty table, and was in the process of cleaning it with a tissue from her bag.

"Let's just eat in peace, all right?" said Fang Mu as he sighed and poked at the potatoes on his plate.

"What? I don't believe it!" Du Yu was still looking back at Deng Linyue, his neck stretched like a giraffe's.

Again Fang Mu turned to look, only to see that Liu Jianjun was now sitting opposite Deng Linyue, and the two of them were chatting freely. This did not seem to be their first meeting.

"See, this is what happens when you wait," said Du Yu, his voice thick with annoyance. He retracted his neck and looked at Fang Mu.

"There's a kind of person who will do anything to help set-up his friend with a girl," said Fang Mu, glaring back at Du Yu, "when all he subconsciously wants is to be with that girl himself."

His mouth full of food, Zou Tuanjie tried to keep from cracking up.

"Bastard!" yelled Du Yu, his face scarlet.

On the way back to their rooms, the three of them ran into Liu Jianjun in the dormitory hallway. A huge smile on his face, he greeted them loudly. Although Fang Mu and Zou Tuanjie responded, Du Yu just stared at the ceiling.

"You see that? What did I tell you!" said Fang Mu to Zou Tuanjie with a smile.

Du Yu smiled as well, and then punched Fang Mu in the shoulder.

The victim was a seven-year-old girl named Jin Qiao. She had been in class three of the second grade at the Jiangbin City University employees' elementary school. Her father, Jin Bingshan, was 42-year-old and the president of the Metropolitan Culture Company. Her mother, Yang Qin, was 41 and an assistant professor of philosophy at Jiangbin City University.

When her body was returned, Jin Qiao had already been missing for over 50 hours. According to her parents, on the night Jin Qiao disappeared, her father was supposed to have picked her up from school, but because he was dealing with some clients at the time, he arrived late and she was no longer there. After alerting the police, the parents papered the city with missing person notices, but for the next two days there was no news, up until the victim's corpse appeared on her parents' doorstep.

At the time of discovery, the victim's corpse was completely naked and covered with wounds. According to the medical examiners, the cause of death was shock resulting from painful, large-scale tissue damage. In other words, Jin Qiao was tortured to death. The examiners also determined that after she was dead, her body was raped. However, because no trace of semen was discovered inside, they suspected that her killer used a condom.

The corpse had been placed inside a large cardboard box, which was soon identified as an old Adidas packing box. In addition to the body, two other objects were found inside, both seemingly inexplicable. One was a videotape, the other a broken piece of some ceramic object.

The videotape was of the standard variety compatible with the average family VCR. No fingerprints were found on its exterior. The tape itself was only 15 seconds long and consisted of a single close-up on a young girl's genitals. She was lying on a black sheet (probably to conceal the colors and characteristics of any other objects in the room), her legs were spread wide, and from beginning to end the camera never moved. The girl didn't either, and this coupled with the color of her skin suggested that she was already dead. Based on her physiology, she did not appear to be older than 14. Later, after the victim's parents were shown the video, they noticed a birthmark on the girl's thigh that identified her as their daughter Jin Qiao.

In her right hand the victim was found holding a piece of an unknown ceramic object, with a surface area of eight-square-inches. This was soon determined to be a broken piece of pottery, likely part of some sort of container, and it appeared to be decorated with pictures of naked men and women. The police then sought the advice of the chairman of the Jiangbin City Ceramic Artists Association. He responded that based on the images on the broken pottery, it looked very much like the work of Grayson Perry, the British ceramic artist who specialized in vases. However, it was extremely unlikely that this was an original.

To begin their investigation of the case, the police decided on the following steps:

First, visit the victim's elementary school, making sure to interview the students and teachers she came in contact with on the night she went missing.

Second, because the crime was so savage, it was very likely to have been done out of revenge. Therefore, a comprehensive investigation needed to be made of Jin Bingshan and Yang Qin's social relationships.

Third, because the box in which the victim was found was fairly large, her killer would probably have needed a car to transport it to her doorstep, but because the driveway was laid in cement, it was impossible to obtain any trace of tire tracks. Therefore, immediate interviews would need to be made with everyone living nearby, to determine whether any suspicious cars were seen on the morning of the murder. At the same time, car rental agencies across the city would need to be investigated for news of any suspicious renters.

Fourth, although the box in which the victim was found likely originated at either an Adidas company store or specialty shop, the killer had already removed any label that might have identified the place from where it was purchased or shipped. This was obviously done to conceal its origin, so a citywide search would need to be made for the source of the box.

Fifth, while undergoing intense torture, the victim had probably attempted to dodge or resist her killer, and police suspected that it was during one such attempt that the victim grabbed the piece of pottery. This meant that the vase from which the piece was broken had likely belonged to the killer. Therefore, all markets in the city that sold this kind of pottery would need to be investigated for clues about its purchaser.

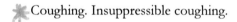Coughing. Insuppressible coughing.

And then endless vomiting.

Leaning on the rim of the toilet, grabbing for the toilet paper. Ripping off a piece and carelessly wiping away the vomit and then throwing it into the toilet and flushing. The filthy paper swirling out of sight.

So dizzy.

With difficulty standing up. A familiar face in the mirror. Skin pallid, unkempt hair.

Smiling at the face.

Eyes shut as the lips curl upwards.

No—must not look at that monstrous smile.

Stumbling back into the living room. Collapsing on the couch. Tightly shut living room windows, thick curtains blocking out the sun. Pale yellow light from a single bulb on the wall. The air stiflingly hot. But then, why does it still feel so cold?

Hair soaked with cold sweat, plastered uncomfortably to the forehead. Forcefully pushing it back with a damp palm. Sniffing.

The room smells of rot.

Striding quickly to the window, throwing back the curtains with a whoosh, and then, as if burned by the sunlight, immediately drawing them closed. Over to the desk now, tearing open the drawer, pulling everything out. At last, a bottle of air freshener. Psh. Psh. Psh. Spraying until there's not a drop of liquid left.

The dense lemon scent burns, but now everything is much more comfortable.

Falling back onto the sofa. Grabbing a book from the floor, flipping through the pages. On one: a large fold-out drawing of the human anatomy.

Get the fuck away!

The book is thrown hard against the wall, hits with a thunk, and falls to the floor with a rustle of paper. Innocently, it lies open.

Body going limp, sliding to the floor. Instantly chilled by the cold tile.

Hands propped at sides, trying to rise, feeling something cold, damp and oily beneath one palm.

Lifting it from beside the sofa. One glance. A small piece of someone's ruined skin.

Throat suddenly clenching. And then mouth covered, scrambling to the bathroom, no time to get the toilet lid up before the horrid sound of retching echoes off the walls.

Although bent like a bowstring, although stomach twitching violently, only a few mouthfuls of yellowish liquid fall into the bowl. Despite tear-blurred vision can still feel drops of mucus trickling down the lips.

Again that face in the mirror. Tiredly wiping long trails of saliva hanging from the mouth. Staring at the face. It was someone else, the face was just as pale but it was someone else.

Laugh! Open your mouth and laugh.

The stranger in the mirror cackled right back.

Looking back into the living room, at the photograph on the computer screen.

You'll never defeat me.

15 WRONG WAY

Fang Mu took a few quick steps over the grass and then hurried down the little path back to his dormitory. When he reached the building he saw Liu Jianjun, who was wearing a suit and tie and talking to Deng Linyue just outside. Seeing Fang Mu, Liu Jianjun waved enthusiastically, and Deng Linyue gave a very polite smile. Fang Mu waved back at them distractedly and then rushed into the building.

Five minutes earlier, Du Yu had called Fang Mu from their dorm room, saying that one of Fang Mu's college classmates was there to see him.

Since graduating from the Teacher's College, Fang Mu had essentially lost touch with all of his old friends, so he found it extremely surprising that one would come for a visit.

When he opened the door, someone sat up on his bed, and then in a thick Dalian accent said, "Sixth Brother, you're back."

For several seconds Fang Mu was stunned. Then without saying a word, he walked over and gave the visitor a big hug.

"Eldest Brother," said Fang Mu with a smile. *(Translator's note: In Chinese dorm rooms, it is customary to refer to one's roommates based on their age—as in Eldest Brother for the oldest guy, and then Second Brother, Third Brother, Fourth Brother, etc. Because China's dorms are often quite packed, it is not unusual to have up to six "brothers" in one room.)*

Eldest Brother was rather taken aback by this sudden show of affection. Clapping Fang Mu on the back, he said, "My man, you look exactly the same."

As they released each other, Fang Mu had tears in his eyes. Embarrassed, he quickly wiped them dry. "Eldest Brother, what are you doing here?"

"I just happened to be in the city on business, so I figured I'd stop by and see you. Man, I never expected Jiangbin City University's security to be this tough. They made me register my ID number before they'd even let me up here."

"Some serious stuff has happened here over the last little while, so they're being pretty strict with outsiders."

"Oh, what kind of stuff?"

"Two students were murdered," interjected Du Yu.

"Jeez, that kind of thing seems to be happening everywhere," said Eldest Brother with a frown. Then when he noticed how Fang Mu's expression had changed, he quickly switched topics.

"You guys' dorm is pretty nice. Is this standard for graduate students?"

"Yep," said Fang Mu. "But, Eldest Brother, what have you been doing?"

"Just muddling along. I'm sure you've heard how hard it is for college graduates to get jobs these days. I've been working in the legal department of a state-run company in Dalian. The company's been having some trouble lately, so we've had to put forth some suits on their behalf, and collect from some debtors. You know, 'This isn't enough money', or 'This will do for now'—that kind of stuff. In fact, that's why I'm here today; to go see a company about some money they owe us."

Fang Mu laughed and said, "Have you been in touch with any of the other guys?"

"Second Brother went into the army. The Eldest Brother from Room Three-Fifty-One joined at the same time, and he told me recently that Second Brother is now a company-level cadre. After graduation, Fifth Brother went to Guangzhou to become a lawyer, and I hear he's doing pretty well. But truth be told, I haven't been great at keeping in touch."

Eldest Brother's voice fell. "After what happened with Third Brother—when Fourth Brother died and you barely survived—you remember what it was like. We had been six close roommates, and then only four were left. Afterwards, none of us wanted to talk about it, we were all just looking forward to the day we could forget it even happened, so it was only natural that we would gradually fall out of touch."

Noticing that Du Yu had been listening in, Fang Mu took Eldest Brother's arm and said, "Come on, Eldest Brother. You've traveled all this way; let me treat you to something to eat."

At a small restaurant just outside the university gates, Fang Mu and Eldest Brother drank until their faces were red. After all, they had once been as close as brothers, so having not seen each other for two years, it was only natural that they had a lot to talk about. At first they kept interrupting one another, like a pair of old men competing to see who had the best memory, though as if by tacit agreement they both carefully avoided bringing up that tragic event. Instead, they did their best to recall all the hilarious stories and brilliant remarks they could remember from their college days, and when they couldn't think of anything else to say, they just laughed idiotically and took another drink.

After they had more or less drunk their fill, Eldest Brother suddenly clapped himself on the forehead and said, "That's right, I almost forgot. Did that journalist ever come talk to you?"

"Journalist?" said Fang Mu, a little confused. "What journalist?"

"Wasn't there a journalist that wanted to interview you?" said Eldest Brother, looking even more confused himself.

"Interview me?" said Fang Mu. "Interview me about what?"

Eldest Brother sighed. "What else? That thing with Third Brother."

Fang Mu sobered up fast. "What exactly are you talking about?"

"No need to get so excited. About three months ago I got a call from someone who said he was a reporter for the Changhong City Evening News. He asked me if I was your classmate, and I said I was. Then I asked him how he had gotten my number. It was in the alumni book, he said. Then he told me he was investigating what happened with Third Brother, because he wanted to write an article about the mental health needs of university students."

"What did you tell him?"

"Nothing much, just what I knew. However, I began to have a feeling that what this guy was really interested in wasn't Third Brother; it was you."

"Interested in me?"

"That's right, for example what your personality was like, how you behaved after everything happened. I think it was because you were the only survivor."

Fang Mu thought for a moment, and then asked, "What was this guy like?"

"While I can't say anything for sure, his voice didn't sound that old, around thirty, more or less, and he was very polite." Then, noticing that Fang Mu's brows were drawing tighter and tighter, he asked: "What's wrong? He never interviewed you?"

"No." Fang Mu shook his head.

"That's strange. What could this guy have wanted?" said Eldest Brother, visibly puzzled.

Fang Mu was thinking the same thing. He thought of the person that Librarian Zhao had mentioned over the summer.

Who was he? And what was he after?

Zhao Yonggui's trip to Hegang City turned out to be a big waste of time. At first, however, it seemed promising. Once there, he was informed by the local police that while in high school, Wang Qian was strenuously courted by a male classmate named Yan Hongbing. The problem was, his method of professing his love was a little excessive; any boy that came in contact with Wang Qian would inevitably be beaten up by Yan Hongbing and some of his hooligan friends. One time, Yan Hongbing happened to run into Wang Qian while she was being tutored in physics by a male teacher; as a result, this man was later beaten so bad he ruptured his spleen. This incident caused so much fuss that if the College Entrance Exam hadn't been coming up, Wang Qian might have changed schools. Afterwards, Wang Qian began attending Jiangbin City University, while Yan Hongbing, who failed to graduate, became a jobless vagrant, and traveled twice to Jiangbin City University to pester her. The second time, however, he was soundly beaten by Qu Weiqiang and his soccer teammates.

"Just you wait," Yan Hongbing was reported to have said at the time, "sooner or later, I'm going to take care of you." And as it happened, at the time of the 7/1 double murder, Yan Hongbing had left Hegang City, and his whereabouts were unknown.

This piece of information closely conformed to the murder motive suggested by Professor Qiao, and Zhao Yonggui grew excited about the prospects. So, when the Hegang police informed him that Yan Hongbing had suddenly returned, he asked them to detain him, and then drove straight through the night to Hegang to begin his interrogation.

The result was greatly disappointing. Although the story about Yan Hongbing pestering Wang Qian at Jiangbin City University turned out to be true, a short time after that he had gone to Guangzhou and found work as a hired goon in an underground gambling hall. Then, while participating in an armed fight in mid-June 2002, Yan Hongbing was severely injured. On the day of the crime he was still in a hospital in Guangzhou undergoing treatment, and under strict police supervision to boot.

So when Tai Wei emerged from the director's office and then, while heading back down the hallway, once more came across Zhao Yonggui leaning against the window and smoking sullenly, he knew exactly what was meant by the phrase 'misery loves company'.

Because right then, Tai Wei's mood was no better.

Not only had the hospital murder case reached an impasse, there were also zero leads in the recent killing of the little girl. So far, all preliminary investigations into the case had come back with nothing.

On the day of her disappearance, nearly all of Jin Qiao's classmates were promptly picked up by their parents. Only one, a little girl, recalled that when she was heading home, Jin Qiao was still standing outside the school doors, as if waiting for someone. And because the teacher in charge was celebrating her father-in-law's birthday that evening, she had left as soon as school was out. No one noticed who Jin Qiao ended up leaving with or where they went.

Although Jin Bingshan and Yang Qin were originally both professors at Jiangbin City University, Jin Bingshan later left to form an arts and entertainment company with some of his friends, while his wife continued to teach. But whether at the university or in society at large, they both had excellent reputations and no enemies. And while Jin Bingshan did work in the business world, he kept his hands clean, and was never known to have engaged in illicit relationships with any other women. Therefore, the possibility that this was a crime of either passion or revenge could essentially be eliminated.

Interviews with those living near the crime scene also brought miniscule results. According to Jin Bingshan, when he returned home at roughly 2 a.m. that morning, the box was discovered; it was not yet there and he did not register its appearance until five hours later, when he tried to leave and found it blocking the door. Therefore, at some point between two and seven in the morning, the killer must have transported the box containing Jin Qiao's corpse to her parents' doorstep. At this time of year, the sky would already have begun to brighten by 6 a.m., meaning that the killer most likely dropped off the box at some point between two and five. Incidentally, this also happened to be the time when most people sleep their deepest. So when police asked the building residents whether they heard the sound of someone moving something heavy that morning, or saw a suspicious car parked outside, nearly all of them just shook their heads. Only one, a middle-aged man with prostate issues, said that while he was getting up to use the bathroom at around 4 a.m. he heard the sound of a car engine outside. As for the model, license plate, or driver, he never even looked.

As for the box itself, police checked Adidas company stores and specialty shops across the city. They learned that boxes like it were originally used for shipping sportswear, and that after it arrived at a store and was unpacked, it would either be sold to a salvage station or occasionally taken home by one of the employees. There were over a thousand salvage stations of all sizes across the city; investigating them one by one would take a lot of time.

As for the piece of broken pottery, police discovered that it did indeed come from a replica of a vase by the British artist Grayson Perry. Such replicas were available in arts and crafts stores in every corner of the city. Finding the buyer of this specific piece would be like dredging a needle from the bottom of the ocean.

Neither investigation was going anywhere, so when Tai Wei received orders to report to the director's office, he had sighed and prepared for the worst. Luckily, the director didn't blame him at all; just told him to pay attention to every detail and pursue every lead.

After leaving the director's office and nodding at the equally gloomy Old Zhao in the hallway, Tai Wei returned to his office and slumped into his chair. Then, kneading his temples, he lit a cigarette, opened the case folder and began to read, word by word, page after page.

Several hours later, when Tai Wei finally left PSB headquarters it was almost midnight and he was exhausted. At a small roadside wonton restaurant, he ate a cup of hot soup mixed with spicy pepper flakes and looked over the few lines of notes he had scribbled hastily in his notebook.

While reading aimlessly through the case files that afternoon, he had suddenly thought of Fang Mu and remembered how the kid had once talked about a killer's symbols and needs. With nothing else to go on, Tai Wei had figured he might as well try analyzing the case from this perspective.

In a criminal investigation, the key breakthrough point is determining the killer's motive; that way the range of possible suspects can be reduced. And to a certain extent, what is found at the crime scene will suggest this motive.

For example, in the killing of the little girl, there were certain elements that seemed to distinguish the case.

First, the torture. For an adult, murdering a seven-year-old girl would not be a difficult task in the least. So why had the killer taken the time and energy to torture Jin Qiao to death and then afterwards raped her corpse? If this was done to satisfy some sexual need, then the killer was most likely a sexual psychopath.

Second, the videotape, the 15-second close-up that the killer filmed of the victim's genitals. Was this also meant to satisfy some need? If, for instance, the tape was meant to provide sexual stimulation at a later time, why had the killer taken only 15 seconds of footage? More importantly, why deliver this film to the victim's parents? And if the tape was meant to be part of some twisted collection, why only film the victim's genitals when these just barely distinguished her? What kind of significance could this possibly have to the killer?

Third was delivering the victim's corpse to the victim's parents. Based on similar cases in the past, this kind of behavior was often meant as a kind of challenge or way of showing off. In which case, who was he challenging? The police or the parents themselves?

Gulping down the boiling-hot wonton soup, Tai Wei did his best to follow Fang Mu's example and analyze the case based on the killer's psychological characteristics. However, by the time the soup was finished, he had no choice but to admit that besides copying the kid's frowning expression, the rest of it was beyond him.

Afterwards, standing in the crisp midnight air, Tai Wei made a decision: no matter how much the kid glared at him, he was going to visit Fang Mu tomorrow and see what he had to say.

The situation ended up being much simpler than Tai Wei had expected.

Unlike before, when Fang Mu had regarded Tai Wei like he was some unwelcome stranger, this time he just made sure the door was closed, and then took the case files from Tai Wei and began reading them quietly.

Tai Wei sighed to himself with relief. He knew by now that when Fang Mu was looking over a case, it was best not to say anything. So with nothing else to do, he turned on Fang Mu's computer and began browsing aimlessly. Inadvertently, in one section on the hard drive, Tai Wei came across a folder titled Data. He opened it. Inside were six more folders, the first titled Huang Yongxiao, the last Ma Kai. His heart skipped a beat; these were the cases Fang Mu had previously helped solve. He double-clicked several of the folders, but they were all password-protected. Then, just as he glanced back at Fang Mu and calculated the likelihood that he would tell him the password, the kid opened his mouth.

"You figure out where this thing came from?" asked Fang Mu, pointing at one of the photographs.

Tai Wei walked over and looked. It was the cardboard box that had held Jin Qiao's corpse. The three-leafed Adidas logo was printed on the side.

"Not yet, we're still looking. Why?"

"Oh, no reason," said Fang Mu, turning his attention to a photograph of the broken piece of pottery. "How about this?" he asked after a moment.

"That one's an even bigger headache. Nearly every crafts market in the city sells them. It's going to be very difficult to determine who bought it."

"What could it mean?" asked Fang Mu, staring at the ceiling and seemingly speaking to himself.

"Could the victim have broken it while struggling with her killer and then grabbed a piece in her hand?"

"No way," said Fang Mu, shaking his head. "I'm certain that the killer placed it in her hand after she was dead."

"How can you be so sure?"

"Don't you think it's a little big?" said Fang Mu, indicating the piece's size with his hands. "The killer murdered the victim, raped her, and then filmed her—no way in this whole series of events could he have failed to discover that she was holding this thing in her hand."

"You mean to say..." Tai Wei paused for a moment, and then slowly continued. "The killer placed this in her hand to communicate some kind of message?"

"That's right, but I don't know what exactly this message was supposed to be. Still, I think we can go about determining it in two ways. The first is through the object itself. The second is through the meaning expressed in this British artist Grayson Perry's work. For the latter we'll need to do some research, but as for the former..." Fang Mu trailed off. Then, speaking slowly as if deep in thought, he said, "I believe it has something to do with the identity of the victim. What characteristics does ceramic have?"

"Well, it's fairly hard, but also quite fragile."

"That's what I was thinking myself. I believe this can also refer to the female sex."

"Oh. How do you mean?"

"I'll answer that question in a moment, but first let's discuss the killer himself. I believe he's between twenty-five and thirty-five-year-old, possesses a certain amount of education and artistic taste, and lives fairly comfortably. In person he's clean-cut and urbane. And he suffers from a psychosexual disorder that stems from a history of sexual failure."

"On what basis?"

"First, there's the piece of pottery he placed in the victim's hand, which we tentatively believe represents femininity. In and of itself, this implies that the killer received a good education, and possesses a certain amount of artistic taste," he said. "Very often, this sort of person pays a lot attention to his appearance. Next, in committing the crime, the killer's behavior demonstrated the marks of sexual psychosis. For example torturing the victim; for example raping her corpse; for example filming her genitals. In general, raping the victim's corpse is often the mark of an individual unable to have normal sexual relations with women, and frequently one who has been refused or insulted sexually by women. This sort of person is also likely to possess a strong tendency toward sexual domination and sadism. So for such an individual, a dead woman is far better able to satisfy his need to control the female body than a live one. This is why I guessed that the broken pottery, by being hard and yet fragile, was meant to represent the female sex. It implies both refusal, as well as the fragility to collapse at the first blow. This is how the killer views womankind. Also, the return of the corpse to her parents' home probably also expressed this particular attitude. However..." He hesitated for a moment, "I have to admit to being far from confident in this analysis, because I cannot understand why the killer chose a seven-year-old girl. The majority of individuals with this sort of psychological makeup ordinarily select adult women for their victims, in order to better alleviate their feelings of frustration. But conquering a seven-year-old? I can't imagine that could have been all that satisfying for him."

"Maybe this was the killer's first time, so he intentionally selected an easy target? Or I guess it could all have just been by chance."

"Right now it's still unclear, so it would be best not to draw any conclusions," said Fang Mu, shaking his head. "On another note, the case files say that the source of the car is currently being investigated. Has there been any news?"

"Not yet. After speaking to the cab drivers working the morning of the crime, we turned up nothing, so at this point we're beginning to consider whether the killer might have rented a car or used his own."

"Oh." Fang Mu nodded as if lost in thought. "I think you might as well consider the possibility that someone friendly with the parents committed the crime."

"Why?"

"Because if this was a violent kidnapping, there would have to have been some kind of disturbance outside the school, and someone would have seen. Also, having grown up in that kind of household, the victim would surely have been instructed by her parents not to just wander off with strangers. And anyway, she might only have been seven-year-old, but this isn't like when we were young—someone wouldn't have been able to just lead her away with a piece of candy. Therefore, I think it's highly likely that this is a case where the perpetrator was familiar with the family. And after using this familiarity to get the little girl to drop her guard, he kidnapped her."

When Tai Wei was about to leave, Fang Mu asked him how things were progressing on the hospital murder case. Tai Wei hesitated for a moment, and then admitted that Fang Mu's suggested line of attack hadn't worked out. Fang Mu did not look disappointed in the least, but instead just frowned and stared out the window for some time.

"How about the seven-one case?" he said at last.

"I'm not entirely sure. As you know, that case is being handled by the State Enterprise and Nonprofit Institution Investigative Division, so I don't hear much about it, but I suspect they're as stumped as us." Seeing Fang Mu's frown grow deeper, he asked, "Why, what are you thinking?"

Fang Mu said nothing.

"Wait, are you thinking," Tai Wei hesitated for a moment, "that all these crimes were committed by one person?"

After a long time, Fang Mu slowly shook his head. A thin, bitter smile played across his lips. "I myself am finding it difficult to say what exactly I'm thinking," he said, meeting Tai Wei's eyes. "Rationally, this does not seem like the work of one person, because in all three crimes, the murder method, the victims, the characteristics of the crime scenes, and those of the killer's own psychology were much too different. Still, I can't shake the feeling that there's something connecting them." Noticing that Tai Wei was now following his every word with bated breath, Fang Mu smiled awkwardly and said, "However, this could all just be in my imagination. You shouldn't take it too seriously."

As Fang Mu was walking him out, Tai Wei seemed to suddenly think of something. "Did you ever read that letter Ma Kai wrote to you?" he asked.

Fang Mu hesitated for a moment before admitting the truth. "No. I burned it."

Tai Wei was extremely taken aback. "You burned it?" The way he saw it, that letter had been an almost ideal document for the study of criminal psychology, so for someone this interested in the field—not to mention this concerned with empirical research—to simply burn it up without even reading it was mindboggling. He was about to ask why when he saw that the words "Don't ask!" were practically scrawled across Fang Mu's face.

Jeez, thought Tai Wei, what was that saying again? Oh, yeah; geniuses are all crazy.

16 THE NUMBER KILLER

Dragging a broom and dustpan, cleaning woman Zhang Baohua climbed wearily to the fourth floor of the Multidisciplinary Building. This was supposed to be Tian Cuixia's responsibility. Zhang Baohua didn't know how that old shrew had gotten so lucky, but after getting divorced, she had been able to marry the boss of a snack food wholesaling company. And then recently, after the wife of Pang Guangcai, one of the electricians from the maintenance department, was killed, police had come snooping around and discovered that he and Tian Cuixia had once had an affair. Even though she was proven to have had no part in the murder, she was obviously not going to stick around there any longer, so without even a word of warning, she quit. Since there already weren't enough cleaners to begin with, the maintenance department had had no choice but to temporarily assign the job of cleaning the Multidisciplinary Building to Zhang Baohua. Her reward would be an extra 200 renminbi a month.

After quickly cleaning several rooms, Zhang Baohua glanced down at her watch. It was already almost 7 a.m. According to regulations, the whole building had to be finished by eight. Thinking of the three floors she still had left to clean, Zhang Baohua massaged her waist and then pushed open the door to Room 404.

Huh? she thought. What were people doing studying here this early?

Amid the empty desks in the classroom two people sat side by side. In the faint morning light, Zhang Baohua could just make out that one of them was dressed all in red.

If they had come there to study, why'd they leave the lights off? Hmph, she thought, they probably just snuck in here last night to have sex.

Curling her lips in contempt, Zhang Baohua switched on the light.

Eating as fast as they could, Fang Mu and Du Yu hurried to the Multidisciplinary Building, but when they arrived they discovered that there was no reason to worry about being late for class. Several hundred students and teachers were already gathered outside the building, the scene as noisy as a food market. But although everyone was saying something different, they all wore the same panicked expression.

What had happened?

Fang Mu was about to ask one of the students beside him, when he noticed police cars parked on the street side of the building, their lights flashing. His face fell. Could someone else have died?

Abandoning Du Yu, he did his best to squeeze through the crowd. When he finally made it to the front, a policeman abruptly blocked his way.

"Can't you see the police tape?" he asked.

Behind him, a blue-and-white cordon separated an empty space in front of the building from the crowd of onlookers. The main door was wide open, and policemen could be seen rushing up and down the stairs. Through the window of the on-duty room, Fang Mu watched one of the building attendants haltingly explain something to an imposing veteran officer. In the chair beside them sat a cleaning lady. She was holding a cup of water with both hands and shaking all over, her eyes absolutely blank.

Suddenly there was a disturbance within the crowd. It was the dean, a rather heavy man, doing his best to wade through the onlookers. Once he had pushed his way to the middle, he lifted the loudspeaker he was carrying and turned it on.

After clearing his throat, he began to speak at the top of his lungs. "Students, teachers! All classes in the Multidisciplinary Building have been canceled for the day! Makeup times will be posted at a later date. As for all other buildings, classes will proceed as scheduled. Again, all classes in the Multidisciplinary Building are canceled for the day! Classes in all other buildings will proceed as scheduled!"

An excited murmur ran through the crowd, for even though they were all terrified of what might have happened inside the Multidisciplinary Building, the prospect of skipping class that morning was still enticing. Yawning, students who had been up all night returned to their dorms to get some sleep, while those who hadn't yet eaten hurried to the dining hall. Whoever was inside the building, whatever had happened to them—it all seemed much less important than catching a few more hours of sleep or eating a good breakfast. After all, the lives of other people were just that— other peoples'.

Very quickly the crowd dispersed. Figuring that even if he waited around no one would tell him what was going on, Fang Mu also turned to leave. But just as he was about to walk away, he spotted Tai Wei's jeep parked outside the building.

Fang Mu was surprised. What was he doing here? Shouldn't this case be handled by the State Enterprise and Nonprofit Institution Investigative Division? And if so, why was he getting involved?

Fang Mu thought for a moment, and then he pulled out his cell phone and called Tai Wei.

The phone rang for a long time before Tai Wei picked it up. He sounded exhausted.

"Who is it?" he grunted.

"It's me. What's going on?"

"Oh, Fang Mu. How'd you know I was at your school?"

"I saw your car. What are you doing here? What exactly happened?"

"There weren't enough people on duty so I'm helping out for the time being. It's another goddamned murder."

"Who?" asked Fang Mu, his voice anxious. "What happened?"

"Don't ask. Right now I'm extremely busy. I'll contact you in a few days." Then without saying anything more, Tai Wei hung up.

Although it was clear from his abrupt tone that Tai Wei was upset, this was hardly surprising. Even as a cop, to be faced with one murder after another like this was enough to make someone curse-out their best friend.

And indeed, at that moment Tai Wei really did want to curse someone out. Zhao Yonggui had already run to the fourth floor bathroom to throw up, and although Tai Wei wanted to do the same, at least one of them had to remain at the scene at all times, so he had no choice but to stay put.

So summoning up his courage, he turned around and faced a sight unlike any he had ever seen before.

They were in a fairly large classroom, with enough seats for 80 people. In the fourth row sat the victim's corpse. Its skin had been peeled off.

Because nearly every inch of skin had been removed—including from the corpse's face—it was difficult to determine its gender. But given the adipose tissue remaining on the victim's chest, it was most likely female.

The skinless corpse sat at the desk with its face lowered, as if filled with shame. The crown of its head, once covered by long, thick hair, was now a bloody mess. A tapestry of muscles and veins covered its body, as if the victim were wearing some motley red-and-blue attire. Without any lips to cover them, the corpse's white teeth glistened brightly in the light of the flashing cameras.

Next to the corpse, a plastic male mannequin sat quietly. A strange kind of outfit was stretched tightly across its muscular frame. On closer inspection, this was revealed to be blood-spattered human skin. A pair of breasts hung loosely from the mannequin's chest, the nipples already dark purple. If this was a woman's skin, then its owner was most likely the corpse sitting at the next desk. Sitting next to its bloody, ravaged female companion, the mannequin looked perfectly innocent. The thin smile that crossed its lips made the crime scene photographers shudder as they snapped its picture.

Dizzy from the constantly flashing cameras, Tai Wei increasingly felt the need to vomit. Breathing heavily, he pulled aside one of the photographers and asked roughly, "Are you guys done yet?" When the man said yes, Tai Wei waved his hand and said, "Everyone else, get to work!"

With that, the medical examiners and crime scene investigators sprung swiftly to action.

Silently, Tai Wei gazed at the two motionless figures before him. The sun was climbing higher in the sky, and the once dark classroom was now filling with light. As bright rays poured through the window, he grew distracted, and for a moment he imagined that he was a teacher, and these two "students" were his class. But what would he be teaching them? Human anatomy?

Suddenly, one of the medical examiners gave a shout. Then a moment later, he cried: "Tai Wei, come look at this!"

His reverie interrupted, Tai Wei quickly walked over.

"What is it?" he asked.

"See for yourself," said the medical examiner, clearly astonished. He pointed at the corpse's head.

Tai Wei looked to where he was pointing. Two thin black cords ran from somewhere inside the desk drawer, up the corpse's body, and then into either ear.

It was a pair of earphones. As Tai Wei reached out to open the drawer, the medical examiner quickly tried to stop him. "Be careful," he said, "inside there's probably a —"

Ignoring him, Tai Wei slowly opened the drawer. A small CD stereo had been placed neatly within.

After putting on a pair of rubber gloves, Tai Wei carefully lifted the stereo out of the drawer. Through the plastic covering, he could clearly make out the sound of a rapidly spinning disc.

This horrifying, skinless corpse was actually listening to music.

Tai Wei signaled for the medical examiner to remove the corpse's earphones.

Confronted by this strange scene, the medical examiner started to tremble, but composing himself, he reached forward and removed one of the earphones. However, when he tried to take out the other it wouldn't budge. Redoubling his efforts, the medical examiner gave it a much stronger yank, but rather than pull out the earphone, he instead nearly tore the stereo from Tai Wei's hands. Although Tai Wei was quick enough to hold onto it, the force of the maneuver caused the earphone cord to pop out of the stereo.

Instantly an explosion of noise erupted within the classroom, so deafening it seemed like a sledgehammer was smashing against the skull of every cop in the room. One of the men who had been carefully examining the back of the classroom was so surprised that he immediately fell onto his backside, but no one laughed. Everyone was too busy staring with fear and alarm at the stereo in Tai Wei's hands.

As for Tai Wei, he very nearly threw the screeching thing to the ground, but then he quickly got ahold of himself and hit the "Stop" button.

Her head lowered, the female corpse seemed to be secretly laughing at Tai Wei and the rest of the cops, while beside her, jostled by all the commotion, the straight-backed mannequin clothed in human skin appeared to rock with amusement.

The event that morning caused a great deal of discussion across campus, and as the days passed and Fang Mu waited to hear the real scoop from Tai Wei, he also did his best to collect what clues he could about what actually took place. He listened to both official news and rumor, and heard stories true and obviously false. But a few things were certain: someone had been killed in the Multidisciplinary Building that morning, the victim was a woman, and from what he had heard, the crime scene was truly horrifying.

Sure enough, Tai Wei showed up at Fang Mu's dorm three days later. As soon as he walked inside and saw no one else was there, he flung himself onto Fang Mu's bed.

"You have anything to eat?" he asked. "I'm starving."

"Just instant noodles," said Fang Mu. Noticing Tai Wei's unkempt hair and bloodshot eyes, Fang Mu thought he looked more like a migrant worker who hadn't eaten in days than an officer of the state.

"Let me go to the dining hall and buy you something," said Fang Mu.

"Don't worry about it. Instant noodles will do fine. And if you have some hot Sichuan pickles to put on top, that would be even better."

Fang Mu poured some boiling water into a bowl of instant noodles, and then added a pack of Sichuan pickles whose month and even year of expiration were totally unknown. Before the noodles were remotely soft, Tai Wei began wolfing them down, all the while pointing at the black briefcase he had brought with him.

"Take a look at what's inside," he said, his mouth full of food.

The victim was a sophomore physics student named Xin Tingting. She was 20-year-old and from the city of Zhouxi in Sichuan province. When the crime was committed, she had already been missing for 36 hours. However, because she had numerous online friends and had left the city unannounced to meet them on previous occasions, none of her roommates had been concerned and no one had notified any of her teachers.

The victim's body was left in Room 404 of the Multidisciplinary Building. It was found by a cleaning lady, who in the dim morning light believed that the victim was wearing red clothing. But when she turned on the light, she discovered that in fact the corpse had had all of its skin peeled off.

According to the interviewer's notes, the cleaning lady had seen two people when she entered the room. So without lifting his head, Fang Mu asked Tai Wei, "Who was the other person?"

Tai Wei stopped chewing at once. Based on the look on his face, he seemed to be remembering something awful.

"It wasn't a person," he said, forcing himself to swallow the food in his mouth. "It was a plastic mannequin."

Fang Mu frowned. "A plastic mannequin?" he repeated, and was about to ask more when he saw that Tai Wei had already begun to retch. Fang Mu quickly pointed at the trash can beside his desk.

Feeling rather embarrassed, Tai Wei gulped down several mouthfuls of water and cleared his throat. Then pretending as if nothing had happened, he said, "Damn, I ate way too fast."

When Fang Mu didn't respond, but rather just gave him a long look with a hint of derision in his eyes, Tai Wei got a little annoyed.

"All you students are real wusses, you know that?" Tai Wei snapped. "From what I've heard, none of you are willing to even step foot in that classroom anymore. Small wonder, given that it's Room Four-Zero-Four on the fourth floor. With that many fours, it's bound to be unlucky." *(Translator's note: In Chinese, the number four is pronounced almost the same as the word for death.)*

Fang Mu smiled and asked again, "So a plastic mannequin, huh? What kind, and where are the crime scene photographs?" But then, with no warning whatsoever, he suddenly leapt to his feet and cried, "Wait! What did you just say?"

Caught completely off guard, Tai Wei swallowed the water in his mouth too fast, and started coughing violently. Fang Mu immediately began hitting him hard on the back, all the while continuing to loudly ask, "What did you just say?"

"What did I say when?" said Tai Wei, panting for breath. "Are you trying to scare me to death or something?"

"Think," said Fang Mu anxiously. "What did you say just now—it was something about the number four."

"Oh, um, I was saying… The fourth floor, Room Four-Zero-Four. What about it?"

Fang Mu didn't respond, just stared at the corner of the room, lost in thought.

Tai Wei watched him, completely baffled. After a while, he realized the kid was mumbling something under his breath: "One, two, three, four…"

Just as he was about to ask him what was going on, Fang Mu turned around and began to speak. "Tai Wei," he said slowly, a strange light flashing through his eyes, "you need to combine the cases. It's the numbers."

"What numbers?" asked Tai Wei, even more confused.

"I can guarantee that all of these murders were committed by the same person, because at every crime scene the killer left behind a number," said Fang Mu, sitting down on the bed. "It's just that this number doesn't refer to the individual victim per se, but rather to where the crime falls in the overall sequence. At this point, murders one through four have already happened."

"I don't understand."

"In the seven-one double murder, the male student whose hands were cut off—what do you remember about him?"

"That case I don't know much about, but I think he was the goalie for the school soccer team."

"What number jersey do goalies usually wear?"

He paused. "I don't know, but the French goalie Barthez wears number sixteen." On the day that Fang Mu had nearly been killed by Ma Kai, Tai Wei had happened to notice this piece of information while walking past the TV in the on-duty room.

Getting back on topic, Fang Mu said, "Number one, they generally wear number one. And I know for certain that Qu Weiqiang did, too, because I went to his jersey retirement ceremony."

"One. Now I understand. The hospital murder took place in Observation Room Two. That was two. But what about three?" Scratching his head, Tai Wei puzzled over this question.

But Fang Mu had long since thought of the answer.

"The packing box that the little girl's corpse was delivered in," he said slowly. "Do you still remember what it looked like?"

"That Adidas box?" said Tai Wei, not seeing where this was going. "What was special about it?"

"The three leaves," said Fang Mu, smiling bitterly. "I should have noticed it much sooner."

But Fang Mu wasn't the only one upset; Tai Wei now felt the same way. At that moment he clearly recalled the trademark logo that had been printed on the side of the Adidas box—the three-leaved trefoil. He had looked at that box hundreds of times. Why had this thought never occurred to him before?

"Room Four-Zero-Four on the fourth floor, and the corpse was even found sitting in the fourth row," muttered Tai Wei. "Obviously, this was four."

In an instant, it seemed as if the two people sitting in Room 303 were enveloped by a heavy sense of fear, one that came with the smell of blood. For a moment, neither of them spoke. Fang Mu looked at the ground. Tai Wei looked at him. All the while the fear slithered back and forth between them like a long serpent, smiling wickedly, baring its poisonous fangs, and shooting out its forked tongue as it arrogantly enjoyed their terror and helplessness.

After a long time, Tai Wei forced himself to say: "How many more will there be?"

Fang Mu took a deep breath, and then shook his head. "I don't know."

The dorm room fell once more into silence. After some time had passed and Tai Wei felt a little better, he asked: "Couldn't this all just be a coincidence?"

"I don't think so," said Fang Mu, his expression grave. "Not only have the crimes been numbered one through four, they've all taken place around

Jiangbin City University, and when the victims weren't students, they were the family of faculty members. This is too much to be simply coincidental."

Suddenly he stood up, grabbed the thick folders of case data, and dropped them down on the desk with a bang.

"I recommend that you combine these cases into one," Fang Mu said, eyes now blazing as he stared at Tai Wei. "As for me, I will continue to analyze the murders committed thus far. I hope…" he paused to lick his dry lips, "that we can stop him at four!"

Xin Tingting's cause of death was mechanical asphyxiation, the murder weapon most likely a length of rope. Because trace amounts of the sedative Alprazolam were found in the victim's bloodstream, she was believed to have been drugged prior to being killed. Afterwards, the victim's skin was entirely peeled off, and then draped like clothing over the plastic mannequin that had been placed next to her. As demonstrated by photographs of the scene, even though the victim was nearly 5'7", her skin was still a little small for the male mannequin to wear. Except for its torso, arms and thighs, all of which had been forcibly covered, the rest of the mannequin's plastic body was revealed. Although the killer's method of skinning the victim made clear that he was no expert, the neat and meticulous stitching he had done to make this set of "clothes" for the mannequin showed that he was a careful, patient individual.

A CD stereo with a disc still playing inside was also found at the scene. From the stereo display, it seemed that the disc had been playing since 1:45 that morning—which must have been roughly the time that the killer placed the corpse and mannequin in the classroom.

The song that the corpse happened to be listening to was an old one: "Revolution 9" by The Beatles, from their popular self-titled CD.

The police and Fang Mu found this discovery extremely perplexing. Killing a person, skinning her—these things obviously carried deep significance. But making a corpse listen to music, what was that supposed to mean?

Although more than a few people felt the rationale for combining the investigations was a little farfetched, it was ultimately given the director's approval and a special team was formed, with Tai Wei and Zhao Yonggui in charge. All the abandoned leads from the three previous murder cases were once more taken up and thoroughly investigated. Initially, two of these were given precedence above the rest.

The first was the source of the heroin used in the hospital murder. A drug like that was not the sort of murder weapon a person just happened across. Therefore, police believed that if they investigated heroin buyers across the city, they might be able to identify the killer himself and at the very least may learn some of his characteristics.

The second important lead was the car. Previously, Fang Mu had suggested to Tai Wei that the killer was probably a car owner, and on this point the police happened to be thinking the same thing. Their reasoning was that the first, third, and fourth murders all took place in a different location than where the bodies were found, and therefore would have required the killer to transport his victims. Were he to have moved them on foot, not only would he be wasting time and energy, he might also be discovered. Because Jiangbin City University's three gates—at its north, east and west entrances respectively—closed every night at roughly 11 p.m., any cars that tried to get in afterwards would be discovered by campus security. As a result, the police began to consider the possibility that the car came from somewhere inside campus.

One week later, the officers investigating the two leads reported back to the special team. The group responsible had spoken to informants among the city's addicts, but had not found any buyers who fit the description of the killer. They did, however, learn one important piece of information. While one of the addicts was returning home from buying heroin late one night in mid-September, he was attacked in the street and his wallet and the heroin he had just purchased were both stolen. Although the man had been injured, he had not reported the crime to the police for fear of being arrested himself. Police later interviewed the addict in question, but he had nearly lost his mind to the ravages of drugs and could remember nothing about the person who had mugged him. In the end, police had no choice but to send him to a prison labor camp.

The group responsible for locating the killer's car set to investigating the source of all the cars frequently parked on campus. They found nothing. However, while later searching the school boundaries for entry points, one sharp-eyed policeman located a hole in the iron fence on the north side of campus. One of the bars had been sawed off and then replaced so that the fence still appeared continuous while still allowing someone to easily remove it whenever they wanted. The hole itself was big enough for an adult to climb through. Once inside, it was a one-minute walk to the Multidisciplinary Building (scene of the fourth crime), and a five-minute walk to the track and field stadium (scene of the first crime). Tire tracks had been left on the street beside the fence, but too much time had already passed to identify them. All the same, police decided that, until proven otherwise, this was where the killer had entered the campus.

From these findings, along with the analysis of the Department of Public Security's criminal psychology research division, it was determined that the killer was relatively well-off, strong-bodied, and intelligent, and quite familiar with the campus of Jiangbin City University as well as the surrounding area.

This conclusion was essentially identical to the one Fang Mu had reached earlier.

It was a bright afternoon in late fall, while Fang Mu and Tai Wei were sitting on one of the benches beside the basketball court. Tai Wei had just told Fang Mu their latest find: the factory that produced the plastic mannequin from the fourth murder had been found. However, over a hundred stores in the city sold this model, so it would be very difficult to determine who purchased it. Although Tai Wei said "We're still working on it," Fang Mu could tell that he wasn't very optimistic.

The sun was unusually pleasant, and Tai Wei leaned back and stretched. It felt as if the sunlight was slowly entering the spaces between his bones, warming him to the core. The sensation was delightful. Lighting a cigarette, he slumped back against the bench, thinking how nice the day would be if only he didn't have to worry about the grisly case before them.

Beside him, Fang Mu was thinking the same thing. Bathing in the warmth of the sun, he felt his muscles ache and his eyelids grow heavy. Over the past week, Fang Mu had been studying the case day and night, poring over the data, taking notes, and avoiding Du Yu, who was now more curious than ever. Seriously short on sleep, all he wanted to do at that moment was lie down and rest for days. And yet even on this blissfully warm day, with his eyes comfortably shut and his body relaxed, all the words and photos from the case files continued to flash through his mind, as if someone had taken a knife and carved them onto the surface of his brain.

The police analysis had not been wrong—this guy was inordinately smart. If they were hoping he had gotten sloppy and left some major clue behind, they were going to be out of luck. The only way to catch him would be through meticulously analyzing his behavior and then piecing together a picture of the man himself. And yet, what exactly could Fang Mu hope to learn from these increasingly puzzling cases?

This was what had most perplexed Fang Mu over the past several days. Through research and personal experience, he knew that in committing their crimes, serial killers always acted in a way meant to satisfy some psychological or emotional need. This sort of behavior was often known as a serial killer's personal mark. Determining and then analyzing a serial killer's personal mark was critical to cracking the case. First of all, this behavior was the basis for identifying several murders as the work of one individual, and second, it was a window into the killer's overall motive. And because the personal mark often accurately reflected the character, lifestyle, and experiences of the killer, it could lead to important clues found at the intersection of the killer, his victims, and his chosen crime scenes.

Without a doubt, the killer had meticulously arranged for the number of each crime to be hidden somewhere within the crime itself—this was not just some coincidence. At this point, not knowing anything more about their meaning, there was no choice but to understand these numbers as a kind of provocation. As for the rest of the killer's unusual behavior, could any of it be seen as his personal mark?

Superficially, some of it did seem possess the characteristics of a personal mark: dismembering Wang Qian, and then transporting Qu Weiqiang and cutting off his hands in the first crime; placing a piece of broken ceramic pottery in Jin Qiao's hand, filming her genitals and then returning her to her parents in the third crime; skinning Xin Tingting in the fourth crime. All of this behavior clearly required that the killer expend additional time, patience and skill, while also increasing his risk. And all of it was far in excess of what he needed to do avoid detection; rather, it seemed to have been performed for his own satisfaction.

Even so, this was what most puzzled Fang Mu. Because from said behavior, which at first might seem to so obviously display the killer's personal mark, it was not only impossible to determine how the killer's obsessions were either increasing in force or shifting from crime to crime, it couldn't even be claimed that there was any consistent information about the man at all. In other words, these so-called examples of the killer's personal mark were unable to fully reflect the killer's character or his psychological characteristics.

During the first crime, after the killer raped Wang Qian, he dismembered her and then pieced her back together. According to Professor Qiao, this came from a desire to "build her anew." And as for Qu Weiqiang, the severing of his hands after he was killed was supposedly motivated by jealousy. But at this point, the investigation had found no evidence that this had been a crime of passion. And the syringe that was plunged in Wang Qian's breast also remained unexplained.

During the second crime, a middle-aged woman had been killed. She was not raped, and the crime did not appear sexually motivated. As for the pornographic manga found in her bag, Fang Mu believed it had been placed there in an attempt to dishonor her. But again, the information currently available about the crime could not prove this point.

During the third crime, the killer sexually tortured the victim to death, filmed her genitals and placed a piece of broken pottery in her hand. All this demonstrated a psychosexual disorder, as well as a violent need to control the female body.

During the fourth crime, the killer skinned the victim and then clothed the male plastic mannequin beside her in her skin. This demonstrated a tendency toward transvestism. From the standpoint of academic sexual psychology, transvestism may dispose a person toward torture fetishism, but it is extremely rare for a torture fetishist to transform into a transvestite, and almost unimaginable for such a thing to occur in so short a length of time.

If this was a case of multiple personality disorder, then most likely there weren't just two or three personalities at work here, there were a whole bunch.

When this guy got out of bed each morning, he probably had no idea who he was going to be that day.

What kind of person were they dealing with here?

"I just had an idea," said Tai Wei, who up until then had been lounging idly and not saying a word. "I'm sure you've noticed it yourself. Every one of these murders has at least one unexplainable element that does not appear to have anything to do with the crime itself. The syringe in the first murders, the pornographic manga in the second, the CD in the fourth. These all seem to hint at something about the killer's methods and the victims themselves."

"Oh?" Fang Mu said. "Tell me what you're thinking."

Sitting up, Tai Wei turned to him, his eyes bright. "Actually, I've had a feeling about this ever since I heard about the first crime scene, where a syringe was discovered in the victim's breast. Because the thing is, during the second crime, the victim was killed in a hospital. You think that's a coincidence? And don't forget how the manga found in her bag was filled with scenes of torture porn, and then the third victim just happened to be tortured to death."

Chopping the air with his hand, Tai Wei continued. "I think that every one of these murders can be looked at in two ways. In all of them, the elements that don't seem to fit are actually hinting at the characteristics of the next crime."

Fang Mu said nothing. In fact, this sort of thought had occurred to him as well. Although Tai Wei hadn't mentioned the broken pottery from the third crime, Fang Mu had already done a good deal of research on the piece as well as Grayson Perry, its creator. As he discovered, Perry himself was a transvestite, and in the fourth crime, the killer had dressed a male plastic mannequin in the female victim's skin, demonstrating a desire to change genders.

If this hypothesis was correct, then they were faced with two questions. First, what was the killer's motive? And second, what was being hinted by the CD left at the fourth crime scene?

Exhausted, Fang Mu massaged his temples. The degree of difficulty in figuring out what was going on in the mind of someone this psychologically unstable was enormous.

"Regardless," Fang Mu said, "I think the next victim will be someone from this school and…"

"And will somehow be related to the number five," said Tai Wei, gloomily completing his thought.

They both wondered if they should tell everyone on campus to avoid everything related to the number five. At a loss, the two of them gazed at all the people passing by, cheerful smiles on their faces, hearts full of hope for the beautiful future they knew life held in store for them.

Lecture Theater 5.

Men's Dormitory 5.

Dining Hall 5.

The fifth lane on the racetrack.

The fifth basketball court.

…Perhaps more…

Even though the sun was shining just as brightly as before, Fang Mu and Tai Wei felt a cold breeze blow through them.

It was already late fall.

17 PIGS

It was fated to be an unusual day.

Before noon, Professor Qiao summoned Fang Mu to the Psychological Consultation Room. First he asked him whether he had been involved in any of the investigations taking place on campus. Muttering to himself about how Professor Qiao himself had already asked him to analyze one of the cases, Fang Mu initially just hemmed and hawed.

But when Professor Qiao narrowed his eyes at him, Fang Mu admitted everything he knew about the situation thus far. When he was done, Professor Qiao frowned and successively smoked two cigarettes. Then, strangely enough, he just spoke a few stock sentences reminding Fang Mu to be careful, and waved him out the door.

Fang Mu sensed that Professor Qiao was dissatisfied with him, but when he considered that this meant the professor might now join the case, and how much easier this would make it to catch the killer, he felt a little better.

Later that afternoon, something happened in the private study room that mortified Fang Mu.

Tai Wei had photocopied several documents and given them to Fang Mu, who hoped to find some more clues hidden within. So he had retreated to a remote corner of the private study room and started to read. He preferred it, as Du Yu and Zhang Yao had occupied the dorm room and were doing their thing.

By the time Deng Linyue saw Fang Mu and walked over, he was already looking at several pages that had been photocopied from the pornographic manga. He didn't even notice her.

"Hey," she said, smiling at him. "You read comics, too, huh? Which one is this?"

When Deng Linyue bent over to get a better look, Fang Mu tried to cover the pictures of stark-naked flesh bound in rope, but it was already too late.

Deng Linyue stared blankly at the pictures for several seconds. Then she blushed to the tips of her ears.

"Um, you have very...unique taste," she said. Then not even daring to glance at him, she spun around and ran off.

Fang Mu hurried to explain, but by then she had already left the room.

"Oh, hell!" Fang Mu yelled, tossing the papers onto the desk. This is just not my day, he thought.

As if the day hadn't been chaotic enough already, Tai Wei called him around nightfall.

"I'm at Caijia Village," he said, his voice agitated. "Find a cab and get here as fast as you can!"

"What's going on?"

"No time for questions; this one's big. Get here now. When you're nearby, call me and I'll come meet you." Saying this, Tai Wei promptly hung up.

Caijia Village was located on the outskirts of Jiangbin City, and all its residents were registered as city dwellers. Although there was no land there to farm, the people kept to their rural traditions. After dark, they merely ate dinner, turned out the lights, and went to sleep. So even though it wasn't yet 7 p.m., the village was almost totally dark. Almost, that is, because one section was still lit up and there Fang Mu could see the bright flash of police lights.

When he saw Tai Wei standing by the side of the road smoking a cigarette, Fang Mu felt his spirits plummet. Even from a distance, he could see Tai Wei was stooped over, his collar unfolded and his hair blown in all directions by the fall wind. Thanks to the jeep headlights beside him, Fang Mu could make out Tai Wei's downcast expression. Even after knowing him all this time, Fang Mu had never seen Tai Wei look like this.

Fang Mu jumped out of the cab and walked toward him. Seeing him coming, Tai Wei tossed away his cigarette, turned to him, and actually grinned.

I know how you're feeling, thought Fang Mu, but don't smile. It's terrifying.

Once they were inside the jeep, Tai Wei absentmindedly asked him, "How much was the cab ride? I'll pay you back."

"Don't worry about it."

Tai Wei didn't seem to want to make a big deal over such a small thing, so he said nothing and just kept driving.

A few minutes later, Tai Wei and Fang Mu drove into a small courtyard. An enormous, hundred-watt spotlight shone onto the courtyard, making it bright as day. The faces of all the people milling about looked pale as ghosts in the light. They got out of the jeep.

"You're finally here," one of the men said suddenly. He was crouching by the corner of the courtyard wall.

Fang Mu looked toward the sound of the voice. The man was a medical examiner. Fang Mu had seen him before during the Ma Kai case.

Another man was crouched beside him, a cigarette in his mouth. After glancing up at Fang Mu, he looked away and said nothing.

Fang Mu recognized this man as well. He was named Zhao Yonggui. He had been one of the two policemen present when Professor Qiao invited him to the Psychological Consultation Room.

Right now everyone in the courtyard was staring at Fang Mu. For a moment, he didn't know what to do.

Then Tai Wei called out to him from a corner of the courtyard. "Over here!"

Walking over, Fang Mu could smell a strong odor coming from that direction. When he reached Tai Wei, he saw that he was standing within a pigpen made of crushed brick, wooden planks, and tree bark.

Fang Mu carefully stepped inside. Thanks to the powerful police spotlight, every inch of the pigpen was immediately visible.

The mud was six inches thick. Pig feed was everywhere. The feeding trough had fallen down and was now half-submerged in the mud. It was indeed a sorry way to raise pigs.

At that moment, however, none happened to be in sight. And even though the mud-covered figure lying absolutely still in the muck before him did closely resemble one, Fang Mu was certain that it was a person.

"Who...is that?" he asked, his voice shaky.

Tai Wei didn't respond, just handed him an evidence bag. Inside was a mud-caked passport. It was open.

Fang Mu could make out a picture in the upper-right corner. In it, a blond-haired, blue-eyed white man grinned vapidly. According to the card, his name was Thomas Gill, he was from the United States, and he had worked for the foreign teachers administrative department at Jiangbin City University.

The victim was a foreigner. It was just as Tai Wei had said—this one was big.

Suddenly Fang Mu looked up and glanced all around, as if he were searching for something.

Tai Wei knew what he was looking for, so he handed over another evidence bag. Inside was a watch, just as mud-caked as the ID booklet. But Fang Mu could still see that the hour hand, minute hand, and second hand were all stopped at five.

Fang Mu stared at the watch. This was the fifth murder.

"How about it, Tai Wei?" yelled the medical examiner, a touch of impatience in his voice. "Can we get started?"

Tai Wei turned and motioned for them to begin processing the scene, and then looked back at Fang Mu. "I made them wait for you to observe the scene before they could begin examining it," he said, "although some police from the local substation did manage to disturb a few things before we arrived. Anyway, I know that seeing the scene in its original state is extremely important to criminal profiling." He gave Fang Mu a very self-satisfied wink.

Fang Mu forced himself to squeeze out a thin smile.

Two policemen wearing rain boots then hopped into the pigpen. After struggling to pull the corpse out of the mud, they laid it on a plastic tarp that had been placed in the middle of the courtyard.

The victim was small in stature, looking to be about 5'6", which meant that in the U.S. he was probably considered quite short. Although his body was caked with mud, several of his wounds were still visible. Some were so deep that the bones stuck out.

"Damn," said the medical examiner, frowning as he slipped on a pair of gloves, "it looks like the pigs have been nibbling on this guy for a while. You go handle your business, Tai Wei. With a body like this," he pointed at the corpse, "it's going to take me a little while."

Tai Wei nodded and then led Fang Mu into the house.

Navigating the chaos of farm tools and cooking utensils that had been placed haphazardly in the central room, they made their way into the inner room of the house.

Just like outside, it was ablaze with light. A bony man who looked like a farmer was sitting earnestly on a small stool in one corner of the room. He was the homeowner, and seemed to be the one who had called the police. Sitting on the edge of the kang bed were two policemen, while an interview notepad had been placed on the kang table in between the two parties.

As soon as Tai Wei and Fang Mu entered, the two policemen stopped the interview and stood up. In the corner of the room, the owner also quickly stood up.

Tai Wei waved for him to sit down and then grabbed the notepad and flipped through a few pages. After a moment, he turned to the owner, who was still nervously standing in place, and said, "Repeat for me everything you just said to these two men."

A miserable look on his face, the owner said, "Chief, I've already told it multiple times and I still haven't eaten yet. Besides, my pigs are over at Second Son Wu's house, and I know that cheapskate would never feed them for me."

After the "Chief" promised to buy both the farmer and his pigs dinner, the man very reluctantly began to talk.

"Yesterday I got in a big fight with my no-good, spendthrift wife," he said, "after which she returned to her parents' home. Once she was gone, I went and played poker at a little store nearby, and then came home around five that afternoon. As soon as I entered the courtyard, it occurred to me that I hadn't fed the pigs all day, so why weren't they screaming for food? They still seemed to be doing all right, weren't making a sound. But in any case I heated up a pot of swill and then went to go feed them. While feeding them, I decided to save some electricity—it's so expensive out here in the countryside, sixty-eight cents per kilowatt hour, you guys in the city only pay thirty-nine cents, right?"

At this point the man launched into a nearly two-minute-long tirade against the government's policies toward farmers, which only ended when Tai Wei was forced to remind him to stay on topic.

"Oh, what was I talking about again?" the farmer said. "That's right, saving electricity. So I kept the light off, but as I looked around I could tell something was wrong. I only own four pigs, so what were five doing in the pen? At first I thought one of my neighbor Second Son Wu's pigs must have jumped the fence, and just as I was feeling really happy about that possibility, I noticed that it was just lying there and not eating, so I prodded it with my stick, but still it didn't move. That's when I shined my flashlight over on it and, my God, it was a person! So I called the police and someone from the local substation came out here, showed me his badge, and then called you guys."

At this point the medical examiner entered the house. He turned on the faucet in the central room and washed the mud off his hands.

From the inner room Tai Wei called out to him. "How's it look out there?"

"Cause of death was shock due to blood loss," said the medical examiner, shaking the water from his hands as he walked into the room. "We still have to take a closer look at some of the places that were eaten by the pigs, but it's clear he was stabbed at least fourteen times."

Nodding toward the farmer, he continued. "It's no surprise he took the victim for one of his pigs. This was one heavy guy, at least two hundred pounds. Your pigs have been eating well." Noticing that everyone was now frowning and looking like they wanted to vomit, he cackled with laughter.

Tai Wei muttered the word sicko under his breath and then turned to Fang Mu, only to find the kid was staring off into the corner, mumbling to himself.

"Pig...pig...pig…" he murmured.

Tai Wei was about to ask him what he was talking about, when Fang Mu abruptly turned to the farmer and asked: "You just said that when you first saw the victim, you thought he was a pig, right?"

The farmer nearly jumped with surprise at the sudden question. "Yes," he said, "that's right. It was dark and I couldn't see any of the pigs clearly. Besides, with him lying face down in the pigpen like that, what was I supposed to think?"

Fang Mu turned and looked at Tai Wei. Although the kid's face was ghostly pale, his eyes were shining bright.

"Where's the CD?" Fang Mu asked.

"What CD?" For a moment, Tai Wei had no idea what he was talking about.

"From the last crime, Room Four-Zero-Four! The one the skinless girl was listening to!" Fang Mu was now so agitated his voice was almost incoherent.

"It's at headquarters. Why, what are you thinking?"

Before the words had even left Tai Wei's mouth, Fang Mu had already leapt to his feet and was on his way out of the room.

"Come on," he said, "we need to get that CD!"

Tai Wei drove back at lightning speed, keeping his siren on the whole time. By the time they reached the station, everyone in the Material Evidence Division had already gotten off work.

"We're out of luck," said Tai Wei helplessly, as he turned to Fang Mu and shrugged. "All we can do is wait until tomorrow."

"Unacceptable!" yelled Fang Mu. His answer was short, but utterly decisive.

Having no other choice, Tai Wei called one of his colleagues from the Material Evidence Division. Thirty minutes later, the CD stereo was sitting before their eyes.

Fang Mu turned it on, put on a pair of headphones, and then silently listened to the music.

Tai Wei didn't know what exactly Fang Mu was trying to do, but he figured that the kid already had a pretty good idea about the connection between the CD and the fifth murder case, so it would be best not to disturb him. Lighting a cigarette, he sat beside Fang Mu and watched him in silence.

Fang Mu listened to one song after another, pausing every now and then to jot something down. Some songs he listened to all the way through, others he skipped after only the first few lines.

At last, he came to one song that seemed to really interest him. He listened to it over and over again, rapidly scrawled two words in English, and then circled those words many times over.

Tai Wei quickly leaned over to see what he had written.

"Helter Skelter."

"Helter Skelter?" asked Tai Wei, confused. "What's that supposed to mean?"

Fang Mu had drawn his circles with so much force that he'd punctured the paper, giving it an appearance that aligned with the mindset represented by the two words.

Fang Mu slowly removed his headphones and, ignoring the fact that the CD was still playing, lit a cigarette from the pack on the table and began to smoke. Tai Wei noticed that the kid's hands were shaking slightly.

"Charles Manson," said Fang Mu in a low voice.

Tai Wei felt he had heard this name before, and vaguely recalled that it belonged to the leader of some perverse religious cult. What did he have to do with this murder?

"Charles Manson was the infamous leader of the Manson Family cult," said Fang Mu, "which was active in the U.S. in the late sixties and early seventies. He planned to incite an apocalyptic war by killing white people and then starting a race war between the whites and the blacks. His first group of victims included the wife of the famous director Roman Polanski, their unborn child, and four other people who happened to be staying in their house. The second group was the family of a supermarket executive. There the Manson Family scrawled the words 'Kill the Pigs' on the wall of the crime scene. According to Manson, he had received instructions to start his apocalyptic war by a Beatles song. That song," Fang Mu pointed at the CD player, "just happens to be on the same CD as Revolution 9. It's called Helter Skelter."

Tai Wei listened to all this in stunned silence. Finally, he asked, "So what you're saying is, the killer copied Charles Manson?"

"That's right," said Fang Mu in a quiet voice. "I'd been wondering why the killer left the victim in a pigsty, and then when the owner of the house mentioned how he had mistaken the corpse for one of his pigs, I instantly thought of Charles Manson. There are numerous historical examples of serial killers doing things to shame their victims after they're dead, for example placing them under public signs that read 'No Dumping Trash,' or positioning a young man and woman so it looks like she's giving him oral sex. That's why I guessed that the pornographic manga found in the hospital murder had been left there to dishonor the victim. However, the most classic example of a serial killer who labeled his victims pigs was Charles Manson. And since I had a faint idea that it was a rock song that inspired him to commit his murders, I therefore deduced that this song had to be on the CD from the fourth murder case." Fang Mu slumped tiredly against the table. "And sure enough, I was right."

After thinking for a moment, Tai Wei said, "So do you think the previous crimes were copying the style of other serial killers?"

"It's possible, but I can't say for sure until I do some more research." Fang Mu stood up. "I'd better be heading home; we'll need all the time we have."

Tai Wei stood up as well. "I'll take you," he said.

"Don't worry about it," said Fang Mu, waving his hand. "You need to get back to the scene and make note of anything that doesn't seem to fit. More than likely..." he paused to lick his dry, cracked lips, "you'll find some clue to crime number six."

Six. At the sound of this ordinarily harmless number, the faces of both men turned grim.

All through the night, Fang Mu sat at his computer doing research. At last, when light began to fill the sky, he crawled exhaustedly into bed and fell asleep with his clothes on. He slept straight until noon, when Du Yu finally woke him up.

After eating a hurried meal in the dining hall, Fang Mu rushed to the library.

Since it was still lunchtime, the library was silent and no one else was around. Fang Mu looked at his watch. It wasn't yet one, so there was still more than half an hour before the reading rooms opened. He then walked upstairs to the third floor reference room, placed his bag on the terrazzo floor, and sat down and leaned against the wall, hoping to nap until the place opened.

After closing his eyes, Fang Mu drifted in and out of sleep for about 15 minutes before being awakened by the sound of steps echoing from the stairwell. He heard a man speaking softly.

"Yes... I know... It's not what you think... Well, how about next week...?"

A second later, the speaker appeared in the same corridor as Fang Mu. When he saw him sitting there, the speaker suddenly stopped in place, said, "I'll call you back in a little bit," and then hung up his phone.

With difficulty, Fang Mu forced his eyes all the way open.

It was Librarian Sun.

Surprised, Librarian Sun looked down at him. "What are you sleeping here for?" he asked. "You'll catch a cold if you're not careful." After helping Fang Mu up, he pointed at the chilly terrazzo floor. "You shouldn't go around thinking that being young means you're invincible. You could get hemorrhoids sitting on the cold floor like that."

"Thank you, sir," said Fang Mu, rubbing his head in embarrassment.

Librarian Sun looked at his watch. "Seems you're pretty early today. The library's not even supposed to be open yet. That's okay though, I'll let you in." Saying this, he unlocked the big door to the reference room.

As soon as the door was opened, Fang Mu hurried over to the stacks. One after another, he grabbed The United States Encyclopedia of Crime, The Encyclopedia of Criminology, and Criminal Profiling, as well as several other books, and then holding them in a wobbly pile, walked over to one of the tables and sat down. Through force of habit, he immediately took out a pack of cigarettes, but after thinking about it, he put them away.

At that moment, Librarian Sun walked over. Smiling, he said, "Since the library's not yet open, it's okay to smoke." Then he noticed the pack in Fang Mu's hand. "Well, well, well," he exclaimed. "Hibiscus King—that's a very high-quality brand."

"One of my teachers gave me them," said Fang Mu, a little embarrassed. "Librarian Sun, would you like one?" He offered him a cigarette.

In response, Librarian Sun produced a pack of Hibiscus King cigarettes from his own pocket and, waving them slightly, said, "Already got a pack. Just make sure you don't get ash all over the place." Then he walked back to his desk, sat down and began reading a book, puffing away on a cigarette all the while.

For the rest of the afternoon Fang Mu did nothing but research and take notes. Besides getting up every now and then to find new books and return old ones, he barely moved.

People came and went. Sometimes the reference room was noisy, sometimes it was quiet. But none of this affected Fang Mu in the least. Every bit of his attention was focused on the materials before him. Floating down the river of humankind's criminal history, he brushed past butchers of all kinds, from hulking behemoths to wretched wraiths. Hurtling through the decades, he read about crimes so blood-drenched that they threatened to soak the very pages of his notebook, and entered the minds of criminals from 10, 50, even 100 years ago. All the while, he felt himself drawing steadily closer to the truth.

By the time he was finally so exhausted that he could write no more, the sky outside was already growing dark. Massaging his temples, he got up and walked to the water cooler, filled a paper cup full of cold water, and downed it in one gulp.

By now he was the last person left in the reference room. He looked at his watch. The library would be closing soon. Returning to his table, he slowly gathered up his belongings. All of a sudden, he felt an extreme tiredness creep over him.

How am I this exhausted?

His hands and feet felt as if they were filled with lead, his eyelids fought to close, and his chair felt more comfortable than it ever had before...

The sun is blazing hot. Out on the sunbaked basketball court with all my friends from the dorm, wearing shorts and no shirts, playing ball. Third Brother is being too competitive. We had to win, and if we lost he wouldn't let us leave.

The dorm hallway. Passing silent, grim-faced students, blankets held tightly over their shoulders. Sun Qingdong from Room 351 is sitting in front of the door to the bathroom stall, shaking all over. Someone whispers to me: Zhou Jun died in there.

The library. Flipping through the pages of a book, the sound like a tree full of dry leaves rustling in the breeze. Shock as I look at the library card at the back of the book, at all the familiar names that have checked it out.

The little market. Her hair fluttering, Chen Xi laughs and says, 'It's up to you. Which one do you think is the best?'

The Route 25 bus station. Chen Xi rests her head against my shoulder.

The student club. Savagely, the demon raises his axe high. Blood spurts into the air. Chen Xi's pale, tranquil face.

Room 352. Wang Jian and Fourth Brother's bodies lie twisted amid the flames. A scorched odor fills the air. Wu Han stands before the door. Slowly, he turns around. Panicked, I say, 'You were the seventh reader.' Smiling thinly, he walks slowly toward me, the military dagger in his hand.

Then he whispers, 'Actually, you and I are the same...'

No...

Suddenly Fang Mu leapt to his feet, startling the dark shape before him so it moved back a few steps.

"Are you okay?"

It was Librarian Sun. Fang Mu could see his own disturbed, sweat-soaked face reflected in the glasses perched on the bridge of the librarian's nose.

"Oh, uh, I'm fine," said Fang Mu, taking his hand from out of his bag, where he had been grasping the handle of the military dagger.

"The library is about to close," said Librarian Sun, still badly shaken, "so when I saw you lying on the desk fast asleep, I figured I'd go wake you up. I didn't expect you'd scream and leap up like that. Scared me half to death."

"Sorry," said Fang Mu, "I was just having a bad dream." He forced himself to smile.

"Don't worry about it," said Librarian Sun, patting him on the shoulder. "You may be young, but you still need to take care of yourself."

Fang Mu nodded, but said nothing more. After gathering his things, he grabbed his bag and left the reference room.

The deceased was one Thomas Gill, 41, a white male from the United States, formerly in charge of hiring at the Jiangbin City University foreign teachers administrative department. On the night of the murder, he took a cab from the school gate to the nearby Evening Breeze Jazz Club. There he had several drinks, but no one paid attention to what time he left. This above information was gleaned from his cab driver, who often picked up people outside the school gates, and the staff at the club.

Cause of death was shock due to blood loss. According to the autopsy, by the time his body was discovered, the victim had already been dead for at least 15 hours. He had been stabbed a total of 21 times in the chest by a sharp blade measuring five to seven inches in length and approximately 1.5

inches in width. Based on the location and appearance of the victim's wounds, the killer seemed to be a right-handed adult man standing between 5'7" and 5'10".

Other than the victim's watch, which had been set to 5:25:25, none of his belongings had been touched. His money, bank card, and credit card were all still in his wallet.

Based on an investigation of the crime scene, it was determined that the pigpen where the victim was found was not the scene of his murder. Since the victim was quite heavy, the killer had probably used some sort of vehicle to transport his body. The testimony given by the individual who reported the crime and the results of the autopsy both indicated that the victim was probably left in the pigpen between 10 a.m. and 4 p.m. Police interviewed people living near the crime scene in hopes of finding someone who had seen a suspicious vehicle that day, but they came away with just about nothing. Only one person, a roughly 70-year-old woman, said that on the day the body was discovered, she happened to spot a white car parked near the crime scene. Unfortunately, she was unable to provide the car's make, model or license plate number. And because so many cars had driven past the crime scene by now, even if the killer's car had been parked there, its tracks would be impossible to find.

Interestingly, according to the victim's coworkers, he had been gay. This made police suspect that perhaps the killer was gay as well, or rather had merely pretended to be so that he could trick the victim into accompanying him to the murder scene, where he then took the man's life.

The U.S. and Chinese heads of state had visited each other's nations at the end of 2001 and the beginning of 2002. This was perhaps even more significant for the new American president, who was making his first visit to China. A high-ranking U.S. military officer was also set to visit China at the end of the year, and now the whole world was watching as military relations between the two countries appeared to warm. Therefore, the U.S. consulate in Jiangbin City was paying close attention to this case and had spoken on multiple occasions with the city government and Public Security Bureau in hopes of obtaining a speedy resolution.

The special investigation team could feel the pressure.

Another bright afternoon. As usual, Tai Wei and Fang Mu were sitting on the bench beside the basketball court, a stack of absurdly thick folders beside them.

First, Tai Wei updated Fang Mu on their current progress investigating the case. Fang Mu listened closely, rarely interrupting. Finally, with a downcast look on his face, Tai Wei said that they still hadn't found any clues as to the next murder. Fang Mu thought for a moment, and then grabbed one of the case folders and began reading.

While he was looking through the evidence photos, Fang Mu paused on one of the pictures for a long time. In it, the contents of the victim's wallet were spread out on a table. In addition to a bank card and credit card from the Industrial and Commercial Bank of China and a certain amount of U.S. dollars and Chinese renminbi, Fang Mu also saw a strangely-colored bill, but because it was halfway covered by some of the other items, he couldn't make out its denomination or form of currency.

"What's this one?" asked Fang Mu, pointing at the unknown bill. "The one in the middle."

Tai Wei looked over. "Oh, that one. It's British. Five pounds."

Fang Mu frowned. "Why would he be carrying British currency in his wallet?"

"He's a foreigner," said Tai Wei casually. "They always walk around with foreign currency."

"Yeah, but this guy's an American. For his day-to-day life, all he should need in his wallet are dollars and renminbi. Why carry around pounds? And why only five?"

This question stumped Tai Wei. Scratching his head, he said, "Maybe… maybe it had some sentimental value for him. Why?" He looked at Fang Mu. "Are you thinking this is a clue to the next crime?"

"I can't say for sure," said Fang Mu, shaking his head. "I just think it's a little peculiar. I'll have to do some more research."

"All right. So how's it been over here? You found anything?" Tai Wei looked over the stack of documents Fang Mu had brought along. He knew the kid was going to tell him what was inside, but he was too impatient to wait.

As Fang Mu nodded, his eyes became calm and resolute.

"Things are beginning to come into focus," he said.

"Really? What do you mean?"

"Hold your horses; let's do this one thing at a time." Fang Mu laid the folders from the first four cases in a row. Tai Wei noticed that atop each of the four stacks he placed several sheets of photocopied text.

"Let's start by looking at the second case," said Fang Mu. "At the scene of the first crime, the female victim was found with a syringe stuck in her chest. I believe this was meant to hint that the second crime would take place at a hospital, or that at the very least it would have something to do with the medical profession. Sure enough, it was committed at the school hospital, the victim was a forty-three-year-old woman, and the cause of death was heroin poisoning." Here Fang Mu paused, took the photocopied papers from atop the second stack and handed it to Tai Wei. "Take a look at this."

Taking the papers from him, Tai Wei looked at them. They appeared to have been copied from various books and journals, and each was covered with Fang Mu's underlines and scribbled notes.

"It's probably a little disorganized," said Fang Mu. "Why don't you look through it while I narrate?" Then, speaking slowly, he began. "What you're looking at are some documents on the infamous British serial killer Harold Shipman. In 1963, when Shipman was seventeen, he knelt at his mother's bedside and watched her die of cancer at the age of forty-three. This incident was an enormous blow to him, and it became the turning point of his whole life. For this reason, he decided to study medicine. Before she died, his mother had been in such pain from her illness that for a long time she had been forced to rely on heroin and morphine to get through each day. Therefore, Shipman desired to kill others by using a lethal combination of these drugs. With his mother dead, he could not tolerate other middle-aged women getting to live their own safe and happy lives."

Tai Wei had forgotten to look at the documents in his hands, but rather had stared open-mouthed at Fang Mu this whole time. Unperturbed, Fang Mu continued to speak in the same slow, calm manner: "In 1970, he graduated from medical school, and soon became known as an unusually skilled and highly ethical family doctor. However, he was never able to truly forget what had happened to his mother. In 1984, Shipman began using heroin to kill his own patients, selecting as his victims mainly women around the same age as his mother when she died. By the time he was arrested at the end of 1998, he had poisoned a total of two-hundred-fifteen people to death."

It took Tai Wei a long time to gather his thoughts. At last, he said, "So what you're saying is, the killer was copying Harold Shipman's criminal method?"

"Exactly. Now as you'll recall, the victim at the second crime scene was found with a pornographic Japanese manga in her handbag. Its contents included scenes of torture fetishism and homosexuality. I believe this comic was meant to be a clue to the third crime, during which a seven-year-old girl was tortured to death." Saying this, Fang Mu took several more photocopied papers and placed them in Tai Wei's hands.

"These documents are about the infamous Japanese serial killer Tsutomu Miyazaki. He was born prematurely, leaving him with deformed carpal bones in both hands. Because of this, he developed an inferiority complex from a young age. Although he did not like to interact with other people," he said, "he loved watching pornographic anime. When he was arrested, police discovered over six thousand titles of pornographic anime in his apartment, much of which was focused on torture fetishism. Miyazaki committed his first murder in 1988. The victim was a four-year-old girl. After strangling her to death, Miyazaki raped her corpse and then filmed a close-up of her genitals, which he later used to masturbate. In October and December of that year, and then in June of the following, he committed three more murders. The victims were all little girls no older than seven, and after torturing each to death, he raped their corpses. Most perversely, in January of 1989, the killer returned to the site where he had buried the first victim's body and collected her decomposed remains. Then he packed them in a cardboard box and sent them to her family. Inside, he also left a short, cryptic note describing the crime. Later, he would also send similar notes to several relatively large newspapers. Then, in July of 1989, Miyazaki was arrested. In 1996, the Tokyo district court sentenced him to death; however, he is still appealing the charge to this day."

Hearing all this, Tai Wei muttered to himself. "This…this is simply identical to the Jin Qiao case." Then, too impatient to wait for Fang Mu, he grabbed the documents stacked on top of the fourth case folder and said, "What about this one? Who was he copying here?"

"Ed Gein, the infamous American serial killer." For some reason, whether exhaustion or something else, Fang Mu's voice had grown quiet and his expression was even gloomier than before.

"When the body of Jin Qiao was discovered, she was holding a broken piece of ceramic pottery in her hand. This piece came from a copy of a vase originally created by the British artist Grayson Perry, who is a transvestite. The most famous transvestite serial killer in history was Ed Gein. For his whole life, Gein lived under the stern and tyrannical eye of his mother. When she died, he placed her corpse in a special room in his house and then sealed it off, like a holy tomb. At first, to stave off loneliness, he would dig up the bodies of recently buried women, and then touch and enjoy the sight of them. Later, he began skinning these corpses and sewing them into dolls. In the end, his perversity intensified, and within three years he killed three middle-aged women. He would later turn their body parts into 'handcrafted objects', which included clothes made of human skin and a bowl made of a human skull."

Fang Mu pointed at a photograph on one of his photocopies. "Here, these are the clothes made of skin. After Gein was captured, he admitted to longing to know what it felt like to have breasts and a vagina. When he wore the human skin-clothes he had sewn, he would fantasize that he was his own mother. Have you ever seen The Silence of the Lambs?"

Tai Wei nodded.

"The plot of that movie was adapted from the life of Ed Gein," said Fang Mu, picking up some of the case files that Tai Wei had brought for him. "In the fourth crime, the CD that the skinned girl was 'listening' to was a clue to the next murder, in which the killer imitated Charles Manson. After claiming to have received instructions from The Beatles song Helter Skelter, Manson began what he hoped would become an apocalyptic race war by slaughtering bourgeois whites. As I said before, not only did Manson write something at each crime scene calling the victims pigs, he also always referred to his murders as 'pig butchering'. Before you is all the information I have gathered over the last two days. I believe that the killer is modeling his crimes after history's most famous serial killers and is leaving a clue at each scene that hints at whomever he will be copying next. In my opinion, the sixth crime will most likely have something to do with that five-pound note."

For a moment Tai Wei appeared lost in thought. Then, as if something had just occurred to him, he said: "What about the first crime? You never said who he was copying there."

Frowning, Fang Mu said, "I've also been racking my brains about the first crime. There are too many historical examples of serial killers who dismembered their victims after murdering them. Based on the method used by our killer, it's extremely difficult to judge who exactly he was imitating. However, one of his motives for the crime was definitely jealousy, I'm certain of that. Think of the risk he took transporting Qu Weiqiang's body from his apartment all the way to the soccer field. That's got to mean something."

After thinking for a moment Tai Wei said, "What about Professor Qiao's idea about the killer wanting to rebuild Wang Qian anew. Could that be some kind of clue?"

Fang Mu didn't reply. Picking up the folder from the first case, he flipped directly to the crime scene photographs.

Wang Qian's body lay on the floor, cut into six parts and pieced together in a spread-eagle position.

Fang Mu stared at the photograph, as well as its accompanying description.

All of a sudden he seemed to notice something, and his brow furrowed in concentration.

"Head to the north, feet to the south... head to the north, feet to the south..." he muttered to himself, before abruptly asking: "Where were the door and window located at the crime scene?"

After thinking about it for a moment, Tai Wei replied, "I think it was a north-south arrangement. The door was north and the window south. I remember Old Zhao saying to me at the time that the victim's head was pointed towards the door and her feet towards the window."

"What you're saying is, when the police entered the room, this is what they saw?" Saying this, Fang Mu thought for a moment, and then rotated the photograph. Wang Qian's spread-eagle body was now upside-down, her head, arms and legs pointing in five different directions.

Fang Mu's swept his eyes across the victim's head, torso, arms, and legs. Suddenly his breathing grew rapid. Pulling his cell phone from his pocket, he quickly dialed a number. Tai Wei could see his hands were shaking.

After a few seconds, Fang Mu heard Du Yu's voice on the other end: "Hello?"

"It's Fang Mu. Du Yu, do you still remember what that five-pointed star on our door looked like?"

"Five-pointed star? What five-pointed star?"

Fang Mu leapt to his feet in agitation. "The one from the night of the World Cup finals! We watched the game at a restaurant, came back, I went to the bathroom, and then when I returned to our room, you were wiping something off our door. You said it was a five-pointed star. Do you remember or not?"

"Oh, now I remember. Yeah, that's what happened. What made you think of it now?"

"That's none of your concern! I just need you to tell me, what did that five-pointed star look like?"

"It had five points man, what else can be said? As I recall it was pretty damn ugly, too."

"C'mon, just think; was there anything else special about it? For example…"

"Oh yeah, I just thought of something. The five-pointed star, it was upside-down."

"…Upside-down…" said Fang Mu, seemingly speaking to himself. All of a sudden, his face was ashen.

"That's right. It was drawn with one point down and two points up. Why do you want to know? …Hey, Fang Mu, can you still hear me? Hello, hello…?"

Ignoring him, Fang Mu slowly hung up the phone.

Looking as if all his energy had left him, Fang Mu leaned back against the bench, his eyes empty. From Fang Mu's conversation with Du Yu, Tai Wei more or less understood that on the eve of Qu Weiqiang and Wang Qian's murders, someone had drawn an upside-down five-pointed star on Fang Mu's door. Now he wondered what it was supposed to mean.

"What's the significance of an upside-down five-pointed star?" asked Tai Wei.

Fang Mu seemed to be so scared that he had begun to tremble. It took him a long time to reply. At last, lips shaking, he said, "Richard Ramirez. American serial killer. On multiple occasions between 1984 and 1985, he snuck into peoples' homes, killed all the adult men, raped the women and children, and then dismembered their corpses. Once he was finished, he would leave behind the same symbol at every crime scene: an upside-down five-pointed star. Sometimes he would leave it on the wall, sometimes on a mirror, and sometimes directly on the bodies of his victims."

He pointed at the crime scene photograph. "Wang Qian's head is facing the door and her feet are facing the window so that when police entered the room she would have looked just like an upside-down five-pointed star. Ramirez was different than other serial killers. Not only did he lack any trademark method of murdering his victims—he'd shoot them, beat them to death, slit their throats, strangle them—he also didn't seek out any particular kind of victim. He killed children under five, men and women over seventy, and people of all races and walks of life. As a result, he was extremely difficult for police to catch. At last, Ramirez was arrested in 1985 and sentenced to death in 1989."

With that, Fang Mu dropped his head and said no more.

Lighting a cigarette, Tai Wei slowly organized his thoughts.

"Richard Ramirez, Harold Shipman, Tsutomu Miyazaki, Ed Gein, Charles Manson," he said at last, seemingly lost in thought, "it really does seem like this guy is copying famous serial killers from history. And he even left a clue to the first crime on your door—the five-pointed star…"

The moment these words left Tai Wei's mouth, he abruptly stopped talking and his eyes went wide. The cigarette in his hand was immediately forgotten. For several seconds he sat there, stunned. He then turned to face Fang Mu, who was trying to light a cigarette, but his hands were shaking too much to use the lighter.

At last, with what seemed great determination, Tai Wei slowly said: "Fang Mu, I think this guy is coming for you." He gave the kid a careful look. His face was now deathly pale. "He's testing you, trying to see whether you can guess who he'll be copying next. No one else on campus understands this stuff as much as you do."

Tai Wei spoke slowly and softly, but to Fang Mu, each word felt like a bullet shot straight at his heart. "You think so?" he asked at last. "No way, that's impossible." Lighting a cigarette, he inhaled deeply, and then turned to Tai Wei and forced a smile.

What kind of smile was this? Tai Wei had to wonder.

Disheartened. Indignant. Despairing. Terrified. Was he trying to convince himself that this was all just a coincidence?

Don't be such a fool, Fang Mu thought as his thin, self-deceiving smile twitched involuntarily.

Time passed and the sky grew dark. To Fang Mu, it began to seem as if all the dim shapes around him were growing nearer. The basketball hoops, the chain-link fence, the trees, even the dorms all appeared to come alive, and with the deepening darkness they seemed to be secretly laughing at him, as if they were closing in on him, malice in their hearts, step by step.

He felt his throat become dry, his mouth bitter, and his head spin. At last, unable to stop himself, he bent over and began to vomit.

Tai Wei sat there motionlessly, watching as Fang Mu retched so violently that his body appeared to split in half.

His heart was filled with sympathy and misery.

18 THE YORKSHIRE RIPPER

Fang Mu lay in bed all day. He didn't eat, didn't drink, didn't say a single word; just stared at the ceiling and ignored everyone. Although Du Yu was already accustomed to this sort of behavior, he had a vague feeling that something was different this time.

Tai Wei came by later that night.

When Tai Wei entered the dorm room, Du Yu was trying to convince Fang Mu to have some of the dinner he had bought for him. Tai Wei saw that a lunch tray was still sitting on Fang Mu's desk, the food long since gone cold.

Du Yu nodded at Tai Wei as he came into the room and then motioned helplessly in Fang Mu's direction.

Only a day had passed, but Fang Mu had already thinned out considerably. His chin was even sharper than usual and his eyes, still staring motionlessly at the ceiling, appeared startlingly huge.

Tai Wei sat down next to Fang Mu's bed and looked at him for several seconds. "You fasting?"

Fang Mu made no response. His eyes didn't even move.

Tai Wei chuckled and picked up Fang Mu's dinner tray. He gave it a good sniff.

"Mmm, smells delicious. Stewed chicken and potatoes with rice. What's this one?"

"Sweet and sour crispy-fried fish balls," said Du Yu, looking at Fang Mu as he answered. "It's an appetizer."

"Wow, what a considerate friend you have!" said Tai Wei. "You'd better eat this quick."

Fang Mu briefly dropped his gaze from the ceiling. "Thank you," he said quietly, and then rolled over to face the inside of the bed.

Du Yu looked at Tai Wei and shrugged helplessly. Tai Wei just smiled and waved his hand to show he didn't mind.

The three of them sat there in silence. After a little while, Du Yu picked up his backpack and water bottle and motioned to Tai Wei that he was going out. Then left, quietly shutting the door behind him.

Now it was just the two of them. Tai Wei looked at Fang Mu, who was still lying there motionless with his face to the wall. Sighing, Tai Wei pulled out a cigarette and gloomily smoked it.

By the time the cigarette had burned all the way down, Fang Mu still hadn't acknowledged his visitor in the least. At last, Tai Wei started to talk.

"Partner, I completely understand how you're feeling right now. I might be a cop, but if I had an opponent like this, I'd be just as scared as you. But scared or not, hiding out in your room all day is no kind of solution. If he wants you dead, then no matter how much you try to escape, sooner or later he's going to find you. That's why we need to strike first!"

Seeing that Fang Mu still hadn't moved, Tai Wei continued. "Today I looked over all of Ma Kai's known acquaintances and didn't find anyone suspicious; therefore, I don't think the problem came from that end. I've also already spoken with the Changhong City PSB and asked for their assistance in investigating if any of the family members or accomplices of the criminals you put away are trying to get revenge." He paused for a moment before continuing. "I know I didn't ask your permission. You're not going to be mad at me, are you?"

Suddenly Fang Mu sat up, startling Tai Wei.

"Is it possible for you to shut your mouth for even a second and not chatter on like an old woman?" Fang Mu yelled.

Doing his best to keep his cool, Tai Wei began: "I understand how you're feeling right now –"

"You don't understand shit!" said Fang Mu roughly. "I'm not afraid at all. Even if he were hiding under the bed right now with a knife in his hand I still wouldn't be afraid. This isn't the first time I've faced someone who wanted kill me, and it won't be the last!" Suddenly his voice choked with sobs. "Why did you need to kill all those people? If you want me dead then do it! Kill me right now! Why end so many lives for no reason?"

He jumped up and knocked all the books off his shelf, then fell dejectedly back onto the bed.

"Son of a bitch..." he said beneath his breath. As he closed his eyes, a tear dropped down his face and onto his pillow.

Tai Wei looked at the books scattered across the floor, and then at the frail young man lying on the bed before him. Now that he knew the real reason Fang Mu was feeling so down, he couldn't help but feel a measure of respect for the stubborn bastard.

Love and duty. No emotions were more precious than those.

Tai Wei stood up, studying the dejected student on the bed. Bending over, he slowly picked up all the books, blew the dust from their covers, and then placed them neatly back on the bookshelf. When he finished, he sat beside the bed. He fixed his eyes on Fang Mu.

"Kid, get up and eat!"

His tone was firm and absolute. All traces of his previously comforting manner were gone.

Noticing this, Fang Mu opened his eyes and looked at him.

Tai Wei didn't avoid his gaze at all. In his eyes, Fang Mu read the trust and encouragement.

As if he was giving a pistol to a diehard partner, Tai Wei placed a spoon in Fang Mu's hand.

"Partner," he said, "we've got to keep going. I don't know how many more victims he's planning on killing, but we need to do everything we can to stop him before more people die. Don't think any more about the ones who have already gone. When you're dead, you're dead; you feeling guilty is not going to bring anyone back. This is your fate, Fang Mu. Great power demands great responsibility, and it's useless to try and hide from it. Catching the killer is the best consolation you can give to his victims. But before all that," he said as he placed the food in front of Fang Mu, "at the very least, you need to not starve to death!"

Fang Mu looked at the food before him. It was still steaming a little. He looked at Tai Wei. The man's expression was deadly serious.

For several seconds the two of them stared at each other in silence. At last Fang Mu took the plate of food and began to eat ravenously.

Damn, that's delicious, Fang Mu thought.

When he finished eating, Fang Mu leapt out of bed and stretched. The tightness in his chest relaxed with each breath and his whole body felt much more alert.

He then summarized some of his recent thoughts for Tai Wei. Even though he had been lying in bed, tormented by anger and guilt for the past day and night, he had still been closely analyzing the details of the case. His mind had not been idle. As he saw it, the reason the killer was targeting him had to have something to do with one of the cases he had helped solve. Even though Tai Wei had not asked his permission before contacting the Changhong City PSB, Fang Mu agreed that at present it was their only feasible lead.

"And as for the numbers," he added, "I believe they have some special significance."

"Oh?" said Tai Wei, his tone curious. "What are you thinking?"

"I don't know if you've noticed, but from the five distinct crimes that have occurred so far, there have already been six victims. However, the numbers left at the crime scenes have only been one through five," Fang Mu said. "I found this strange when I first noticed it, because if the numbers corresponded to the victims, this would demonstrate that the killer was showing off and trying to provoke us. But what does it mean if the numbers actually correspond to the crimes themselves? It means that the killer doesn't care about the number of victims killed, but rather the number of crimes committed—or in other words, the number of people he has copied. With this line of thought, this number is most likely fixed, meaning that the killer probably already knows exactly how many people he is planning on copying.

"Because," Fang Mu paused, "if this is a test, then like all tests, it must have an end, at which point it will be determined whether or not I've passed." He looked calmly at Tai Wei and smiled.

Seeing the smile on the kid's lips, Tai Wei felt chilled to the bone. Since he was young, Tai Wei had experienced his share of tests, but none had ever made him feel as thoroughly terrified as this one.

To imagine taking a test where every answer had to be written with a pen dipped in blood was both terrifying and daunting. If answered correctly, then the test was over and everything was okay. But if anything was answered incorrectly, then one person was going to disappear from the world. And it probably wouldn't just stop at him or her.

And more terrifying yet, before they had even realized it was a test, each of the first five questions had been crossed out with a bloody X. They would never have the chance to get those questions correct.

"In that case," said Tai Wei, "what's the total number going to be?"

"Seven, nine, eleven," Fang Mu said, deep in thought. "It has to be an odd number. It's unlikely to be eleven, because that would make the crimes go on for too long. He's probably anxious to face-off with me, and I doubt he's patient enough to wait until then. Seven." He nodded thoughtfully. "Seven seems to be the most likely."

"Why seven?"

"I'm a psychological profiler, so I think he wants to have a bit of a psychological competition with me. And in psychology, seven is considered an unusually attractive number."

"Attractive?"

"That's right. For example, when it comes to remembering strings of numbers, people are generally able to remember one or two less or one or two more than seven. From five to nine, in other words. After nine, most people's memories become hazy. So when people try to remember fairly long chains of numbers, such as pi, for instance, they often break them up into groups. In addition, there are many notable parts of human history that happen to involve seven, such as the seven days in a week, seven notes in the diatonic scale, seven colors in the visible spectrum, seven deadly sins, the seventh..." Suddenly Fang Mu stopped talking and the color drained from his face.

"The seventh what?"

"Oh, nothing." Very quickly Fang Mu's expression returned to normal.

Tai Wei lowered his head, as if he were considering something. After some time, he looked up. "Fang Mu."

"Yeah?"

"What were you just about to say?"

Fang Mu stared at him for several seconds. Then he smiled. "I don't know. If I really am part of this test, then I must be the last part. And if I'm not part of it, then my time's going to come immediately after it's over. In short, I can't escape."

Seeing the calm look on Fang Mu's face, Tai Wei didn't know what to say. The kid was discussing his own murder in the same manner as one might discuss football or the weather or some other totally inconsequential topic. It was absurd.

Tapping the gun on his waist, Tai Wei said slowly, "I won't let anything happen to you."

Fang Mu smiled indifferently. "I hope that's the case. But like you said, this is my fate. If I really am meant to die, then there's no avoiding it."

He walked to the window and looked out. Through the frost that was already covering the glass he could vaguely make out the streetlights below, as well as the students who passed beneath them, talking and laughing loudly.

"Death," said Fang Mu quietly. "Actually, heaven has already been looking after me."

Then with one by the bed and the other at the window, the two men in Room 313 lapsed into silence. Fang Mu looked outside and Tai Wei looked at Fang Mu.

The light through the window gave him a slightly golden silhouette. After a while, Tai Wei got up and stood beside him.

"Assuming you're right," said Tai Wei slowly, "then there's still two more." He looked out at the darkening campus. Even now it was still buzzing with life.

After a long time, Fang Mu spoke. His voice was soft and sounded as if he were speaking only to himself.

"There's still two more."

The days grew colder and colder. Soon girls had no choice but to abandon their more fashionable, revealing clothing for heavier attire. And as the summer colors quietly vanished from campus, the whole place became much lonelier and more desolate.

Great swaths of leaves were now daily blown from the trees by the fierce autumn wind and floated gently to the ground. When stepped on, they crackled softly, as if not yet resigned to their fate. The day before a light snow had blanketed the ground, but now the ground was covered in mud and slowly rotting leaves. It seemed as if overnight the once bustling campus had been filled with the air of death.

But what the students found truly unsettling wasn't this bleak scenery; it was the presence of all the stern-eyed policemen constantly hurrying about.

The special investigation team had already been stationed at the campus for over a week. They could be seen in academic buildings, dining halls, dorms, and library, either in uniform or plainclothes. Many students, used to their previously unencumbered lives, felt increasingly uncomfortable, and a sense of antipathy slowly spread among the student body. Nearly every day some kind of dispute between a student and a police officer was reported to campus security. For the pair of provosts individually in charge of student affairs and campus management, every day was a headache. They each prayed for no one else to die and that the police would catch the killer as soon as possible.

Unlike his peers who were either indifferent to or annoyed by these recent developments, Fang Mu was much more concerned with the progress of the investigation. As Tai Wei had requested, no word of Fang Mu's connection to the case was being aired for the time being and all investigations into his background were conducted in secret. This allowed Fang Mu to continue searching undisturbed for clues to the sixth crime. Of course, unless he was forced to be elsewhere, Tai Wei was by the kid's side nearly every day—just in case.

Today was another busy afternoon. Fang Mu was in the reference room poring over the thick book before him while Tai Wei was sleeping soundly at the next table over, flecks of saliva hanging from the corners of his mouth.

The reference room was crowded. It was almost finals, and with everyone busy writing their term papers, students were constantly arriving to checkout books. When they saw Tai Wei passed out on the table, more than a few eyebrows were raised, and Librarian Sun kept worriedly glancing over at the brand new edition of 200 Years of Western Crime (1800-1993) propped under the policeman's head.

Fang Mu rubbed his temples in exhaustion and then flipped to the next page. While reading one of the paragraphs, his breath suddenly caught in his throat.

He quickly read it again two more times, his face reddening with excitement. He jumped out of his seat, ran over to Tai Wei, and shook him awake.

"Hey," he said, "you need to look at this."

Tai Wei leapt to his feet in surprise, saliva hanging from his mouth, one hand going to his sidearm.

"What's going on?" he cried.

At the sound of his voice, everyone in the reference room looked up in surprise. One student who had been climbing a stepladder to reach a book on the top shelf was so startled he fell to the floor.

Ignoring all the displeased looks around him, Fang Mu merely smiled apologetically at Librarian Sun, who appeared stupefied, and impatiently placed the open book in front of Tai Wei.

Buttoning the holster on his gun, Tai Wei awkwardly looked down. He immediately frowned. When he had finished reading, he took out a pack of cigarettes and placed one in his mouth. Seeing this, Fang Mu quickly pulled him out into the hall.

The two of them smoked in silence in the stairwell. When their cigarettes were half gone, Tai Wei looked at Fang Mu and asked probingly: "The Yorkshire Ripper? You think that's who the killer's going to copy next?"

"I think it's a definite possibility." Fang Mu tossed his cigarette to the floor and slowly crushed it with his foot. "You just read it yourself. That five-pound note matches him perfectly."

Tai Wei nodded and thought back on what he had just read.

Dubbed the "Yorkshire Ripper", a British man named Peter Sutcliffe had killed thirteen women between 1975 and 1980. His method of choice was to beat his victims over the head with a ball-peen hammer and then stab them in the chest with a screwdriver. After killing them, he liked to place a five-pound note in one of their hands.

"In that case, do you think the next victim will be a woman?" asked Tai

Wei.

"If he's really going to copy the Yorkshire Ripper, then yes, there's no doubt about it." Saying this, Fang Mu watched a group of girls cheerfully emerge from a yoga class at the other end of the corridor.

"Well, shit," said Tai Wei, forcefully throwing his cigarette to the floor. "I'll go call everyone together and figure out some way to stop this. How many female students do you have here?"

"About four thousand."

"Christ!"

That afternoon, the more observant students noticed that some curious new people had arrived on campus and some equally curious things were taking place. Security personnel were increased in all the women's dorms and a room on the sixth floor of each was cleared out and converted into an on-duty lounge. In the women's bathhouse, the sixth shower stall was locked, as was the number six locker in the women's changing room in the gymnasium. In the academic buildings, keen-eyed, well-dressed women with a bulge at their hips could also be seen strolling near number six classrooms, women's bathrooms, and along sixth floor hallways.

All the tools belonging to the maintenance department – especially hammers and screwdrivers – were individually registered and workers were required to sign them out whenever they needed to use them. On campus, vehicles were frequently stopped and examined. Students became more concerned about their civil rights than ever before, and on several occasions their resistance turned physical. After this state of unrest persisted for another week, the police and school administrators finally held an emergency meeting. The ultimate result was that police checks would be limited to men over 30-year-old, and unless it was absolutely necessary, students would no longer be interrogated. With that, the atmosphere on campus settled down a little.

While strolling past the gymnasium one Wednesday afternoon, Fang Mu happened to glance over his shoulder. Sure enough, Tai Wei was following him a short ways back. Fang Mu couldn't help but sigh.

The sight of a policeman shadowing a student all day, every day, had already made a lot of people suspicious. Fang Mu suggested that Tai Wei take care of some of the other campus security work, saying that he didn't need to follow him all the time. "I'm going to be the final one," he had said. "So he's not going to do anything to me now." Although Tai Wei had seemed to agree, Fang Mu still constantly noticed the policeman over his shoulder.

Around noon that day, Fang Mu had received an unexpected call from Xing Zhisen of the Changhong City PSB. Old Xing was the same as always. After barely a word of greeting, he immediately asked Fang Mu how the investigation was going. He then told him flatly that they had already looked into all the old cases Fang Mu had helped solve and they had turned up nothing. Although Old Xing ended the call by telling Fang Mu to take care of himself and that if he needed anything, not to hesitate calling, Fang Mu still felt a little disheartened. After anxiously circling his room for a few minutes, he decided that he might as well go out.

At that moment, several members of the student union were hanging a posting on the bulletin board outside the gymnasium when Fang Mu got there. Liu Jianjun was among them. The poster was huge, and on it a basketball player was leaping towards the hoop, ball in hand. Fang Mu recognized him as Su Jun, star of the provincial basketball team. Because the bulletin board's aluminum frame was a little uneven, the poster would not lie flat. With a hammer in hand, one of the students had climbed up a ladder and was pounding the frame back in place.

Instantly a plainclothes cop appeared beneath him. With a cold look in his eyes, he asked, "Where's the registration slip for that hammer?"

Glancing contemptuously down at him, the student said, "I don't have one."

Liu Jianjun, who was helping to hold up the poster, quickly explained. "It doesn't belong to the maintenance department. It's from our dorm."

As soon as he heard this, the cop walked over and pulled on the student's pant leg. "Get down."

"What do you think you're doing?" yelled the student.

"Give me your student ID card!"

"I don't have it!" returned the student, shaking the cop off his leg.

The cop's face went dark and he kicked at the ladder. "Get down here!"

The student staggered atop the ladder, nearly falling. Now he, too, was enraged. "You trying to kill me?" he yelled, pointing the hammer at the cop's face. "You can't catch the killer, so you've decided to throw your weight around with the students, huh? You guys are real brave. How the hell did our country produce trash like you?"

The cop's face immediately set hard as steel. He reached up and pulled the student off the ladder.

Fang Mu hurriedly tried to break it up, but before he could say anything, Tai Wei had sprinted over and grabbed the cop, who had just begun rolling up his sleeves.

"What's going on?" Tai Wei asked the student. "Where's your student ID?"

By now the student was a little afraid. "I didn't bring it," he said quietly.

Liu Jianjun quickly spoke up. "He's a chemistry major. His name is Qin Dahai. I can vouch for him."

"And who are you?" asked Tai Wei.

"I'm at the law school. My name is Liu Jianjun." He pointed at Fang Mu. "He can vouch for me."

Fang Mu quickly turned to Tai Wei and nodded.

"Then whose hammer is this?" said Tai Wei, looking at Fang Mu.

"Our dorm's," he said.

Tai Wei took the hammer and weighed it in his hand for a moment. Then he passed it back. "Keep an eye on it. Don't lend it out and don't lose it. I hope you can support our work here."

"Yes, sir," said Liu Jianjun, quickly nodding his head. He pulled on the sleeve of the other student. The miffed student softly and reluctantly said, "Yes, sir."

The plainclothes cop was still livid. Patting him on the shoulder, Tai Wei said, "All right, go on and get back to work."

"These little brats," muttered the cop, still fuming. "We work from dawn to dusk to protect them and the bastards still don't –"

"Enough!" yelled Tai Wei, cutting him off. "Get back on patrol."

"Yes, sir!" The cop glared once more at the student, and then spun around and walked off.

When he was some distance away, Tai Wei shook his head and sighed. "It's not their fault. They've been working day and night recently. Now they're exhausted, so it's no wonder tempers are flaring a little."

Fang Mu smiled to show he understood. When he turned back around, he saw that Liu Jianjun and the other students were still awkwardly standing around. He hurried to smooth things over.

"What are you guys up to? Is some event coming up?"

Liu Jianjun gave a big smile. "Tomorrow night the provincial basketball team is going to play our school team in a friendly match." He pointed at the poster. "Su Jun will be there, too. You know the guy's on the national team, right?"

"Whoa! That's awesome." Fang Mu couldn't help but feel a little envious.

"Man, I told you! You should have joined the team. You could be competing against one of the top players in the country."

"I wouldn't have a chance," said Fang Mu, laughing and playing it cool, although inside he really wished he could take part as well.

He looked back at Tai Wei. The guy was frowning deeply. Fang Mu knew exactly what he was thinking. Working security at an event this big would be astronomically difficult. There would be a ton of spectators and a million things to watch for. The scene did not lend itself to being easily controlled. If they messed up, the killer could use this as an opportunity to strike.

Of course, none of this had occurred to Liu Jianjun.

"Tomorrow you'll have to come and cheer me on!" he said, glowing with excitement.

By then Tai Wei had already started walking away. Fang Mu gave Liu Jianjun a quick "I'll be there", and hurried to catch up with Tai Wei.

"How the hell did the school not tell us about this sooner?" asked Tai Wei angrily. He shook his head and waved Fang Mu away. "You get back to your dorm. I need to go and figure out how we're going to secure this thing. Oh, and be careful."

Having no choice, Fang Mu just nodded and said, "Okay."

The following evening, the basketball game began on schedule in the school gymnasium.

The gymnasium was a fully functioning sports arena, with a court that conformed to international standards and retractable bleachers that could seat over 2,000 people. Although the game wasn't set to begin until 7:30, by 6 p.m. students had already filled every seat and even the aisles were packed tight.

Zou Tuanjie and the rest of the diehard fans had long since hurried to the stadium and saved seats, two of which belonged to Du Yu and Fang Mu. The two of them waited until nearly 7 p.m. to begin strolling over to the stadium. As they reached the stadium steps, Fang Mu saw Deng Linyue and a group of girls walk past, chatting happily. A teacher standing nearby yelled impatiently, "Let's go, let's go! What took you ladies so long? Hurry up and get changed."

"Cheerleaders," said Du Yu, staring at all the gorgeously dressed girls. He grinned. "With beauties like that cheering him on, Liu Jianjun will be showing off for sure."

After squeezing through the jam-packed crowd and stepping on more feet than they could count, Fang Mu and Du Yu finally arrived at their seats. Before they could catch their breath, the sound of whistles and excited applause filled the stadium, followed by an earth-shattering roar. Looking up, Fang Mu saw a pack of scantily-clad girls run out to center court and begin dancing, with Deng Linyue in the lead.

At once everyone's attention shifted from thoughts of the game about start to the sight of the girls' legs, particularly their thighs. Du Yu's mouth was hanging wide open and his eyes were fixed straight ahead. Fang Mu found this hilarious and he reached over and handed him a tissue.

"What's this for?" asked Du Yu.

"To wipe the saliva off your mouth."

Du Yu laughed and socked Fang Mu on the arm.

After a few minutes, the cheerleaders' dance routine ended. A very loud and clear noise sounded overhead, announcing that the game was about to start.

Suddenly, as the announcer began to speak, all the lights in the gymnasium went out, save for the spotlight, which shined brightly on the entrance to the court. The players from the provincial team appeared first. They ran out under the light, one enormous athlete after another, as their familiar names echoed throughout the gymnasium. They stood imposingly across center court. The last to emerge was Su Jun, the member of the national team, and as soon as his name was announced, the crowd erupted, screaming and whistling so loud that it seemed the roof would blow off the building.

Next came the members of the Jiangbin City University team. As they entered the arena under the glare of the spotlight, they appeared much more flustered than their professional counterparts. One point guard even slipped and fell as he was about to reach the court, causing the whole crowd to laugh good-naturedly. As team captain, Liu Jianjun was last to enter, and Fang Mu noticed that when he appeared the cheerleaders seemed to scream extraordinarily loud. Liu Jianjun made a point to grandstand as he ran out, waving at all the spectators.

The game began. Although the members of the provincial team were treating it like a practice match, the play was obviously one-sided. Compared to the professionals – whose average height was around 6'4" – the students looked tiny, clumsy, and scared. At the end of the first quarter, the provincial team was already leading 35-6.

When the second quarter started, the provincial team eased up, rarely using their physical superiority to drive to the hoop. Instead, they hung around the perimeter and launched jump shots. At the same time, the school team's offense started to pick up. Leading the attack was Liu Jianjun, playing especially ferocious. One time he even hit a turnaround jumper while being guarded by Su Jun himself. In retaliation, when it came time to block, Su Jun made no more than a symbolic effort, his tiptoes never leaving the floor. Fang Mu noticed that every time Liu Jianjun scored, he would face the screaming, dancing cheerleaders and fiercely pound the left side of his chest. Looking closer, Fang Mu saw that unlike his teammates, Liu Jianjun had drawn a big "D" onto his jersey, right over his heart, using what appeared to be felt-tip marker.

D for Deng, thought Fang Mu, smiling to himself. This guy...

At halftime, the provincial team still held a significant lead. But the student spectators didn't care at all about who won or lost. For them, the most important thing was seeing their sports heroes in person. They were excited to learn a dunk performance would take place during halftime, and of course the professionals would be the stars of the show. However, what made the crowd proudest was the news that a fellow student would be joining the show. This student was none other than Liu Jianjun. Although only 6'1", he could jump astonishingly high.

Liu Jianjun made three attempts. Although he missed one, his other two dunks were brilliant. After each, he turned toward the cheerleaders, roared once, and pounded his left breast. The cheerleaders responded with high-pitched screams. Frequently they would nudge Deng Linyue, looks of envy in their eyes. For her part, Deng Linyue kept fairly cool. But although she was hardly going wild with outward excitement, her eyes never left Liu Jianjun.

The second half began. Perhaps because he had been so active during the first two quarters, Liu Jianjun seemed a little sluggish at first, so the coach subbed him out to take a breath. Rather than heading straight for the bench, however, Liu Jianjun walked over to where the cheerleaders were and said something to Deng Linyue. Her expression seemed a little surprised, but she still nodded her head, blushing slightly.

"Aw, you don't have a chance anymore," grumbled Du Yu as he watched what was happening on the sidelines. "This guy's really stolen the show tonight."

"So what?" said Fang Mu. "You're such a broken record, always going on and on about something I never even cared about to begin with!" He stood up. "Let me by."

"Where are you going?"

"To the bathroom. Why, did you think I was trying to find a place to be alone so I could cry over my broken heart?"

Moments later, Fang Mu was outside the gymnasium. Compared to the noise and excitement of the arena, the gymnasium corridor felt unusually desolate. He hurried toward the bathroom, wanting to get back as soon as possible so he could keep enjoying the game. Rounding one corner, he nearly bumped into two stern-looking policemen in SWAT gear. Seeing them, his spirits fell.

You can't relax now, he told himself grudgingly. The killer is still out there somewhere.

In a flash, all that was going on in the gymnasium no longer meant a thing to him. He even forgot that he had been heading to the bathroom. Instead he just stood there, watching the two policemen walk away until they disappeared around the corner.

He looked out the window beside him. Although it was pitch-black outside, he could still make out a police car parked beside the gymnasium, its red and blue lights flashing soundlessly.

After watching it for a few moments, he turned and walked slowly and distractedly back to the arena. Once he'd returned to his seat he could no longer focus on the game. Scanning the bleachers, he spotted one plainclothes cop after another. Although they appeared to be moving carelessly through the crowd, they were still wary: nerves taut as a bowstring, ready to fire at a moment's notice.

Fang Mu glanced back. Sure enough, Tai Wei was in the bleachers behind him. Seeing Fang Mu looking at him, Tai Wei made a small wave.

Expressionlessly, Fang Mu turned forward again. He didn't know why, but his spirits had sunk within him.

After the game ended, Liu Jianjun and Su Jun were both voted MVP. Gripping his trophy, Liu Jianjun waved at the whole crowd, his face glowing with happiness. Next it was time for both teams to take group pictures. Camera flashes lit up the stadium.

Most of the spectators had already begun to leave, with only the most diehard fans waiting behind to get Su Jun's autograph, Du Yu among them. Since Fang Mu wanted to get back early, he waved goodbye to Du Yu and left.

It was cold outside, especially after leaving the hot, jam-packed arena, and Fang Mu couldn't help but shiver. He noticed Tai Wei standing nearby, hands clasped behind his back.

Seeing Fang Mu, Tai Wei waved him over. "Got a cigarette?" he immediately asked.

Fang Mu nodded.

"Give me two, one for me and one for him," said Tai Wei, pointing at the plainclothes cop standing beside him.

Fang Mu took out two cigarettes and handed them over. He lit one for himself.

For a while the three of them smoked in silence, each taking deep drags. At last Tai Wei said, "Damn, I was going nuts out here. We just got out of the stadium, but had no cigarettes, and there was no way I could leave and go buy a pack." He pointed at the flood of people leaving the arena.

Fang Mu thought for a second, and then passed him his half-full pack. "Take this."

Tai Wei accepted it without a word of thanks. "Where are you off to?"

"Back to the dorm."

"By yourself?"

"By myself."

Tai Wei thought for a moment and then said, "Don't go back yet; wait here with me. When all this is finished I'll take you back."

Fang Mu was about to refuse when Tai Wei waved his hand conclusively, as if to say it had already been decided.

After everyone had left, Fang Mu went with Tai Wei as he circled the campus, mostly paying attention to several women's dormitories and various areas where couples were known to meet up. Fang Mu felt extremely awkward patrolling these latter areas, like he was no different than a Peeping Tom. By the time Tai Wei yawned and said he would take Fang Mu back to his dorm, nearly an hour had passed.

As the two of them walked past the gymnasium, chatting casually, Fang Mu happened to glance in its direction. He immediately stopped walking.

"Look!"

Tai Wei looked to where he was pointing. Dim light could be seen through the gymnasium's blue glass windows. "It looks like it's coming from the basketball court," Tai Wei said, glancing at his watch. "The place should have been cleared out a long time ago. What are people still doing inside?"

They exchanged a look and then hurried toward the gymnasium doors.

While toweling off her wet hair, Deng Linyue stared absently at the "9" nailed to the door of her locker.

During the game just now, Liu Jianjun had told her to wait for him alone in the gymnasium afterwards.

What was he planning? Deng Linyue felt a little nervous.

To be honest, Deng Linyue felt all right about Liu Jianjun, but she didn't like him in that way. Although a lot of people mistakenly thought she was his girlfriend, he had yet to express his feelings.

Perhaps tonight, she thought, he will say those three words to me.

Outside the locker room, she could hear the teacher supervisor organizing the changing room keys.

"Three, four, five...seven, eight, ten, eleven... Wait, where's nine? Who's using number nine?"

"Deng Linyue," Deng Linyue called. As soon as she spoke, someone knocked on the door to the locker room.

"Linyue, you're not ready yet?"

"I'm going to stay a little longer," she yelled toward the door. "You all go on without me."

"Such a dillydally! Tomorrow you'll have to bring the key to the student union yourself," the teacher decided.

Deng Linyue heard the teacher and all of her fellow cheerleaders walk away.

She continued on about her tasks. When she was all ready, she left the locker room and locked it behind her.

As she did, her cell phone beeped. It was a text from Liu Jianjun.

"I'm waiting for you at the basketball court, " it read.

Taking a deep breath, Deng Linyue pulled on her backpack and left the locker room.

The basketball court was completely empty, which made the huge space feel incredibly vast.

Deng Linyue glanced at the stands all around her. There was no sign of Liu Jianjun. "Where is he?" she muttered to herself, strolling aimlessly to center court.

Peng... peng... peng!

A rhythmic, banging sound suddenly echoed within the gymnasium, startling Deng Linyue. Looking around again, she saw that a basketball had been launched from up in the stands and was now bouncing on the court.

When the ball bounced over to her she stopped it with her foot and picked it up. It was a brand-new Spalding. Deng Linyue + Liu Jianjun was written in gold on each of its eight sections. It was beautiful.

Deng Linyue smiled to herself. This boy really was quite thoughtful.

Just then, Chyi Chin's The Moon Represents My Heart began to play over the loudspeakers. *(Translators' note: Chyi Chin, a famous Chinese pop music star.)*

In the enormous arena, the sound of his magnetic voice filled the air:

"You ask how deep my love's for you... How much do I love you? ...My feelings are true, my love is deep, the moon represents my heart..."

Deng Linyue looked up at the broadcast booth above the stands. A light was on inside, and she could see someone standing there and waving at her.

It was Liu Jianjun.

Before long the song ended and after a few seconds of silence, she heard Liu Jianjun's voice reverberating throughout the arena.

"Linyue, today has been a very special day for me," he said. "Not just because I got to compete with my idol on the same court, but more importantly, because today I will tell the girl I love how I feel about her..." His sweet-sounding voice was amplified by the loudspeakers, giving it an unexpectedly soul-stirring charm.

Looking up at the vague figure in the broadcast booth, Deng Linyue felt as if her whole body was filling with happiness.

Love. This was love.

What girl wasn't a little vain? It nearly made her blush. What girl wouldn't want her boyfriend to be tall and handsome? What girl could resist a romantic offensive like this?

"Linyue, I –"

A sudden, sharp bang split the air.

Suddenly all the lights in the arena went out and Liu Jianjun's heartfelt words abruptly stopped.

Plunged at once into darkness, Deng Linyue was momentarily stunned. At a loss, she waited for several seconds and then shakily called out, "Liu Jianjun...?"

The broadcast booth was pitch black as well. There was no response.

She cried out several times. In the vast, open gymnasium, her voice echoed back and forth, the sound frighteningly clear.

"Don't scare me!" she yelled, on the verge of tears. "I don't like it!"

Suddenly a spotlight switched on. The pale beam shined all the way from the top of the stands to the court, enveloping Deng Linyue.

Blinded by the light, she cupped a hand over her eyes and looked to where it was coming from.

Uncertain, she thought she saw someone walking down the stands.

Then the sound of steady footsteps reached her ears and she knew she hadn't been wrong.

"Liu Jianjun, is that you?"

The figure didn't respond, just kept walking towards her, neither fast nor slow. With the spotlight beam shining behind him, Deng Linyue couldn't make out his face, but she could tell it was a man.

As he drew closer, Deng Linyue was finally able to determine that it wasn't Liu Jianjun; this man was nearly half a head shorter than him.

"Who...who are you?" she wanted to run, but her legs felt too weak to move.

When at last the man stepped onto the basketball court, she could now see that he was wearing a black windbreaker and was carrying something in one hand.

Twenty feet, fifteen feet, ten feet...

As the man drew closer and closer, Deng Linyue's whole body began to shake. At last she saw his face.

The black hood of the windbreaker covered the upper half of his face, while his nose and mouth were tightly hidden behind a surgical mask.

She saw his mouth move behind the mask, but he wasn't speaking – it looked like he was smiling.

At last Deng Linyue reacted. With a cry of alarm, she threw the basketball at the man, and then turned and ran.

But the man was too fast. He leaped forward and grabbed hold of her hair. He raised his other hand and savagely brought it down to strike her.

But Deng Linyue's hair was still damp from her shower and it slipped out of his hand. The hammer that was supposed to come crashing down on her head instead smashed into her shoulder.

She gasped in pain. Her legs went limp and she collapsed to the floor.

Laughing darkly, as if amused, the man slowly stepped to her.

She tried to scramble away in terror, her arms and legs flailing protectively. "I'm begging you, don't..."

The man was completely unmoved. He stepped to her and put one foot on her leg and raised the hammer again.

"Stop!"

Like a thunderclap, a voice roared from the arena entrance, followed by a bang. A bullet shot through the air, nearly hitting the man.

The surprised man's attention went to the entrance.

Two figures there sprinted towards him. With no left time to think, he turned and fled.

When the two figures reached the terrified and cowering Deng Linyue, one of them yelled, "You wait here!" Then pistol in hand, he took off after the man.

Shaking, Deng Linyue felt someone help her up into a sitting position. Her whole body was in pain. Lacking even an ounce of strength, she could do nothing but lean softly against the person behind her. Struggling to look back, she saw it was Fang Mu, his face filled with worry.

"It's you?" His voice was surprised. "Are you okay?"

She feebly shook her head.

"Where are you hurt?"

"My...my shoulder..."

He sighed with relief. With some effort he knelt down and helped her to lean against his chest. He grabbed his dagger and dragged the sheath off the blade with his teeth.

Deng Linyue closed her eyes halfway, content with her rescuer. Her body suddenly drained of energy, she lay limply against his chest.

But Fang Mu hadn't relaxed in the least. Gripping the dagger handle tightly, he felt his palm fill with sweat. Before long it seemed like the thing would slip out of his hand.

Another gunshot ripped through the gymnasium. Fang Mu and Deng Linyue both jumped in surprise, but then silence followed.

Neither was sure what it meant. A lone gunshot?

Had the killer been hit?

Fang Mu looked around nervously. Besides the nearby spotlight beam, everything else was obscured. On the dark bleachers, it seemed as if a million hidden creatures were leaping and dancing. He did his utmost to pick up any suspicious sounds from his surroundings, but besides his and Deng Linyue's breathing, the gymnasium was silent.

When his eyes finally adjusted to the darkness, he saw that a basketball was sitting in front of him.

"It was just you in here?" asked Fang Mu, lightly shaking Deng Linyue.

She weakly opened her eyes. "No. Liu Jianjun is here, too."

"Where is he?" he asked quickly.

She feebly waved a hand toward the top of the stands. "In the broadcast booth."

He had to go check it out. He tried to gently but hastily place Deng Linyue back the floor.

With newfound strength, she grabbed tightly onto his shirt. "Don't go, don't go. Don't leave me here, I'm begging you!"

He struggled for a moment, but was unable to free himself. He was about to get angry when someone's urgent footsteps sounded behind him. Gripping the knife, he quickly spun around. Several flashlights shined in his eyes.

"Whoever's there, drop it!" someone called.

Fang Mu heard the sound of guns being cocked. He quickly put his hands up. "It's me, Fang Mu."

Several people ran forward. Fang Mu saw that the man in the lead was the plainclothes cop who had argued with the student on the ladder the day before.

He shined his flashlight at Fang Mu and Deng Linyue. "It's you? What's going on? Where's Tai Wei?"

Fang Mu didn't have time to answer him. Pointing up at the broadcast booth, he said, "Quick, someone's still up there."

The plainclothes cop signaled to the officer beside him. "You, follow me!"

Then the two of them sprinted up the bleachers, guns in hand.

Watching them duck inside the broadcast booth, Fang Mu silently prayed: Don't let him be dead. Please don't let him be dead.

Their flashlight beams swayed inside the booth.

When everything was silent for a while, Fang Mu could wait no longer.

He yelled up to the booth. "How is he?"

The plainclothes cop stuck his head out of the booth. "He's fine. Still alive."

Fang Mu sighed with relief, and then turned to the two cops beside him. "Tai Wei ran that way after the killer. You guys need to go help him!"

"No need."

One hand over his face, Tai Wei emerged from the darkness. He was holding something in his other hand. He looked up to the officers in the booth. "Turn on the lights!"

A few seconds later there was a rumble and the arena was suddenly bright as day.

For the first time Fang Mu got a clear look at Tai Wei. His face was bleeding and in his hand he held something long and slender wrapped in tissue.

Did he get him? Fang Mu wondered. What happened to his face? What's he holding?

With so many questions flooding his mind, he found himself momentarily unable to say anything.

Tai Wei also didn't look like was in the mood to immediately explain anything. Frowning, he watched his two fellow officers struggle to carry Liu Jianjun down to the court.

"How is he?"

"He's fine; just out cold."

Tai Wei looked over the half-comatose Deng Linyue. The worry in his expression eased when he saw her.

He told the four policemen to get the two injured students to the hospital as fast as possible, and then turned and showed Fang Mu what was in his hand.

It was a screwdriver.

They looked at one another in silence.

It was the Yorkshire Ripper, just as they had expected.

"Shit, that guy ran fast as hell and he definitely knew his way around the gymnasium," Tai Wei said. "I was chasing him toward an intersection when I saw him turn and hurl something at me. I ducked my head but still didn't dodge it." He pointed at his gashed face. The wound had opened across his cheekbone and was still oozing blood. "I fired at him in surprise, but I think I missed. Anyway, slowing down those few steps was all it took. In a second he had rounded the corner and was gone." He shook his head, clearly annoyed.

He nodded to the screwdriver. "Afterward, I turned around and picked this thing up."

Fang Mu looked at the tool, seemingly deep in thought. Suddenly he pointed at something next to Tai Wei's feet. "What's that?"

Tai Wei bent over and picked the object up. It was a key fastened to a small iron fob by a rubber band. The word Women was written on the fob. Tai Wei turned the key over.

"Six?" said Tai Wei.

"Nine?" said Fang Mu, standing beside him.

They looked at one another. Was it 6 or was it 9?

"This thing…" Fang Mu looked again at the key. "It seems to be a key for the women's locker room."

"The women's locker room?" said Tai Wei at once. "Then it must be nine, because the number six changing room is definitely locked."

Fang Mu thought for a moment, and then took the key and walked off.

Tai Wei followed Fang Mu into the women's locker room. After looking high and low, Fang Mu found locker six. He tried the key in it, but it didn't open.

"Hey, over here there's another number six," said Tai Wei with surprise. He pointed at one of the lockers.

Fang Mu walked over. Nailed to the outside of the metal locker was the number six. He slipped his key inside, and it opened with only the slightest bit of effort.

He pushed lightly on the number. It absurdly spun round and round: 6, 9, 6, 9…

Tai Wei walked over and took a closer look. He discovered that the top of the two rivets holding the number in place had been unscrewed.

"This locker was originally number nine," he said, looking at Fang Mu. "Then someone got tricky and switched it to six."

Six...6.

The corners of Fang Mu's mouth curled into a faint smile.

That someone didn't get his way this time.

19 THE MEANING OF LOVE

"Uh-huh… Okay, I understand. Then keep it that way for now. Bye."
Fang Mu hung up the phone and pointed at the tangerines on the fruit
stand. "How much per pound?"

Tai Wei's tone had been gloomy when he had spoken with Fang Mu just
then over the phone. As he'd told Fang Mu on the night of the attempted
murder, the police had made a huge effort and spent vast manpower
combing the campus in search of the killer. However, they hadn't found a
single clue. Because of this they still needed to be stationed on campus for
the time being.

Fang Mu understood exactly how Tai Wei was feeling. He had finally been
within striking distance of the killer, only to watch him escape from out of
the palm of his hand. This was something that no cop could endure. He
was probably going over and over every aspect of the event in his head: If
only he had been a little faster… If only he had pulled out his gun more
decisively… If only he had fired more accurately…

For his part, Fang Mu was much more at ease. Perhaps it was because they
were approaching the problem from different perspectives. Tai Wei, for
his part, was comparatively concerned with how soon he cracked the case.
While Fang Mu also wanted to catch the killer as soon as possible, having
stopped the man from committing another murder was even more
important to him. After being questioned by the police on the night, Fang
Mu had returned to his dorm and had a long and restful sleep. The next
morning, when his fellow students heard the news, they started coming in
droves to ask him what had happened, Fang Mu was still asleep.

After sending the last of them away, he and several of his friends decided to go visit Liu Jianjun in the hospital.

Carrying the fruit that they had bought at exorbitant prices from the stand near the provincial hospital entrance, Fang Mu and the others signed in inside and then headed to the third floor inpatient department. While Du Yu scowled as he searched for Ward 312, Fang Mu proceeded straight to the end of the hall where two police officers were standing guard outside one of the doors. Since one of them recognized him, no further questions were asked and they were allowed inside.

The bed beside the window was already surrounded by people, all of whom looked back at them as they entered. Fang Mu recognized two of them as the cops who had rushed to the gymnasium the night before.

They nodded at Fang Mu in greeting and then one turned back to the doctor and said: "So what you're saying is he's not fit to answer questions in his current condition?"

"Isn't that obvious?" said the doctor gruffly. "He's still half-comatose. How are you going to ask him anything?"

The two cops looked at one another helplessly and then silently left the room.

After placing the fruit on the windowsill, Fang Mu gave Liu Jianjun a long look.

Liu Jianjun's head was wrapped in bandages and his skin was deathly pale. His eyes were half-closed and an oxygen mask covered his mouth. He looked terribly weak.

Fang Mu's heart fell. Liu Jianjun's injuries were far worse than he had imagined. When the two policemen had carried him down to the court the night before, they had said he was "fine". Now it looked as if the word only meant was that he was still alive.

Fang Mu looked down at the health record hanging beside his bed. At the top of it was written simply: "Depressed skull fracture."

"Depressed?" he said quietly. The killer had probably hit him with a blunt object – a hammer, he guessed.

Liu Jianjun's roommate, Zou Tuanjie, was sleeping beside the bed.

Du Yu nudged him. "How is he?"

Zou Tuanjie yawned and said, "He finished surgery last night. The doctors said there's no threat to his life, but he's going to have to stay here for a little while so they can monitor him."

A sudden burst of noise sounded from the hallway. A man was heard arguing with the policemen on the other side of the door while a woman cried. "I'm his mother," she said through her sobs. "How can I not be allowed see him?"

The door opened and a travel-worn, middle-aged couple walked quickly inside. After anxiously scanning the crowded ward, they hurried over to Liu Jianjun's bed.

Before she had even reached his bedside, the woman began to wail.

Zou Tuanjie jumped to his feet and hurried to support her. "Come on, Auntie," he said consolingly. "Please sit down. Jianjun is going to be fine."

Liu Jianjun's mother sat down beside him. As big tears rolled down her face, she held one hand over her mouth, seemingly worried she would wake up her still-comatose son. She leaned over and lightly stroked his face with her hand.

Liu Jianjun's father softly read the words on his son's health record. "Depressed skull fracture?" Fear and sadness were written across his face.

"Don't worry, Uncle," said Du Yu quickly. "The doctors have already finished his surgery. They said he's not in any danger."

The father nodded, his expression relaxing slightly. He looked at all the young men. "You guys are Jianjun's classmates? What exactly happened?"

Du Yu looked at Fang Mu. "I don't know the specifics. However," he said, nudging Fang Mu, "this guy saved Liu Jianjun's life."

Liu Jianjun's father turned to look at Fang Mu as his mother grabbed Fang Mu's hand.

"Child, please tell Auntie, what on earth happened?" she implored. "Who did this?"

"Auntie, I also don't know what exactly happened," Fang Mu told them. "I was just lucky enough to be there in time."

She suddenly got down on both knees and, choking with sobs, said: "You wonderful child. Auntie is so grateful. I only have this one son...thank you, thank you."

Fang Mu quickly helped her up, his face red from embarrassment.

"Auntie...Auntie, don't do that... It was nothing..."

After he finally convinced Liu Jianjun's mother to return to her seat, Fang Mu knew he couldn't stay there any longer. More than anything else, the mother's endlessly grateful eyes were too much to bear.

After all, Liu Jianjun's attack had been because of him.

Looking once more at his comatose friend, Fang Mu's heart grew heavy. He balled his hands into fists.

Son of a bitch! I swear I'll catch you.

Not wanting to let Du Yu and the others see the change in him, he quietly left the room.

Back in the hallway, Fang Mu felt much better. Suddenly he really wanted a cigarette. After looking at all the doctors and nurses passing back and forth, he decided to find a bathroom and covertly smoke there.

He was strolling down the hallway toward the bathroom when he unexpectedly saw Tai Wei sprinting up the stairs.

"Hey, you're here, too?" Tai Wei asked upon seeing Fang Mu.

"Yeah, I came to see my friend."

"The boy? How is he?"

"His life's not at risk, but he's still in a coma. What are you doing here?"

"I'm going to go ask the girl what happened. She's here, too, on the fifth floor. Want to come?"

After thinking about it, Fang Mu nodded and followed him up.

Deng Linyue's police protection was much tighter than Liu Jianjun's. Four cops in SWAT gear were standing guard outside her door. The room itself was very spacious and outfitted with every amenity, and she was the only occupant. It looked like an upscale two-bedroom apartment.

Also inside Fang Mu and Tai Wei found a dignified, very well-kept woman arguing with two policemen.

"Wait a few days and we'll see," she was telling them. "How can you expect Linyue to answer any questions in the condition she's in?"

The two policemen appeared to be in an awkward situation. "We understand your daughter's condition very well," said one with distinct politeness. "But she is the only person to have been in close contact with the killer. The sooner she can provide us with any helpful clues, the sooner we can crack this case."

"Well, that will just have to wait!" said the woman decisively. "My daughter must be fully rested." Then seeing Tai Wei enter the room, she snapped, "Who are you?"

The two policemen looked back and nodded. "Captain Tai."

"You're their commanding officer? Perfect," she said. "Then I'll ask you; when can those doorkeepers outside leave? Or do you take us for criminals as well?"

"For now they're going to have to stay put," said Tai Wei, looking around the empty room. "Where's your daughter?"

Deng Linyue's mother didn't answer him. Instead, a dark look covered her face. "Well then, is my husband going to have to give your department director a call?"

Tai Wei met her eyes for a moment. "I can't give you all the specifics," he said coldly, "but it is very likely that the killer is still after your daughter." He paused. "So then, how about it? Still want us to leave?"

All the color immediately drained from the woman's face. After several seconds she managed to squeeze out a few words. "In…in that case, perhaps things should continue like this for now."

A toilet was flushed in the bathroom, and then two nurses emerged and helped Deng Linyue into the room.

Her face was deathly pale and her hair was tied up in a bun. She wore a cast on her shoulder and her arm hung in a sling in front of her chest. Seeing Fang Mu, she smiled weakly and said, "It's you." Then nodding toward the woman, she continued. "This is my mom. Mom, it was these two who rescued me."

Deng Linyue's mother looked a little embarrassed. As if to make up for her disrespectful behavior from before, she forced a smile and waved for them to each have a seat.

The two nurses helped Deng Linyue to lie down and then placed the blanket over her. They raised the bed so she could talk comfortably with her visitors.

Curled up under the snow-white covers, she smiled at Fang Mu. "Thank you for coming to visit me."

"I came to visit Liu Jianjun." As soon as the words left his mouth, Fang Mu realized they were a bit rude, so he quickly added: "And you as well."

For a moment, she looked a little embarrassed, but she quickly regained her composure. "Oh, how is he?"

"He finished surgery, and the doctors have said he's no longer in danger."

Deng Linyue's mother snorted disdainfully.

Opening his briefcase, Tai Wei took out a notebook and pen. "Ms. Deng, would you be able to tell me a little about what happened last night?"

At once Deng Linyue's face grew even paler. Her breathing sped up with anxiety and her eyes filled with tears. Obviously, she was not yet able to get past what had happened to her.

Seeing her daughter's reaction, Deng Linyue's mother quickly spoke up. "I told you not to ask her. Can't you be considerate of the victims? Come back in a few days and we'll see." She rose to her feet, her expression telling them to head for the door.

Having no other choice, Tai Wei placed his pen and pad back in his briefcase. "All right then, make sure to rest up," he said to Den Linyue. He turned to her mother as he stood up. "We'll be back in a few days."

Fang Mu was about to follow him to the door when Deng Linyue called him back.

"Fang Mu," she said, doing her best to sit upright, "what room is Liu Jianjun in? I want to go see him."

Her mother cut off the idea at once. "I won't allow it! How can you go see him in the state you're in?"

Tai Wei gave the mother a dark look, and then turned and strode out of the room.

Helpless, Fang Mu gave Deng Linyue a little wave and then quickly followed Tai Wei out. As soon as they left, they could hear Deng Linyue and her mother arguing quietly.

"Christ!" said Tai Wei, lighting a cigarette. Ignoring the "No Smoking" sign in the hallway, he took several deep drags and then said, "That woman is too goddamn difficult!"

Not knowing whether he was talking about Deng Linyue or her mother, Fang Mu vaguely tried to calm him down, saying "Well, she is in a delicate situation."

"The whole thing's a mess," continued Tai Wei. "The father's some senior cadre, and so far he hasn't been willing to cooperate with us in the least." He tossed his cigarette away. "These are our two witnesses. One's in a coma, the other won't talk. How the hell are we supposed to continue the investigation?"

He waved to a nearby policeman: "You! Go ask the doctors when the boy is going to wake up."

The policeman immediately nodded and then sprinted downstairs.

For a few moments Tai Wei just stood there, hands on his hips, nearly panting with rage. Suddenly he said: "So what do you think is going to happen next?"

Fang Mu was caught off-guard. "What? What do you mean happen next?"

"What's the killer's next move going to be?" asked Tai Wei impatiently. "Will he look for another opportunity to finish off the girl? Or if he chooses someone else for the sixth murder, who's he going to copy this time?"

"How should I know?" replied Fang Mu angrily.

But Tai Wei had a point. What was the killer going to do next?

This time the killer had failed to complete his crime, and had also not left any clues behind at the scene. It brought up many questions: How were they supposed to prevent the next murder? What kind of victim was he going to choose? Deng Linyue or someone else instead? Everything was unknown.

It was as if an empty white space had suddenly appeared on the test paper in the middle of an exam. What were the next questions going to be? No one knew.

"Oh, it's you?"

"Yeah. Were you on the phone? I don't want to disturb you."

"It's no problem. I just finished."

"You asked me to come by. Is something up?"

There was a laugh. "It's nothing important. You just haven't been here in a while. I want to see how you were doing."

"Oh, I'm doing fine. Your complexion is looking a little off. Are you sick?"

"Oh, it's nothing. Just a little cold."

"You have a temperature?"

"No. Really, it's nothing."

"Should I go with you to the doctor?"

"No, no, no. Now back to my question. How are you?"

"I'm good."

"Still scared of roll call?"

"I don't think I am. I really have to thank you. I feel like I'm just about over it completely."

"Really? Are you certain about that?"

A few days later Liu Jianjun finally began to speak. Haltingly, he did his best to tell the police what happened that night. According to him, he had planned to tell Deng Linyue he loved her in the gymnasium after the game. He had borrowed the key from the stadium caretaker at lunch the day before, and had also asked him all about operating the broadcast booth's spotlight and microphone. Then during the game, he told Deng Linyue to wait for him on the basketball court after everyone had left. Everything went as planned, but just as he reached the most critical part of his romantic display, someone suddenly attacked him from behind and knocked him out. He had no idea about anything after that.

Eventually, Deng Linyue was also able to calmly recall what happened to her that night, and she described it for the police in detail. But because of the darkness and her extreme terror at the time, she could only attest that the killer was a man standing at least 5'7".

Fang Mu and Tai Wei had also seen the killer that night, and in fact Tai Wei had even chased him, but because of the darkness and their distance away, the attacker hadn't made a distinct impression on either of them.

There was something else the police were interested in, too: How had the killer known that Deng Linyue would be in the gymnasium by herself?

He had specifically removed a screw from the locker she was using that night, changing the 9 to a 6. This showed that he had already made Deng Linyue his target, and his actions made it clear that he knew she would be using locker nine and would be alone in the arena after the game. In which case, he had to be among those privy to this information.

This thought encouraged the police to no end, because it meant the scope of their investigation could be drastically decreased.

But after looking into it, they found themselves disappointed again.

Liu Jianjun said that he hadn't told anyone about his plans for that night. This meant that there were only two times when someone else could have overheard what was going on. First, while Liu Jianjun was borrowing the key from the arena caretaker and asking him how to use the equipment. Or second, when he asked Deng Linyue to wait for him after the game. But according to Liu Jianjun, no one else had been around while he spoke to the caretaker. As for the caretaker himself, a police investigation confirmed that he had nothing to do with the crime. Therefore, this first possibility was eliminated.

As for the second possibility, police closely investigated the cheerleaders and fans that had been near Deng Linyue at the time, and confirmed that none of them had been involved.

The investigation into the locker number also similarly ground to a halt. According to the other cheerleaders and their teacher supervisor, when they received their locker room keys in the gymnasium corridor, they were surrounded on all sides by a throng of fans streaming into the arena, so it would be impossible to determine who might have heard what locker number Deng Linyue had received.

In other words, the unfortunate events from that night did not help the police make any substantial headway toward cracking the case.

What was most preoccupying Tai Wei, however, were a pair of the numbers: six or seven? Which one would be next?

The way Fang Mu saw it, the killer was an exceptionally cruel individual dead-set on carrying out his plan. He would not give up easily, so the next victim would likely still be number six. As for whether he would try again for Deng Linyue or choose someone else, at this point it was impossible to say. This was why Fang Mu and the police both felt that they should maintain tight security over the girl while continuing to monitor all areas on campus relating to the number six.

Fang Mu went to visit Liu Jianjun several more times, his motive having less to do with their friendship than his own guilt.

Liu Jianjun had suffered a depressed skull fracture, which had caused serious brain bleeding. Although he was no longer in critical danger, some of the effects would be permanent. On several occasions, when Fang Mu had watched him drink rice porridge from a bowl, Liu Jianjun's head and hands would begin to violently shake and this often spread to his entire face and body. Seeing this, Fang Mu felt the strong impulse to throw himself before Liu Jianjun and ask for his forgiveness. But he never did. Instead he would just quietly leave the ward, hide himself in the bathroom and smoke one cigarette after another.

Zou Tuanjie secretly told Fang Mu that Deng Linyue had only visited once, after which she never returned. But as soon as Liu Jianjun was first able to walk, he had struggled up to the fifth floor to go see her. At the time, Deng Linyue's relatives had blocked him from going inside, claiming she was asleep.

So Liu Jianjun had just stood there, tears streaming down his face as he yelled incoherently at the closed door. "I'm sorry! I'm sorry! I'm sorry!"

To Fang Mu, this insight felt like a knife to the heart.

The Jiangbin City University school authorities also visited Liu Jianjun several times. After determining the extent of his injury, they recommended that he take a year off from school to get better. Liu Jianjun's parents were extremely grateful to them. However, their son's graduate advisor told them in private that in this matter the school bore a clear responsibility, and that they should sue for just compensation. But his parents, both of whom came from working class backgrounds, would not go along with this. The way they saw it, their son had nearly been disabled from the attack, so for the school to offer him a year off was already an enormous kindness. How could they repay that with a lawsuit? Hearing this, all Liu Jianjun's advisor could do was shake his head and sigh.

Amazingly, only two weeks later Deng Linyue was back on campus.

Even though she had been the killer's main target, her injuries were much lighter than Liu Jianjun's. Thanks to the cotton jacket she had been wearing the night of the crime, her shoulder blade had suffered only a minor break. Add to this the superb care and proper nutrition she had received in the hospital, she was able to quickly return to school.

When Du Yu passed this information on to Fang Mu, he didn't pay much attention to it; he just thought it was strange that Deng Linyue hadn't returned to her hometown. When Tai Wei heard the news, he put it another way: since it was highly likely that the killer would make Deng Linyue his next target, the safest thing for her would be to return home for the time being.

Then something far more surprising happened. That afternoon, Deng Linyue unexpectedly gave him a call.

"Hello, is this Fang Mu? It's Deng Linyue."

"Oh, how are you?" he asked her.

"I'm fine. So it's like this: I want to treat you to dinner. Are you free?"

"Treat me to dinner?" The phone call surprised him, and the invitation shocked him. "Why?"

"To thank you. If it weren't for you, I probably wouldn't be here."

"You don't have to do that. It was just good timing, that's all."

"Oh no, I won't let you decline. I'm treating you and that's that! Wait for me outside the school gates at five o'clock tonight." Saying this, she hung up.

Fang Mu sighed and hung up the phone. When he turned around, he saw that Du Yu, nosy as ever, had been listening in. "What should I do?"

Without a shred of embarrassment at having eavesdropped on his friend's conversation, Du Yu grinned and said, "You go of course. What else needs to be said?"

Fang Mu shook his head. "I don't want to go. It seems...too awkward."

"Ah, stop being such an old lady and go. You want me to lend you some cash?" Du Yu reached for his wallet.

Fang Mu was about to make fun of him, tempted to say, You're so excited it's like she invited you, when his spirits suddenly fell. "If you're still thinking the same thing as before, then I'm not going to go."

Du Yu abruptly stopped what he was doing. The smile disappeared from his face. "What are you trying to say? That since Liu Jianjun is still lying in the hospital I'm trying to get you to take advantage of the situation? Don't forget," he said, looking Fang Mu in the eye, "that when a girl invites you out you need to go. It's a matter of etiquette."

Fang Mu thought about it and realized his friend was right. It was just one meal; refusing would seem a little narrow-minded. "All right, I'll go."

At 5 p.m. Fang Mu approached the school gates as planned. From far away he could already see Deng Linyue's tall, slender frame.

"Sorry I'm late," he said when he reached her.

"You're not," she said. "I just got here early. I was worried you wouldn't come."

He just smiled in reply.

"I also realized I don't know what you like to eat. Where should we go?"

"Wherever. I like everything." He pointed at the line of small restaurants outside the school gate. "Why don't we grab something at one of these places. We don't need to do anything too expensive."

"No way, not after you saved my life." She smiled and tilted her head. "Let's go downtown and find something a little nicer."

After they hailed a cab, Deng Linyue told him she was taking him to the restaurant at the Shangri-La. Fang Mu nearly jumped out of his seat in surprise – that was a five-star hotel. At a place like that, dinner for two would cost at least a thousand renminbi, so he firmly declined.

Deng Linyue didn't argue. Laughing, she said, "Then we won't go. I once ate a meal there that cost over 3,000 renminbi and not one dish was any good."

In the end, the two of them decided on a Korean restaurant called Papa's.

The restaurant was mostly filled with young couples. The warm tones, dim lighting, and sultry-voiced singer expressing her emotions onstage all gave the place an air of romance.

The waiter enthusiastically recommended the "Sweetheart Meal" to Fang Mu and Deng Linyue, but Fang Mu immediately declined and ordered the barbecue meal instead.

Du Yu was continually mentioning this place to Fang Mu, but until then Fang Mu had never been. First of all, he had no girlfriend, so for him to go and spend that kind of money seemed a little stupid. And second of all, he had always thought that Korean food was only good for cold noodles and kimchi and not much else. When the waiter brought the food over, however, Fang Mu discovered that not only was it beautifully prepared, it smelled unexpectedly delicious as well.

He was not a talkative person, so he just buried his face in his food and ate. Deng Linyue didn't seem to care and stayed silent as well.

Eventually Fang Mu began to feel that just eating in silence as they were was a little awkward, as well as impolite, so for the first time he looked up at Deng Linyue. Just then she was spooning soup into her mouth. Her arm movements still looked a little stiff.

"Your injury..." he said, "how is it?"

She did not immediately answer him. After putting down her spoon, she laughed brightly and said, "I thought you were planning on ignoring me the whole meal."

He was a little embarrassed. "Of course not. It's just that I'm not much of a talker."

She laughed again. "Oh, I figured that out a long time ago." Realizing that she was talking about that time in the dining hall, he was even more embarrassed.

Seeing his discomfort, Deng Linyue quickly changed topics. "My injury is essentially fine," she said, rotating her arm slightly. "It just hurts a little sometimes. But I don't think it's a big deal."

"Why didn't you go back home to get better? I'm sure it's a lot nicer there. Safer, too."

"My family was saying the same thing, but I didn't want to go. Oh, that's right." She leaned forward slightly. "Last time that policeman said that the killer might try to attack me again. Is that true?"

After thinking about this for a moment, he decided not to tell her the real situation to avoid scaring her unnecessarily. "The guy's just a lunatic. And he's not necessarily going to come after you again. You don't need to worry."

"Gosh, I don't know what's been going on with our school this year; so much bad stuff has happened." She sucked on her straw. Suddenly, her expression grew mysterious. "So, master sleuth, are you helping the police investigate the case?"

Fang Mu was taken aback. "Not at all. I hardly have that kind of talent."

"Humph, you don't have to hide the truth from me. At the last assembly I heard the provost commend you." A girlish pout came to her lips. "Besides, if you're not helping the police solve the case, how come you were with a policeman the night you saved me?"

"I already told you, it was just a coincidence."

"Liar. I've heard what the kids at the law school say. Out of everyone in the criminology department, your grades are the best. Oh, I get it." Her eyes went wide and her voice dropped to a whisper. "Do you need to keep it a secret? I also heard from some classmates that you're an undercover agent sent by the PSB to infiltrate our school. Is that true? Like Stephen Chow in Fight Back to School?"

Fang Mu didn't know whether to laugh or cry. It was hard enough for the average guy to deal with an immature girl like this, let alone someone like him, who had barely any experience with the female sex.

"I'm not some undercover agent. I'm an average student. I just happen to be…quite interested in a few aspects of criminology."

"Oh, in that case you admit that you've helped the police solve cases?" Her tone grew excited. "Can you tell me about it? I've loved reading detective novels since I was little."

He felt a little uncomfortable. He didn't really want to discuss this stuff with her.

"Forget it; it's all really scary. It's not appropriate for a girl to hear."

"Don't patronize me. I've got strong nerves," she told him with a steady look.

He had no other choice. "Fine."

Over the next hour, Fang Mu told her about Ma Kai, the "vampire case." At first he deliberately underplayed his role in the investigation, but as he watched Deng Linyue rest her chin on her palms and stare fixedly at him, every now and then exclaiming "Oh no!" or "My God!" He felt an unexpected faint sense of pride and a desire to show off. By the end, especially when he was describing his one-on-one conversation with Ma Kai, during which he had nearly been killed, Deng Linyue had her hand over her mouth in concern for him. Her brows were knit over her worried expression, and he couldn't help but feel a little conceited.

When the story was over, she placed a hand over her heart and stared at him with disbelief. "You're so brave. My God, I never would have thought I'd have a friend like this."

He just laughed. Turning his head, he caught a glimpse of his self-satisfied face in the window beside him, which immediately embarrassed him.

What am I doing?

To hide his discomfort, Fang Mu called for the check. It was obvious that Deng Linyue was reluctant to leave, but she didn't argue.

As they left the warm and cozy restaurant, the air outside felt especially cold. He was about to hail a cab when she stopped him. "Will you take a walk with me? I'm a little full after that meal."

After thinking about it, he agreed.

Side by side, the two of them strolled slowly down the sidewalk. Feeling a little ashamed of his arrogant behavior at the restaurant, the normally laconic Fang Mu was even quieter than usual. Deng Linyue also seemed to be thinking about something and didn't say a word either. The silence continued for a while, both of them quiet, just walking along.

The streetlights lengthened and shortened their shadows, and now and then they would blend together, as if they were embracing.

As local Bus 25 rumbled past, Fang Mu turned and watched it until it disappeared around the corner.

After they had walked for some time, Deng Linyue suddenly asked, "How is Liu Jianjun?"

"I went to see him a few days ago. The situation's not that good; some of the damage is going to be permanent." He turned to looked at her. "You…why didn't…?" As he was still considering the best way to put it, Deng Linyue had already grasped what he was going to say.

"I know that all of you probably think I'm heartless," she said slowly. "Honestly, I've really wanted to go see him, but my mom won't let me. She feels that if he hadn't asked me to wait for him in the gymnasium, I never would have gotten hurt. The one time I did sneak over there, his parents were both very cold, as if they thought I was the reason this happened to him. I didn't think this was fair at all, but I didn't get angry at them. After all, they've suffered enough already."

"Do you love him?"

She laughed softly and shrugged. "I don't know. As you're probably aware, he's been pursuing me for a long time, since before you and I were even introduced. To be honest, I do really like him. Whether it's his education, his looks, or how he treats me, I have nothing to complain about. We come from very different backgrounds, but that's not something I care about. And all my friends are always saying we should be together. But I never had that special feeling for him, the one that would let me count on him completely, would let me completely relax. That night I was almost there, but…" She shook her head and smiled bitterly.

Fang Mu was silent. He didn't know whether to console her or feel sympathy for Liu Jianjun.

"Let's talk about you," she said, regaining her previous cheer. She tilted her head toward him. "So, do you have a girlfriend? I don't think I've ever seen you with a girl."

"Me? No, I don't have one."

She laughed. "So then what is it? Are you too involved fighting criminals to have time for one?" She skipped ahead to face him and began walking backwards so she could see his face. "Or are your tastes too unique?" Blushing, she gave him a mischievous wink.

Fang Mu's face turned bright red. "That was for an investigation... You wouldn't understand if I told you...in any case..."

Seeing that he was at a loss for words seemed to delight Deng Linyue, and she laughed happily.

A small fireworks stand sat under one of the streetlights ahead of them. The owner was walking back and forth, lighting one sparkler after another and periodically waving them at the passersby. Very few people were buying, however, and in the dark street the burning sparklers looked unusually lonely.

"Wow, this long until Spring Festival and they're already selling fireworks?" said Deng Linyue. "Come on, let's go take a look." Full of enthusiasm, she ran ahead.

Fang Mu sighed, lit a cigarette, and inhaled deeply.

When she waved for him to join her, he held up his cigarette, indicating that it wasn't safe, and he'd be there when he was done.

After saying something to the stand owner, Deng Linyue handed him several bills. Beaming with joy, the man placed the cash in his pocket, handed her a big box of fireworks, and then started up his pedi-cab attached to the front of the stand and drove off.

The box in her hands, Deng Linyue walked back toward Fang Mu, a big smile on her face.

"How come you bought so many?"

She laughed. "I've loved this stuff since I was a little kid. The owner said that if we didn't buy him out he couldn't return home, so I figured I might as well get them all."

"The problem is, where are you going to set them off?" He looked at the box she'd set down. There had to be at least 50 fireworks inside.

"We'll do it right here." She held out her hand. "Can I borrow your lighter?"

"Are you crazy? If the cops see you shooting fireworks in the middle of the street they'll give you a huge fine."

She giggled. "When they see I'm with the master sleuth, they'll let us off, won't they?"

Having no other choice, Fang Mu took a look around. He recalled that there was an elementary school ahead.

"Let's head that way," he said, pointing in the direction of the school. He tossed away his cigarette, bent over and picked up the box of fireworks. As they walked along the street, Deng Linyue trotted behind him, a look of endless excitement on her face.

He smiled at her.

Just like a little kid.

When they reached the empty school playground, Deng Linyue impatiently lit one of the sparklers with Fang Mu's lighter. Holding it as it crackled to life, she jumped and danced, swinging her arm in a small circle while the sparkler glittered in the darkness.

Standing to the side, Fang Mu smoked and looked worriedly into the fireworks box. How long would it take for the whole box?

"Let's do one together." Seeing that he was just standing there, she warmly invited him to join in.

He wasn't interested, but to spare her feelings, he lit a sparkler and swung it around.

In the flickering light, his mind began to wander. The girl silhouetted before him looked just like someone from the deepest part of his memory.

Sadness suddenly welled up inside him.

Noticing that he was staring at her, Deng Linyue blushed slightly and walked over to him.

"Are you okay?" she asked softly.

"I'm fine." He ducked his head and lit another cigarette.

Looking at the sparkler in her hand steadily burning away, Deng Linyue said thoughtfully, "The first time I saw you I felt you were someone with a story. But I also knew you were the kind of person who doesn't like to open up about himself to other people. That's why getting to talk with you this much tonight has made me so happy; because I…I really want to understand you."

Her gaze dropped as her voice grew slowly softer. "Do you remember how I said that Liu Jianjun never made me feel like I could relax completely, like I could completely rely on him?" She paused for several seconds, and then, with what seemed a great deal of determination, looked up. "That night, lying against your chest, I really felt that way."

Fang Mu said nothing. His hands began to tremble.

Thinking back on what happened, Deng Linyue spoke as if she were talking only to herself. "At the time I was so afraid. Of course, I'd been scared before, like when I saw a cockroach or had a bad dream, but that night was different. That was the kind of fear that makes you feel sick from the inside. My mind kept saying the same thing over and over: 'I'm going to die, I'm going to die.' It felt like I was the only person left on Earth; that there was no one who could save me. But then you appeared, at that very moment you appeared. Leaning against your chest, I could feel your breath, your heartbeat. I knew that I had been rescued, that I was safe. No one could hurt me, because you were by my side."

Fang Mu looked down. Although Deng Linyue didn't see it, a huge teardrop rolled down his face.

Chen Xi, I loved you more than anything. And yet I was too late.

Deng Linyue slowly leaned against him, resting her head on his shoulder.

"You said that man might try to get me again. If he does," she said, looking up at him, "will you protect me?"

Will you protect me?

She was standing with her back to him in the market; their shadows entwined under the streetlight; her head on his shoulder at the bus stop; soft sounds in the night... Are you still awake? Chen Xi was dressed in white; her long hair fluttering; her face serene in the crime scene photograph...

I will protect you...

At last Fang Mu began to sob. Turning, he saw Deng Linyue, her eyes full of tenderness.

These past few years, I've been so tired.

Unable to help himself, he reached his arms around her and her warm, soft body leaned against his chest. Seconds later a pair of warm, supple lips pressed against his own.

20 CAT AND MOUSE (I)

After accompanying Deng Linyue back to her dorm, Fang Mu suddenly felt the need to take a walk alone.

Once he reached the outdoor stadium, he began strolling around the track. For a long time his mind was totally empty. Only when the cold made him start to shiver did he finally come back to reality.

I kissed a girl today?

The details of the kiss were blurry, the feel of her lips, their twining tongues. It was not the unforgettable experience he imagined his first kiss would be. When he had struggled out of the vortex of his memory and seen Deng Linyue pressed sweetly against his chest, his first thought had been, My God, what have I done?

When he had dropped Deng Linyue off at the women's dormitory moments ago, she had looked at him as if she didn't want him to leave, but Fang Mu knew he couldn't stay another second.

Why did I do this?

Was it because of loneliness? Or something else?

When did I get so weak?

At last he was too tired to walk any farther. Leaning against the flagpole at the north end of the stadium, he exhaustedly closed his eyes.

The ice-cold flagpole quickly sent a chill through his body, the sensation like a snake wriggling inside him. Although terribly uncomfortable, he still didn't want to move. He lit a cigarette, inhaled deeply, and then slowly exhaled while looking up at the starlit sky.

The cigarette smoke mixed with his vaporous breath. It obscured the stars, and also obscured the people watching down on him from above.

By the time Fang Mu got back to the dorm it was almost curfew. Du Yu was playing Counter-Strike. When he heard Fang Mu come in he quickly turned around and said, "You're back?"

Afraid he would ask for details, Fang Mu just nodded, and then grabbed his washbasin and headed for the bathroom.

The bathroom light was broken again. In the darkness, Fang Mu filled the basin with cold water and dunked his head. He shivered, but his mind felt clear and light.

Suddenly, something furry brushed quickly past the back of his leg. He was so startled that he swallowed a mouthful of water. He immediately looked up, wiped the water off his face and looked around. A small black and yellow cat was watching him from the bathroom doorway.

Fang Mu knew it was Tom, Meng Fanzhe's cat.

Feeling both curious and amused, Fang Mu cupped his hands full of water and pretended he was about to splash the pet. But for some reason, the cat wasn't scared at all. He just tilted his head and kept looking at Fang Mu.

Fang Mu opened his hands, and as he did a thin stream of water spilled out.

Fast as lightning, Tom leapt away. Instead the water spilled on the foot of someone who had just entered the bathroom.

"Oh no, I'm sorry," said Fang Mu quickly. Looking up, he saw it was Meng Fanzhe. "Oh, it's you. My bad."

Meng Fanzhe smiled to show he didn't care.

Tom had fled the bathroom, but he didn't go far. He sat in the corridor and watched them through the doorway.

As Meng Fanzhe looked at Tom, his eyes filled with affection. "He's really cute, isn't he?" he mumbled to himself dreamily.

"He sure is," said Fang Mu. Suddenly his humor returned, and he added, "Jerry."

Meng Fanzhe turned and looked at him. "Jerry?" He laughed and then looked down, as if thinking something over. "Jerry...Jerry..."

Without another word, Meng Fanzhe abruptly turned and walked out the doorway. Seeing this, Tom raised his tail and silently followed his owner.

Feeling a little embarrassed at having made fun of the guy, Fang Mu grabbed his bar of scented soap and looked off toward where Meng Fanzhe had disappeared.

When Meng Fanzhe had looked at Tom, love hadn't been the only thing in his eyes.

There had also been a trace of pity.

When Fang Mu returned to his room, Du Yu was still at his computer, tirelessly waging war. "Hey, so how was it?" he asked without turning his head.

"How was what?"

"Your romantic date."

"What's there to say? We just ate dinner." Suddenly feeling a little guilty, Fang Mu quickly tore off his clothes and burrowed under the bed covers. He closed his eyes and pretended to go to sleep.

After a while he heard Du Yu finally turn off his computer and climb into bed. A few minutes later he was snoring away.

Fang Mu wasn't able to sleep at all. With his eyes tightly shut, he did his best to eliminate two words from his mind.

Liu Jianjun.

He didn't dare think of the name.

At 6:30 the next morning, Fang Mu was awakened by a beeping from his phone. Hazily opening his eyes, he saw that it was a text message.

"Let's get breakfast together."

The number was unfamiliar. He thought for a second and then checked his phone's call record. It was Deng Linyue's cell number.

His sleepiness disappeared at once. Sitting on his bed, he mulled it over in his head. At last he decided not to go.

A half-hour later Du Yu woke up. Pretending to have just awakened himself, Fang Mu accompanied him to the bathroom and washed up, and then the two of them left for the dining hall.

The moment they walked out of the front door of their building, they saw Deng Linyue waiting outside, her face red from the cold. She had her hands in her pockets, and was hopping up and down to stay warm.

Seeing Fang Mu, she didn't complain; just smiled and said, "You finally came down."

Du Yu's surprise was obvious, but seeing the bright flush on Fang Mu's face, he tactfully said, "I'll catch up with you later."

Once Du Yu had walked away, Deng Linyue said quietly, "How come you're so late? Didn't you get my text?" She looked closer at his eyes. "Or didn't you hear it?"

"Oh, I…didn't hear it."

"Did you get to sleep too late?" She blushed slightly. "Or maybe you didn't sleep at all!" She giggled.

He avoided her eyes. "Let's…just go get something to eat."

As if he had something to hide, Fang Mu took Deng Linyue to a table in the far corner of the cafeteria. His precautions were hardly necessary, however, as lots of people familiar with them kept casting astonished glances in their direction – especially members of the basketball team. They craned their necks to get a better look at the pair tucked away at the corner table.

While Fang Mu was on pins and needles as the team members began whispering among themselves, Deng Linyue didn't seem to care at all. Whenever she noticed anyone looking at them curiously, she just stared right back until the other person turned away.

After what seemed like forever, Fang Mu and Deng Linyue finally finished eating breakfast. He then bid her a brief goodbye and hurried toward the door. But before he had even gotten outside, he heard Deng Linyue's voice calling for him to wait.

She walked quickly over to him, her face slightly red from the hurry, giving him a scowl. "Fang Mu, are you embarrassed to be with me?" Her tone was even more hostile than her eyes.

"…No."

"Then why are you treating me this way?"

"…I…"

"Do you feel like you're betraying Liu Jianjun?" Her voice grew softer now. "I already told you, Liu Jianjun and I were never a couple. Just because he was pursuing me and then got injured doesn't mean I can't love the person I choose."

He could say nothing.

She waited a moment, and then seeing he wasn't going to say anything, she sighed and continued more softly. "If you don't like me, please tell me directly." She paused. "If you think that because we kissed you're now responsible for me, then you need to forget that. We're all adults, so there's no reason to believe anything so ridiculous." She glanced at her watch. "Don't you have class?"

"Yeah."

"Then you'd better hurry. You don't want to be late."

He hesitated for a moment. Realizing that just turning and leaving would be a bit cruel, he said, "You don't need to worry about us. I'll give you a call a little later today."

She looked a little happier at this, the smile coming back to her eyes. She asked quietly, "Can we see each other tonight?"

"If I'm not busy, then yeah, I think so."

"Okay." She smiled. "Now get going, and look after yourself."

A few moments later, Fang Mu was panting as he ran up to the second floor. Zou Tuanjie was standing in the hallway near a classroom, cell phone in hand. Seeing Fang Mu, he abruptly asked, "Have you seen Meng Fanzhe?"

Fang Mu shook his head. "No, why?"

"The guy's already missed a ton of classes, including a bunch where the professor took attendance." Zou Tuanjie glanced back into the classroom. "Just now the professor let slip that if Meng Fanzhe misses another class, the professor won't let him defend his thesis when it's time to graduate."

"Are you calling him?"

"I just did," said Zou Tuanjie, waving the phone helplessly. "He didn't pick up."

Fang Mu looked at his watch. Class was about to begin. With no time to say anything else to Zou Tuanjie, he immediately turned and sprinted to his classroom down the hallway. As he ran, he wondered what was going on. Meng Fanzhe was no longer afraid of roll call, so why wasn't he going to class?

It was night in the private study room.

Fang Mu absentmindedly flipped through the book in front of him. Deng Linyue sat quietly beside him, translating an article from English. She was very quick, stopping only now and then to check the dictionary or softly read a sentence aloud.

Fang Mu knew he wasn't absorbing a thing. Looking up, he glanced aimlessly around the room. He abruptly turned toward the entrance to the room, watching it. No one was there.

Humph, he thought, guess that guy really did keep his word.

That afternoon Tai Wei had stopped by. At first he just made fun of Fang Mu, laughing about how he'd been "lucky in love," and that the "beautiful girl had fallen for her heroic savior." Fang Mu knew he was talking about Deng Linyue, and he wasn't surprised that this guy knew all about their recent activity. In fact, he wouldn't have been surprised if Tai Wei had been sitting one table over from them at the restaurant that night.

When Tai Wei was finished joking around, his expression turned serious, and he said that because Fang Mu and Deng Linyue were probably both being targeted by the killer, if they were going to be together, then the police would have to keep a close watch on him. The idea annoyed Fang Mu, and he told Tai Wei that if he went through with that, their relationship would take a nosedive. At first Tai Wei tried to explain why this was necessary and then attempted to play on Fang Mu's emotions. Still Fang Mu wouldn't agree, so Tai Wei had no choice but to give up. Still, he insisted that no matter how Fang Mu felt about it, the police were going to increase their protection of him, albeit according to the prerequisite of "not influencing Fang Mu and Deng Linyue's personal lives." Noticing that when Tai Wei said "personal lives" with a bit of good-natured innuendo,

Fang Mu couldn't help but laugh and lighten up a little.

As Fang Mu climbed to his feet in the study room, Deng Linyue inquisitively looked up at him. When he motioned to the pack of cigarettes in his hand she just nodded, a sliver of disapproval in her eyes.

Standing in the hallway a moment later, Fang Mu lit a cigarette and looked around. Suddenly someone popped their head out of the stairwell at the end of the hall and then disappeared. Even though it had only been for a split second, Fang Mu immediately recognized the man as one of the officers under Tai Wei.

Jeez, now he's getting other people to follow me.

Shaking his head, Fang Mu leaned against the wall and smoked in silence. After a while, he looked back down at the entrance to the stairwell. It was black as a cave. Although there wasn't a sound coming from it, he was sure the cop was still there. After a moment of thinking, an idea occurred to him. He looked at his watch; it was 7:26 p.m. Tenth period was about to end.

One of the classrooms nearby was lit up. He could faintly hear the sounds of a lecture underway inside.

Making up his mind, he went back into the study room and walked quickly over to Deng Linyue.

"Get your things," he said quietly.

She gave him a puzzled look.

"The police are following us," he said, smiling mysteriously. "Let's play a little joke on them."

Deng Linyue nodded excitedly. She hurriedly threw her things into her book bag, pulled on her jacket and then in a voice both nervous and eager, whispered to him, "What should we do?"

Fang Mu told her she should first sit back down, put her phone on vibration and keep cool. She nodded and did as he said.

A few minutes later, the bell rang to signal the end of class. Fang Mu silently counted to ten and then took Deng Linyue's arm. "Let's go."

The two of them walked quickly out of the study. The instant they were through the door, he glanced down to the end of the hall. Sure enough, the cop was standing outside the stairwell.

Fang Mu led Deng Linyue toward the class that had just let out. It had been held in a large classroom capable of seating nearly a hundred students. At that moment a huge crowd of them were swarming out the door and filling the hallway.

Fang Mu and Deng Linyue slipped into the throng. Just as they were passing by the classroom, they quickly walked inside.

As he led Deng Linyue to the back of the room, Fang Mu dialed her number on his cell phone.

When they reached the back of the room, Fang Mu cracked open the rear door and carefully glanced out into the hall where he could see the exiting students. As expected, the cop was caught up in the crowd of students, craning his neck and looking all around.

Deng Linyue nudged Fang Mu and held up her vibrating cell phone. "What should I do?" she whispered.

"Answer it and then don't hang up." He turned and saw that the crowd and policeman were heading toward the rear door of the building.

He looked back at Deng Linyue. "Go. Together we're too big of a target, so we need to split up. You head that way." He pointed in the direction opposite where the policeman was going. "Go to the first floor and then wait for my instructions."

"Okay." Shaking from excitement, she gripped her phone in one hand and headed down the hall.

Fang Mu then turned and walked quickly toward the policeman, who was constantly scanning the area ahead, completely unaware that his target was actually behind him. Carefully concealing himself behind a group of students, Fang Mu made sure to stay roughly 15 feet behind the cop at all times.

As he walked, the man took out his cell phone and made a call.

Fang Mu carefully drew closer and did his best to listen in.

"…I don't see them…" the cop said, unaware of Fang Mu. "What floor are you on…the sixth? I'll head to the back door… Exactly, you take the front… Fast as you can."

Just as he had thought. Fang Mu smiled, slowed down and then put the phone to his ear. "Where are you now?"

"First floor. You?" Deng Linyue was panting, but she still sounded nervous and excited over the phone.

"Get to the front door as fast as you can. You need to be out of the building before the police get here."

"Okay, and after that?"

Fang Mu thought for a moment and then said, "Head to the old bunker; we'll rendezvous there. Don't hang up."

By the time Fang Mu had followed the policeman down to the first floor, very few students were going in and out of the back door. The cop ran to the doorway, looked all around, and then headed back inside and sprinted to the reception office. He asked the woman on duty several questions, but she just shook her head in confusion. The cop then hustled back to the door and stood beside the entrance, staring closely at every student who passed.

Fang Mu hid in a corner, thought for a moment, and then whispered into the phone, "I'm going to hang up for now. I'll call you soon."

"Okay, be careful." Deng Linyue giggled.

Fang Mu dialed another number. A few seconds later, a frosty female voice sounded over the receiver: "Welcome to the Jiangbin City University telephone directory. Please dial the extension you wish to call now. For the operator, press zero."

Fang Mu pressed zero. A few seconds later, another woman's voice said:

"Hello, who would you like to reach?"

"What's the extension for the reception room at the rear of the Education Building?"

"Two-five-eight-three."

Fang Mu dialed again. "Hi, is this the reception room? I'm from the special investigation team. I believe one of our officers is by your office... Yes, that's the one... Can you please give him the phone?" He watched as the woman on duty ran out of the reception room and waved at the policeman.

"Officer, there's a call for you," she said.

The policeman looked confused, but he still hurried after the woman.

Laughing to himself, Fang Mu hung up the phone and ran toward the door. After ducking under the reception room window, he slipped out of the building.

The old bunker was located in the northeast corner of Jiangbin City University. It had been accidental discovered by construction workers while they were expanding the campus. Experts were later hired to investigate the site, and they determined that it was a former Kuomintang underground prison. The place was divided into two floors made entirely from concrete. There were eight large prison cells on the top floor as well as an above ground entrance. On the bottom floor there were two huge cement pools. According to the experts, it had been used as a water dungeon.

Because it was a historical site, the school did not disturb it, and after the matter was discussed with city authorities, it was decided that the bunker would be left in its original state. Since neither side could agree who should be responsible for repairing the site, the matter was left unresolved. Now the bunker was mainly used to store old desks and chairs.

Panting, Fang Mu sprinted to the bunker. When he reached it he didn't see Deng Linyue anywhere. His heart fell, and he quickly dialed her number.

She picked up almost immediately. She was also breathing hard, and he could hear wind blowing in the background from her side of the phone.

"You got away?" she said.

"Yeah. Where are you?"

"I'm almost at the bunker. Are you already there?"

"Yeah," he said. "Why'd it take you so long to get here?"

She laughed. "Oh, I kept feeling like someone was following me, so I went through the supermarket and then the dining hall, and then I made two loops around the dormitories. I had to lose my tail! ...Okay, I see you now. I'm hanging up."

Fang Mu thought the image of Deng Linyue "losing her tail" was prettily amusing. As he put away his phone, he saw her skipping toward him.

In an instant she hopped right in front of him. Her cheeks were rosy and her eyes shined amid the evening darkness.

"How exciting!" she said. "Just like an action movie."

Although she looked thrilled, Fang Mu actually felt a little nervous. He looked around. No one was around. Not far behind them stood the top of the old bunker. The structure was dark and quiet. It looked like some enormous, crouching beast that was ready to pounce at a moment's notice.

A cold breeze blew past. He couldn't help but shiver.

"Let's go. This place is too isolated."

"What? Are you scared?" She winked mischievously.

"You're not?"

"Nope, not as long as you're with me." Her voice was firm and yet warm.

He didn't say anything. His enthusiasm for risk-taking had passed and now he didn't know what to do with her.

Suddenly his phone rang. Answering it, he heard Tai Wei's worried voice sound in his ear.

"Fang Mu, where are you?"

Fang Mu's mouth fell open in surprise. "At school."

"What's your location? Is Deng Linyue with you?"

"Yeah, she is. Don't worry, we're both safe."

"Okay, but where exactly? I'll have someone come get you."

"Don't bother. I'll call you soon." Afraid that Tai Wei would yell at him, Fang Mu quickly hung up.

"Come on, we should head back," he said, taking Deng Linyue's arm. "Otherwise Tai Wei is really gonna let me have it."

As Fang Mu walked Deng Linyue back to her dorm, she seemed to emerge from her previous state of nervous excitement. She didn't say a word the whole way.

When they reached the dorm, she stopped and looked down, as if she was waiting for him to say something.

He stood there silently for a while, feeling the awkwardness. At last he managed to say, "You...should really head up to your dorm."

She sighed quietly, lifted her head and stared at him for several seconds. Finally, she said softly, "You're not going to give me a kiss before you go?"

He immediately flushed bright red. "Right here...? It's a little crowded, isn't it?"

At first she didn't reply; just gazed off into the distance. After a long time she spoke in a hushed manner. "Fang Mu, there's something I've been wanting to ask you."

"Yeah?"

"That night we…when we kissed, you were so emotional. Crying, in fact. Can you tell me why?"

When he didn't respond, she asked, "Was there someone you…once loved and were never able to forget?"

He turned his back to her, not wanting her to see his eyes fill with tears.

"Can you tell me?" she asked gently.

After a long moment, his trembling voice finally answered. She leaned closer to hear.

"There was once a girl I really loved," he admitted, "but I never told her how I felt...and then before I could, she died…"

She made a muted gasp, shaking her head. "My God. How did she die? Was she sick?"

"No." He closed his eyes and made an effort to summon all his fortitude. "She was murdered. The killer was one of my roommates."

"What? But…why?" She couldn't suppress her astonishment.

Fang Mu could no longer reply. He couldn't even stand upright. Crouching down, he buried his face in his hands, his shoulders twitching violently as the memories caught up with him again. He felt a small hand press tightly against back, and then Deng Linyue's arms wrapped around his shoulders. Her face closed in to his and he felt her hot tears fall on his neck.

"I'm sorry," she whispered. "I'm so sorry. I shouldn't have asked you. I know there's pain in your heart. I'm sorry, I'm sorry..."

Deng Linyue held him close, as if she was trying her best to ease his shaking, and in that moment, her comfort eased into him.

She closed her eyes, absorbing his pain. He needs my protection, too, she thought, as I need his.

Fang Mu held his phone away from his temple as he slowly climbed the stairs. Tai Wei was shouting angrily on the other end of the line. Fang Mu didn't have to hold it close to his ear to hear what the cop was saying.

"...I'm telling you right now, you pull this again and I won't be so forgiving!" came Tai Wei's irate tone.

At this point Fang Mu already deeply regretted his rash behavior from before, so he understood how Tai Wei felt. If either he or Deng Linyue had been nabbed by the killer after they split up and left the Education Building, the consequences would be too awful to contemplate.

And so Fang Mu endured the tongue-lashing and repeatedly promised that it would never happen again. Once Fang Mu had said everything he could, Tai Wei abruptly hung up.

Du Yu wasn't around when Fang Mu got back to his dorm, but there was a note on his desk. It was from Du Yu, saying that he and Zhang Yao were going to an all-night movie theater and he wouldn't be back until tomorrow.

Fang Mu secretly thanked his lucky stars. If Du Yu were around to see his red eyes, he would definitely ask what was wrong. After getting yelled at by Tai Wei, Fang Mu had no desire to get tangled up in yet another person's endless questions.

Fang Mu took off his jacket and grabbed his toiletries from under his bed. He grabbed his washbasin and left the room.

While brushing his teeth in the bathroom, he heard loud cursing from the other end of the hallway. Moments later, a stainless steel food bowl and several books came flying out of one of the rooms.

With his toothbrush still in his mouth, Fang Mu walked out of the bathroom. He could see someone standing in the hallway outside of the room, swearing at whoever was inside; however, the person inside was saying nothing – just throwing one thing after another into the hallway. Clothes, books, basketball shoes, bedding – a huge pile had soon formed outside the room.

Fang Mu knew it was Meng Fanzhe's dorm room and that the guy cursing in the hallway was Wang Changbin, Meng Fanzhe's roommate. Which meant that the person throwing all the stuff out of the room had to be Meng Fanzhe.

What was going on? Fang Mu wondered. Meng Fanzhe was normally a decent, well-behaved guy. What had made him flip out like this?

If it went on much longer, Fang Mu was pretty sure it would come to blows.

He ducked back into the bathroom and after quickly spitting out his toothpaste, grabbed his toiletries and hurried over to Meng Fanzhe's dorm room.

A bunch of people were already there, watching what was going on. Wang Changbin was no longer swearing, now just standing there with his hands on his hips, angrily watching Meng Fanzhe throw item after item out of the room. At this point he looked more helpless than enraged.

Just as Fang Mu walked to the front of the crowd, Meng Fanzhe threw what seemed to be Wang Changbin's final possession out of the room and then slammed the door in Fang Mu's face.

Looking at all the stuff on the floor, Fang Mu asked Wang Changbin:

"What's going on? How did this happen?"

"That SOB is crazy!" said Wang Changbin gloomily.

Zou Tuanjie and several other guys crowded around and helped Wang Changbin pick up his stuff

"Why don't you crash in my room for the night?" Fang Mu offered to

Wang Changbin. "Du Yu's not coming back until tomorrow."

"No need," said Wang Changbin, firmly refusing. He pointed at Zou Tuanjie. "I'm staying in his room, Liu Jianjun's not around either."

Fang Mu nodded and then turned back to the door. When he tried to open it, he found it was locked.

He knocked lightly. There was no response.

He tried again, a little louder this time. "Meng Fanzhe," he said, "it's me. Why don't you open the door?"

Something shattered against the door and then fell to the ground. It sounded like a glass cup.

Fang Mu jumped back in surprise.

Now other people were getting angry. Zou Tuanjie held Fang Mu back. "Just leave him alone. He's out of control."

Unable to do anything else, Fang Mu crouched down and helped Wang Changbin organize his things.

After everyone had helped Wang Changbin move into Zou Tuanjie's room and put his stuff away, Wang Changbin took out a pack of cigarettes and handed them out. While they all smoked, someone asked him what exactly had happened.

"Man, don't even ask," he said."You know that cat Meng Fanzhe's been raising? Normally he treats it like it was his own son. But the thing is just so goddamn annoying. Not only has it shit on my bed who knows how many times, once it even pissed on one of my textbooks. The smell was so bad that when I brought the book to class the next day, everyone around me was covering their noses."

Several people laughed. Interrupting them, Zou Tuanjie said, "You guys normally get along pretty well. Why didn't you say something to him?"

"We do normally get along well, and if that's all that had happened I actually wouldn't be this mad," said Wang Changbin, pulling at his hair impatiently, "but you guys don't understand. For some reason this guy has recently changed a hell of a lot. Every day he's either sitting in the room staring into space or off missing somewhere, and he never goes to class. I've tried talking to him several times, but he just ignores me. Then late one night I woke up to go to the bathroom, and when I opened my eyes he was sitting straight up in his chair mumbling something to himself. At first I was puzzled. If he was memorizing something why didn't he turn on the light? But then when I listened closer I heard what he was saying. Can any of you guess what it was?"

Wang Changbin paused for effect and looked around the room. Seeing that everyone was staring at him with bated breath, he looked satisfied and said, "He was saying his own name! Meng Fanzhe, Meng Fanzhe, Meng Fanzhe – the same words over and over again. This scared me wide awake, and although I wondered whether he was maybe talking in his sleep, I was too scared to say anything."

"Then what happened?" someone asked.

"After he said his name a while longer, he suddenly began pulling his hair and smashing his head against the wall so hard that he cried out. By then I was scared stiff, and I didn't move an inch until he fell asleep. I stayed like that until dawn." There was a slight quiver in Wang Changbin's voice as he spoke. It was obvious that the events of that night were still frightening for him. "Living with this guy is too much. Like today, for instance. I told him how the teacher had read his name again and again and when he wasn't there had gotten really angry. Then without even saying a word, the psycho just started throwing all my stuff out into the hallway. I yelled at him, but it was like he didn't even hear."

This story unsettled everyone. When it was over, they all said a few vaguely reassuring words and then went their separate ways.

After returning to his dorm room, Fang Mu turned off his computer, lay on his bed and shut his eyes. But he was unable to sleep.

Meng Fanzhe had been chanting his name in the middle of the night like he was reciting a spell. Thinking about this, Fang Mu knew it had to be somehow related to his fear of roll call. But that fear had already disappeared – not only had Meng Fanzhe said as much, but Fang Mu had also seen him say "Here" with his own eyes. And yet his recent behavior was extremely abnormal, so what exactly was going on?

As Fang Mu understood him, Meng Fanzhe had a weak personality, and Fang Mu doubted that he could have overcome his roll call phobia all by himself. He must have undergone psychotherapy with a professional. So given the sudden change in Meng Fanzhe's behavior, Fang Mu had to wonder: Had something gone wrong with the therapy?

Fang Mu turned the matter over and over in his head but didn't get anywhere. At last he decided to find an opportunity to talk to Meng Fanzhe the next day.

That night the nightmares arrived on schedule.

The burning dorm. The dead classmates. Wu Han's distorted face before him.

Actually, you and I are the same.

When Fang Mu struggled awake, his first reaction was to grab for the knife under his pillow. As his breathing slowly calmed, he realized that his clothes were soaked with perspiration.

Sweat was dripping down his head and sticking uncomfortably to the back of his neck. With difficulty, he climbed to his feet, grabbed his towel and a bar of soap, and headed to the bathroom to wash his face.

Only one light was on in the hall, its beam very dim. Still, Fang Mu immediately noticed several dark red stains on the floor.

Crouching down, he wiped his finger across one of the stains. Its surface had already dried, but some of it still came off on his finger He rubbed his fingers together. It still felt a little wet. He brought his finger to his nose and sniffed. The smell was sickly sweet.

It was blood.

The hair on the back of his neck immediately stood up.

He looked around in a panic. The hallway was empty. There was no one in sight, only tightly shut doors.

He looked back down. Several more spots of blood had dripped onto the floor. They seemed to lead into the bathroom.

Fang Mu slowly stood up and tiptoed toward the bathroom.

Was someone hurt?

Or maybe it was merely a nosebleed?

As the pitch-black entrance to the bathroom drew closer and closer, Fang Mu's heartbeat sped up, until it seemed as if the sound was echoing off the walls of the hallway. He couldn't help but feel that if someone was in the bathroom, they would hear it beating.

At last he reached the entrance.

He looked inside.

The bathroom was as dark as a cave and smelled strongly of blood. Someone was standing by the sink tearing something apart. All Fang Mu could see was the movement of the person's head and shoulders. A wet, squishing noise was coming from his mouth. He seemed to be chewing.

Fang Mu quietly reached for the light switch and turned it on.

In an instant, the fluorescent light buzzed to life and the bathroom was bright as day. Having grown accustomed to the darkness, Fang Mu's vision blurred and he felt dizzy. He quickly grabbed for the door frame to keep from falling over.

The person at the sink was also startled, and he abruptly spun around.

It was Meng Fanzhe.

In the intense fluorescent light, the rims of Meng Fanzhe's eyes looked green and his eyeballs pure black. Their whites were nowhere to be seen.

The area around his lips was bright red and thick, red liquid dribbled from the corners of his mouth. Looking closer, Fang Mu could see that several black and yellow hairs were stuck to his lips.

He was so shocked that for several seconds he and Meng Fanzhe just stared at one another, neither of them saying a word.

At last, in a faltering voice, Fang Mu asked, "Meng Fanzhe, what are you doing?"

For an instant, he was certain he saw a murderous look pass through Meng Fanzhe's eyes, but then it disappeared and they were filled with only helplessness and despair.

"I..." He suddenly smiled, but almost at once the smile vanished, his gaze fell, the corners of his mouth drooped, and with a voice that sounded like he was on the verge of tears, he said, "I don't know..."

Fang Mu noticed that Meng Fanzhe was holding something in his hand. He focused closer on it. It was the furry, blood-soaked leg of an animal. From the looks of things, it appeared to belong to a cat.

He looked past Meng Fanzhe. The sink behind him was a horrible sight. Bloody flesh, internal organs, fur, and skin lay everywhere. Some of it still seemed to be steaming.

Walking past Meng Fanzhe, Fang Mu cautiously drew closer.

It was just as he thought. The animal whose parts were scattered in and around the sink was none other than Meng Fanzhe's cat – Tom.

Fang Mu looked around. He didn't see a knife or any other sharp object.

Meng Fanzhe had torn Tom apart by hand while the cat was still alive.

Fang Mu turned around and looked at Meng Fanzhe. He hadn't moved an inch and was still staring at the entrance, as if none of the carnage had anything to do with him at all.

Fang Mu tugged on his sleeve and then pulled the cat leg from his hand and threw it in the sink.

As if in a daze, Meng Fanzhe did nothing to stop him; in fact he made no resistance at all.

Fang Mu stood in front of Meng Fanzhe and looked into his eyes. "Fanzhe," he said slowly, "can you hear me?"

After a long time, Meng Fanzhe's eyeballs slowly rotated toward Fang Mu, and he nodded slightly.

"Can you tell me what happened?"

The corners of Meng Fanzhe's mouth moved. Then, as if he had suffered a stroke, half of his body slowly turned and he pointed at the cat in the sink.

"Tom… They all hate him…so I can't…rely on him…any longer…"

Looking into Meng Fanzhe's dull eyes, Fang Mu did his best to understand what he had just said.

"What do you mean, 'rely on him'?" He shook Meng Fanzhe's shoulders. "Come on, speak!"

Fang Mu's actions caused Meng Fanzhe's body to sway violently, and he seemed to become much more lucid.

"I don't know, I don't know!" he cried, roughly wiping his mouth. When he saw that his hand was covered in blood and cat hair, he grew so frightened that he immediately tried to rub his face clean, but all he did was smear himself with blood.

"What exactly is going on?" asked Fang Mu in a low voice. He caught Meng Fanzhe's hand and held it tightly.

Only then did Meng Fanzhe seem to realize that it was Fang Mu standing before him. "Is that you, Fang Mu?" His body went limp at once. Tears streamed from his eyes and mucus dripped from his nose. "Help me, help me, please. I don't know what I've done; it's like I was dreaming…"

Fang Mu put his hands under Meng Fanzhe's armpits for support and did his best to hold him up.

"I will, I will help you. Now tell me, what is going on?"

Meng Fanzhe's gaze went to the sink. At once his senses seemed to return. Shaking with fear, he pointed at Tom's remains. "I didn't do it, I didn't do it…it wasn't intentional…"

He leapt at Fang Mu and grabbed at his collar, his eyes full of fear and desperation. "Don't tell anyone," he entreated. "Please don't tell anyone. I'm not crazy... I didn't mean to do it. I didn't mean to. I'm not crazy…"

He pushed Fang Mu away, shot toward the sink and picked up the bloody flesh and fur. He looked all around, his mouth still moving nonstop. "Gotta take care of this now. Can't let anyone else see…gotta take care of this now, now, now!" He spun around in place, looking wildly for somewhere to put his cat's remains.

Fang Mu was so disturbed by all this that for a moment he had no idea what to do. At last he picked up the big plastic trash can from the doorway – normally used for throwing out leftover food – and signaled for Meng Fanzhe to put the remains in there.

Meng Fanzhe forced Tom's skeleton into the dirty water at the bottom of the trash can. He then ran into one of the stalls, grabbed the wastepaper bucket and dumped its contents in on top. Next he hurried to the sink, turned on the tap, and let the water wash away the bloodstains. When it wasn't rinsing fast enough, he used his bare hands to scrub the sink clean.

After the last cat hair disappeared down the drain, Meng Fanzhe grabbed a mop from behind the door and vigorously scrubbed the blood from the bathroom floor.

At a loss, Fang Mu could only watch as Meng Fanzhe rushed to clean every inch of the bathroom. A million thoughts were going through his mind at once.

At last Meng Fanzhe stopped and leaned exhaustedly against the wall, panting heavily.

Cautiously, Fang Mu asked, "What happened? Can you tell me?"

Meng Fanzhe shook his head weakly. "I don't know. But recently I've been feeling so strange. I'm constantly forgetting what I've been doing, and there are all these things in my room that I don't remember having brought there."

Fang Mu thought for a moment. "Do you want to go see a doctor?"

Meng Fanzhe shook his head repeatedly. "No, no, no, that's not necessary." Then as if thinking aloud, he said, "I will get better, yes, I will definitely get better. I don't need to rely on anyone else…"

He muttered this over and over again, as if he had no faith in himself.

Fang Mu watched him silently. He had no idea what he should say.

Suddenly Meng Fanzhe stood up straight. Forcing a smile, he looked at Fang Mu and said, "I…I'm gonna go back to my room. Will you…" he dropped his eyes, "keep this a secret for me?"

"All right. However, I still recommend that you see a doctor."

"Okay, I understand. If I think it's necessary, I'll go. See you later." Then he walked unsteadily out of the bathroom and back down the hall toward his room.

The bathroom was quiet once more. The only sounds were the gurgle of water rushing through the pipes and the hum of the fluorescent light overhead. For a long time Fang Mu just stood there, barely moving a muscle. He looked at the spotless sink, and then at the trash can. What the hell was going on with Meng Fanzhe tonight? His behavior made no sense at all, was just utterly strange.

Even stranger than that first day in class.

21 3+1+3

Early the next morning, Fang Mu knocked on Meng Fanzhe's door. There was no answer. He knocked again and again, almost 20 times, but there was still no response. He looked through the small window in the door. No lights seemed to be on inside. He didn't know whether Meng Fanzhe had already gone out or just didn't want to answer.

All that day Fang Mu could think of nothing but Meng Fanzhe. The fellow student's pale face and cavernous eyes seemed to always be hovering in front of him.

A behavioral scientist for the FBI once proposed a related theory. If an individual manifested at least two distinct traits while young, the likelihood of him committing crimes later in life would be fairly high. Among those traits were continuing to wet the bed past a certain age, starting fires, and torturing animals or smaller children. These types of behaviors were caused by weak self-control coupled with strong anti-social impulses. And, from the perspective of behavioral science, the need to torture animals often came from anxiety caused by feelings of powerlessness and loss of control in daily life.

So what was making Meng Fanzhe feel powerless and out of control?

And the other important question: What would he do next?

Meng Fanzhe had a weak personality, but he was kind and sweet-natured. Tearing a living cat apart and then eating it was not something a person like him would do. And it had been obvious to Fang Mu that last night, while Meng Fanzhe was mutilating Tom, he was in a very confused state.

What had caused Meng Fanzhe to begin acting this way?

"Tom… They all hate him…so I can't…rely on him…any longer…"

Rely on him?

If Meng Fanzhe had been relying on Tom, what had the cat been protecting him from?

Rats?

Fang Mu knew Meng Fanzhe was afraid of roll call. Perhaps he was scared of rats as well.

Keeping a cat would give him a subconscious feeling of protection and would cause his fear of rats to disappear, at least to a certain extent.

The problem was that this would make him reliant on this source of protection, and should it ever go away, not only would his fear of rats resurface, it would probably be even stronger than before.

If Fang Mu was right, then by killing his treasured Tom – whom he most likely saw as his protector – Meng Fanzhe was essentially burning all his bridges, or rather, destroying the basket in which all his eggs had been placed.

A person who could do something like that was dangerous.

Fang Mu was just as lost in thought that night while studying for class.

After being ignored by him for half the evening, Deng Linyue finally spoke. "What's on your mind?"

"Oh, nothing really." Realizing that he had been acting a little cold, he turned to her and smiled apologetically.

She didn't smile back, just looked down and continued reading. After a while, she said quietly:

"Are you thinking about a certain someone?"

"Who are you talking about?" For a moment he didn't know how to react. He had no idea when she could have met Meng Fanzhe.

"You know…the girl who's always on your mind."

He stared blankly for a moment, and then shook his head helplessly. "I'm not. Don't get so carried away."

She looked searchingly into his eyes, obviously not believing him. "Will you tell me about her?"

"No!" He stopped the conversation in its tracks.

Deng Linyue didn't say another word to Fang Mu for the rest of their time together. When he walked her back to her dorm, she didn't ask him for a hug or a kiss like usual. She just said, "I'll see you later," and walked to the door, leaving him alone on the sidewalk.

With no other choice, Fang Mu turned to go. After walking only a few dozen feet, he turned and looked back. Deng Linyue was still standing in the doorway of the women's dormitory, looking in his direction.

He started to walk towards her, but before he had gone more than a few steps, she spun and hurried upstairs.

He hesitated for a moment and then walked over to the dorm. He waited for fifteen minutes before deciding that Deng Linyue wasn't coming back out. He shook his head, turned, and left.

Is this what love looks like?

After returning to his dorm, Fang Mu first went to Meng Fanzhe's room. Even though he could see from the doorway window that no lights were on, he knocked anyway.

No response, just as he had expected.

He had already talked to Zou Tuanjie, who said that Meng Fanzhe still hadn't come to class that day, and no one had seen him all day.

Where had he gone?

When Fang Mu returned to his room Du Yu was already there, but much to his surprise, he wasn't playing Counter-Strike. Instead he was sitting at his desk with a serious look on his face.

"What are you doing?" asked Fang Mu. Having grown accustomed to Du Yu always having a smile on his face, Fang Mu found his current expression to be a little amusing.

"Do you have a moment?" Du Yu asked, turning an unhappy look on him. "I wanted to talk to you."

"About what?" Fang Mu couldn't help but feel a little baffled.

"About you and Deng Linyue."

He stared at Du Yu for several seconds. "Are you just curious? Or is it something else?"

"It's not that." Du Yu paused for a moment. "I just wanted to talk to you as a friend."

Fang Mu pulled his chair over and sat down, and lit a cigarette. "What do you want to know?"

"Are you and Deng Linyue…really a couple?"

Fang Mu hesitated for a moment. "I…suppose we are."

"What do you mean 'you suppose?'" Du Yu brought his chair closer to Fang Mu. "Do you love her?"

For a moment Fang Mu was silent. He took several drags from his cigarette. "To be honest, I don't know."

He really didn't know. Several days ago, the name Deng Linyue had meant only victim to him. Now, however, she was his girlfriend. The whole process had been like an unrealistic dream that he had fallen into without realizing it.

It wasn't the first time this problem had occurred to Fang Mu. In fact, he had been trying to avoid thinking about it for the past several days.

He had avoided it because he had grown accustomed to his new life.

Accustomed to a girl's warm eyes looking at him adoringly.

Accustomed to someone caring deeply about his daily life.

Accustomed to having a soft, sweet-scented body beside him.

And accustomed to those hugs and kisses that made him tremble inside.

Du Yu was watching him, waiting for more of Fang Mu's reply. He sighed. "Actually," he said, speaking slowly, "as your friend I really support you and Deng Linyue being together. And Yaoyao and I both feel that you two are very good for each other. It's just that you became a couple so fast that, especially right now, it really surprised everyone." He paused. "You know what everyone's saying about it, right?"

Fang Mu suddenly realized exactly why Du Yu had been so serious about wanting to discuss the subject with him. It was because of Liu Jianjun.

Seeing that Fang Mu wasn't going to say anything, Du Yu answered the question himself. "They're saying that you took advantage of Liu Jianjun's injury to steal his girlfriend."

Fang Mu laughed hollowly. This was hardly the first time others had misunderstood him. Wasn't he called a freak all the way back to the beginning of school? Well, he still didn't give a damn.

"Is that what you think, too?" Fang Mu asked at last.

"Of course not! I know you too well to think that." Du Yu paused, and then quickly added, "However, I'm still not totally clear about what exactly happened."

Fang Mu had no desire whatsoever to keep discussing this topic with Du Yu, but when he saw the firm and trusting look in his roommate's eyes, he thought for a moment longer and then told him everything that Deng Linyue had said about her relationship with Liu Jianjun.

After listening, Du Yu was quiet for some time. But when Fang Mu lit his fifth cigarette, Du Yu suddenly seemed to come to some internal conclusion and jumped up and placed his hand firmly on Fang Mu's shoulder.

"I support you, brother," he said rather loudly. "You did nothing wrong, and neither did Deng Linyue. Next time I hear someone criticize you, I'll tell them what really happened!"

Fang Mu was about to tell him he really didn't need to do anything like that, but when he saw the self-sacrificing look on Du Yu's face, he just laughed and nodded.

With this weight lifted from his mind, Du Yu slept soundly that night. Fang Mu, however, couldn't get to sleep. To his roommate, his explanation had probably seemed perfectly reasonable, but it did nothing to relieve Fang Mu's self-doubts.

Do I really love Deng Linyue?

He had always known that he had the power to see into other people's hearts, and there was no doubt in his mind that Deng Linyue loved him. But could he say the same?

It is difficult for a doctor to treat himself.

At that moment, Fang Mu understood what the old saying meant. He felt like a flashlight – able to illuminate the darkest corners, but unable to shine a light on himself.

Perhaps this was how it had to be.

Everyone had a road they must walk. Some were smooth, others bumpy.

Mine, thought Fang Mu, is covered in thorns and beset by danger on all sides. There will be blood and monsters and regret and sadness, and my only company will be nightmares and the spirits of the dead.

I've already walked so far. And I'm so tired

His thoughts drifting, Fang Mu gradually fell asleep. His doubts had not been answered, but he had already begun to wonder whether that even mattered.

All he knew was that when Deng Linyue held him, he felt so warm.

The next day Tai Wei came to see him.

As soon as he walked inside, he tilted his head and looked at Fang Mu. He chuckled. "Well, you're looking pretty good."

He knew Tai Wei was trying to make fun of him about Deng Linyue. He ignored him.

Tai Wei had grown a lot thinner lately and looked a little green around the eyes. He appeared not to have slept well in some time. "Why didn't you go with Ms. Deng to the study room today?"

"Her parents came to visit her today and took her out to dinner." In fact, all day she had been hinting that Fang Mu should go with them, saying she really wanted her parents to meet him, but he never agreed to go. Perhaps it was because he still had such a bad impression of her mother from that day in the hospital. Also, he knew that if he did go, it would give the unmistakable impression of a future son-in-law paying his respects to his girlfriend's parents – and that was something he didn't want to do at all.

"So how's it going?" he asked Tai Wei. "Any discoveries?"

"None. We haven't made any progress whatsoever." Then without asking for permission, Tai Wei flopped onto Fang Mu's bed. "Right now all we can do is wait around helplessly. Fuck, man, when is all this going to end?"

The previous afternoon Tai Wei had returned to the city bureau to report to the director. Just as he had walked into the office he happened to pass the deputy mayor and the Jiangbin City American consul coming out. The director hadn't looked too pleased, but he had held his temper and listened to Tai Wei give his report. When Tai Wei finished, the director didn't give any specific comments, just told him to stay vigilant and crack the case as soon as possible. Tai Wei knew that after the fat American was killed, the bureau had been under an enormous amount of pressure. He decided not to wait around and returned directly to Jiangbin City University.

The past few days Fang Mu had been mainly thinking about Deng Linyue and Meng Fanzhe, and hadn't paid much attention to the case. But now that he saw how exhausted Tai Wei looked, he couldn't help but feel a little guilty. Taking out a pack of Hibiscus King cigarettes, he handed one to Tai Wei and then made him a cup of strong tea.

"How about on your end? Anything strange been going on?" Looking like a dignified old man, Tai Wei sipped his tea, his cigarette still hanging from the corner of his mouth. "Of course, besides that time Deng Linyue got pissed at you outside her dorm."

Jeez... thought Fang Mu, glaring at Tai Wei and shaking his head.

Tai Wei chuckled and continued to smoke his cigarette and drink his tea. After a moment of silence, he suddenly asked: "Fang Mu, what kind of person do you think this guy is?"

Fang Mu was taken aback. "Didn't I already tell you in detail about his probable physical and psychological characteristics?"

"You did," Tai Wei said, nodding. "There's something else, though, and I don't quite know how to put it." He gave Fang Mu a scrutinizing look. "For a while I've felt that this guy…is very similar to you."

Fang Mu said nothing. Actually, he had been thinking the same thing himself. The killer had designed each of his murders to challenge Fang Mu, which meant that he had to possess a deep of understanding of criminology, or at least think he did, and at Jiangbin City University, Fang Mu only knew of one other criminal profiler.

Fang Mu's heart fell.

Could it really be Professor Qiao?

Impossible. He immediately rejected this idea. From his professional integrity to his personal morality, Professor Qiao was exemplary. Besides,

Fang Mu knew his skills were nothing compared to Professor Qiao's. There was no need for the professor to compete against him. Also, not only did these crimes require technique, they also demanded strength, and that was something that the old professor no longer possessed.

Almost 20 days had passed since the last crime and the killer had done nothing. The waiting was really akin to torture.

A gloomy atmosphere gradually fell over the room, spreading like the smoke from their cigarettes. Soon Tai Wei and Fang Mu could barely discern the other.

And, as if to mirror the haze, neither could see the man they were seeking. After a while, Tai Wei rose to his feet, sluggishly extended his arm and looked at his watch. "It's almost nine. I'm going to swing by several of the observation points to check things out. You want to come?"

Fang Mu thought about it. Having nothing else to do, he decided to go.

The police were still focusing most of their attention on the women's dormitories and areas relating to the number six. Although the observation points were all different, the policemen standing watch were all exhausted and irritable.

The nonstop battle had been going day and night for over a month. Anyone in their position would feel just as bad.

Fang Mu and Tai Wei visited several observation points, one after another, and each reported that "everything was normal." The sight of his comrades continuing to man their stations despite their obvious exhaustion was too much for Tai Wei, so he and Fang Mu went to one of the little restaurants outside the school gates and ordered several boxes of take-out food. Tai Wei even went so far as specifically asking the owner to put in a little extra meat and vegetables in the orders to back to the officers. Seeing the few sad-looking bills in Tai Wei's wallet, Fang Mu stopped at the supermarket on the way back and bought two cartons of cigarettes. He was going to buy alcohol, too, but Tai Wei stopped him. When they got back with the food, the officers were delighted. After each took a box, they leaned against the walls or crouched on the floor and immediately dug in. The male cops ate crudely, stuffing huge amounts of food that had already gone a little cold into their mouths, chewing roughly before swallowing it down. Every now and then one of them would bite into a bit of sand or small stone from the unwashed vegetables, but then just swallowed that, too. The female cops ate in a group, quietly commenting on the food and exchanging pieces back and forth – a chunk of meat for you, a bit of ribbonfish for me – that sort of thing. And when they had finished, the women still remembered to hand out tissues to all their male comrades who were about to wipe their faces on their sleeves.

But even while they ate, the cops continued to carefully scrutinize everyone who walked past. Even those who were chatting still had their ears perked, listening for any suspicious sounds.

Watching them, Fang Mu couldn't help but be filled with admiration. They were haggard and exhausted and yet still just as alert as a hunter in the forest. While passing out the cigarettes, he made sure to give two extra packs to the officer he and Deng Linyue had tricked. The man obviously didn't hold any hard feelings, giving Fang Mu a grateful smile as he took the packs.

Observing all the officers devour their food, Fang Mu felt a little hungry himself, so he and Tai Wei decided to share a box. He was astonished at how good it tasted. Even though he was eating it while leaning against a cold wall, even though the rice was far from fresh and a chilly wind was blowing all the while, Fang Mu still felt it was the most delicious meal he'd had in days.

After they ate, Tai Wei brought Fang Mu back through all the observation points once more. By the time they finished it was almost eleven that night and the campus was empty. Dormitory lights were blinking out one by one. After a long, noisy day the only sound left on campus was the cold wind.

Fang Mu and Tai Wei hurried down the empty street towards Fang Mu's dorm. Just as they arrived, Tai Wei suddenly stopped and looked behind them.

"What is it?" Fang Mu asked. He looked back. Not far away stood a lonely streetlight, illuminating the patch of street underneath. Everything else was shrouded in darkness and the campus was silent.

"Nothing," said Tai Wei. Frowning, he looked around. "I must be hearing things."

They walked single file into the dorm. When they passed the first floor bathroom, Tai Wei suddenly stopped and held his stomach. "You go on ahead," he said. "That ribbonfish wasn't fresh. I think I'm going to be sick."

Fang Mu nodded. "I've got some herbal meds in my room. You should come get some when you're done." He headed on upstairs.

The stairwell was eerily quiet. Every now and then he could hear the faint sound of water running through the pipes. He had been walking all night and now his legs ached a little, so he climbed the stairs slowly, listening to his footsteps echo throughout the stairwell.

Suddenly, he heard footsteps that didn't belong to him.

The steps were coming from somewhere nearby. They were moving neither fast nor slow, and sounded almost careless.

When Fang Mu reached the second floor landing, he stopped and listened closely.

At once the sound of footsteps vanished, as if they had never been there.

Fang Mu held his breath and listened. After a few seconds, he stepped forward and began again slowly climbing the stairs.

Sure enough, the other footsteps started up again as well.

As Fang Mu climbed, he held onto the handrail and glanced down. He could see a long, thin shadow swaying on the stairs between the first and second floor, moving slowly higher.

Fang Mu felt all the hairs on his body stand up. There was no time to think. He bolted up the stairs as fast as he could and into the third floor hallway. When he reached the door to Room 313, his room, he hesitated for a moment, and then ran past it to the far end of the hall. There was a low wall next to Room 320 that was big enough to hide behind. When he passed Room 318, he saw a large shattered mirror leaning against the wall beside the door. The broken mirror had been left outside for the cleaning people to deal with, as was customary. Fang Mu leaned down and grabbed a decent-sized piece and then kept going. When he reached the low wall, he placed the mirror across the hall beside the door to Room 321 and angled it so it reflected the other end of the hallway. Positioned this way, when he crouched down behind the wall he could see what was happening in the rest of hall without revealing his location.

After a few seconds, a vague figure appeared in the mirror.

He was walking at a steady pace and appeared to be about 5'9" and very thin. He kept one hand inside his pocket while the other swung freely back and forth at his side.

For some reason, Fang Mu suddenly felt that the figure looked extremely familiar.

All the while the figure continued to walk closer and closer. Then, without any warning, he stopped. Judging from his position, Fang Mu guessed that he was standing outside Room 313.

The person stood there for several seconds, and then suddenly extended one arm and began moving it across the door.

Fang Mu frowned, wondering what was the man was doing.

Looking into the blurry mirror, he did his best to determine what was going on, but he still couldn't make it out. Taking advantage of the fact that the person was still facing the door, Fang Mu quickly popped his head out.

It was Meng Fanzhe.

Fang Mu sighed with relief and came out of his hiding place.

"Hey, it's you."

Meng Fanzhe snapped his head around and stared blankly at Fang Mu approaching.

Fang Mu was taken aback. It had only been a few days, but Meng Fanzhe already looked a lot more haggard than the last time he'd seen him. His face was deathly pale, the skin around his eyes dark, and his cheeks sunken. His hair, which looked like it hadn't been washed in a long time, stood up in tufts all over his head.

Fang Mu's eyes fell to the hand that Meng Fanzhe had just been moving across the door. In his long, thin fingers he held a felt marker.

At once Fang Mu thought of the five-pointed star. He stopped walking. He asked guardedly, "What are you doing?"

Seeming not to hear, Meng Fanzhe just continued staring dully at him.

Fang Mu cautiously took another step toward him. "Meng Fanzhe, what are you doing?"

Before Fang Mu's very eyes, Meng Fanzhe's empty, lifeless eyes suddenly filled with wild ferocity. The muscles in his face twisted. He opened his mouth, revealing frighteningly white teeth, and let out a deep, animalistic roar.

"Aghh!"

Fang Mu was so startled that he jumped back two steps. Before he could say anything, Meng Fanzhe pulled out the hand that had been in his pocket the whole time. In it was a huge box-cutter.

Fang Mu's senses alerted. "What are you...?"

Meng Fanzhe flicked his finger and the blade shot out, glittering coldly. Gripping the knife, he muttered something and began walking toward Fang Mu. Suddenly he raised his arm overhead, the blade catching the light, and then lunged forward.

As Meng Fanzhe's arm swung down, Fang Mu leapt back, feeling the blade whistle past his nose and then slice through the fabric of his jacket. "Are you out of your mind, Meng Fanzhe?" he shouted, dodging backwards.

"It's me, Fang Mu!"

But his words were useless. Seeing that his previous attempt had fallen short, Meng Fanzhe raised the knife again and went straight for Fang Mu's neck.

Fang Mu hurriedly ducked down, avoiding the blade, and then darted behind Meng Fanzhe and kicked him savagely in the back of the knee.

Meng Fanzhe fell forward onto the floor. Immediately Fang Mu leapt forward to pin him down, but Meng Fanzhe was too fast. Before even standing up, he swung the blade backwards.

Fang Mu tried to dodge, but he was a second too late. The knife edge sliced one of his fingers. Blood spurted.

Meng Fanzhe got to his feet and advanced on Fang Mu, growling under his breath. In the overhead light, Fang Mu could clearly see Meng Fanzhe's clenched jaw and the white froth surrounding his mouth, much like a mad dog. Squeezing his bleeding finger, Fang Mu hastily walked backwards.

Suddenly the sound of hurried footsteps came from behind him. He spun around. From out of the darkness at the other end of the corridor appeared Tai Wei, one hand going to his sidearm as he ran toward them.

In the blink of an eye, Tai Wei was beside him. With a taut face, the cop pulled Fang Mu behind him and raised the gun. "You all right?" he asked. Without waiting for an answer, he yelled toward Meng Fanzhe, "I'm a police officer! Put the knife down now!"

This had no effect on Meng Fanzhe. He seemed oblivious to Tai Wei. He just kept staring at Fang Mu and continued to walk closer, closing the distance between them.

Tai Wei cocked the hammer of the gun. "Put the knife down now or I'll shoot."

Fang Mu nervously grabbed Tai Wei's arm. "Don't fire; he's my classmate."

Tai Wei stared at Meng Fanzhe a few seconds before easing the gun hammer. He holstered it and took a combat stance.

One after another the doors along the hallway opened. Having heard the commotion, various underwear-clad students stuck their heads out to take a look. Once they saw what was going on, however, they gave an alarmed cry and shrunk back inside their rooms, keeping their doors cracked just wide enough to observe the scene.

Du Yu also came out into the hall. After standing there helplessly for a few seconds, he grabbed a broom from inside his room and ran behind Fang Mu. Shaking with fear, he said, "Meng Fanzhe, don't do anything crazy now."

Meng Fanzhe let out another growl and then swung the knife.

Tai Wei quickly stepped forward, grabbed Meng Fanzhe's knife hand, and twisted his wrist. Despite the pain, Meng Fanzhe did not release his grip on the blade, so Tai Wei gave his knee a hard kick. At last the knife clattered to the floor. Tai Wei yanked Meng Fanzhe toward him, grabbed his collar, and tossed him forward. Meng Fanzhe smashed into the wall, falling roughly to the floor. He curled up in pain.

Tai Wei rushed forward, flipped him over, and held him down with his knees on his back. He cuffed the student's hands together.

Lying on the floor, Meng Fanzhe could do nothing but pant for breath.. Tai Wei took out his phone, dialed, and then said simply, "Dormitory Five, Room Three-Thirteen. Get here as fast as you can." He hung up and turned to Fang Mu. "What happened here? Who is this guy and why'd he want to kill you?"

Fang Mu didn't respond to the question, just stared blankly at Meng Fanzhe as he groaned and breathed heavily on the floor. Fang Mu could only think of a single word.

Why?

By this time the hallway was filled with noise. Nearly everyone who lived on the floor had run out of their rooms to see the excitement. Several yelled out in surprise: "Isn't that Meng Fanzhe?" "What's going on?"

Suddenly Fang Mu rushed forward and knelt beside Meng Fanzhe. In a loud voice, he said, "Can you hear what I'm saying? What's going on with you?"

Meng Fanzhe's eyes were closed, his breathing labored. He made no response.

Fang Mu let go of his bleeding finger, grabbed hold of Meng Fanzhe's shoulders and shook him forcefully. "Talk to me, Meng Fanzhe. What were you doing just now? Why do you want to kill me?"

Meng Fanzhe's eyes opened at once, flashing the same murderous look as before. Twisting his body, he mustered all his strength and lurched at Fang Mu, trying to bite him.

Fang Mu fell backwards onto the floor as Tai Wei stepped forward and kicked Meng Fanzhe in the face.

"Keep still!" he yelled.

Unfazed, Fang Mu crawled forward and grabbed hold of Tai Wei's leg. "Don't hurt him," he said. "Something is definitely wrong here! He's not normally like this…"

Meng Fanzhe's mouth was cut from the blow and as the blood trickled down his ashen skin, his appearance changed beyond recognition.

Fang Mu's wounded finger had also split open and the blood ran down his fingertips and onto the floor. Before long, a small pool had formed.

Seeing that Fang Mu was bleeding, Du Yu quickly grabbed his arm. "Come back to the dorm. I've got bandages."

His mind blank, Fang Mu let Du Yu pull him to the door of Room 313. When they reached the entrance, Fang Mu suddenly remembered that Meng Fanzhe had been drawing something on their door, so he pushed Du Yu off and looked closely at it.

The door appeared empty. Meng Fanzhe didn't seem to have written anything.

After sweeping his gaze across the surface, Fang Mu began inspecting the

door inch by inch. Suddenly, he noticed something on the room number.

In-between the "3", the "1" and the "3", Meng Fanzhe had written two "+" signs with his felt-tip marker.

"Three plus one plus three…" muttered Fang Mu. Suddenly, he felt a chill pass through his entire body.

Seeing Fang Mu standing motionless in front of the room door, Tai Wei turned to two of the students nearby. "Watch him for me," he said, pointing at Meng Fanzhe, who was still writhing on the floor. He walked over to Fang Mu.

"What is it?" Tai Wei asked.

Fang Mu didn't respond, just stared dumbstruck at the numbers.

Tai Wei followed his gaze. A few seconds later, Fang Mu heard the cop's breathing suddenly quicken. He looked over. Tai Wei's eyes were locked on the room number, his face registering shocked realization.

By this time the other police had arrived at the scene. "What should we do, Captain?" one of them yelled to Tai Wei. "Interrogate him here or take him back to the station?"

Tai Wei just waved his hand. "All of you, get over here right now!"

Once the officers had all crowded around the door, Tai Wei pointed at the number. "Comrades," he said, his voice shaking slightly, "we got him. This is the guy!"

The police all turned to the room number. After a few seconds of silence, shouts of accomplishment suddenly erupted from the group. Filled with the rush of relief, they congratulated and jostled each other. One of the female officers even rushed through the crowd and hugged Tai Wei.

Squeezed in the middle of this madly happy group, Fang Mu was knocked to and fro. But there wasn't a hint of a smile on his face. He just stared blankly at the door number, that single word still the only thing in his mind.

Why?

"All right, all right," said Tai Wei, waving his hand for silence. In a confident tone, he yelled out: "Everyone on your marks! Let's get to work!"

After giving a brief shout of agreement, the officers all attended to their own tasks. They sealed off the crime scene, collected evidence, determined the suspect's identity. It was the typical follow-up.

Before long, all the onlookers were told to disperse, leaving only Meng Fanzhe lying on the floor and Fang Mu still standing in the doorway.

Two of the cops lifted Meng Fanzhe off the floor, and then with one man grabbing each arm, they began dragging him toward the first floor. Fang Mu tried to run after them, but he was stopped by Tai Wei.

"You need to go to the hospital," the cop said. "Your wound looks deep."

"It's fine," said Fang Mu impatiently. "I need to talk to him; something about this doesn't seem right to me."

Tai Wei seemed a little annoyed by the remark. "Anything that doesn't seem right will be cleared up once we start interrogating him. Little Zhang," he said, waving to one of the officers nearby, "take Fang Mu to the hospital."

The cop nodded and walked over. Having no other choice, Fang Mu followed him downstairs.

A number of police cars were parked at the entrance to the building, lights flashing. Fang Mu saw Meng Fanzhe sitting in one, his head down. Police officers were sitting on either side of him, holding his arms tight.

The cop who was taking Fang Mu to the hospital waved him over to a nearby police car. As Fang Mu walked toward it, he kept his eyes on Meng Fanzhe, as if he hoped to find some clue in his face. It was then that Meng Fanzhe looked up at him.

At once Meng Fanzhe leapt at the window, but now the murderous look was gone from his eyes, replaced instead by one of bottomless fear and despair. He knocked against the window as hard as he could, yelling soundlessly, tears streaming down his face.

The two cops quickly restrained him, beating him about the face and the body.

Fang Mu ran forward, wanting to open the door. But just as he reached the rear bumper, the car suddenly sped off, knocking him to the ground. By the time he climbed to his feet, the car had already turned a corner and was nowhere to be soon, leaving only the sound of its siren echoing across campus.

22 CAT AND MOUSE (II)

Fang Mu's wound wasn't long, but it was very deep. After cleaning it out, the tired-looking doctor on duty at the hospital closed it up with two stitches. When Fang Mu left the examination room, Little Zhang, the cop that had escorted him, was on the phone. Seeing Fang Mu emerge, he quickly hung up. He then asked him a few brief questions about his injury, and said that he would take him back to the school.

Fang Mu shook his head. "Take me to the city bureau."

"Absolutely not." Little Zhang's tone was firm. "Captain Tai ordered me to take you back to school."

"I was the victim of this crime. Don't you have to take my statement?"

Little Zhang seemed stumped by the question, but after hesitating for a moment, he still insisted on taking Fang Mu back to his dorm.

"Well, I don't need an escort!" Fang Mu yelled. "I can get there myself!" He stormed out of the hospital.

As soon as he was outside, he hurriedly hid around the side of the building. A few seconds later he saw Little Zhang sprint out after him. The cop looked all around, swearing beneath his breath. Then he hopped into his car, started it up, and sped off.

When Little Zhang was far enough away, Fang Mu left his hiding place and walked straight to the line of cabs waiting outside the hospital.

The entrance to the city bureau was ablaze with light. Cars packed the courtyard. After hopping out of the cab, Fang Mu approached the heavily-armed policeman guarding the entrance.

"Officer Tai asked me to come and give my statement," he told the cop.

The cop nodded and went into his sentry box to make a call. A few minutes later, Little Zhang came running out of the building.

"I knew you were going to follow me here!" Little Zhang snapped at Fang Mu. "Don't say anything else. As soon as you finish your statement you're leaving. Captain Tai said he'll contact you in a few days."

Fang Mu had no choice but to follow him as he walked away.

After bringing Fang Mu to one of the detainment rooms, the cop told him to wait there a moment and to not do anything stupid, and then left the room.

As soon as he left the room, Fang Mu snuck out after him. The corridor was jammed with people. Uniformed and plainclothes police officers hurried from one room to the next. Occasionally someone would look suspiciously at him, but no one ever stopped to say anything. As he walked, he kept hearing things like, "Bring these documents to the third floor as fast as you can" and "To the interrogation room."

Everyone seemed to be paying close attention to what was happening on the third floor.

Doing his best to stay inconspicuous, Fang Mu hurried up to the third floor.

A large iron door stood open at the end of the corridor. Beyond that was another room. Its back wall was all glass. At the moment, over a dozen policemen were standing quietly near the glass wall. Fang Mu could hear Tai Wei's voice coming from within the crowd.

"...At that moment I feigned having diarrhea, and hid in the bathroom and listened for sounds of movement," he was saying. "Sure enough, I soon heard someone climbing the stairs, so I quietly followed behind him.

After he entered the third floor hallway, I watched as he walked a few steps, stopped, and then walked a little farther, until he was standing in front of Room Three-Thirteen. There he seemed to either knock or write something on the door – I couldn't tell at the distance. Afterwards the victim spoke briefly to him, and since I figured that they knew each other, I turned to leave. But before I had gone ten feet I heard the sound of fighting, after which I restrained him and then brought him back here..."

Fang Mu walked quietly farther into the room. Everyone was watching Tai Wei with bated breath, so not a single person noticed him.

"Can you guarantee that this is the killer?" asked one of the listeners, a stern-looking man with a beer belly.

"I can!" Tai Wei's voice and expression were both resolute. "First of all, we discovered that he had indicated the number seven on the victim's door; second, one of my men from the special investigation team recently finished checking the scene – including the suspect's room – and he just called me to say they made a huge discovery."

Several female officers now rushed over and handed several thick stacks of documents to Tai Wei. After briefly flipping through them, he turned to the fat, grave-faced man and said, "Director, we can begin."

The director nodded. "Then let's get started."

Everyone turned toward the glass wall. Not daring to get too close, Fang Mu did his best to catch what was happening through a space in the crowd.

The wall was actually a one-way mirror. On the other side of it was the interrogation room.

Inside that room, it was sparsely furnished, containing only a single table with a lamp, two chairs on one side and one on the other. Two policemen sat side by side, one flipping through the documents that had just been given to him, the other writing something on a piece of paper. The chair opposite them was fixed to the floor, appearing horribly cold and uncomfortable. A camera monitored the scene from the ceiling. It was equipped with a microphone, which amplified all the sounds within the interrogation room and transmitted them to the room on the other side of the glass wall where the onlookers observed.

The small door on the right side of the room opened and Meng Fanzhe was led in by two policemen. His hands and feet were shackled.

He kept his head down and appeared extremely weak, swaying when the police forced him into the chair. The blood had already dried around his mouth and his face was covered with dark red splotches.

The two policemen stared at him for several seconds. Then the older one said: "Name?"

Keeping his head down, Meng Fanzhe made no response.

The other officer turned the desk lamp to face Meng Fanzhe. Enveloped by the bright light, Meng Fanzhe's body made a twisted shadow on the back wall of the room.

"Name?"

Meng Fanzhe still said nothing. He was so motionless he could have been sleeping.

The older officer calmly lit a cigarette and opened one of the files in front of him. "Where were you on the morning of July 1, 2002, between one and three a.m.?"

No response.

"Where were you on the morning of August 10, 2002, between eight and nine a.m.?"

Still no response.

The other officer looked at the mirror on the wall behind him. He knew that many of his colleagues as well as the director himself were all watching from the other side. Turning back to Meng Fanzhe, who was still sitting as lifeless as a block of wood, he couldn't help but be shamed into anger.

Slamming a fist down on the table, the interrogator yelled, "Meng Fanzhe! Don't think that if you stay silent everything will be okay. According to the code of criminal procedure –"

Before he could finish what he was saying, Meng Fanzhe's head suddenly jerked up. Although he was facing the bright light, his eyes were wide open. If looks could have killed, the two officers opposite him would have been dead instantly.

"Aghh!" The same wild howl that Fang Mu had heard in the hallway roared again.

Although shackled to the chair, Meng Fanzhe struggled forward with all the strength he had, looking like he might snap his fetters at any moment and leap on the two officers. The younger one was so startled by the outburst that he recoiled back in his seat. The two cops standing behind Meng Fanzhe hurried to hold him down, but in that moment he seemed to have acquired superhuman strength at odds with his feeble appearance. Despite their superior size, the cops were unable to control him as he thrashed about in his confines, and one was nearly bitten in the commotion.

One of them pulled out a police baton and raised it.

Behind that two-way mirror, Fang Mu was in motion. "No!" He suddenly dove against the glass and pounded it with his fists.

Everyone observing froze at his outburst. After standing there stunned for two seconds, Tai Wei blurted, "Fang Mu?"

Fang Mu spun around and grabbed Tai Wei's arm. "Don't hurt him…"

"Who are you?" asked the director, cutting him off.

"Oh, he's the one that the suspect attacked," said Tai Wei quickly. "I asked him here to take his statement." He turned around and whispered to Fang Mu, "Go downstairs, I'll be there in a little bit."

"Tai Wei," said Fang Mu, pulling on his arm almost entreatingly, "let me

Profiler

talk to him. I'm positive something's up. There's no way he's the killer."

"Absolutely not!" Tai Wei threw him off and then whispered sternly, "Where do you think you are? Get downstairs now."

Fang Mu was adamant. "It can't be him; he's nothing like the person I predicted..."

The director, who had been standing to the side and aloofly watching all this, now spoke: "Tai Wei, is this the so-called genius you told me about?"

Realizing that it was already too late to hide anything, Tai Wei had no choice but to tell the truth. "Yes, sir." he said. "This is the one."

The director snorted disdainfully and turned to look into the interrogation room. Meng Fanzhe was still struggling, and had thrown both the cops off of him. One took out his electric baton, turned it on.

"Get out of the way!" he yelled to his comrade. Barely had the other officer moved, than the first officer pressed the baton against Meng Fanzhe's shoulder.

At once Meng Fanzhe's eyes went wide and his body bent like a bow as the current surged through him. The cop prodded him several more times, and after each Meng Fanzhe howled in pain and writhed like a fish on a chopping block. In moments he was no longer struggling, just slumped over in his chair, his whole body shaking.

With a hard look on his face, the observing director said, "We won't interrogate him tonight. Just lock him up for now; tomorrow we'll get some experts over here to give him a psychological assessment." He turned and walked out, glaring furiously at Tai Wei as he passed.

Tai Wei tried to explain, but the director had already passed. Helplessly, he just shook his head and turned back to the interrogation room where Meng Fanzhe was being dragged out of his seat like a dead dog. For a moment Tai Wei stood there with his arms crossed. Without turning his head, he said, "Take him back."

"Yes, sir," said Little Zhang. He grabbed Fang Mu's arm. "Let's go!"

Fang Mu tried to argue, but the cop pulled him roughly away.

The whole way back to the dorm, Little Zhang didn't say a word, just sped through the city streets. Fang Mu didn't want to talk either. He stared at the ink-black sky through the car windshield, his mind blank.

Arriving at the campus, Little Zhang tightly gripped Fang Mu's arm and marched him swiftly up to the third floor of Dormitory 5. By then Fang Mu's whole body ached and he had long since given up resisting.

The hallway was filled with noise and packed with onlookers. Some were students wearing nothing but underwear and a blanket over their shoulders; others were campus security guards who had just heard the news. Through the crowd, Fang Mu could see that all the lights in Meng Fanzhe's room were on and he could hear one of the cops standing outside yell repeatedly for everyone to move back.

The number for Room 313 had already been taken as evidence, and when the cop escorting Fang Mu tried to open the door, he found it was locked.

"Who here lives in Room Three-Thirteen?" Little Zhang yelled into the crowd.

Du Yu was also out watching the commotion, but when he heard this he came running over and opened the door.

Pushing Fang Mu into the room, Little Zhang said, "Don't go running off anywhere." Then he turned to Du Yu and said, "You keep an eye on him." He walked out and slammed the door.

Hands at his sides, Fang Mu just stood there for several seconds. Then he slowly walked over to his bed and collapsed on it.

Giving him a worried look, Du Yu said cautiously, "Fang Mu, you want something to drink?"

Fang Mu didn't say anything, just slowly shook his head. He lay there only seconds before he suddenly leapt out of bed, threw open the door, and ran toward Meng Fanzhe's room. He pushed through the crowd gathered there until he had reached the doorway. He lifted the police tape stretched across it and headed inside.

A number of police were already inside inspecting the scene. Little Zhang was among them. Seeing Fang Mu enter, he rushed over to stop him.

"What the hell are you trying to do now?" he asked.

"What have you guys found?" asked Fang Mu anxiously.

The other cops just looked at one another.

Now Little Zhang was angry and he turned Fang Mu around and led him towards the door. "Get out of here. This isn't your business. If we find anything, Tai Wei will let you know.

Fang Mu shoved the cop's hand off of him and darted back into the room, yelling, "Just what have you guys found?"

"Fang Mu!" Little Zhang yelled, sliding a pair of handcuffs from his belt. "You're obstructing police business. Don't make me do this!"

Pushing through the crowd, Du Yu grabbed Fang Mu and pulled him away, saying quietly, "Brother, let's head back now; you can figure the rest out tomorrow."

Still fuming, Little Zhang turned to one of the security guards standing nearby. "Make all these students return to their dorms! They're getting in the way of our work!"

One after another, the security guards sprang into action. "Everyone back to your dorms," they told the curious students. "Anyone who sticks his head out again will receive a public criticism... No, a demerit in their permanent record!"

After being dragged by Du Yu back inside their room, Fang Mu stood by the door for a long time, his breath coming heavily. Before he could even catch his breath, he suddenly tore open one of his desk drawers, grabbed several thick brown paper folders, and tossed them on the desktop with a thud. He pulled several stacks of files out of them and began studying each in silence.

Du Yu stood some distance away, cautiously trying to see what Fang Mu was looking at. He could just barely make out several pictures of blood-soaked murder scenes and could hear his roommate whispering to himself.

"Impossible," Fang Mu murmured. "It can't be him… It can't be him…"

Where am I?

My head hurts so bad, like it's gonna explode…

What did I do…?

…

"Do you have a lucky number?"

"No, I don't really believe in that kind of stuff. Anyway, the reason I came this time was –"

"Let's not get ahead of ourselves. Do you know which number the majority of people like the most?"

"I don't know. Is it…eight?"

"Only Chinese people think that way. And mainly just the nouveau riche and low-class, rural moneybags. *(Translator's note: The Chinese word for eight is pronounced ba, meaning "to get rich.")* Look, you're smiling. I told you, don't be anxious."

"I'm not anxious, it's just that I feel…I feel like we've sort of taken a step backward. Because the past few days in class, I started to be afraid of roll call again."

"Oh? When did this begin?"

"The last time…the last time we met."

"Don't worry; this is very normal. Some things need to be repeatedly reinforced before you can reach the optimum result."

"I hope you can help me."

"All right, but you must follow what I say exactly. Do you understand?"

"Yes."

. . .

My God, now I remember…

Fang Mu, are you dead?

. . .

"What should I do? Tell me, what should I do?"

"Don't worry; let me think."

"I embarrassed myself so badly today. I was in front of so many people and I just couldn't say 'here'…"

"Perhaps we should change tactics; however, this other tactic will probably seem a little harsh. Are you sure you can handle it?"

"I…"

"If you can succeed, you will eliminate this fear forever."

There was a pause.

"But if you feel that you are simply a weak person, then forget it. I can't help you."

"…I…I'm willing to try."

"Very good. Now I want you to lie down on that couch. Relax, and then we will began."

There was a moment.

"You are now in class. Try and imagine it. Your classmates are all around you. There are so many people... The teacher takes the attendance sheet...begins reading the names one by one...Meng Fanzhe!"

Pause.

"Meng Fanzhe!"

He writhed uncontrollably, sweat pouring down his face.

"Meng Fanzhe!"

"Meng Fanzhe!"

"Meng Fanzhe!"

"Meng Fanzhe!"

"Aghh!"

…

It's so cold...

My arms and legs won't move. I want to hold my shoulders, but I can't...

Help me, help me...

…

"Are you scared of death?"

"Of course; who isn't scared of death?"

"Actually, there's nothing scary about death. What do you do when you feel unhappy?"

"Um, play video games, or hole up and sleep for a long time."

"Is that so? Actually, death is just a much longer kind of sleep. In it you can forget all your troubles. Many people would rather die than lose their dignity. Have you heard of Hemingway?"

"Yeah, The Old Man and the Sea."

"When faced with an incurable disease, he chose to kill himself rather than forfeit his dignity. To be honest, sometimes I really envy him."

A pause.

...

What should I do?

Did I kill someone?

I'm finished...

...

"Have you ever noticed that seven is a very interesting number?"

"Oh, is that so?"

"Think about it. There are seven days in the week, seven colors in the spectrum, seven notes in the diatonic scale. Therefore, seven symbolizes satisfaction."

"Oh, is that so?"

"And when you're satisfied, there's nothing else to worry about, isn't that right?"

...

I'm a murderer...

Everyone will know that I'm a murderer...

For the rest of her life my mother will be filled with shame...

I'm twenty-four...

My life, this is how it ends...

...

"Take this…go back to your dorm room…search your surroundings, find the number seven…there you will fulfill all your desires…"

…

It's hopeless…

It's hopeless…

…

Fang Mu didn't fall asleep until nearly four in the morning, and he was still at his desk.

He awoke later that day to the noise of people bustling about outside. A feeling of discomfort hung over him. His chest hurt from having been pressed against the edge of the desk and his body felt heavy. He struggled to stand up. A blanket lay on the floor behind him. He figured Du Yu must have placed it over his shoulders.

His finger ached, too. Blood had leaked through the gauze. He must have reopened it in the commotion last night.

But he didn't care about any of this. Reaching unsteadily for the cup on his desk, he downed the lukewarm water in one gulp.

Too impatient to wash his face, he quickly organized his things and got ready to leave.

He had to see Meng Fanzhe that day. All the clues indicated that he could not be the killer. However, some questions remained, and only Meng Fanzhe could answer them.

As Fang Mu opened the door to leave, he bumped into someone standing the hallway.

It was Tai Wei.

"You're just in time. Take me to see Meng Fanzhe." Saying no more, Fang Mu took hold of Tai Wei's elbow and tried leading him toward the door.

But Tai Wei didn't move. "It's too late."

"Huh?" Fang Mu stopped and looked back at him.

"Meng Fanzhe is dead," Tai Wei said somberly.

Fang Mu stared at him for nearly half a minute, until Tai Wei pulled him back inside the room.

"We'd better talk in here," he said.

Fang Mu stood in the center of his room, staring blankly out the window. He didn't look at Tai Wei, didn't say a word.

"This morning before dawn – " Tai Wei began.

Fang Mu suddenly raised his hand to stop him from going on. He crouched down and put his head between his knees as the events caught up with him, his whole body shaking fiercely.

Tai Wei waited for Fang Mu to calm down a little before slowly helping him to sit on the bed. He handed him a cigarette and lit it for him.

With a dull look on his face, Fang Mu put the cigarette in his mouth and inhaled viciously. He smoked the cigarette before turning to Tai Wei. His voice was hoarse as he asked, "How did he die?"

"He smashed his head against the wall," Tai Wei said simply.

"Why did no one stop him?" Fang Mu asked in an almost demanding tone.

"We had already taken all the necessary precautions," Tai Wei insisted. "We shut him inside the detainment room and shackled his hands and feet to the chair. At first, the guard on duty heard him crying, and then he heard something thumping. But when he ran inside it was already too late."

"His hands and feet were both shackled, so then how...?"

Tai Wei smiled wryly. "You're not going to believe this. Meng Fanzhe managed to get both his hands and feet out of the shackles. In all these years, I've never seen anything like it." He shook his head. "The skin on his hands and feet was torn off, and the metacarpal bones in both his hands were broken." He gestured with his hands. "It's hard to imagine just how determined this kid was to die."

The room was silent for some time. At last, Fang Mu asked without expression, "What's the bureau's opinion on this?"

Tai Wei hesitated for a moment. "The preliminary conclusion is that he killed himself to escape punishment."

"On what basis? Don't tell me you decided he was the killer because of what happened last night."

Doing his best to keep a calm tone, Tai Wei said, "Fang Mu, I understand how you're feeling. However, we wouldn't just suspect someone without any evidence. Meng Fanzhe may not have said anything to us during the interrogation, but we discovered these in his dorm room." He took a stack of documents out of his briefcase and handed them to Fang Mu.

As Fang Mu looked through the files, Tai Wei explained further.

"This picture is of a black sheet," he said as Fang Mu examined a photo. "After comparing it to the one that Jin Qiao was lying on in the video, we feel they're very similar. We also found a number of possible bloodstains on it. They're examining it at the crime lab right now and the results should be in by this afternoon..." He nodded to the next photo Fang Mu studied. "This is a hammer. After Liu Jianjun was attacked, we analyzed the wound and made a rough prediction of the weapon that could have caused it. This size hammer is exactly what we were thinking of. And there's this, look here," he said as he pointed at a picture of over a dozen books. "These were also found in Meng Fanzhe's dorm room. They're all about human anatomy, Western criminal history, and serial killers. You remember all those books we looked through in the library? Well, they were all in his room. We've already sent someone to check out Meng Fanzhe's library record... This little plastic bag we found in the pocket of one of Meng Fanzhe's jackets. Inside was a small amount of powder. The lab already determined that it's heroin —"

Fang Mu cut him off. "What about the car? The killer needed a car to commit his crimes, so where's Meng Fanzhe's? And you don't expect me to believe that he killed Jin Qiao and skinned Xin Tingting in his own dorm room, do you?"

"Renting a car would not have been a problem. And he most likely also rented a place somewhere off-campus to commit his crimes."

"Rented a place? Then why'd he bring all this stuff to his dorm room? Wouldn't it be a lot safer to just leave it in his apartment?"

For a moment Tai Wei couldn't respond.

The door suddenly opened and Deng Linyue ran in, breathing heavily. Du Yu followed behind her, a tray of food in his hands.

Deng Linyue froze when she saw Tai Wei, but rather than say hello to him, she immediately turned to Fang Mu. "Are you okay? You're not hurt, are you?"

Seeing the gauze on his finger, she made an alarmed outcry, rushed closer and took his hand.

"My God! You're injured and it's still bleeding! We need to get you to the hospital." She looked Fang Mu up and down, speaking rapidly before he could reply. "You're not hurt anywhere else, are you? I'm sorry, I'm sorry; I only just heard the news. I came too late."

She seemed about to cry, but Fang Mu pushed away her hand and continued to stare at Tai Wei, waiting for him to answer his last question.

Tai Wei ignored Fang Mu's questioning look and opened the documents to the photo of the hammer.

"You came just in time," he said to Deng Linyue. "Look here. Was this what the killer was holding on the night of the crime?"

Deng Linyue looked at the photo. "It seems…like it was. Yes, it does look like it." But noticing Fang Mu's stern expression, she quickly added, "I'm not really sure. Aren't all hammers the same? Oh, I don't know, I don't know!"

Tai Wei glared angrily at Fang Mu, slammed the folder closed, and then stood up. "I'm going to go. Keep your phone on and don't run off anywhere in the next few days. As soon as there's any news, I'll let you know." He grabbed his briefcase and left.

The dorm was enveloped in silence. Du Yu looked at Deng Linyue, and then at Fang Mu. He pointed to the food on the desk. "You should eat something, Fang Mu. I bought you breakfast."

When Fang Mu didn't say anything, Deng Linyue smiled apologetically and said, "Thank you, Du Yu."

"I guess I'll be going then," Du Yu said, grabbing his backpack. On the way out, he whispered to Deng Linyue, "Make sure you look after him."

After Du Yu left, the dorm room fell into an even more unbearable silence. For a while Deng Linyue sat quietly beside Fang Mu, but when she saw that he wasn't going to say anything, she took the food tray and tried to hand it to him. "You should really eat something."

When Fang Mu wouldn't take it, she scooped a spoonful of rice porridge and lifted it toward his mouth.

He turned his head away. "I don't want to eat. You should go. I want to be alone for a while."

Having no other choice, Deng Linyue placed the tray back on the desk. In a soft voice, she said, "I'll stay with you."

He shook his head. "Don't bother. You should head back."

She bit her lip. Her voice rose despite herself. "Do you really…find me so awful?"

He considered her for a moment, and then said helplessly, "No. There's just nothing you can do to help me."

"There's nothing I can do to help? How can you not need my help at a time like this?" She suddenly stood up. "I know your emotions are painfully raw at this moment, and although I don't understand what happened or why that person wanted to kill you, I still want to be a consoling shoulder for you. Can't you be a little warmer to me?"

"No!" His voice leapt to an angry tone. "Do you really understand me? Do you know what kind of person I am? Do you know the burden you'll have to bear if you're with me? You can't do it!"

"What makes you think I can't? After what I went through, what else could be too much for me?"

Not wanting to argue with her any further, he stood up and opened the door. "Either go or don't go, but if you stay, I'm leaving!"

Tears were now running down her face. Deng Linyue could only stand there and stare at him for several seconds. Then she bolted past him and ran out of the room.

As Fang Mu watched her figure disappear down the end of the hall, he was awash in both unspeakable guilt and exhaustion.

Deng Linyue, you don't understand. The scariest part isn't knowing what he's going to do; it's having no idea when he's going to do it.

One day later, Tai Wei called to tell Fang Mu that the blood on the black sheet was proven to be Jin Qiao's. This, combined with Tai Wei's account of the killer's appearance from when he'd chased him through the gymnasium and the library record which proved that Meng Fanzhe had taken out all the books in May of 2002 – which closely conformed to the dates of the murders – made it appear Meng Fanzhe really had been the perpetrator.

That day, Meng Fanzhe's mother arrived at the school.

Meng Fanzhe's father had been dead for a long time, so his mother was there alone. As soon as she heard the news, she hopped on a train and rushed to Jiangbin City. Because her heart was not strong, she had already fainted twice in the university president's office.

It was Zou Tuanjie who told Fang Mu the news. When Fang Mu saw the woman himself, it was noon of that same day.

An older, white-haired woman, she was escorted by two policemen up to

Meng Fanzhe's room to gather his effects. As soon as she saw the police tape outside his door, she began to sob.

Several students from the law school, including Fang Mu, stood outside Meng Fanzhe's room and watched his mother haltingly open the door. As soon as she walked inside, she looked all around, as if she was expecting to see Meng Fanzhe and hear him say, "Mom, you've come." After her gaze swept the room, she knelt beside his bed, pulled his blanket beneath her nose and inhaled as intensely as she could. She began to wail, an anguished cry of misery and loss. After she cried for a long time, the policemen reminded her why she was there. She slowly stood up and organized her dead son's belongings.

Because the majority of Meng Fanzhe's things had been taken by the police as evidence, there only remained enough affects to fill his mother's small travel bag. As she left the room, holding the last things her son had left on this earth, she suddenly said to one of the policemen, "Would I be able to see the boy that my son attacked? I just can't believe my son could ever kill someone."

The man's eyes rested for a second on Fang Mu's face down the hall before he said tersely to the woman, "No, that won't be possible."

At once everyone's eyes fell on Fang Mu.

He paid no attention to them, just watched as Meng Fanzhe's mother hobbled down the hall and then disappeared through the door at the end.

The watching students weren't yet ready to leave. They continued to crowd the hall, and every now and then one would look over at Fang Mu and whisper something to the people around him.

With what seemed to be a great deal of determination, Zou Tuanjie walked over to him. "Fang Mu, why did Meng Fanzhe want to kill you?"

Fang Mu stared at him for a few seconds. "I don't know."

Fang Mu really didn't know. For the past two days, he had been going over and over everything that had happened between him and Meng Fanzhe, and he couldn't find a single motive for the guy to want to kill him. There was also too much of a disparity between Meng Fanzhe and the killer Fang Mu had theorized; while he often reminded himself that his profiles were never going to be perfectly spot-on, these differences were simply too great.

However, a few things were undeniable: Meng Fanzhe had marked the equation of "7" on Fang Mu's door, and then tried to kill him. Also, a lot of evidence had been discovered in his dorm room.

Still, Fang Mu couldn't picture Fang Mu as the sly and ruthless individual who had committed all the crimes, especially not after seeing him pressed against the window of the police car, crying soundlessly. Fang Mu just kept telling himself again and again, It's not him, it's not him.

In that instant in the police car, Meng Fanzhe was obviously begging for him to help.

Was this really how the killer would behave?

Soon after, the special investigation team began pulling out of Jiangbin City University campus. Prior to their departure, Tai Wei went to tell Fang Mu about the latest developments in the case. After searching through Meng Fanzhe's belongings, police had not found any sort of receipt from a car or apartment rental, nor had they discovered anything else that indicated he had rented either of these things. Still, based on the rest of the evidence, they were positive that the murders were his doing. Since he was now dead, the police decided to close the case.

After listening to this, Fang Mu was silent for a moment. "In other words, your conclusion is that Meng Fanzhe was the killer?"

Tai Wei nodded. "That's right."

"Do you really believe he was the killer? Or would you just prefer to believe it?"

Tai Wei made an effort at self-control at what sounded much like an accusation. "What do you mean?"

"Meng Fanzhe was not the killer!"

"What's your evidence?"

Fang Mu hesitated.

"Intuition? What's more reliable: intuition or facts?" Tai Wei's annoyance turned to a low level of rage. "Do you take us all for idiots?" he asked testily. "There's no denying that you've been a huge help to this case, but we've done our part as well!"

"How about the motive? What was Meng Fanzhe's motive?"

"Shit! Can't you see the guy was a lunatic? Since when do lunatics need a reason to kill people?"

Fang Mu scowled back at him. "Could a lunatic have planned such precise murders? Could he have copied all those other serial killers?"

"He...he probably didn't lose his mind all at once..."

"Really?" Fang Mu flung his cigarette far away.

Tai Wei continued to smoke impatiently. Suddenly his eyes narrowed on Fang Mu. "Maybe you're just being difficult because you're simply ashamed that the profile you predicted fit someone completely different than Meng Fanzhe. Is that really it?" He laughed, and then added in a stinging tone, "And especially since all this happened in front of your girlfriend?"

"Go fuck yourself!" Fang Mu bit back at him, and stormed off.

Rather than return to his dorm, Fang Mu headed to the library. For the past few days he had practically lived there, taking out all the books that had been found in Meng Fanzhe's dorm room and reading through them one by one. He hoped to find some clues about the course of Meng

Fanzhe's psychological transformation, and although he knew it was probably hopeless, at the moment it was the only thing he could do.

Actually, he could completely understand where Tai Wei was coming from. They had been working on the case for nearly half a year; add to that the foreign pressure from the Thomas Gill murder, and everyone was just hoping to solve it as soon as possible. However, he refused to accept the verdict. Meng Fanzhe was not the killer – of that he was sure; but he had no way of proving it.

Suddenly his phone rang. All the students reading nearby glared in his direction. Frowning at him, Librarian Sun nodded toward the hall, indicating to answer it outside.

Fang Mu waved at him apologetically, grabbed his phone and ran out into the hall.

Flipping open his phone, Fang Mu saw the number wasn't in his phone book. When he looked at the area code, his heart skipped a beat – it was from Suijing City.

Meng Fanzhe's hometown.

"Hello?" he said into it.

He heard an old woman's voice on the other end. "Excuse me, is this Fang Mu?"

"That's right. Who am I speaking to?" he asked politely.

"I'm Meng Fanzhe's mother."

His mouth fell open. How did she get his number? "Oh, hello, Auntie. What did you want to talk to me about?"

"Well, I believe you already know what happened with Meng Fanzhe. Yesterday I finished organizing his final affairs..." Her voice choked with sobs. "And I just got home earlier today. After resting for several hours, I unexpectedly discovered that there was a letter in our mailbox. When I looked at it, I saw that it was from Fanzhe, and that he had sent it several days ago. I checked the date and it was the very day that all this happened."

He felt as if his heart was about to stop. "Meng Fanzhe...sent you a letter?"

"That's right. The letter is really confusing. He mentioned a bunch of strange things and said they had to with some doctor that he had met recently. He also wrote that if anything ever happened to him that I should give the letter to you, and he gave me your phone number and said that you were the only one who could help him..." At this point, she began to moan in pain.

"Auntie, Auntie, are you still there?" he asked anxiously. "What's wrong?"

"I'm here. My heart isn't doing too well. Just now...it felt a little agitated..."

"Is your medication nearby?"

"Yes. Wait a moment, I'm going to go take some."

Through the receiver, Fang Mu could hear the sound of footsteps. Then a drawer was opened, pills rattled in a bottle, and a faucet was turned on.

After a little while, Fang Mu again heard Meng Fanzhe's mother's voice. "Hello?"

"Auntie, I'm here."

"How can I get you the letter?"

"Auntie, please tell me your address. I'll come get it now."

"Okay, write this down: apartment four-zero-one, building three of number six, Golden Pedestal residential area, eighty-three North Riverbend Street, Baita District in Suijing City. Got that?"

After copying down the address, Fang Mu read it back to Meng Fanzhe's mother. Then he warned her: "Auntie, whatever you do, don't leave the house. Wait for me and then we'll figure everything out."

"Okay."

After hanging up, Fang Mu went back into the reading room and returned all the books to their shelves. He quickly collected his things and hurried back to his room.

It was already 3:50 p.m. and it would probably take him around three hours to get to Suijing City. Fang Mu doubted he would be able to make it back that night. After returning to his dorm, he opened his drawer to find that he had only a little over 100 renminbi. He packed himself a small bag, left Du Yu a note saying that he wouldn't be back until tomorrow, and grabbed his bank card and ran to the local sub-branch at the campus gate.

The bank was filled with elderly men and women collecting their pensions, and there was a long line at the ATM outside. Fang Mu looked at all the old people in their thick glasses who were checking the figures in their bankbooks again and again, and weighed his options. At last, feeling helpless, he lined up at the back of the queue for the ATM.

The line wriggled slowly forward. Fang Mu kept looking nervously from his watch to the distant ATM. When it was finally his turn, he took out 1,000 renminbi and then sprinted over to the cab stand in front of the school gates.

By the time Fang Mu reached the long-distance bus station it was already 4:30. With a sinking feeling, he learned from the attendant at the ticket counter that the last bus for Suijing City had just left. Hearing this, Fang Mu jumped in a cab and headed to the train station.

Luckily, there was still another train to Suijing City leaving at 5:10. After buying a ticket, Fang Mu went to the train station supermarket and bought some bread and a bottle of water, and then sat quietly in the waiting room until his train arrived.

When he had seen Meng Fanzhe eating his cat alive in the bathroom that night, he had had a feeling that someone was giving Meng Fanzhe psychotherapy – and that there had been an error in his treatment, bringing his mind to the brink of collapse. Then on the night when Meng Fanzhe had gone raging mad and tried to kill him, Fang Mu began to suspect that someone might be controlling his classmate.

Meng Fanzhe's mother had just told him that the letter mentioned a doctor. This seemed to give preliminary proof to Fang Mu's suspicions. And if this person really did exist, then he was certain to have had something to do with the murders.

Fang Mu could feel he was getting closer and closer to the truth.

It made him burn with impatience, and as he waited, time seemed to pass much slower than usual.

The train traveled steadily along the tracks, sounding its horn with a kind of rhythm.

The train was much emptier than Fang Mu had expected, and he was even able to find himself a seat. The train attendant told him that it was a local train, making all the stops, so they wouldn't be arriving at Suijing City for another four hours and 40 minutes.

It was hardly a long journey, but since Fang Mu knew that at its end laid the answers he had long been searching for, the wait felt unbearable.

He sat next to the window, watching the sky gradually darken. Every now and then the train would stop at a station and a smattering of passengers would get on, holding bags of all sizes.

The dress and social status of the each of the passengers was different, but almost everyone looked anxious to return home.

What was home? Hot food, warm slippers, a familiar bed, and the affectionate scolding of one's family members.

Perhaps Meng Fanzhe had thought these same thoughts when he took this train home, maybe even wearing the same sort of expression.

Fang Mu laid his head against the cold window as the image of Meng Fanzhe pressing his tear-streaked, frightened face against the cop car window appeared in his mind.

Save me, save me, Fang Mu.

Fang Mu closed his eyes.

Fang Mu walked out of the Suijing City train station at a little before 10 p.m. He bypassed all the pimps incessantly touting, "Lodgings, pretty girls, very cheap," and hurried out to the public square where the cabs were parked.

His cell phone suddenly rang. He pulled it out and looked at it. It was Deng Linyue. After thinking about it for a moment, he decided to answer.

"Hey."

"Where are you?" Deng Linyue hadn't contacted him for a few days, and her voice was a little cold.

"I'm off-campus."

"Where? I'll come meet you."

"It's too far. I'm outside the city, in Suijing City."

"Suijing? What are you doing there?" Her voice sounded surprised.

"Don't worry about that right now," he said, hailing a cab as he spoke. "I've got some pretty important stuff I need to take care of. I'll tell you about it when I get back."

"Oh…all right. Well, make sure you look after yourself." She paused, and then added, "I'll be waiting for you."

After hanging up, Fang Mu told the driver where he wanted to go, and then suddenly realized that he should probably give Meng Fanzhe's mother a call.

He dialed her number and the phone rang and rang. No one picked up. It didn't seem right at all, so Fang Mu urged the driver to hurry up.

They crossed the city, the streets gradually emptying out. At last the driver stopped in front of a residential neighborhood.

"Seventeen bucks," the driver said, pointing at the meter. As Fang Mu handed him a 50, he looked off at the nearby apartment buildings.

"A fifty? You don't have any change?"

"No, just keep twenty for yourself," said Fang Mu hurriedly, not wanting to delay any longer.

"Sure thing, boss," said the driver with a smile. "Wait a second, I'll give you a receipt." The printer attached to the meter buzzed to life and spat out a receipt. Ripping it off, the driver handed it to Fang Mu along with 30 renminbi.

Fang Mu got out and walked inside the Golden Pedestal residential area. The place had obviously been around for a while. The buildings were all made in the old style, with outdoor walkways running alongside the apartments. Squinting, he did his best to make out the cracked and faded building numbers. Luckily the place wasn't that big and he quickly found building six.

After reaching unit three, Fang Mu carefully climbed the stairs. He soon reached the fourth floor. He looked around. Apartment 402 was to the left, 403 to the right. He walked left and found the apartment all the way at the end of the hall.

He was met by an old-fashioned wooden door. New Year's blessings from the beginning of 2002 were still stuck to the outside. He knocked lightly. When there was no response, he glanced at the window beside the door. All the lights inside appeared to be off.

Could she already be asleep?

Fang Mu knocked again. Still no response. He pulled lightly on the door handle and to his surprise, it opened.

"Anyone here?" he yelled, sticking his head inside.

No answer.

A sense of foreboding suddenly came over Fang Mu. He pulled the dagger from his pocket, unsheathed it, and slowly entered the apartment.

The apartment was pitch-black. Not a single light was on. Fang Mu stood in the entryway for several seconds. He could vaguely make out a hallway ahead of him. A door was to his left. Through it he could see the dim shapes of a stove and range hood. He assumed it was the kitchen. To his right was a small window. A few potted plants sat on the sill.

Fang Mu walked carefully forward. The hallway was about 16 feet long. When he reached the end everything was just as dark as before, but he could tell that the space in front of him had opened up. Probably the living room.

Fang Mu stopped at the entrance to the living room and forced his eyes to adjust to the darkness. At the same time, he listened closely for any sounds of movement.

Gradually, he began to hear strange rustling noises coming from within the living room. It sounded like someone turning the pages of a book, or tiny claws moving across cotton.

Fang Mu was focusing as hard as he could on the sound when he suddenly felt something scurry across his foot. Startled, he jumped back and slammed into the wall, feeling as if his heart was about to leap out of his chest.

It was then that he remembered the lighter in his pocket. He pulled it out and flicked it on. A small flame emerged and the scene before him was finally revealed.

It was in fact the living room. At its front sat a cabinet with a TV inside. Facing the TV was a couch, the back of it before Fang Mu.

From the thin light of the flame, he could vaguely make out several strands of gray hair hanging over the back of the couch.

"Auntie?" he asked haltingly.

The hair didn't move at all.

The lighter had already begun to burn Fang Mu's hand, but he ignored this and walked slowly toward the sofa, gripping the knife as tightly as he could.

As he got closer to the sofa, his heartbeat sped up, his teeth chattering nervously, and his hand began to shake so badly that he thought for sure he would drop the lighter.

Just when he was about to reach the sofa, the lighter suddenly went out and Fang Mu's eyes were plunged once more into darkness. Flicking at the burning-hot lighter, he shuffled forward. Right as his knee brushed against the sofa, the lighter clicked on and a huge flame shot out.

A bloodless face, its eyes and mouth wide open, suddenly appeared before him.

Meng Fanzhe's mother was half-sitting, half-lying on the sofa, her face upright and her hair falling over the back. One of her hands gripped her chest, the other held onto the sofa cover. Her eyes were bulging and her mouth was gaping wide, a terrified look on her face.

And she was dead.

A big black rat sat on one of her legs. Provoked by the flame from Fang Mu's lighter, it didn't try to hide at all, just stared at Fang Mu with its small red eyes.

When the lighter began to burn Fang Mu's hand, he was finally shaken out of his state of terror and forced back to reality. Panicking, he swung his dagger all around in blind defense, frantically searching his pocket for his cell phone.

At last he found it. Flipping the phone open, he was about to dial Emergency when he heard hurried footsteps outside the apartment.

Suddenly several flashlight beams shot into the apartment through the window beside the door. Blinded by the light, Fang Mu covered his eyes with his hand.

In that instant, he noticed that two strange symbols had been written in the condensation on the window glass. It had been too dark to notice them before.

"Who's there? Put the knife down now!" a man shouted. "Now! Or we will open fire!"

Fang Mu heard the sound of guns being cocked. He hurriedly tossed his dagger on the floor and put his hands up.

Several cops pounced on him and forced him to the ground. Struggling to lift his head, Fang Mu tried to see what exactly had been written on the window.

"Goddammit, you still don't want to cooperate, huh?" Someone struck Fang Mu across the face.

He tasted blood. With his head still spinning, he twisted weakly around. "The window..." He mumbled repeatedly over and over: "The window... What's on the window...?"

23 CHRISTMAS EVE

Shortly after falling asleep at around three in the morning, Tai Wei was woken by the ringing of his cell phone.

Stumbling out of bed, he grabbed for his phone and flipped it open, his eyes still closed. "Hello?"

"Is this Officer Tai?"

"Yeah. Who's this?"

"I apologize for waking you," said the voice over the phone. "I'm Li Weidong from the Baita PSB substation in Suijing City. Do you remember me?"

Li Weidong? Tai Wei did remember him. Once when Tai Wei had gone to Suijing City to arrest an armed fugitive he had made contact with the Baita substation. As he recalled, Li Weidong was quite a drinker.

"Oh, it's you, Weidong. Nice to hear from you."

Li Weidong gave a slight, embarrassed laugh. "I know it's very late, and I really am sorry, but there's something I need to discuss with you. Do you know a Fang Mu?"

All of Tai Wei's sleepiness immediately disappeared. "Fang Mu? Yes, I know him. Why?"

"At this moment he's in our custody."

"In your custody? What happened?"

"An old women died in our district last night, and he was found at the scene."

"Are you saying…?"

"No, it's not that. The results of our medical examiners just came back, and at this point there's no evidence that he was involved. However, when we asked him what he was doing there, he said he was investigating a crime and asked us to call you."

"Oh, I understand." Tai Wei knew exactly what had happened. Suijing City was Meng Fanzhe's hometown, and the dead woman was most likely his mother. "Weidong, tell me if this sounds acceptable. For now, don't interrogate him. I'd stake my life on Fang Mu not having had anything to do with the woman's death. I'm going to head over there right now. Once I'm there we can figure all this out."

"Fine by me," said Li Weidong, without hesitation.

Tai Wei rushed over to the Suijing City Baita substation. By the time he arrived it was already 6:30 a.m. Li Weidong was waiting for him in the courtyard.

With no time for proper greetings, Tai Wei got right to the point. "Where's Fang Mu?"

Li Weidong led him to the entrance of the detainment room. Through the small window in the door, Tai Wei could see Fang Mu curled up asleep on one of the benches, a police-issue sleeping bag wrapped around him. Part of his face was bruised.

"You guys hit him?" Tai Wei asked, frowning.

"Yeah," said Li Weidong, laughing with embarrassment. "He was struggling like crazy at the scene last night. He probably got struck a few times."

When they were back in Li Weidong's office, Li Weidong politely handed Tai Wei a cigarette.

The cigarette burned away between Tai Wei's fingers, his impatience growing. "So what exactly happened?"

"It's like this," Li Weidong said. "Last night we received a call from a resident of the Golden Pedestal residential area on North Riverbend Street. He said that while making a call out on the terrace he happened to notice someone standing in front of an apartment on the fourth floor walkway across from him. The man continued to watch this person as he made his call, and saw that after knocking a few times, the person walk inside the apartment. The caller said he was surprised to see that the person did not turn on any lights. Then, when he saw a small flame appear inside, and noticed that the intruder had pulled out a knife, he was so startled that he called us immediately. Because some of the men from our substation happened to be in the area breaking up a gambling ring, they were able to quickly swing by." He paused for a moment. "When we arrived at the scene and saw the dead woman, we realized that the situation was very serious, so we brought the kid back here."

"Was the dead woman named Dong Guizhi?"

"Yeah," said Li Weidong, surprised. "How'd you know?"

"She's the relative of the suspect in a case we were investigating recently," said Tai Wei simply. It was clear to him Fang Mu had gone to Suijing City because of Meng Fanzhe.

"Did he say anything about what he was doing at the crime scene?"

"At first he didn't say, just kept telling us that we needed to go back to the scene and look at the marks on one of the windows," Li Weidong said, "saying it was extremely important. So while we questioned him, we notified one of the officers at the scene to check the window for any marks."

"Marks? What marks?"

"Who knows? The officer inspected the window that Fang Mu was talking about. The inside of it was covered in water droplets and was marked by nothing, and the outside had already been wiped clean by all the neighbors who pressed against it to see what was going on. The officer didn't find a thing."

"Then what happened?"

"Then Fang Mu told us to look for a letter at the crime scene and told us the date it was sent. I relayed this information to the officers at the scene. They searched through a huge stack of letters, but didn't find anything from the day Fang Mu was talking about. After that, he gave us your number and told us to contact you."

Tai Wei didn't say anything further, silently smoking. When his cigarette was gone, he looked at his watch. It was almost seven. "Can I take him back with me now?"

"I'm afraid not," said Li Weidong. "As of right now, Fang Mu is still too tied up in the case. However, my fellow officers are working as fast as they can, and if all goes well, we should reach a preliminary conclusion on the case soon."

At that moment a young policeman walked into the room, carrying several large plastic bags. Some were filled with soybean milk, others with deep-fried twisted dough sticks and stuffed steamed buns.

"Put them in here," said Li Weidong, indicating several stainless bowls on the desk. He motioned to Tai Wei. "Why don't you have something to eat? You must be hungry, too." He turned back to the young officer. "Take several steamed buns to Fang Mu and give him some hot water, too."

While they ate, Li Weidong asked Tai Wei about the case he had mentioned. Since it was already closed, Tai Wei decided there was no harm in talking about it, so he briefly described the particulars to Li Weidong.

"No wonder," Li Weidong said with a smile. "Yesterday when we were about to question the kid, he quickly listed all his rights before we even had time to read them to him. He sounded like he was even more familiar with criminal procedure than we were. It figures that he's a grad student."

As he finished speaking, an officer with heavy bags under his eyes opened the door and looked to him. "Weidong, can I have a word with you?"

Wiping his mouth, Li Weidong turned to Tai Wei. "You keep eating. I'll be back in a little bit."

Li Weidong was gone for more than an hour. When he returned, it was with Fang Mu.

When they entered the room, Fang Mu continued to ask Li Weidong his most-pressing questions. "Did you find the letter? What was written on the window?"

Ignoring him, Li Weidong turned to Tai Wei and said, "Everything's been pretty much straightened out. In a moment I'll need you to sign a few forms and then you can take him back."

Fang Mu's dissatisfaction with the matter was still evident on his face, but Tai Wei gave him a glance that told him not to say anything else. He tossed Fang Mu a cigarette. Fang Mu caught it, looked over at Li Weidong, and then sat reluctantly in one of the chairs and lit the cigarette..

"So there's no problem?" Tai Wei asked Li Weidong.

"Nope. Our medical examiners worked through the night to make an autopsy of the corpse, which confirmed that the woman died of a heart-attack," Li Weidong said. "As it turned out, the old lady had a serious case of rheumatic heart disease. We found a number of rats while investigating the apartment and believe that one of them probably scared her to death. Also," he said, pointing at Fang Mu, who was sullenly smoking, "we found a train ticket and taxi cab receipt in one of his pockets. We contacted the cab driver and he remembered Fang Mu well because he had given three renminbi more than the fare. The driver confirmed the time he had dropped him off, which was over an hour after Dong Guizhi had died."

Not seeming to care that he had just been freed of suspicion, Fang Mu asked again: "What about the letter? And the marks on the window?"

Li Weidong looked at him. "We couldn't find the letter you were talking about, and as for that window, there were no marks when we checked. Take a look at this picture if you don't believe me." He took a picture out of the folder he was holding and handed it to Fang Mu.

Fang Mu studied the picture for a long time, turning it in every direction. At last, without saying a word, he placed it on the table and stared unhappily at the floor.

"Although we still don't understand why you were at the crime scene, we have determined that this was merely a coincidence," Li Weidong said. "Therefore, once we take care of a few formalities, you'll be free to go."

"It wasn't a coincidence!" Fang Mu suddenly yelled in agitation.

"Keep quiet!" Tai Wei roared. He turned to Li Weidong. "In that case, let's take care of this stuff so I can take him back."

Li Weidong nodded and left the office.

Tai Wei looked back to Fang Mu. "You want them to keep you locked up in here? If not, then the less you say, the better!"

Fang Mu didn't reply, just took a deep drag on his cigarette.

After the paperwork was finished, Tai Wei and Fang Mu were allowed to leave. While retrieving his personal belongings, Fang Mu discovered that his dagger was no longer there, and when he asked the policeman in charge, he was told that the knife had been confiscated. Finding this unacceptable, Fang Mu demanded that they return it to him, refusing to leave if they did not.

Seeing no other choice, Tai Wei went to find Li Weidong again, and at last they got the dagger back.

After politely refusing Li Weidong's invitation to get something to eat, Tai Wei took Fang Mu to the jeep and they headed back to Jiangbin City. As soon as Fang Mu was inside, he lay down in the back and fell into a gloomy sleep.

Seeing the exhausted expression on Fang Mu's face, Tai Wei sighed and turned up the heat in the jeep.

After driving for over an hour, Tai Wei saw in the rear-view mirror that Fang Mu had sat up and was drowsily licking his cracked lips.

"You're awake?" Tai Wei noted. He passed Fang Mu a half-full bottle of water.

Fang Mu emptied the bottle in one gulp. He leaned silently against the seat back and stared out the window, still dazed.

"Talk to me," Tai Wei insisted. "Why did you go to Meng Fanzhe's home?"

Fang Mu didn't immediately respond. After a while he said slowly, "Meng Fanzhe's mother called me and said that before her son's incident, he had sent her a letter. In it he mentioned my name, and said that if anything ever happened to him, she should give the letter to me."

"Oh? And what did the letter say?"

"I don't know. You heard him yourself; they didn't find it at the scene."

"Then what were those marks you were talking about?"

"When the police arrested me," Fang Mu said wearily, "I saw what appeared to be symbols written onto the window glass. But now they're gone."

"Symbols? What did they look like?"

Fang Mu thought for a moment. "I'm not sure. They didn't look Chinese. It was almost like...eh..." He thumped his head. "I just can't remember."

"Forget it; don't think too much about this," said Tai Wei as they passed a truck. "And make sure you take it easy when you get back. You're lucky the old lady's death was just an accident or I never would have gotten you out of there so fast."

"It was not an accident!"

"How is a heart-attack not an accident? Or are you saying someone killed her?"

"When I entered the apartment, the door was unlocked. Does that sound normal to you?"

"She was probably just careless, accidentally let in a few rats and then was so startled that she had a heart-attack."

"Not only was the door unlocked, the lights were all off…"

"Maybe she was about to go to sleep?" It sounded more like a question than a statement as Tai Wei said it.

"Are you wearing your daytime clothes when you turn off the lights to go to sleep?"

For a moment Tai Wei was tongue-tied. Then after thinking for a while, he said, "The old lady probably just got back and forgot to shut the door. Maybe she was feeling really tired, so she lay down on the sofa to take a nap. After sleeping for a little while, she suddenly felt something crawl across her body. So, she reached out to see what it was, discovered it was a rat, and then had a heart-attack and died." He looked back at Fang Mu in the rear-view mirror. "Well, what do you think?"

Fang Mu snorted in disbelief at the scenario. "If you don't want to believe me, fine, but don't act like I'm an idiot!"

Insulted, Tai Wei glared angrily at him in the mirror. He continued driving, not saying a word.

After the jeep traveled in silence for a while, Fang Mu suddenly asked, "While going through Meng Fanzhe's things, did you find any hospital receipts or medical records or things like that?"

"No, why do you ask?"

"Meng Fanzhe's mother said that in his letter he mentioned a doctor."

"A doctor?" Tai Wei's hands tightened on the steering wheel. "How can there be another doctor?"

"What do you mean another?" asked Fang Mu immediately.

"Um… Do you still remember the letter that Ma Kai wrote you?" He avoided Fang Mu's eyes. "In it he also mentioned a doctor."

Fang Mu lunged forward. "You read the letter?"

"I just glanced over it," Tai Wei quickly explained, shrugging. "When he gave it to me, I honestly couldn't resist taking a look at it, but before I could actually read it I was ordered to go take care of something else."

"What did it say?"

"Like I said, I only read a few sentences, but basically he was saying that he was not a bad person, and that he had previously gone to a doctor for treatment, but unfortunately this had not gotten rid of his illness."

When Fang Mu didn't say anything for a long time, Tai Wei looked at him hovering at the seat back. "What? Are you thinking that these doctors are the same person?"

Fang Mu shook his head. "I don't know."

For a moment Tai Wei was lost in thought, attention back on the road. "You shouldn't think about this stuff anymore," he said at last. "Meng Fanzhe's case is already closed. Get some rest when you get back and you'll feel a lot better."

"You don't think it's suspicious that the letter has disappeared?"

Tai Wei was silent for a moment. "Fang Mu," he said slowly, "it's not that I don't believe you; it's just that Meng Fanzhe was this woman's only child, and the amount of pain she must have been in would have made it difficult for her to control herself. I'm certain that she was never able to accept that her son could have actually done these terrible things, and was noting every suspicious detail as evidence to help her reverse the verdict. As for that letter, I truly doubt that it ever existed. She probably just wanted you to come see her and used this as an excuse."

"Reverse the verdict? Then why didn't she just call you guys directly?"

"You were his victim. Perhaps what the old lady wanted to know most was why Meng Fanzhe wanted to kill you."

Fang Mu snorted in disillusion this time. He lay down on the back seat again, not saying a word.

Tai Wei looked back at him. "You hungry?" he asked after a few thoughtful moments. "Want me to grab you some food at the gas station up ahead?"

There was a weighty pause, and then he finally heard Fang Mu's muffled voice reply, "I'm fine. Thanks."

Tai Wei just shook his head helplessly, and stepped on the gas.

It was almost noon when they arrived at the Jiangbin City University gates. Tai Wei invited Fang Mu to get something to eat at one of the little restaurants nearby, but Fang Mu stiffly refused, grabbed his bag, and headed into campus without looking back.

Tai Wei watched him disappear into the crowd of people walking through the gate.

"Stubborn bastard," he muttered to himself, and then shut the door, got back in, and started up the jeep.

As the engine idled, he sat with his hands on the steering wheel, lost in thought. After hesitating for some time, he pulled out his phone and dialed.

"Hello? Brother Tai?" Li Weidong's voice sounded over the receiver.

"Yeah, it's me. You guys really didn't discover that letter at the scene?"

Li Weidong laughed. "What is it? You don't believe me?"

"No, no, no. I was just asking."

"Well, we really didn't find it. You want me to send someone over there to look again?"

"Yeah, that would be great." Tai Wei quickly added, "Also, could I trouble you guys to check one more time for any signs that someone else might have entered the apartment?"

"All right. However, we've recently been focusing on gambling and automobile theft, so our numbers are a little limited. When I get a chance I'll definitely send someone over there to check, and if they find anything I'll let you know."

"Thanks a lot. Now I've got some stuff to take care of, so I'll talk to you later." After hanging up the phone, Tai Wei looked back toward the campus entrance. Crowds of students were walking in and out, talking and laughing, their faces free of worry.

Could there really have been a letter?

Could the killer really be someone else?

Could we really have made a mistake?

These were possibilities that Tai Wei could not accept.

Du Yu wasn't around. That was lucky, because otherwise there would have been no end to the questions.

Fang Mu tossed his backpack onto his chair and then lay heavily on the bed.

His whole body hurt and the bruises on his face were still swollen. When he lay against the pillow, the pain made him groan.

With difficulty, he rolled over. He really wanted to go to sleep, but although he closed his eyes, he stayed wide awake. Two vague shapes refused to leave his mind.

The symbols on the window.

He got gingerly out of bed and sat at his desk. Grabbing a piece of paper and a pen, he tried as hard as he could to remember what he had seen the night before, and as he thought, he drew.

In fact, he wasn't even sure whether what he saw was man-made or just random smudges in-between the droplets on that window. Bit by bit, as his memory grew, the symbols took shape.

There was a total of two shapes. The one on the left looked a little like a "9" with a short horizontal line through the middle, while the one on the right sort of resembled the letter "A".

Fang Mu picked up the piece of paper and looked at it from every possible angle, but he still couldn't figure anything out. He tossed it aside, took out a cigarette, and glumly smoked it.

Someone had reached Meng Fanzhe's house before him, snatched the letter, and killed Meng Fanzhe's mother. From this he could deduce two things: First, this person knew about the letter and knew that Fang Mu was going to the house as well. Second, he knew Meng Fanzhe's mother had heart problems and was scared of mice.

Fang Mu thought back to when he had received Meng Fanzhe's mother's call in the library. Had there been anyone else around? Who were they? But he couldn't remember a thing. At the time he had been so engrossed in what she was saying that he hadn't paid any attention to the scene around him.

At the time he had considered having Meng Fanzhe's mother read him the letter over the phone, but fearing that this might get her too excited and worsen her heart condition, he'd decided against it. In the long run, however, it seemed that this decision had cost her life.

Exhausted, he leaned back in the chair and closed his eyes.

Meng Fanzhe had raised a cat, which meant that he was probably scared of rats. In fact, people's fears were mostly acquired from experiences earlier in life. So Meng Fanzhe's fear of rats probably came from his mother. Perhaps when he was young he saw his mother become terrified of a rat, and as a result, gradually developed this fear himself.

In which case, someone who knew that Meng Fanzhe's mother was scared of rats would also be someone who deeply understood Meng Fanzhe.

And the only person who could have gotten Meng Fanzhe to reveal such personal information was probably that doctor.

If this person really existed, then Fang Mu's initial deduction was correct: At first, this doctor had given Meng Fanzhe a certain amount of psychotherapy, helping him to overcome his fear of roll call, and probably also his fear of rats; it had been he who suggested Meng Fanzhe get a cat. In this way, Meng Fanzhe would have begun to deeply trust and rely on this doctor, even to the point where he would do whatever he was told.

In which case, beginning with the 7/1 double homicide, had Meng Fanzhe carried out all these murders under this doctor's control?

Most likely not. Fang Mu rejected this possibility almost immediately. First, although Meng Fanzhe had a weak personality, he was still a law graduate student and would have never agreed to kill someone. Second, even supposing that the doctor hypnotized Meng Fanzhe, the likelihood was still very low. Although movies often depicted hypnosis as being almost supernaturally powerful, from a criminal justice standpoint, it had never been proven that a person could be hypnotized into committing a murder; not to mention that no one under hypnosis could be capable of planning and carrying out crimes as detailed and meticulous as these.

In which case, could this doctor have been responsible for all the murders?

Fang Mu couldn't help but shiver.

What kind of person is this, and why is he after me?

Someone knocked on the door, jolting his thoughts. When Fang Mu opened it, Deng Linyue stood there.

He subconsciously turned his head as soon as he realized it was her, but she had already seen the bruises on his face.

A small gasp escaped her. "My God, what happened?"

"It's nothing, it's nothing," he mumbled, waving her into the room.

But she wouldn't let up so easily and insisted that he tell her what happened.

Unable to dissuade her, he had no choice but to explain everything.

When he had finished, Deng Linyue didn't say anything in response, just wordlessly sat beside his bed.

After a long silence, she asked, "Is this…really what you want to do?"

"What do you mean?"

She looked up. Placing her hand on his knee, she looked into his eyes and said, "You don't want to just be an ordinary person? Studying hard, graduating, and then going abroad with me? That's not good enough for you?"

Fang Mu looked down and said nothing. He gently moved her hand away and shook his head.

"Why?" she asked, her eyes filling with tears. "Do you think your life is normal? Do you think you're happy like this?"

His voice was soft as he spoke. "No."

"Then why are you doing this?" Deng Linyue suddenly jumped to her feet. "Are you a policeman? Is this your duty? Or is someone forcing you?"

When she saw that he wasn't going to respond, she bit her lip in an attempt to calm down. "Fang Mu, I admit that the reason I love you is because you're someone who has experienced a lot. There's an indescribable sort of force around you, and this made me curious. It also captivated me, and made me feel secure. But after I fell in love with you, I found that this force also scared me." The questions seemed to come tumbling out. "Why does so much death always seem to follow you? Why must you always place yourself in such dangerous situations? After what he did, that boy Meng deserved to die, so what does that have to do with you? Why do you have to get yourself tangled up in it? Why do you have to cause so much pointless trouble?" She paused. "When you were doing all this, did you ever think of me?"

Fang Mu looked up. "Meng Fanzhe isn't the killer. The killer is someone else."

"Then so what? Why don't you just not worry about it? Why don't you just let the police do their jobs? Why don't you just be a normal student?"

He smiled bitterly and shook his head. "Impossible." He held her attention. "There are so many things... You just wouldn't understand."

"What wouldn't I understand? Tell me!" She sat down beside him and wiped away the tears forming. Her eyes never leaving his face.

He looked steadily into her bright and innocent eyes. He opened his mouth to speak, but all he managed to say was, "You...don't need to know."

She stared at him until he looked away.

After a few long moments, she dried her eyes and slowly stood up. She walked to the door. "No matter what," she said in a quiet, soft tone, "I hope you know that regardless of what happens, I will always be by your side."

She opened the door and left.

For an instant Fang Mu wanted to call her back, hold her close, and whisper to her, "I'm sorry... forgive me."

But he didn't do a thing, just sat there and watched her disappear.

A few days later, Tai Wei called to say that Li Weidong had sent police to recheck the apartment, but because the scene had already been fairly heavily disturbed, it was impossible to determine if someone had been there before Fang Mu arrived. Additionally, interviews with the neighbors had turned up nothing of value. The police also searched through the apartment several times, and were certain that the letter Fang Mu mentioned was not at the scene.

Although Tai Wei didn't offer any official opinion over the phone, his position was already clear: the letter did not exist. Someone had to be lying, but whether this was Fang Mu or Dong Guizhi, he didn't know.

Fang Mu didn't feel like arguing with him, so after saying a few brief words, he quickly got off the phone. Sensing that Deng Linyue had been listening in to his conversation, he said without looking over at her: "That was Tai Wei. He called about the Suijing City investigation."

Sure enough, Deng Linyue had been true to her word. For the past few days, she had stuck close to Fang Mu at all times, except when they were asleep. No matter what time he left his dorm, she was always waiting for him outside.

But she was also speaking less and less. Even when they were eating, she often wouldn't say a word. Many times, Fang Mu would happen to look up at her and find that she was staring back at him.

The look in her eyes was no longer the warm, soft gaze from when they first got together; now it carried the hint of a close examination. It made him nervous when she looked at him like that, and when their eyes met he often had to look away in defeat after a few seconds.

At night, when he would walk her back to her dorm, Deng Linyue would always stand silently outside of it several minutes. He stood beside her, smoking or just looking off into the distance, not saying a word either. Often, she would turn and walk into her dorm without the least bit of warning, and though Fang Mu waited for her several times, he never saw her turn and come back as she had that one night before.

They hadn't kissed in a long time.

At one point Zhang Yao came to talk with Fang Mu. She told him that over the past few days Deng Linyue had been acting very strangely. Often Zhang Yao wouldn't see her all day, and then when Deng Linyue returned to the dorm at night, she would go straight to bed. One time, Zhang Yao woke to find Deng Linyue crying under her covers late in the night. When she asked her what was wrong, Deng Linyue just answered that she'd had a nightmare and wouldn't say anything else.

With the hint of a threat in her voice, Zhang Yao told Fang Mu that Deng Linyue had once asked her if she had made the right choice in being with

Fang Mu. "If you don't start acting a little nicer to her," Zhang Yao said, "I'm afraid she might dump you!"

Fang Mu didn't really care whether Deng Linyue dumped him or not, but hearing how sad she sounded, he couldn't but feel a little sorry. When she invited him to a Christmas party, he immediately said yes.

For Jiangbin City University students, Christmas was easily one of the best-loved holidays. Even though it was a foreign holiday, these black-haired, yellow-skinned students celebrated it with even more fervor than Chinese New Year. By mid-December, all the restaurants, flower stores, and gift shops around the school had begun promotional activities, the campus was covered with over-the-top advertisements and posters, and everywhere one looked was the image of that red-hat-wearing, white-bearded old man. Girls began looking forward to the gifts they would receive, while boys began saving their money, either for a gift that would make their girlfriend smile or one that would capture the heart of a girl they'd long admired.

Despite the festive atmosphere, Fang Mu hardly caught the Christmas fever. Previously, when he had been single, he had never given any thought to the holiday. But although he still felt the same way, when Du Yu asked him if he wanted to go shopping for Christmas gifts, he forced himself to tag along.

Du Yu strolled around the Guomao shopping mall as patiently as a girl, frequently stopping to ask Fang Mu what he thought of some item or whether another was actually so nice. Each time Fang Mu just shrugged and said: "It's all right." Soon Du Yu began to feel that having Fang Mu help him choose a gift hadn't been the smartest idea in the world, so he ignored him and kept looking on his own. Freed from his duties, Fang Mu walked leisurely along after him, hands in his pockets.

He may have been bored, but this kind of relaxed afternoon was hard to come by. After being so tense for so long and after all the terrible things that had happened, he found it truly satisfying to stroll around, with a light heart and an empty mind.

While passing a counter covered with little knick-knacks, Fang Mu happened to catch sight of a small glass globe. The glass gleamed so brightly that he stared at it for an few extra seconds. Noticing this, the young saleswoman immediately called him over in a warm and enthusiastic tone. Seeing no reason not to, Fang Mu walked over to take a closer look.

The globe was actually a music box, or at least made up the upper half of one. Underneath it was the musical portion, a small and square box made of plastic. Inside the glass globe was a scene in miniature: a young man and woman standing side by side under a streetlight, with her leaning happily against his shoulder. Small white flakes were scattered around inside the globe, looking much like snow.

The saleswoman flipped a switch on the bottom and at once the miniature scene came to life. The streetlight inside switched on, the snowflakes swirled through the air, and tinkling music started to play. All the while, the two sweethearts were pressed close, snow floating all around them.

A ghost of a smile crossed Fang Mu's lips. It was snowing.

He thought of the smell of bare branches in the cold air.

... of the crunch of feet walking through snow.

... of a long ponytail tickling his face.

He then thought of two new sweethearts under a streetlight, first standing apart, and then pressing together.

"It's even prettier if you look at it at night," said the saleswoman, interrupting Fang Mu's thoughts.

"How much is it?" he asked, taking out his wallet.

By the time he finished paying, Du Yu had emerged from the crowd, a small plastic bag in his hand.

Seeing Fang Mu, he smiled. "So you bought something, too. What is it?" He grabbed the paper box out of Fang Mu's hand and opened it. "A music box? Where's your creativity? This kind of thing hasn't been popular in years."

Fang Mu laughed. "How about you? What did you get?"

Du Yu chuckled. "Actually, mine is a little over the top." He carefully removed a small, exquisite-looking box from the plastic bag. "It's Poison perfume by Dior, four-hundred-fifty renminbi."

"You sure got some deep pockets, huh?"

"I'm positive Zhang Yao is going to like this," said Du Yu, beaming with joy.

12/24: Christmas Eve.

The foreign languages grad school class of 2003 had rented a large conference room in one of the downtown hotels for the Christmas Eve party. Everyone was splitting the bill. The only requirement was: If you were in a relationship, you had to come as a couple.

Dinner was buffet-style, and while everyone ate, people took part in various skits and performances. Having no interest in this, Fang Mu sat at a table beside the window, quietly eating a plate of fried chicken and fruit salad and looking at the heavy car traffic outside.

The room was very hot and the window beside Fang Mu was covered in water droplets. Bored stiff, he used his finger to draw a design on the glass. After a little while, he realized that he had been drawing the two strange symbols he had seen that night at Meng Fanzhe's house.

What did they mean?

From the start, Fang Mu had been certain that Meng Fanzhe was not the killer. In which case, if it really was the doctor who had arrived at Meng Fanzhe's house before him, then whatever he had written on the window must have been meant for Fang Mu to see.

Could it have been a clue to the next murder?

He looked at the symbol on the left, the "9" with a line through the middle, and shook his head.

If Deng Linyue had been six and he had been seven, then there was no way the next one could be "nine". Therefore, the symbol before him most likely wasn't nine.

Besides, this 9 had been written very strangely. Not only was there a line through the middle, but also, unlike the way most people write 9; where the bottom half slants slightly to the left, this one ran straight down, almost perpendicular to the ground.

Rather than a 9, could it instead be the letter q?

As for the one on the right, no matter how he looked, it appeared to be an A.

Then if they were both letters, why was one uppercase and the other lowercase?

While Fang Mu was racking his brains over this question, Deng Linyue's reflection suddenly appeared in the glass.

She had been dancing for a while, and now her face was red from the heat and she kept fanning her neck with her collar. "What are you thinking about?" she asked.

"Oh, nothing really."

"Why aren't you over there having fun?"

He laughed. "I can't dance. You should go enjoy yourself; don't worry about me."

She covered his hand with her own. "Then I won't go either," she said softly. "I'll stay here with you."

At that moment, the student who was emceeing the party called loudly, "Next we're going to exchange presents. Time to show your S.O. how deep your love goes!"

Taking her hand away, Deng Linyue rifled excitedly through her bag. In the blink of an eye, she was holding a small gold-colored metal box.

She presented it to Fang Mu. "This is for you! Merry Christmas!"

"Oh, thank you." Taking the beautifully-made box from her, Fang Mu saw that the word "Zippo" was written on the side. He understood: It was a lighter.

"Open it up and took a look." Deng Linyue's chin was resting on her palms, her elbows on the table, an expectant look in her eyes.

He opened the box. Inside was a limited-edition Eternal Star Zippo. He knew its market price had to be over 1,200 renminbi. Lifting the cover, he flicked the flint wheel, and a flame whooshed out of the top of the lighter.

"Like it?" she asked, winking at him. "But I still don't want you to smoke too many cigarettes. Now, how about mine?"

Fang Mu hesitated for a moment, then handed her the wrapped box.

Beaming, Deng Linyue undid the wrapping paper. As she took out the box, a boy at the next table noticed it and snorted derisively. Looking over, Fang Mu saw that the boy was just placing a ring on his girlfriend's finger.

"Wow, how beautiful," Deng Linyue said, ignoring the boy. She smiled and held the music box to her heart. "Where's the on switch? Oh, don't tell me; I want to find it." Reaching under the box, she flipped it on and the music began to play.

The streetlight glowed. The snowflakes whirled.

She set the globe on the table and resting her chin on her crossed arms, watching the two sweethearts press together at the center of the snow globe. She watched all the way though, until the song ended.

"I love it," she said, carefully placing the music box in her bag. She looked up at Fang Mu and smiled sweetly. "Thank you."

At the next table, the girl was complaining that the ring was too small. Sweating, the boy there finally managed to squeeze it onto her pinky.

Seeing this, Fang Mu and Deng Linyue couldn't help but look at each other and laugh.

Du Yu and Zhang Yao walked over, arm in arm. She had given him a pair of Nike basketball shoes and he already had them on.

"What do you think? They're Scottie Pippen Nike Air Throwbacks. Slick, huh?" Du Yu smiled with pleasure.

"Enough," said Zhang Yao with a smile. "Look how pleased you are with yourself." She nudged his head playfully, and then turned to Deng Linyue. "Linyue, we're going to go do karaoke soon. You guys should come!"

Deng Linyue looked at Fang Mu, as if waiting for his approval.

Du Yu pulled Fang Mu over to him and said, "You don't need to ask – he's coming for sure!"

Three cabs pulled up out front of the Night Flyer karaoke club and let out more than a dozen young people. Before Fang Mu had even gotten out, he saw Du Yu emerge from the cab ahead of him talking on his cell phone. A few seconds later, however, whoever he was speaking to must have hung up, leaving Du Yu staring at the screen with a baffled look on his face. When Zhang Yao walked over to find out what was going on, the phone suddenly rang again. Although Du Yu picked it up and said "Hello" a few times, it seemed as if the person on the other end wasn't saying a word, so he hung it up and shrugged at Zhang Yao. She just stood there, a suspicious look on her face.

Everyone else then filed into the club, leaving only Fang Mu, Deng Linyue, Du Yu, and Zhang Yao outside. Gesturing wildly, Du Yu was trying to explain something to Zhang Yao, but she just smiled coldly, as if she didn't believe anything he was saying.

Deng Linyue walked over and said something to Zhang Yao, and then clasped Fang Mu's arm and led him into the club.

"What happened?" he asked her.

"I don't know; probably some kind of misunderstanding. We should just go inside and let them be for now," she told him. "Zhang Yao said that she'd come in soon."

After renting two private rooms and ordering beer and snacks, everyone began belting out the karaoke tunes. Unable to withstand the peer pressure, Fang Mu joined in and sang I Haven't Loved You Enough with Deng Linyue.

Du Yu and Zhang Yao never came back inside.

Eventually, Fang Mu called Du Yu, but he didn't pick up. Deng Linyue then called Zhang Yao, but she didn't answer either. Beginning to worry, Fang Mu grabbed his coat and said he was going to look for them. When some of the other boys heard this, however, they all sat him back down on the couch, laughing.

"Come on," one said. "Those two have been together for a long time. It's Christmas Eve; why do you want to disturb them tonight?"

Thinking it over, Fang Mu had to agree. If the two of them had gone to a hotel together, then he would clearly just be spoiling the fun.

By 3 a.m., everyone was exhausted. Unable to hold out any longer, several people had already fallen asleep on the couch, slumped at odd angles. Those who still hadn't had enough were singing tiredly or sitting around the table, drinking beer and chatting.

When someone suggested they tell scary stories, the others immediately agreed.

So people began regaling each other with tales of mountain village zombies and haunted offices. A few of the more cowardly girls hid behind their boyfriends' backs, revealing only their eyes as they listened in abject terror.

"Aw, that's all a bunch of bull," said one of the boys. "If you want to hear something scary, you'd better listen to him." He clapped Fang Mu on the shoulder, who had fallen asleep. "And everything he says will be true."

At once everyone perked up.

"That's right. Didn't you help the police investigate a bunch of cases, Fang Mu? Let's hear some stories."

"I heard you helped them solve those murders that the law school student committed. You have to tell us what happened."

"Yeah, I heard the murderer almost killed you, too. You've gotta tell us the story."

As Fang Mu looked around at all the curious faces, he suddenly remembered the scene before him when the provost had called him up onstage during the assembly.

They didn't care at all about the pain of the victims, or about the fate of Meng Fanzhe. To them, other people's deaths were nothing more than an exciting topic of conversation.

"There's nothing interesting to tell," he said pointedly.

Having been all set to hear some behind-the-scenes stories, the listeners groaned with disappointment. Unwilling to give up, several of the girls who had been hiding behind their boyfriends tried to provoke him, saying, "Don't be so selfish, tell us something." One of them even grabbed Fang Mu's arm and, ignoring her glaring boyfriend, swung it back and forth. "Come on, handsome," she said. "Let us hear one. Crime stories are my favorite; they're so exciting."

Fang Mu stared right into her eyes until she sensed his mood. Feeling a little frightened, she let go of his arm.

"Exciting?" He laughed, and the corners of his mouth curled into a faint smile. "If someone peeled off all your skin and then sewed it into clothing for a mannequin to wear, would you think that was exciting?"

The girl covered her mouth, her face paling at the description. "What's your problem?" her boyfriend yelled angrily. "You don't want to talk about it, fine, but what? Are you trying to threaten her?"

As the others quickly tried to smooth things over, Fang Mu grabbed his jacket and backpack and stormed out of the room.

When he was only a few steps down the hall, he heard Deng Linyue call his name. She quickly caught up to him.

"Don't be angry. They didn't mean anything bad by it." As she took his arm, a pleading look flashed through her eyes. "Why don't you stay for a little while?"

He lightly pushed her arm away. "I can't. You guys have fun. Don't stay too late."

He turned and walked away. He didn't look back once.

24 THE SIXTH LANE

Unexpectedly, Du Yu was already back in their dorm room. When Fang Mu walked in, Du Yu was leaning back in his chair and talking on the phone, still wearing his garish new Nikes. A half-empty beer bottle was on the desk.

"What are you doing back here?" Fang Mu peeked behind the door. "Where's Zhang Yao?"

Du Yu waved for him to be quiet and listened closely to whoever was on the phone. After a few seconds, he threw it against the desk with a bang, grabbed his beer, and took a huge gulp.

Fang Mu frowned. "What's wrong with you?"

Putting the beer down, Du Yu burped and said, "I'm…I'm fine."

Noticing his roommate's red eyes, Fang Mu asked again, "Seriously, what is it?"

"Man, I don't even know myself," said Du Yu at last. Then, as if he was finally letting something out that he had been holding back a long time, he continued. "Right when we arrived at the karaoke club someone called me, but when I picked up, the person on the other end was silent. Then just as I hung up, they called me again and still didn't say word. While I was standing there confused, Zhang Yao became suspicious and demanded that I tell her what was going on."

Fang Mu laughed. "I'm not surprised. If I were Zhang Yao and I saw someone was calling you that late, and especially on Christmas Eve, I'd be suspicious, too. Not to mention, you do have a wandering eye."

"I swear to God," said Du Yu, talking faster, "I've never done anything to dishonor Zhang Yao."

Fang Mu chuckled. "All right, I believe you. Then what happened?"

"Then she got angry and stormed off. When I tried to stop her, the crazy woman turned around and slapped me across the face." He rubbed his cheek as if it still hurt. "After that I was too pissed off to care, so I ignored her and caught a cab back here."

Fang Mu looked at his watch. It was almost 4 a.m. "Where is she now? Back in her dorm?"

"I don't know; no one's picking up the phone in her dorm room. I called her cell several times, but every time she just hangs up immediately."

Fang Mu smiled. "She's probably just still angry at you. Tomorrow – oh, I mean today – you'd better just humor her."

Du Yu didn't respond directly, just glared at his cell phone and muttered, "This girl, man. Her temper is too goddamn bad, and I normally just put up with it." He kicked his leg out, causing one of his shoes to fly into the corner of the room.

"Jeez, don't take it out on the shoes, man."

Fang Mu was in slippers. He shuffled over and grabbed the shoe. Just as he was about to pass it back to Du Yu, he saw something that made him freeze.

The word "AIR" was written on either side of the shoe in huge letters, and on both sides the designer had very skillfully transformed the shape of the A and the R. On the outer side, the R was placed beside the toe cap, while on the inner side, it had been subtly altered and was sewed by the heel of the shoe in a fluid way that looked extremely well-coordinated.

This meant that the placement of the A and the R was reversed on either side, and through some minute tweaks in their design, the two letters looked very similar.

It made Fang Mu think. Could the right-hand symbol he had seen on the window that night have actually been an R?

R? What was that supposed to mean?

When Du Yu saw that Fang Mu was staring blankly at his shoe, he asked curiously, "What's up?"

Coming back to reality, Fang Mu shook his head and said, "Oh, nothing." Then he tossed the shoe back to Du Yu.

"Jeez, a little softer, please. These are brand new."

This guy, thought Fang Mu. How come it wasn't a problem when he was the one kicking his shoe into the corner of the room?

Smiling to himself, Fang Mu grabbed his washbasin from beneath his bed and headed to the bathroom.

After he finished washing up, he returned to the room to find Du Yu on the phone again.

"Well," he said, "did she pick up?"

"Her phone's off," said Du Yu, tossing his phone on the desk. "What the hell? Where could she have gone?"

"There's nothing to worry about. It's really late; I'm sure she's just asleep." Fang Mu took off his glasses and then hopped in bed and pulled the covers up.

Du Yu didn't seem ready in the least to go to sleep. He just continued to lean back in his chair, staring at his shoes, lost in thought. After a while, he suddenly said, "Fang Mu." His voice was slightly trembling.

"Yeah?"

"You don't think…something happened to her, do you?"

"I don't think so." Fang Mu paused. "People were out all over the city tonight; nothing bad could have happened. You should get some sleep and not worry about it."

Du Yu stood up and walked anxiously around the room several times. Then he once more grabbed his phone and dialed.

"Hey, where'd you run off to...? Oh, Deng Linyue. Did Yaoyao come back yet?... Oh, I see... Yeah, he's here... You want to talk to him?... Oh, okay. Talk to you later."

Du Yu sat heavily at his desk. Without turning around, he said, "Deng Linyue asked if you were back."

"What about Zhang Yao?"

Du Yu didn't say anything.

"Maybe we should go look for her," said Fang Mu, reaching for his pants.

"No way!" yelled Du Yu suddenly. "Let her be an idiot if she wants!" He leapt to his feet, strode over to the door and angrily switched off the light. "Go to sleep!"

At 6:30 in the morning Fang Mu was woken by the sound of his ringing phone. He groggily sat up and reached for it, only to see that Du Yu was still sitting at his desk, phone in hand.

"You didn't sleep at all?" Fang Mu asked.

Du Yu's face was covered with stubble and he looked a lot more haggard. Squinting his eyes, he nodded at Fang Mu.

Fang Mu noticed that Du Yu's other hand was holding his stomach. "What's wrong?"

"My stomach hurts a little. I probably drank too much last night."

Fang Mu climbed out of bed and pulled on his clothes. "Come on. Let's grab some porridge at the dining hall and then find Zhang Yao."

The dining hall was fairly empty. Most people had probably stayed out late the night before and were sleeping in. Fang Mu had Du Yu find them seats while he went and bought them breakfast.

Two girls were standing beside him, scooping tea eggs onto their plates and chatting about the party they'd went to the night before.

When Fang Mu had stacked his tray high with food, he headed back to his table. As he passed the two girls, he happened to hear one of them say, "…It's really strange. It's so cold out today, but for some reason the pool's full of water…"

Fang Mu suddenly slowed his pace, and as he walked toward where Du Yu was sitting, he looked back at the two girls.

Abruptly, he placed his tray on one of the tables beside him and began running for the exit.

R was for river!

The symbol on the left wasn't a q – it was an uppercase G! Water droplets had dripped down the two letters, elongating them, which had made the G look like a q with a line through the middle.

GR. Green River!

The Green River Killer.

As Fang Mu burst out of the dining hall doors, he knocked a male student to the ground, but at this point he no longer cared.

Run! Run! Run!

Don't die! Don't die! I'm begging you…

He sprinted over the withered yellow lawn, darted around the tennis courts… He could see the outdoor swimming pool, its gray water rippling faintly.

No matter who you are, don't die!

He ran around the chain-link fence bordering the pool as fast as he could. The branches from the pine trees surrounding it struck his face, but he felt no pain. When he reached the entrance, he saw that the chain lock had already been pried off and was lying curled on the ground like a dead snake.

He pulled open the gate and ran inside.

Before him was a huge pool, already filled with water. He circled it, anxiously searching the depths. Before he had gone more than a few steps, he saw something moving underwater in the deepest part of the pool.

Someone was down there.

My God! The thought froze in his mind.

Without thinking, he took several hurried steps and then dove headlong into the pool.

The ice-cold chill spread from the tips of his fingers to the bottom of his feet. In a flash, he felt like he was going to suffocate.

When his feet touched bottom, he kicked off hard and rose back to the surface. With his head above water, he oriented himself, took a deep breath, and dove back under.

Although the water was extremely murky, Fang Mu could still see a young woman standing on the bottom of the pool. She was wearing a yellow tube top, short leather skirt, and black platform heels. Her arms were slightly raised and her head drooped, and her dyed-blonde hair fluttered with the movement of the water.

Fang Mu swam over, grabbed her clothing, and pulled as hard as he could, but she didn't move at all. Looking down, he saw that her ankles were tied to the drain with a piece of thick rope. This was why the girl had looked like she was standing up at the bottom of the pool.

Fang Mu swam back to the surface and dug wildly through his pockets. When he found the dagger, he put it between his teeth, took another deep breath, and swam back down.

As soon as he reached the bottom, he used all his strength to hack the rope in half. At once the girl's feet lifted off the bottom. Grabbing her clothing, he struggled to swim her back to the surface.

At last, using his final bit of strength, he heaved the girl onto the side of the pool. There she lay, eyes closed, not moving at all. With no time to rest, Fang Mu slapped the girl back and forth across the face, trying to wake her up. He head lolled, but her eyes did not open.

Wake up, please wake up! I'm begging you!

Lifting the girl's upper torso, he desperately shook her back and forth. The movement caused some water to trickle from her mouth. Seeing this, Fang Mu quickly hoisted her onto his shoulder and ran like madman back and forth beside the pool.

A few students who were walking by the pool caught sight of this frightening scene and ran to get a closer look. Dumbstruck, they watched as a man, who appeared to be a lunatic, sprinted about with a corpse held over his shoulder.

Fang Mu's hair had already frozen solid and his pant legs and shirt sleeves were stiff from the cold. Shivering all over, he continued to run rigidly back and forth, carrying the girl all the while.

More and more people continued to surround him. Some called the police, some whispered to each other, some cried softly, and some screamed aloud.

Fang Mu wasn't aware of any of this. His mind blank, he ran mechanically, repeating the same thing over and over to himself.

Wake up, wake up, I'm begging you...

At last, his strength gone, his legs went limp and he collapsed to the ground. The girl fell beside him.

Panting for breath, he crawled over, laced his hands over her chest and pushed down forcefully. After doing this several times, he pinched her nose closed and breathed deeply into her mouth.

Wake up! Wake up...

He repeated this several times, but the girl still didn't show any response. Still he gritted his teeth and continued on, hot tears rolling down his face.

Wake up, please wake up!

Fang Mu felt a pair of hands on his shoulders. It was Du Yu.

"Enough, Fang Mu, give it up. She's dead."

Fang Mu pushed his hands away and again placed his mouth over the girl's.

Taking hold of Fang Mu, Du Yu pulled him away from the girl. But as he did, Fang Mu reached out and, unwilling to give up, grabbed onto her hair.

The two of them fell to the ground. In Fang Mu's hand was a blonde wig.

The dead girl's hair was short and black.

Du Yu sat on the ground and stared at the corpse, his eyes wide. After several seconds he suddenly cried out: "Yaoyao?"

Fang Mu's heart sank. He clambered toward the girl and looked at her face.

Sure enough, despite the heavy makeup, she was Zhang Yao all right.

In an instant, everything around Fang Mu seemed to go silent.

He saw Du Yu kneeling over Zhang Yao's body, holding her and rocking her back and forth, calling out her name.

He saw all the people around them looking around and whispering to one another.

He saw police cars outside the pool area, their lights flashing.

He saw policemen rushing inside, yelling at the crowd to get out of the way.

But he didn't hear a sound. It was as if everything around him had become pure chaos.

Something sickly-sweet was churning in the pit of his stomach. Suddenly, he felt like he was about to explode.

"Aghh!" A howl loud enough to raise the dead roared out of Fang Mu. "Why? Why? If you want to kill me, then come and do it! Why do you have to kill so many people? Come on, kill me! Kill me!"

At once all the faces turned toward him. His features were distorted by anger and anguish, the sounds around him difficult to distinguish.

For a moment, Du Yu stared blankly at Fang Mu. Then he leapt on him and grabbed his collar. "What the hell was going on?" he demanded, shouting. At a loss, Fang Mu just looked away. He saw Deng Linyue staring at him from the crowd, her expression terrified.

Two police officers pulled Du Yu off of Fang Mu, and then someone else hauled Fang Mu to his feet and pushed him toward the exit.

The crowd automatically parted to let them through. All the faces were turned towards them, their expressions suspicious or panic-stricken or both. Fang Mu walked stiffly, a dull look in his eyes as the person behind him pushed him through the crowd and out of the gate. After they had walked for some ways, Fang Mu struggled to look back. It took him a long time to recognize that the man behind him was Tai Wei.

"Let's get you back to your dorm," Tai Wei said, his voice unusually gentle, almost soft, as he held tightly to Fang Mu's shoulders.

When they reached Fang Mu's dorm room, Tai Wei maneuvered the soaking, shivering student onto his bed and wrapped him in his blanket. He tossed him a towel, but Fang Mu just let it fall to the floor.

Sighing to himself, Tai Wei opened Fang Mu's dresser.

"Where do you put your clothes?"

As soon as the words left Tai Wei's mouth, Fang Mu threw off his blanket, staggered to his feet, and tried to run out the door.

Tai Wei quickly stopped him. "Where do you think you're going?"

"I'm...I'm going back there..." Fang Mu mumbled, pushing Tai Wei away from him.

"Oh, yeah, and what are you gonna do?"

"Search the scene!" said Fang Mu, the past hour's defeat suddenly exploding out of him. "Bastard! Bastard! I swear I'll get you!"

Tears welled and fell from his bloodshot eyes. His lips were pale and shaking.

Tai Wei grabbed hold of him firmly. "Let us take care of this."

Struggling with all his might, Fang Mu threw Tai Wei off him. When he flung open the door he ran smack into Du Yu.

Du Yu didn't say a word, just shoved Fang Mu backwards.

Unprepared, Fang Mu fell to his back on the floor of their room.

Before he could get up, Du Yu pounced on him and grabbed his collar.

"Fang Mu, who the hell are you?" The normally cheerful Du Yu instantly changed, his actions those of a man-eating lion, his tear-streaked face twitching with rage.

Fang Mu could only stare back. "What are you talking about?"

"I said who the hell are you?" Du Yu demanded and wrapped his hands around Fang Mu's neck and viciously shook him back and forth. "Just now you said that that person wants to kill you! What's that supposed to mean? That time when your old roommate visited, he said that a bunch of people died in your old dorm room. Why is all this happening? Now I'll ask you again; who the hell are you? Tell me now!"

Du Yu's hands closed tighter and tighter around Fang Mu's neck. Fang Mu could barely breathe, his face turning purplish-red.

Tai Wei intervened and quickly pulled Du Yu off of Fang Mu. Struggling, Du Yu wouldn't give up. "I want to hear it!" he roared. "Who the hell are you?"

Fang Mu sat up weakly, his body racked by a fit of coughing. Eventually he began to retch, spouting a thin strand of saliva that trailed from his mouth and to his chest.   Tai Wei held tightly onto Du Yu, who continued to struggle, still yelling. "If you have something to say, then say it! No more fighting!" Tai Wei warned. "Otherwise I'm gonna stop being so polite!"

"All right!" said Du Yu, making a show of putting his hands up. "I'll stop. Now let him talk!"

Fang Mu slowly climbed to his feet, wiped the corners of his mouth and then took several deep breaths. "That's right. The killer is after me." He gasped for air. He's...testing me...I'm sorry..."

Du Yu glared at him, his jaw clenched. "So you're saying that everyone who was hurt or killed – Deng Linyue, Liu Jianjun, Meng Fanzhe, and..." he choked back a sob, "and Yaoyao... It was all because of you?"

Fang Mu said nothing, just returned Du Yu's stare. He quickly hung his head, nodding.

Du Yu pointed at Fang Mu, his arm shaking. "In other words, you've known for a long time that he was going to kill people," he said through trembling lips, "and probably people close to you. Is that correct?"

Tears fell from Fang Mu's eyes. "I'm sorry..."

Du Yu's pain suddenly burst open again. "Then why didn't you say something sooner? Why didn't you warn everyone? Why did you let so many people die?"

Shaking all over, Fang Mu just mumbled, "I'm sorry...I'm sorry..."

Du Yu rushed forward and grabbed Fang Mu's hair. He struck Fang Mu wildly across the face. "Speak! Speak up, goddamn you...!"

Tai Wei immediately reached for Du Yu, but before he got close, Du Yu abruptly shrunk back.

The dagger was in Fang Mu's hands.

There was a long tear across the front of Du Yu's jacket. He stared dumbstruck at the tear, and then at Fang Mu, who was bleeding from one corner of his mouth.

Du Yu laughed through his misery. "You want to kill me, too, huh? Then do it! Save the killer the effort. Come on!"

"No!" yelled Fang Mu, his voice hoarse. "It wasn't like that. I wasn't intentionally hiding it from all of you… I…"

"Give me the knife," said Tai Wei, stepping between them. "And you," he said, pointing at Du Yu, "do me a favor and get out of here!"

Du Yu glared viciously at Fang Mu, and then turned and left.

At once the room was quiet, the only sound Fang Mu's ragged breathing.

Fang Mu let the blade clatter to the floor and sunk to his heels. He squatted down and began to scream, pulling at his hair as the tears rolled down his face. The only sound was his angry, mournful wailing cry. "Aghh…!"

Tai Wei had never seen Fang Mu cry before, much less sob with the kind of extreme grief he now witnessed. Not knowing what to do, he just stood there, completely at a loss.

Fang Mu cried for a long time, the pent-up emotions releasing. When he had calmed down a little, Tai Wei helped him onto his bed, wrapped him in his blanket and poured him a cup of hot water. After thinking about it, he passed him a cigarette.

His face covered with tears, Fang Mu sat there expressionlessly, taking a drag every now and then from his cigarette. The cup of water he just held. He didn't sip it once.

"You need to change out of your wet clothes, otherwise you're gonna get sick." Tai Wei dug through Fang Mu's drawers and tossed him several pairs of clean clothes.

With much effort, he helped Fang Mu change into dry clothes. Fang Mu's spirits improved slightly after the change of attire and he no longer shivered so badly.

"I was wondering," said Tai Wei tactfully, pulling Fang Mu's chair over beside his bed, "that thing Du Yu just said about your old roommates dying. What was he talking about?"

Fang Mu took several deep drags from his cigarette and was silent for a long time. "When I was in college," he said slowly, "one of my roommates had an illicit relationship with one of the building attendants. Later she became pregnant and wrote him a letter to tell him. My roommate then mistakenly believed that he had placed this letter in one of the books that he had returned to the library. And because of some unkind treatment he received soon after, he suspected that someone must have read the letter and told people what it said."

"Then what happened?"

"He was the seventh person to have checked out the book," Fang Mu relayed. "To avenge himself, he decided to kill every person who checked it out after him. By the time he discovered that no one had actually read the letter, he had already begun to enjoy the feeling of control he found by ending other people's lives. I later discovered that check-out card and realized that someone was going down the list of readers, killing one after another. The victims included one of my other roommates, as well as the first girl I ever loved… I was the only survivor."

"Is this that murder case that happened at Changhong City Teacher's College? I heard that in the end the killer also died."

"That's right." Fang Mu trembled. "He was burned to death. I was…there at the time."

Tai Wei was silent for a moment. "That's when you became really interested in criminal profiling, correct? Everything you've done, all those cases you've cracked – it was all because of this experience, wasn't it?"

Fang Mu tossed away his cigarette. He grabbed his hair with both hands and tried to smooth it down. "I don't know the best way to say this. I've been having nightmares for the past two years. I'm scared of hallways, scared of the smell of roasting meat. I don't dare get close to other people. Only by ceaselessly investigating cases and ceaselessly helping the dead find justice am I able to get a measure of peace... Because," Fang Mu paused, and then his voice suddenly dropped, "in the final analysis, the deaths of all those people – they were because of me."

Tai Wei nodded. Out of all of the human senses, smell stayed in the memory longest. At last he now understood why Fang Mu was such an unusual person, and also why the pain he felt this time, with the killer challenging him by murdering all these people, was so unimaginably severe. "The victim was Du Yu's girlfriend?"

Fang Mu nodded.

"Are you certain that it's the same killer?"

Fang Mu shook his head, smiling wryly. "You still don't believe me." He stared at the floor. "It's definitely him. He understands me extremely well; he knows how important Du Yu's friendship is to me. This was number six. Regardless of whether or not I'm seven, he's trying to destroy me psychologically, bit by bit."

Tai Wei hesitated for a moment, and then said, "When I was at the scene just now, I noticed that the place where the victim had been tied underwater was at the end of lane six."

Fang Mu stared at Tai Wei for several seconds, and then threw off the cover and got out of bed. "Come on," he said. "Let's go to the scene."

The body had already been taken away, but the crowd remained. Fang Mu was surprised to see Professor Qiao among them; he was looking at the pool and frowning. Seeing Fang Mu, he didn't even wave; just turned and left.

The police had placed a filter over the drain to collect any suspicious objects as they emptied the pool. Zhao Yonggui was standing beside the pool, staring at the slowly draining water with his arms crossed and a very dark look on his face.

Tai Wei walked over and patted him on the shoulder. "Find anything, Old Zhao?"

Zhao Yonggui looked at Tai Wei and then at Fang Mu. He shook his head. "Nothing."

His answer didn't surprise Fang Mu in the least. As he watched the cops searching carefully through the waist-deep water, he really wanted to tell them that it was pointless, that the killer wouldn't have left any stray clues behind.

Looking at Fang Mu's red, puffy eyes, Zhao Yonggui said, "You were the first to discover the body, correct?"

"Yes."

"Did you notice anything unusual at the time?"

Fang Mu thought about it and then said, "No, nothing."

"Then how did you know that someone would be in the pool?"

"I heard two girls talking about how the outdoor pool was unexpectedly filled with water. Also, while at Meng Fanzhe's house, I saw two symbols on the window –"

"Enough!" Cutting Fang Mu off, Zhao Yonggui glanced over at Tai Wei. "Are you still insisting that we caught the wrong person?"

For a moment, Fang Mu was speechless, and then as he was about to argue with Zhao Yonggui, he saw Tai Wei nod at him to keep quiet.

"In a little while we're going to take you back to the station to get your statement," Zhao Yonggui said. Without another word, he walked over to the other side of the pool.

On the way to the city bureau, Fang Mu couldn't resist asking Tai Wei, "Why does Zhao Yonggui always act like that towards me?"

Tai Wei hesitated for a moment. "You need to understand his perspective. Although the Meng Fanzhe case was closed without a trial, the bureau commended Zhao Yonggui and me. There's no way he's going to be able to accept your telling him that we made a mistake. Also, I don't think he really trusts in your methods."

Fang Mu considered this for a moment. "In that case, do you trust me?"

Tai Wei was silent for a long time. "We'll see."

It was already afternoon by the time Fang Mu got back from the police headquarters. Standing in front of his door, key in hand, he felt a weighty hesitation. If Du Yu was in the room, he didn't know what he should say to him.

He opened the door. The room was empty. Seeing Du Yu's new Nikes still sitting neatly beside his bed, Fang Mu felt a catch in his throat.

One day ago, he would have been more than happy to list all of Zhang Yao's many faults. But at that moment, all he could think of were her positive qualities.

If only I could open the door right now and see Du Yu and Zhang Yao quickly leap off his bed as if they hadn't just been hooking up, Fang Mu thought, for that I would trade anything.

The room was eerily quiet. Fang Mu found himself desperately wishing Du Yu would appear before him. He felt there was so much he wanted to say to him.

And yet, if Du Yu really did appear, what was he supposed to say?

Should he apologize? But that seemed so pointless. It wouldn't change a thing.

With his thoughts in conflict, he sat there in silence. The sun went down and the moon rose, and then the first rays of dawn lit the morning sky. Fang Mu never moved or said a word. People kept knocking on the door, but he ignored them. All he wanted to hear was the sound of a key sliding into the lock and opening the door. Yet at the same time, he was worried that in that moment he would be so frightened that he would hide.

That whole night Du Yu never returned.

Fang Mu didn't move until, after a day and a night of sitting there and not eating, his stomach began hurting him worse than he could endure. He finally got up and went to the dining hall.

The hall was packed. The recent murder had not affected people's appetites in the least. The victim was someone else; their bodies were their own. So as before, what they cared about most was whether the steamed buns were a day old, whether the soup had cockroaches in it. To them, those were the things that mattered.

There was a long line for food. Head down, Fang Mu went and stood at the end. The person in front of him glanced back. Suddenly the student gasped and jumped back a step. His face filled with fear, he stared at Fang Mu and then grabbed the person next to him, saying, "You see that! It's him! Let's get out of here!"

As the two of them hurried off to another food station, the rest of the line turned and looked back at Fang Mu, who was still standing at the end. Then, as if by tacit agreement, everyone scattered at once, allowing Fang Mu to walk up to the front. As they hurried away, everyone had the same expression on their face: panic.

The cafeteria worker himself was stunned. He stared at Fang Mu for several seconds, and then yelled roughly, "Hey, are you gonna order food or not?"

Gritting his teeth, Fang Mu walked slowly forward, feeling as if the looks from everyone's eyes were stabbing into him like needles.

His vision started to blur and the short distance in front of him suddenly felt as long as a football field. "A bowl of porridge and two tea eggs."

Fang Mu sat in a corner of the dining hall and ate his breakfast. Although he kept his head down the whole time, he could still feel everyone's eyes as they watched him and hear their voices as they whispered to each other.

No one would sit anywhere near him, making the area around his table seem like a strange no-man's land.

It was like he was a poisonous plant with long, spreading vines, and if anyone got too close, their life would be at risk.

After eating half his breakfast, he found his appetite was gone, so he got up and quickly left the dining hall.

As soon as he entered the third floor corridor, Fang Mu saw that a big mess had been made in front of his door. His computer monitor and tower were sitting on the floor, covered by a bunch of his clothes. A crowd of people were standing around his open door, watching the person inside.

Had Du Yu returned?

He hurried forward, reaching his room just as Du Yu threw his blanket out the door. Seeing Fang Mu, Du Yu seemed to pause for an instant, but then he bent over, grabbed Fang Mu's washbasin from beneath his bed, and tossed it outside.

Fang Mu dodged out of the way and the washbasin smacked against the opposite wall, causing his soap and toiletries inside to fall to the floor.

"What are you doing?" Fang Mu asked.

Du Yu didn't respond, just walked over to Fang Mu's bookshelf and knocked all the books onto the floor. Then he picked them up and threw them out of the room one by one. All the people watching outside quickly got out of the way.

Fang Mu didn't move, letting book after book strike his body and legs.

This behavior enraged Du Yu, and he grabbed several more books and hurled them directly at Fang Mu's face and body.

Blood was soon flowing from Fang Mu's nose and mouth, running down his chin and dripping onto his clothing.

Zou Tuanjie had been watching and he couldn't bear to watch this, so he grabbed Fang Mu and pulled him to the side. "Come on, man," he said to Du Yu. "Don't do this…"

The words hadn't even left Zou Tuanjie's mouth when Du Yu hit him in the forehead with a book. Zou Tuanjie gave an outcry of pain and shrank back.

Soon all of Fang Mu's belongings had been thrown into the hall. Clapping the dust off his hands, Du Yu walked out and stared at him for several seconds.

"Beat it!" he barked through clenched teeth.

Wiping his bloody nose, Fang Mu squatted down and began picking up his things.

"Go!" yelled Du Yu, his voice rising in volume.

Seeming not to hear him, Fang Mu patiently organized his things. When he couldn't find the cap to a pen, he began carefully looking for it in a pile of clothing.

"Get out of here," said Du Yu, his voice a little quieter, but still ice-cold. "None of us want to die!"

Fang Mu stopped what he was doing, stood up and turned around. He felt Du Yu and everyone else's eyes boring into his face.

He looked at them one by one. As soon as they met his eyes, almost everyone quickly looked own. Only Du Yu glared firmly back at him.

Fang Mu looked into Du Yu's eyes for several seconds. He slowly said: "I won't leave until I've caught him."

Then he grabbed his blanket and clothes and walked down to Meng Fanzhe's already locked room. With the creak of wood, he swiftly kicked it open. He tossed his things inside, went back to the hallway, collected more, and did the same.

No one stopped him. No one helped him. As everyone else just stood there and watched, Fang Mu picked up the last of his belongings. He walked inside the room that once belonged to Meng Fanzhe and slammed the door shut.

After standing empty for several days, Room 304 finally had a new resident. Fang Mu took the left side of the room, making the bed and placing his things on the left desk and in the left cupboard. Only once everything was neatly put away did he realize that the left bed had been Meng Fanzhe's. For an instant he considered moving his things to the other side of the room, but then he took off his shoes, lay down on the bed, and that was it.

Fang Mu sized up his new lair. No one had lived there after Meng Fanzhe died, so everything was covered in a thick layer of dust. The walls were badly watermarked, as if someone had splashed them with cups of liquid. In short, the place looked awful.

Fang Mu thought and looked around, looked around and thought. After not sleeping for a whole night, his eyelids began to feel heavier and heavier, until sleep won out.

When he awoke it was already night. Even though his stomach was growling from hunger, Fang Mu had no desire to get up. The lights from the dormitory across the way shined into his dark room, sending shadows across the walls that moved faintly.

Feeling a little cold, Fang Mu involuntarily curled up under the covers. By force of habit, he glanced at the other bed across the room, but now there was only a thin straw mattress.

So this is how cold it is, sleeping alone in a dorm room.

Compared to Room 313, which had always been packed full of his and Du

Yu's stuff, Room 304 seemed terribly spacious.

So spacious, in fact, that it made him nervous.

Suddenly Fang Mu wondered whether, during Meng Fanzhe's final days alone in this room, he had also laid here in the dark, silently savoring the feeling of solitude.

Until he truly lost his mind.

Will I go mad, too?

Fang Mu hopped out of bed and looked at the dim lights from the distant dormitory. Seeing them, he felt a little better, a little less alone.

First, he told himself, you need to get something to eat.

But no matter what, he was not going back to the dining hall. He reached out and turned on the light and then grabbed a pack of instant noodles. He shook his kettle. Luckily, Du Yu hadn't broken it. It was empty.

Holding the kettle, he stood in front of his door for several seconds. Then, with what seemed a great deal of determination, he opened it and walked out.

Something fluttered to his feet. Fang Mu picked it up. It was an envelope with a letter inside.

He looked down either end of the hallway. It was very quiet. No one was there.

Fang Mu sat down on his bed and took the letter out of the envelope. It was from Deng Linyue; he recognized her handwriting.

My Dearest Fang Mu,

Please allow me to call you this one final time, and please believe that as I do so, I love you. Perhaps this love will gradually disappear with the passage of time, but at the very least, I firmly believe that at the moment in which I write these words, I do still love you.

406

By the time you read this letter, I will probably already be on my way home. Don't try to find me (although perhaps this is just wishful thinking on my part; you would probably never consider looking for me if I left). I will not be returning to school for some time; I have entrusted my family with handling the necessary procedures to apply for time off.

Perhaps you will despise me. Despise me for leaving without saying goodbye, despise me for my weakness and my cowardice. I am just an ordinary girl, longing to be protected, yearning for a peaceful and romantic life. The instant you rescued me in the gymnasium, I fell in love with you. Just as when a princess is rescued by a prince, I had no choice but to fall in love with you.

And yet I know that you are not my prince. And I am neither as brave nor as strong as I imagined.

Yesterday morning, I saw everything that happened at the pool with my own eyes. When you finally revealed that the killer was after you, my first reaction was fear. I didn't even have the courage to go hug and comfort you; instead I fled back to my dorm by myself. Yes, I was scared, more scared even than that night in the gymnasium. The killer had already murdered your best friend's girlfriend, and I was probably next. Waiting for death is more frightening than death itself – at last I understood what this saying meant.

Why does he want to kill you? Why did he have to kill so many other people? I know you will not be willing to answer these questions, but that is all right. At this point, the answers are no longer important to me. Although I once believed that I was brave enough to stand by you through every trial, when I was truly confronted by the possibility of death, I chose to do the same thing that any normal girl would do.

Forgive me, forgive me for being an ordinary girl who once thought she was something more. Perhaps you never did love me; now I truly hope that is so. Because if it is, then for both you and I, this will be a little easier to bear.

I will pray for you.

Deng Linyue

12/25/2002

Although the letter was short, Fang Mu was still reading it over half an hour later.

His mind and heart were at ease.

He tried to tell himself: She has left you. You should be filled with sadness.

And yet, feeling a chill unlike any he had ever experienced, he couldn't keep from laughing aloud.

Good, very good.

At last, you are alone again.

Though perhaps, you have always been alone.

25 ROOM 304

The victim was a 23-year-old girl from the city of Kaifeng in Henan province. She had been an English language grad student in the Jiangbin City University Foreign Language Department's class of 2003. The cause of death was mechanical asphyxiation, the murder weapon likely a hemp rope. The victim's hymen had already been broken prior to the night of her murder and there was no sign of rape. According to the autopsy and the testimony of the victim's friends, her time of death was determined to have been between 1 a.m. and 5 a.m. on December 25. After the victim was strangled to death, heavy makeup was applied to her face, and then her body was placed in the Jiangbin City University outdoor pool and her ankle was tied to the drain with a hemp rope. The pool was then filled with water.

According to an examination of the scene, the killer used a hammer-like tool to smash the lock on the pool gate so he could transport the body inside. No fingerprints or footprints were found at the scene.

According to the victim's schoolmates and boyfriend, the yellow tube top, short leather skirt, black platforms, and blonde wig that she was wearing when discovered did not belong to her. Her original clothes were not found at the scene.

In addition, a piece of paper was found inside the platform shoes that the victim was wearing. Because it had been underwater for a long time, the writing was unclear. However, it was later identified as a page from the sixth edition of a fourth grade Language and Literature summer reading textbook published by the People's Education Press. This page in particular was from Resplendent Sunset.

According to the victim's boyfriend, on the night before the murder he received two strange phone calls, after which he and the victim got into an argument and she left alone. The police soon located the phone number in question at the telecommunications bureau. They discovered it had never been used to make any other calls besides those two that night. After further investigating the number, they found that it had been purchased from a private seller, and as a result no identification was needed to be shown. Therefore, it is be impossible to determine who had made those two calls.

"Right now, this is all I've found. The case is being handled by Old Zhao and his men, so I had to pull a few favors to even learn this much." Tai Wei passed the case folder to Fang Mu. They were in Fang Mu's dorm room, going through what they could of the evidence report available to them. "Oh, and there's another thing. Over the last few days I've gone to several hospitals around the city, including the one where Ma Kai was treated, and looked into the psychologists they have on staff. You should know, though, that right now I'm only able to investigate this on my own, so my effectiveness is limited. Up 'til now I haven't found anything of value."

Fang Mu smiled at him. "Thank you," he said.

Tai Wei just carelessly waved his hand.

You still believe in me. I can tell, even if you don't say it aloud.

"How's it going over here?" Tai Wei asked. "Any progress?"

Fang Mu looked down at one of the pictures in the folder. In it, a seductively dressed Zhang Yao lay beside the freezing pool.

"What does an outfit like this make you think of?" asked Fang Mu, showing the picture to Tai Wei.

Tai Wei didn't mince words. "A prostitute. This is the classic sex worker getup."

"That's correct." Fang Mu nodded. "This time he was copying the Green River Killer."

"The Green River Killer?"

"That's right. Do you still remember those two symbols I told you about? The ones that were written on the window of Meng Fanzhe's home?" Fang Mu grabbed a piece of paper and sketched something on it. "At the time I thought he had written a lowercase q and an uppercase A. Later I realized I was mistaken, and in fact he had written GR, both uppercase. Because the letters were written on a condensation-covered window, when the water drops slid down it made them look like a q and an A."

"GR? Green River?"

"Exactly. The Green River murders began in 1982 in Seattle, Washington, in the United States. The killer was named Gary Ridgeway. In total he killed over forty-nine people, the majority of them female prostitutes and young women who had run away from home," Fang Mu said. "The bodies of his first few victims he dumped in the Green River, which was located in the southern outskirts of Seattle. The person who discovered the first victim said it looked like she was standing in the middle of the river. This was because the killer had wedged her legs into a crack between some rocks on the river bottom." He shivered. "This was identical to what I saw in the pool that day. Beginning in 1987, the police made Ridgeway their prime suspect, but because they had no evidence and he was twice able to pass a lie detector test, he managed to get off scot-free. Then DNA testing began to be used in criminal investigations. Last year, the police compared a sample of his saliva with the semen that was found in one of the victims. It was a perfect match. Still, even after his arrest, Ridgeway has continued to deny his guilt. Because several of his initial victims were found in the Green River, and because Ridgeway's initials are G.R., he is known as the Green River Killer."

Tai Wei frowned in thought. "The majority of the victims were prostitutes... Is that why Zhang Yao was made to look that way?"

Fang Mu nodded. He flipped through the case files in his hands. "Just now you said that the victim wasn't raped that night?"

"Yeah, why?"

"Hmm, this is rather interesting," said Fang Mu, deep in thought. "It was

Ridgeway's custom to have sex with his victim's before strangling them to death. So if the killer wanted to perfectly copy his crimes, why didn't he have sex with Zhang Yao?"

"There could be a ton of reasons for this. Time, place – perhaps even the killer's mood." Tai Wei chuckled, but then immediately realized that it was inappropriate. His smiled disappeared.

"Mood?" Fang Mu gave a grim smile. "He wanted to destroy me mentally. Now perhaps he, too, is reaching his breaking point."

He reached out and grabbed one of the photographs. It was of the excerpt that had been found in Zhang Yao's shoe.

"Resplendent Sunset?" Fang Mu looked the photograph over. "I remember reading this when I was a kid. I think it was written by Xiao Hong."

Tai Wei moved closer. "You think this is a clue to the killer's next crime?"

Fang Mu thought for a moment. "If nothing else unusual was found at the scene, then yes, tentatively, I believe we can regard it as one. What's the police opinion on the excerpt?"

After hesitating for a moment, Tai Wei said, "Zhao Yonggui believes the paper fell inside the shoe by accident. Therefore, he thinks that there's a kid in the killer's household who's currently attending elementary school. As for the rest of it, I'm not too sure." Tai Wei sighed. "Old Zhao doesn't really want me to take part in this case. Not that he has anything to worry about though – it's already under the jurisdiction of the State Enterprise Investigative Division. At this point all I can do is using some of my connections to find out what's going on."

"All right, then I'll look it up online." Fang Mu sat in front of his computer and searched for the text of Resplendent Sunset. Once he found it, he began reading it slowly and carefully.

Seeming a little bored, Tai Wei grabbed a book from the shelf and flipped through it. He then stood in front of the window, took out a cigarette, and began to smoke.

"Not many people out on campus today," he said.

"Yeah, exams are coming up soon," said Fang Mu absently, his eyes not leaving the screen. "They're probably all inside studying."

"Are you going to have exams soon, too?"

"Huh? Oh, graduate students don't have exams." Smiling without real humor, Fang Mu patted the monitor. "This is my exam."

Tai Wei just shook his head.

Fang Mu's attention returned to the screen, but now he seemed unable to absorb anything he was reading.

Exam?

"Tai Wei…"

Tai Wei had been staring at a tall, beautiful girl standing outside the building, and it took him a moment to register that Fang Mu was talking to him. His voice sounded a little shaky.

"Yeah?" Tai Wei turned around.

Fang Mu was staring at him, his face wearing an inscrutable expression. "I think we've been ignoring something very obvious."

"Oh? What's that?" Tai Wei was suddenly all ears.

"Tell me, what kind of person devises problems to test other people?"

"That's obvious; a teacher, of course." Although Tai Wei casually blurted it out, his eyes immediately widened. "Are you saying that the killer is a teacher at the school?"

Fang Mu nodded. "It's a definite possibility."

"Now hold up." Tai Wei's eyebrows knitted together as he feverishly pondered something. "Previously you said that our man is most likely between the ages of thirty and forty, well-educated, financially stable and clean cut, with a jealous, competitive personality, correct?"

"Yeah, that's what I said."

"In that case, there are way too many people like this on your campus. In my experience, practically all college professors fit this profile."

"We might not know who it is," said Fang Mu, pulling on his jacket, "but I know someone who might. Follow me!"

It was Professor Qiao who opened the door. Although he didn't seem surprised by Fang Mu's sudden visit, his expression shifted slightly when he saw Tai Wei was standing behind him.

He pointed at the slippers placed beside the door, and then turned and walked alone into the study.

After removing their shoes and putting on slippers, Fang Mu and Tai Wei followed after him. Professor Qiao had already lit a cigarette and was sitting on the couch, smoking gloomily, his expression somber.

Seeing the professor's mood, Fang Mu didn't quite know what to say. Tai Wei was first to speak. "Teacher Qiao... Oh, I mean Professor Qiao, how are you, sir?" he said politely. "I'm Tai Wei from the city bureau. This is my police ID."

Professor Qiao didn't even turn his head, just made a brief sound of recognition. Nor did he take the police ID that Tai Wei was holding out for him.

Tai Wei's arm hung awkwardly in the air for several seconds. Miffed, he angrily pulled it back. Seeing that Fang Mu wasn't talking, he poked him hard in the side.

Given no choice, Fang Mu forced himself to say, "Professor Qiao, there is something I wanted to ask your advice about."

"Yes?"

Fang Mu looked at Tai Wei. Then, summoning his courage, he said, "Professor Qiao, do you know anyone on this campus who's fairly adept at

414

psychological analysis?"

Professor Qiao tapped out the ash from his cigarette. "I do."

"Who?" Fang Mu asked. Both his and Tai Wei's ears pricked up at once.

"Me." Professor Qiao paused. "And you."

At once the air in the study seemed to solidify.

Fang Mu stammered: "I…what I was trying to say…"

"That I already know." Professor Qiao then placed the butt of his cigarette in the ashtray on the table, grabbed a book, and began to turn its pages.

When Fang Mu and Tai Wei saw this, they had no choice but to turn to take their leave.

Tai Wei did not look pleased at all. Without even saying goodbye, he left. Fang Mu followed. Tai Wei angrily pulled on his shoes and pounded down the stairs.

After putting on his shoes, Fang Mu looked up to see Professor Qiao standing in front of him. He was watching Fang Mu, his expression meaningful.

"Professor…I…think I'm going to be leaving now," Fang Mu excused hesitantly.

Professor Qiao suddenly reached out and placed one hand on Fang Mu's shoulder. He squeezed it tightly.

"Take care of yourself," he said, then his voice went quiet. "This will all be over soon."

This said, he pushed Fang Mu out the door and then slammed it behind him.

Tai Wei was waiting for Fang Mu in his jeep outside. As soon as Fang Mu got in, Tai Wei stepped angrily on the gas, and the jeep immediately lurched forward.

"That old guy was obviously screwing with us," said Tai Wei, honking impatiently at the bicyclist in front of them. "You think he could be the killer?"

"Don't talk nonsense." Fang Mu was still thinking about the last thing Professor Qiao had said.

"This will all be over soon."

Was it possible that he already knew who the killer was, and was about to bring him to justice?

Previously when Fang Mu had learned that Professor Qiao was joining the investigation, he had felt greatly reassured. Now, however, he didn't feel relaxed in the slightest. Rather, he was even more anxious.

Tai Wei pulled up in front of Fang Mu's dormitory. After Fang Mu got out, Tai Wei turned to him and said, "It looks like we're gonna have to investigate this ourselves. Shit, before this was all easy. But now that I can't look into anything openly, I'm just going to have to investigate things on my own."

"All right. Well, you'd better start by looking into whether any teachers also work in the counseling centers of any of the city hospitals."

"Yeah, I got it. And you be careful." Tai Wei started up the jeep and drove off.

Fang Mu watched as Tai Wei's jeep disappeared around the corner. He looked up at the sky. Huge, lead-black clouds were rolling overhead, seeming to indicate that a blizzard was quietly approaching.

As soon as Fang Mu reached the third floor corridor, he saw that several guys were standing outside Room 313 and sticking their heads through the open door.

Fang Mu's heart skipped a beat. Had something happened to Du Yu?

He walked quickly over. Seeing him coming, several of the students parted to give him a path to the door.

Inside the room, Du Yu was sitting in his chair with his head drooped and a stubbly beard on his face. His pant legs were covered with mud. In front of him stood a man who Fang Mu recognized from the law school office. He was yelling at Du Yu and gesturing wildly.

"If you get caught walking around in the middle of the night with this thing in your possession again, you won't just be dealing with campus security! No, I'll make sure you get sent straight to the police!" He slammed a box-cutter down on the desk. "Trying to get revenge, huh? You think you're going to be able to catch the killer all by yourself? You're just a law student! If you could take him out, then what would we need the police for?"

Du Yu raised his head to argue, but when he saw Fang Mu standing in the doorway, the words caught in his throat and he just stared at him.

Fang Mu looked at the puffy, black and blue bruises covering Du Yu's face. He was about to say something, but when he opened his mouth nothing came out, so he just turned and walked away.

In the middle of the night, the snow finally began to fall.

When Fang Mu happened to look up from his computer screen where he was intensely scrutinizing the textbook excerpt, he saw that the sill outside his window had already accumulated a thick layer of snow.

Picking up a cup of water that had long since gotten cold, he walked over to the window and watched the snowflakes dance and swirl through the air.

His heart suddenly grew warm.

After people die, do their souls live on?

If they do, then Chen Xi, Fourth Brother, Wang Jian…

Help me…

Someone knocked on the door.

Who could it be this late? he wondered.

Grabbing his knife from under the pillow, he tiptoed over and put his ear to the door. He could hear the sound of heavy breathing outside.

"Who is it?"

After several seconds of silence, the person outside said, "It's me."

It was Du Yu's voice.

Fang Mu hesitated for a moment and then opened the door.

A heavy smell of alcohol wafted inside. Du Yu stood in the doorway, his hair disheveled and his face haggard. The bruises on his face looked terrible.

Fang Mu moved to the side and waved for him to come in. As soon as Du Yu walked through the door, he stumbled and then crashed into the doorframe. Fang Mu quickly went to help him, but Du Yu just pushed his hands away. He teetered into the room and sat heavily on the bed across from Fang Mu's.

Du Yu was haggard and unkempt, the stark bruises on his face adding to his miserable appearance. He was gasping for breath, constantly belching from the alcohol. Fang Mu gave him a cup of hot water. Du Yu grabbed it without a word of thanks and downed it in one gulp. Fang Mu tried to stop him, but it was already too late. The water had been nearly 150 degrees, but Du Yu didn't seem to have noticed in the least.

Fang Mu sat down on his bed.

After they had each drunk a cup of water, the two of them silently faced each other from their opposite beds. The space between them was less than nine feet across, but it seemed as impassable as a bottomless abyss.

After a long time, Du Yu cleared his throat and asked hoarsely, "You find him?"

Fang Mu slowly shook his head and said, "Don't pull any more of this crap."

Du Yu sunk once more into silence. A moment later he began to suddenly wail. He buried his head between his knees and tore at his hair. The veins on his hands were all sticking out, as were several wounds that hadn't yet healed. He continued his mournful cry, his voice rising until it was almost a scream, sounding like something being broken apart.

Fang Mu stood and walked over and put one hand on Du Yu's shoulder.

Do you remember how you once put your hand on my shoulder like this?

But Du Yu swung his arm and pushed Fang Mu's hand off him. "Get away!"

Du Yu cried for 10 minutes straight. At last he stopped as suddenly as he had begun.

After grabbing Fang Mu's tissues, he tore off a few pieces and wiped his eyes. He loudly blew his nose and threw the tissues on the floor. He climbed to his feet and walked to the door.

He turned around and said quietly, "When you find him, tell me first." He paused. "If you're still alive, that is." Then he opened the door and walked out.

Fang Mu remained sitting on the bed with his head down until the sound of Du Yu's steps disappeared at the other end of the corridor. He looked up at his closed door. "...Okay."

The room was silent again, as if the visitor from a moment ago had never even been there. Suddenly the room began to feel a little stuffy, so Fang Mu stood up and opened the window a crack.

A strong, snowy wind immediately burst inside, blowing the papers on the desk into the air, where they spun for a moment and then floated to the floor all across the room.

He quickly slammed the window shut as snow rapped against the glass, the flakes seemingly very proud of this surprise attack.

All of the documents that had been on Fang Mu's desk were now scattered about – on the bed, on the floor, all over the place.

After picking them up one by one, Fang Mu discovered he was missing a page. When he looked again, he found that it had floated under the bed.

Crouching down, Fang Mu reached as far as he could under the bed, but he still couldn't grab it.

He looked around the room, but there was no long stick or anything he could use to pull it out. Sighing, he crawled under the bed.

The space underneath was not covered with dust as he had imagined. Instead, as he felt around, he found that there was only a thin layer of the stuff.

His breath caught in his throat at the realization. After pulling out the piece of paper, he grabbed his lighter from the desk and crawled back under the bed.

As the flame burst from the tip of the lighter, the narrow space beneath the bed was illuminated. Moving the light about, he discovered that while there was a thick layer of dust beneath the corners of the bed, the area underneath its middle was quite clean, as if someone had made a point of sweeping it.

Fang Mu looked closely at the clean portion of the floor. He slowly rolled over and lay on his back.

As he held the lighter up to the underside of the bed, shadows fell across several places where the surface appeared uneven.

Fang Mu's eyes suddenly went wide.

All across the bed board a single name had been carved over and over again: Meng Fanzhe.

Some of the characters were written almost neatly, as if they had been carved with a knife. Others were very rough, as if they had been scratched out with a key or something similar.

From the look of things, Meng Fanzhe had not done them all at once.

He twisted about under the bed, shifting his position. Soon he discovered that under the head and foot of the bed Meng Fanzhe's name was written as well.

Fang Mu suddenly realized that during the final days when Meng Fanzhe had lived alone in the room, he had probably crawled under the bed like he was doing now and, trembling, had carved his name into the bed board over and over again.

After lying there for some time, Fang Mu crawled out from under the bed, shaken. Now dust-covered, he sat in the chair and zoned out.

After a few moments of internal debate, he suddenly leapt up and ran to the door.

Throwing it open, he burst into the hallway and looked at the number on the door.

As expected, between the 3, the 0, and the 4, he saw two faint marks. From the look of them, they appeared to be "+" signs.

Someone had made a point of erasing these two marks, but for some reason they hadn't been completely removed. Still, if one didn't look closely, the marks could easily be overlooked.

Just as he had thought. Someone had been controlling Meng Fanzhe.

Seven hours later, Fang Mu and Tai Wei were sitting together in the room.

Tai Wei washed his hands in the washbasin and patted the dust off his body.

"Hypnotized?" he said.

"Yes, I think that's a definite possibility."

"Are you saying that everything Meng Fanzhe did that night was the result of hypnosis? Including writing the plus signs between the three-one-three on your door, and then trying to kill you? Can it really be that powerful?"

"A person can be hypnotized into doing various simple things, but getting them to kill one person in particular is probably outside the realm of possibility." Seeing the puzzled look on Tai Wei's face, Fang Mu clarified: "Meng Fanzhe did not intentionally write the plus signs on my door, nor was his attempt to kill me premeditated. Do you remember how he paused briefly while he was following me that night?"

Frowning, Tai Wei thought back. "Yeah, I do remember something like that happening. He stopped for a little while when he was in the hallway. And you know what? I think it was right outside the door to this room."

"That's right. Now take a look at this."

After leading Tai Wei out into the hallway, Fang Mu pointed at the light marks on his door number.

Tai Wei stared at them, dumbstruck. "My God," he mumbled to himself. "At the time we just looked at your room number. We didn't pay any attention to this one."

"This shows that Meng Fanzhe did not purposefully choose me for his target. Instead, he was merely instructed to search the hallway for the number seven." Fang Mu pointed down either end of the hall. "Right here we have rooms three-hundred-one to three-twenty. Three-twenty-one is the bathroom and three-twenty-two and up are all in a separate section behind a locked door, so he couldn't get to them. Therefore, the only room numbers that could form seven were three-hundred-four and three-thirteen."

"So when he tried to kill you, was that also a result of the hypnosis?"

"At first I was really puzzled by this, too, because like I said, hypnotizing someone into killing a target should be just about impossible. Then I saw the names carved under the bed."

Tai Wei frowned. "What's that supposed to mean?"

"Just wait a minute; first I'm going to give you a simple explanation of what hypnosis is, " Fang Mu decided. "Hypnosis is mainly about causing neurological, biological, and physiological changes through psychological suggestion. For example, hypnosis can be used to cure anxiety and depression and eliminate phobias. It is an extremely complex process and often requires that the hypnotist use various kinds of suggestive signals to help his subject enter a hypnotized state."

"Oh, this stuff I already know," Tai Wei said. "There's a Japanese movie called Hypnosis in which the suggestive signal was something like the sound of metal striking metal."

"Right. Now there's also something called post-hypnotic suggestion. This is when the hypnotist provides his subject with a signal that can still cause him to react even when he is no longer hypnotized. For this post-hypnotic suggestion to remain effective, the subject must have a tremendous amount of trust in his hypnotist and must subconsciously recognize the authority of this signal. From what I know, Meng Fanzhe was someone with a vulnerable psyche, making it very easy for him to become psychologically dependent on other people. In other words, he was an ideal candidate for post-hypnotic suggestion. From that night on, I always suspected that Meng Fanzhe had received this sort of post-hypnotic suggestion therapy, but I could never figure out what the signal was. That was, until I discovered the names."

"Are you saying that those names were the suggestive signal?"

"Correct. Meng Fanzhe had a secret that nobody knew about. He was scared of roll call," Fang Mu said. "Most likely nothing else was impressed as deeply on his mind than his own name. At some point he must have gone to see the killer – in his role as the so-called doctor – for psychotherapy. The killer probably then used Meng Fanzhe's fear of roll call to turn his name into a post-hypnotic suggestive signal. There was one time before that night when I spoke to Meng Fanzhe in the bathroom and discovered that when I said his name, he would undergo a very unusual emotional reaction. Then on the night when he tried to kill me, I initially said a few words to him and he barely even responded; but as soon as I called out his name, he suddenly attacked."

"Hey, I just thought of something," said Tai Wei, his face lighting up. "You remember that night in the city bureau, when we were trying to interrogate Meng Fanzhe? At first he didn't respond at all to any of our questions, but then when one of our interrogators said his name, he went absolutely crazy."

"Exactly. I'm thinking that the killer designed the suggestive signal so that when Meng Fanzhe heard his name, he would attack whoever said it."

For a moment Tai Was lost in thought. He pointed under bed. "So then what was the point of him repeatedly carving his name into the bed board?"

Fang Mu thought about this. "In the days before the incident, Meng Fanzhe had probably begun to realize that something wasn't quite right with his mental state. He once told me that he would often forget where he had been or what he had done, and couldn't remember how a bunch of strange things had appeared in his room – meaning all the evidence you guys found. I'm guessing the killer had also hypnotized him into bringing this stuff back. As a result, I believe he had started to become frightened of himself, and especially of his name. And when people are frightened, they will often choose to hide. The space under this bed," he said, patting the bed board beneath him, "was most likely his hiding place. The thing is, he was probably also pretty dissatisfied with how everything was going. Previously, with the help of this doctor, he had nearly overcome the psychological dysfunction relating to his name. So he forced himself to write his name over and over on the bed board, hoping to convince himself that he wasn't scared of it after all."

Fang Mu paused, and then said quietly, "At that point he must have had a very complex relationship with the doctor, doubting him and depending on him at the same time. That's why he wrote his mom the letter."

In a flash, Fang Mu could almost hear the sound of someone under the bed: breathing rapidly, crying softly, and scratching something out onto the bed board, all the while mumbling indistinctly: "Meng Fanzhe, Meng Fanzhe, Meng Fanzhe…"

Fang Mu clenched his fists.

Frowning, Tai Wei smoked a cigarette and said nothing.

Fang Mu watched him. "How about it? You think this evidence will convince the bureau to reopen the case?"

"I'm afraid it will be very difficult." Tai Wei paused to think for a moment. "First, you were the only person to know about that letter and the GR written on the windowpane. Second, because it seems superficial that the sixth and seventh crimes have already been committed, it would be very tough for the bureau to accept that, in fact, the sixth-lane murder was the killer's actual completion of his sixth crime. And besides, as you well know, the bureau is still firmly of the opinion that you should not be participating in the investigation. So no matter what you say, it's unlikely anyone will believe it."

A dejected look crossed Fang Mu's face.

Seeing his expression, Tai Wei couldn't help but feel for the kid. He patted him on the shoulder.

"Anyway," he said, "did you find anything in that textbook excerpt?"

"Nothing so far." Fang Mu shook his head. "I can't tell you how many times I've scrutinized that thing without finding a single clue." He grabbed a book from his shelf and handed it to Tai Wei. "I took the book that the excerpt came from out of the library, hoping that I might find something. It's called Legends of the Hulan River."

Tai Wei weighed the book in his hands. It didn't feel that heavy. But when he opened it and saw how small the printing was inside, he couldn't help but lose heart. "Jeez, it would take forever to find a clue in here."

"I'm also going to check out the textbook that this excerpt came from. Maybe I'll be able to find something in there."

Tai Wei paused to think for a moment. "You think the killer might have written the clue directly onto the excerpt with disappearing ink or something?"

"I don't think so," Fang Mu said quickly, as if he had long since considered this possibility. "He would have known that the paper would be submerged for some time, and if the ink couldn't reappear then there would be no point of writing it in the first place. I think the clue most likely has something to do with the excerpt itself."

"Jeez, who would have thought that an elementary school textbook would contain the clue to a murder?" Tai Wei stood up and stretched. Suddenly he stopped and said, "You think the next victim is going to be a fourth-grader?"

Fang Mu smiled grimly. "Who knows? Anything is possible."

He looked at the mountain of documents stacked beside his computer. "From tests I've taken in the past, I remember that the last question is frequently the hardest. The teacher would always tell us to first do the easier ones, and then if we still had time, to summon our energy and attempt the final problem."

What was the answer to the seventh question?

It was another cold and dry early winter's morning. Backpack on his back, Fang Mu hurried toward the Education Building. The campus was just as bustling as ever. After slacking off all semester the students were finally getting serious. Final exams were almost there.

During first and second period that day, Professor Qiao had been teaching undergraduate criminology. Because there had been no criminology courses at Changhong City Teacher's College, Fang Mu made a point to sit in whenever he could.

In addition, he hadn't seen Professor Qiao since that time in his apartment. His final sentence, "This will all be over soon," had been making Fang Mu nervous ever since. He really wanted to speak with the professor, but even if they couldn't talk, Fang Mu hoped that Professor Qiao might still give him some unspoken clue.

The classroom was much fuller than usual. Since exams were coming up, students were of the mind that they would be penalized if they didn't show up.

Fang Mu sat down in one of the corners of the room. Recognizing him, some students pointed in his direction, but he just pretended to not see them.

It was already after 8 a.m. and the professor still hadn't showed up.

Up until that point the students had been quietly awaiting the start of class, but now they began to get a little noisy. At 8:15, there was still no sign of Professor Qiao. Some of the more impatient students demanded that the class monitor call him up and see what was going on.

Holding his phone, the class monitor ran into the hall and dialed. He returned a moment later. "His phone's off."

"The dean's office, call the dean's office," someone suggested.

At 8:30, someone from the dean's office hurried into the classroom and announced that class was canceled for the day.

Groaning, the students quickly packed up their stuff and then streamed out of the classroom. Before long, Fang Mu was the only person left.

He pulled out his phone and dialed Professor Qiao's cell. It was off.

He tried his home number. Busy.

He dialed it again and again, but it was busy every time.

An ominous feeling suddenly came over Fang Mu.

That afternoon, his feeling finally became reality.

One of Professor Qiao's older graduate students, who was getting ready to graduate, came to see Fang Mu and asked him if he knew the professor's whereabouts. When Fang Mu shook his head, the older grad student grew anxious. "Shit, man, I haven't finished my thesis yet and now he's missing? I think I might have to temporarily change advisors." The snide comment made Fang Mu suddenly wanted to curse at the guy. But before he could open his mouth, the grad student had walked off.

Forcing himself to calm down, Fang Mu grabbed his phone and dialed Professor Qiao's home number again. It was still busy.

He kept trying. At last he got through.

A worried-sounding woman picked up the phone. "Hello? Who's this?" It was Mrs. Qiao.

"Hi, Mrs. Qiao, it's me, Fang Mu. Is Professor Qiao around?" he asked.

Mrs. Qiao began to softly cry. "Old Qiao hasn't been home for a day and a half…"

"What?" Fang Mu felt as if his heart had been suddenly squeezed in an iron grip.

Professor Qiao was missing.

26 SHIXIONG

Professor Qiao's house was packed full of people. The living room, which was already small to begin with, felt terribly crowded.

There were classmates from Fang Mu's year, as well as some of the professor's older male and female graduate students. Bian Ping, the top-ranking officer from the provincial PSB, was there, too, and when he saw Fang Mu come in he gave him a slight nod.

Fang Mu nodded back at him. Unable to wait any longer, he walked over to the sofa where Mrs. Qiao was drying her eyes. He asked her: "Mrs. Qiao, what happened?"

Her eyes already red from crying, Mrs. Qiao choked back a sob. "The night before last, Old Qiao told me he was going out to see a friend and then left without saying who it was. I waited up for him until after eleven, and when he still hadn't returned, I called his phone, but it was off. I assumed he had probably gone out to dinner and then to a public bathhouse, so I went to sleep. He didn't return all day yesterday, and his phone was still off. I thought he must have gone straight to school, but no one there had seen him, either. Up until now there's been no news at all…"

Suddenly the phone rang and Mrs. Qiao, who only a moment before seemed to have lost all her strength, practically dove for it and grabbed it from the cradle: "Hello? Hello…" Her voice fell. "You bought your ticket? …Tonight? Good, come home and help me find your dad. …Yes, okay, okay."

At last, after hanging up the phone, Mrs. Qiao could no longer control herself, and she began to sob uncontrollably.

Bian Ping stood up and helped her to the couch, consoling her softly.

"You told Qiao Yu to come home?"

"Yes." Mrs. Qiao took Bian Ping's hand. "Little Bian, promise me you'll help me find Professor Qiao. He's an old man; if something bad were to happen to him…"

"Don't think like that, Mrs. Qiao," Bian Ping said quickly. "There's no reason to believe that anything has happened to Professor Qiao. Perhaps…perhaps he just went off somewhere to investigate a case." Then as if he realized that this didn't sound very persuasive, he hurriedly added, "I've already sent my men to look for him; we should be hearing some news soon."

But when the other people around her echoed these words, Mrs. Qiao only seemed to be even more at a loss.

Visitors kept pouring in, the dean of the law school and the president of the university among them. When the phone rang again, Mrs. Qiao once more grabbed it with a look of hope on her face, but as soon as she heard the caller's voice she was once more disappointed.

"Yes… Then you should come by, Little Sun. Okay, see you soon."

Another visitor was on their way over.

After looking around the room, Bian Ping said to the students, "You should all head back. We'll let you know if there's any news."

One after another the students said their goodbyes and left. When Fang Mu walked to the door, he suddenly remembered what Professor Qiao had said to him when they were standing in that same spot only a few days before. Turning to Bian Ping, he said, "Chief Bian, if there's any news, please let me know as soon as possible."

At the moment Bian Ping was speaking to the university president, so he just waved at Fang Mu and said, "I will."

After he returned to his dorm, Fang Mu sat beside his bed and was soon lost in thought. He didn't move until it was almost nightfall.

He couldn't help but connect Professor Qiao's disappearance with what he had said to him.

"Take care of yourself. This will all be over soon."

Unless Fang Mu was wrong, then Professor Qiao seemed to know who the killer was.

Had he tried to catch him single-handedly, and then...?

It was a scenario that Fang Mu was unwilling to consider.

By the time the police began officially investigating the matter, Professor Qiao Yunping had already been missing for 48 hours. They conducted numerous interviews at his workplace and apartment building, and went to the telecommunications bureau to check the call records of his cell and home phone, but discovered nothing of value.

From the time that Professor Qiao went missing, a total of four unidentified corpses were delivered to city hospitals. All four were shown to the missing person's family members, who confirmed that none were the missing professor; nor was any trace of the professor found at any of the city's homeless shelters.

The man had disappeared.

While the police were out searching for Professor Qiao, Fang Mu was also walking every avenue and backstreet of the city. He had no leads and no place in mind. At a loss, he walked down crowded, brightly lit pleasure streets and filthy alleyways, always expecting to turn a corner and see Professor Qiao walking toward him, either from across the street or out of a doorway, or perhaps sitting behind the glass facade of some storefront.

Many times he thought he saw him, only to realize upon closer inspection that it was merely someone of a similar age and build.

Where are you?

Every night, as the sky began to grow dark, Fang Mu would return to campus, doleful and exhausted. After eating a quick, careless dinner, he would collapse on his bed with his clothes still on. Sometimes he would be able to sleep a little, sometimes he would just lie there with his eyes open until the morning light. Then he would get up and do it all over again, returning once more to the crowded city streets to search for the man whose fate was unknown.

Fang Mu was well aware that searching around the clock as he did was pointless; and yet he couldn't stop, couldn't bear to sit quietly in his room and wait for news. He had to do something, for Professor Qiao, and for himself.

And all the while, he avoided thinking about the one thing that was almost certain to be true: Professor Qiao had already been killed.

Fang Mu was unable, or rather not brave enough, to confront this possibility. He preferred to believe that the professor had contracted some serious illness and was lying in some forgotten corner of the city, on the verge of death.

Professor Qiao was the person Fang Mu revered most. This was a different kind of feeling than those he had for Liu Jianjun and Zhang Yao. Fang Mu had never actively sought Professor Qiao's help on the case and had been bluntly refused the one time he tried to ask for his advice. And yet, all along Fang Mu had felt that if he himself was ever killed, Professor Qiao would not stand idly by, but rather would find the murderer and bring him to justice. This was because Fang Mu deeply believed in Professor Qiao, believed in his power and experience – believed that he was his last, best hope.

But now the professor had vanished, his fate unknown. And Fang Mu felt more alone and despairing than ever before.

Sitting in a small street-side restaurant, Tai Wei smoked a cigarette and looked at Fang Mu. The kid was incredibly disheveled.

"Why don't you have a few more bites?" Tai Wei said.

The bowl of soup in front of Fang Mu was still half-full of noodles. Listening to Tai Wei, he picked it up and took several sips.

Tai Wei had met Fang Mu in front of one of the city department stores. At the time, the kid had been eating a piece of bread while scanning the faces of everyone who walked by. It was a cold, windy day, but he hadn't seemed to notice. "You want to order something else?"

Fang Mu shook his head.

Tai Wei studied the unkempt young man sitting before him. It had only been a few days since he'd last seen him, but already the kid seemed much skinnier. His big down coat looked huge on him. Seeing him searching his pockets, Tai Wei pushed the pack of cigarettes that he'd placed on the table toward him.

Fang Mu took out a cigarette, lit it, and then smoked it silently.

Tai Wei sighed.

"I'm telling you, brother, the way you're searching is no kind of method. If you're not careful, you're going to collapse before we even find him."

Fang Mu was silent for a moment. Then he asked, "How are things going on your end?"

"Still no news." Tai Wei shook his head. "This thing is mainly being investigated by the local stations, but Chief Bian Ping from the provincial PSB also pulled a lot of strings and sent people to search outside the city. However, no one's found a thing."

Seeing the news made Fang Mu even more upset, Tai Wei quickly added, "Now don't start thinking anything crazy. If Professor Qiao really did have some kind of accident, someone would definitely have reported it. Therefore, I think he either got sick out of nowhere, or suddenly went senile – which, given his age, really wouldn't be that hard to imagine."

After hesitating for a moment, Fang Mu told Tai Wei what Professor Qiao had said to him that afternoon.

Tai Wei didn't say anything for a long time, just took several vicious drags from his cigarette and then forcefully stubbed it out. "This old guy definitely knows the killer. He tried to protect him, and then got trapped himself!"

Fang Mu didn't like hearing that. "Professor Qiao wouldn't do something like that!"

"Okay, okay, okay." Tai Wei had no desire to argue over the point at the moment. "This is a very important clue. I'm going to discuss it with Zhao Yonggui. I don't care if it pisses him off." He stood up. "Fang Mu, have you forgotten what you're best at?"

Fang Mu frowned. "Huh?"

"Finding people isn't your forte; profiling them is." Tai Wei bent over and stared at him so closely that their noses almost touched. "Let us find Professor Qiao. You need to head back and get some sleep. When you wake up, I want you to make me a profile of this guy." He patted Fang Mu on the shoulder. "Right now you're our last hope."

Their last hope?

Fang Mu was back in his dorm room. As he looked at the documents stacked across nearly every inch of his desk, his spirits suddenly fell.

Tai Wei hadn't been consoling him with what he said – he had been pressuring him. The subtext was clear: If Professor Qiao really had gone to look for the killer, then things did not bode well for him.

Still, he completely agreed with Tai Wei's point of view; they needed to find the killer as soon as possible – for it was the killer himself, not Professor Qiao – who was the crux of the matter. As long as they found him, then they would be able to locate Professor Qiao as well, whether he was alive or dead.

Saving the professor or avenging his death – these things would have to wait. Right now the only thing Fang Mu could do was find the killer.

But when faced with the mountain of documents on his desk, he just sat there dully for over half an hour, unable to absorb a single word.

Over the past few days, he had been so tormented by such excruciating sadness, rage, guilt, and despair that his nerves had reached their breaking point. Now he could barely do a thing. The skill he had once had for perceiving criminal psychology seemed to have vanished.

You need to calm down, thought Fang Mu, as he forcefully massaged his temples.

He lit a cigarette and then forced himself to focus on the materials in front of him.

But instead his eyes fell on the Zippo lighter in his hands.

He repeatedly clicked it open and closed, the sound echoing in his room.

It was the first gift Deng Linyue had ever given him, and it would also be the last.

So whether because of its price or its emotional significance, it should have been precious to him.

And yet Fang Mu had always seen it as just a tool to light his cigarettes or perhaps to shine his way in the dark.

Many things only seemed important in life because of the special significance and sentiments people attached to them. Disconnected from all of this, a limited edition Eternal Star Zippo was no more useful than a one-renminbi plastic lighter.

It was true of people, too.

Liu Jianjun, Meng Fanzhe, Zhang Yao, and now perhaps Qiao Yunping. They were all just victims.

As for me, I'm a psychological profiler.

Fang Mu opened one of the case folders and was met with a picture of Zhang Yao's lifeless face.

Cigarette between his fingers, Fang Mu began to read, one page after another.

The murderer was male, aged 30 to 40 and between 5'6" and 5'8". He was strong, agile and right-handed, highly intelligent, a skillful planner and knowledgeable about a wide array of things. He was well-educated and his parents had been strict but not overly so. The early stages of his life had been smooth and successful, and he had developed an arrogant, very competitive personality. He was cautious and self-disciplined. He was financially well-off, took care of his appearance and was a neat dresser. His social skills were excellent, and he most likely lived with other people. He was skilled at driving a car and probably had one of his own, most likely a top model. He was employed in teaching or a related field, was familiar with the Jiangbin City University campus, and may have worked there as a teacher. He was a master of criminology and criminal psychology, but his medical knowledge – such as his grasp of human anatomy – was less extensive.

After the crimes began, the killer's mental state began to change. At first, his motivation had perhaps been merely to demonstrate his skill in certain areas. But then, as the cops were unable to catch him, and in fact even arrested the wrong person, the arrogant side of his personality grew even stronger. At the same time, however, he probably noticed these psychological changes, and may have even tried to resist them. This would most likely have affected his home life. For instance, the disgust he must have felt at what he was doing probably made him unable to do various things, such as have normal sexual relations (a point which was suggested by the fact that he did not rape Zhang Yao).

In addition, the killer was acquainted with Qiao Yunping, and was both familiar with Fang Mu and understood him very well.

"Criminology Makeup Class."

Fang Mu just happened to see the notice posted in the hall of the Education Building. At first he thought he must have misread, but when he walked closer, he saw that there was indeed going to be a criminology makeup class, and in fact it was scheduled for 8 a.m. that morning.

His heart began beating fast. Could Professor Qiao have returned?

Fang Mu looked at his watch. It was five minutes to eight. With no time to think, he hurried toward the classroom.

But when he reached the entrance, his footsteps slowed. He was filled with hope that as soon as he opened the door, he would see Professor Qiao standing on the dais, about to begin class. After waiting there for several seconds, Fang Mu summoned his courage and pushed open the door.

The dais was empty. The straight-backed, stern-eyed old man was nowhere to be seen.

Moments before the classroom had been filled with noise. Now it went completely silent as all the students turned to look at Fang Mu standing in the doorway. As soon as they realized who it was – not a teacher, just that grad student who often sat in on their classes – they all started talking again. Within moments, the room was once more as noisy as a marketplace.

Head down, Fang Mu walked to the back row of the classroom. Although he was overwhelmed with disappointment, he still hoped that Professor Qiao was merely late.

Time began to move unbearably slowly. All around Fang Mu, the students were yawning, eating breakfast food they had brought from the cafeteria, and continuously chatting and laughing, all while he stared closely at his watch, watching the minute hand move closer and closer to the 12.

Suddenly footsteps sounded from the hall.

Perhaps no one else was paying attention, but despite the noise in the classroom, Fang Mu heard them clearly.

The sound was steady and full of confidence, the pace nimble yet forceful.

The steps grew closer and closer. Fang Mu held his breath.

The door opened.

A man walked inside. It was Librarian Sun.

After entering the classroom, Librarian Sun quietly closed the door, scanning the room quickly at the same time. A moment later, he stepped gracefully onto the dais and placed the folder he was carrying onto the lectern.

"All right, let's begin," he said, smiling faintly at the students sitting silently before him. "Because of some personal reasons, Professor Qiao will be unable to finish the semester with you. Therefore, for the three classes you have left, I will be teaching you the science of criminology in his stead."

He grabbed a piece of chalk. "First I should introduce myself. My name is Sun Pu." He turned around and wrote his name on the blackboard. His handwriting was stylish and yet confident. "You can call me Sun Pu, or Old Sun if you'd like."

A burst of soft laughter rippled through the classroom.

After clapping the chalk from his hands, Sun Pu looked up, just in time to lock eyes with Fang Mu who sat dumbstruck in the back row.

Sun Pu smiled and gave him a slight nod.

Class then began. It was obvious that the moment Sun Pu entered the classroom he had won the approval of almost everyone present. Unlike Professor Qiao's old-fashioned, strict and unavoidably stiff teaching style, Sun Pu had a unique method that was humorous and relaxed and still very incisive. He easily drew everyone's attention to himself.

But as for what he was actually teaching, Fang Mu didn't listen to a word. There was only one thought on his mind.

Why is he the one teaching?

When class was over, the students seemed to have developed a newfound interest in criminology and they crowded around Sun Pu and asked him all kinds of questions. Smiling, he patiently answered each one. When he finally returned to the lectern to organize his materials, he discovered that Fang Mu was standing in the doorway waiting for him.

Looking at him, Sun Pu smiled and said, "Shidi, you still have a question?"

There were numerous things that Fang Mu had wanted to ask, but at that instant he froze. He could only manage, "Shidi?"

"That's right. Professor Qiao never told you?"

"No. This whole time I didn't know that you were also..."

Sun Pu laughed. "There are a lot of things you don't know." He warmly grasped Fang Mu's shoulder, gave it a firm, friendly squeeze, and then pushed him along. "You should get going. If memory serves, you still have two more criminal procedure classes today. You don't want to be late."

Then he turned and walked away, leaving Fang Mu standing there dazed.

For the duration of his two criminal procedure classes, Fang Mu was too distracted to pay attention.

For a long time he had felt like he was standing at the edge of an abyss, doing his utmost to spy the unknowable monster within. Then as the case progressed little by little, the monster slowly began to rise up, its outline growing more and more distinct amid the darkness. And yet there had always been a layer of mist between them, preventing Fang Mu from seeing the beast clearly. All the while, however, he had sensed that the monster was watching him, watching him and laughing to itself. But although the monster was only an arm's length away and Fang Mu could smell the blood on its lips, he had been unable to reach out and touch it.

Now the mist seemed to be growing thinner and thinner.

The dining hall. Lunchtime.

Recently, eating had become nothing more than a burden for Fang Mu. He seemed to have lost all sense of taste. It no longer mattered to him whether he liked something or not; he would order whatever food he could eat fastest.

After carrying his tray to the corner of the dining hall, he sat down and dumped his stewed chicken and potatoes onto his rice. He mixed it up with his spoon and began wolfing it down.

When he happened to look up, he saw several people walk into the cafeteria and head toward one of the booths. Zhao Yonggui and Bian Ping were among them.

Seeing Fang Mu, Bian Ping said something to Zhao Yonggui, who then looked over at Fang Mu as well. Zhao Yonggui then led several people into the booth, while Bian Ping walked toward Fang Mu.

"What are you eating?" Bian Ping asked as he sat down across from Fang Mu. He looked at his bowl. "Stewed chicken and potatoes?" He laughed.

Fang Mu forced himself to smile, but said nothing.

"I always miss the food we used to get here," Bian Ping said. "Although back then we never got anything this good. Still, from the looks of things," he said, pointing at the meager amount of chicken in Fang Mu's bowl, "it seems like even after all these years there hasn't been much progress."

Fang Mu had no interest in making small talk with him. "Has there been any news on Professor Qiao?"

Bian Ping's face fell. "Nothing. That's actually why I'm here today. I wanted to go to the law school and see what was going on."

Fang Mu had nothing to say. His appetite was now gone as well.

"When do you graduate?"

"2004, why?"

Bian Ping snorted and then lit a cigarette. "Then it would seem you're Professor Qiao's most conscientious student."

"Huh? What do you mean by that?"

"None of your fellow students are upset over this like you are. Sure, many of your shixiong and shijie are getting terribly worried, but I can tell that what they're most anxious about is that if no one helps them on their theses, they won't be able to graduate." *(Translator's note: Shijie, elder female apprentice.)* He tapped his cigarette ash on the floor, causing a dining hall worker who was walking past to glare at him. "The top people at the law school asked me to come teach some classes, but when would I have the time to do that? So in the end, Mrs. Qiao recommended someone else for the job."

"Sun Pu?"

"Hey, how'd you know?" Bian Ping's eyes widened with surprise.

"I just sat in on his criminology class this morning. I also heard that he's my shixiong?"

"That's right. He graduated with a masters in '91. I was '86."

"Then why...did he start working in the library?"

"Oh, that's a long story..." Bian Ping smiled bitterly and shook his head.

Just then Zhao Yonggui squeezed out of the booth and waved Bian Ping over.

"All right," Bian Ping said, seeing his gesture, "I'll be there in a second." He looked back at Fang Mu. "Shidi, there was something serious I wanted to talk to you about for a moment. Professor Qiao thought very highly of you, you know. He told me more than once that you were quite gifted, and I also believe that you've got a real talent for this stuff. So then how about it? Want to come work for us after you graduate?"

Fang Mu shook his head. "I've never thought of becoming a policeman."

Bian Ping looked a little disappointed. "Eh, everyone has their own aspirations. However, if you did join the police, I believe you'd be fulfilling Professor Qiao's wishes." He stood up and patted Fang Mu on the shoulder. "Take it easy. If there's any news I'll contact you."

After leaving the dining hall, Fang Mu stood outside for a few minutes. At last he decided to head over to Professor Qiao's house.

Mrs. Qiao was the only person home. As soon as Fang My walked inside, he smelled the strong odor of some kind of traditional Chinese medicine.

"Are you sick, Mrs. Qiao?" he asked as he walked into the kitchen. A very small clay pot was on the stove, filled with a bubbling liquid and sending up steam.

"Aye, how could I not be sick?" she said as he came in.

In the few days since Fang Mu had last seen her, Mrs. Qiao had lost a lot of weight, and her hair was nearly all white.

"You came just in time; in a moment you can help me strain this medicine." She sighed. "I'm sorry there was no one here to greet you. Little Yu left to look for her father again. Now can I get you something to drink?"

Fang Mu hurriedly told her not to worry about it. Then after helping her to lie down on her bed, he rushed back into the kitchen, sieved the medicine into a bowl, and brought it back to her.

"How is everything going at school?" Mrs. Qiao asked after motioning for him to sit beside the bed.

"Well enough. Makeup classes have begun for criminology."

She sighed softly. "The thing my husband disliked most was delaying his students' education. So even though he wasn't around, I couldn't let them keep missing class. There was nothing we could do for the graduate students, but at least we could schedule makeup classes for the undergrads."

Fang Mu was silent for a moment. Then after summoning his courage, he asked, "Mrs. Qiao, Librarian Sun…also used to be one of Professor Qiao's students?"

"That's right. Let me think for a moment." She lightly massaged her temples. "He was part of the class of '91."

"Then why did he go work in the library rather than become a teacher?"

"Aye, that boy has been through a lot." Mrs. Qiao put the bowl of medicine down beside her. "At the time, Sun Pu was the most outstanding student in his class. Old Qiao is rarely the type to praise his students lightly, but back then he would often mention Sun Pu's name at home, and I could tell that he thought very highly of him. After Sun Pu graduated, Old Qiao recommended that the school hire him and arranged for Sun Pu to become his own teaching assistant. Sun Pu has always been driven to excel, and performed superbly in this position. Soon after, before he was even thirty, the school made an exception to their rules and promoted him to associate professor. At the time, Sun Pu was already quite well-known across the province as a very talented young man. Later, however…aye…" Mrs. Qiao shook her head and sighed.

"What happened later?" Fang Mu asked hurriedly.

"As you know, the law school sometimes helps the public security bureau work on cases," she continued. "At the time, Old Qiao had Sun Pu assist him in solving several. After they worked on a few together, Old Qiao decided to see how Sun Pu would do solving some on his own. Sun Pu seemed to have a special gift in this area, and he made expert work of several cases in a row. That's when all the honors and praise started rolling in. Sun Pu was still quite young back then, and he had some trouble keeping himself under control. In 1998, several cases of rape-and-murder occurred one after another on the outskirts of the city. At the time, Old Qiao was out of the country doing research, so the police asked Sun Pu to help them with their investigation. Using your guys' criminal profiling techniques, Sun Pu described the general characteristics of the killer. Soon after, the police arrested an individual who matched these characteristics closely. In the end, however, this person died without making a confession. Because the police had no other evidence, they needed this confession to make the case, but the suspect wouldn't own up. At the time this case was a very big deal and the higher-ups were all demanding that it be solved as soon as possible. The pressure on Sun Pu and the rest of the police was immense. I think this is what made young Sun Pu lose his head, because he soon incited the police to make the suspect confess by any means necessary."

She sighed. "In the end, the man was beaten so badly that he gave in and died. To make matters worse, the real killer was arrested a few days later. Many people were implicated in the killing. Some lost their jobs, others were sent to jail. One of the captains of the unit that was handling the crime, I believe his name was Zhao-something, was also transferred to the State Enterprise Investigative Division. Sun Pu was almost arrested himself, but because there wasn't enough evidence and Old Qiao pulled a lot of strings, he was finally let off. However, there was no chance of him returning to his old position. But because Old Qiao spoke strongly on his behalf to the university president, he was eventually given his job in the library."

So that's what happened, thought Fang Mu. Looking down, he saw the nearly cold bowl of medicine. Hurriedly, he handed it back to Mrs. Qiao. "Why have I never heard about this before?"

Frowning, she drank the rest of her medicine. When she was done, Fang Mu passed her a napkin, which she used to wipe the corners of her mouth. After taking a few deep breaths, she continued.

"You weren't here at the time, and besides, the school did everything it could to keep the incident under wraps. But to tell the truth, it made Old Qiao enormously upset. Ever since then, his temper has been much worse. Sun Pu has come by to see him a number of times, but Old Qiao has always just forced him to leave, even when he's brought gifts with him. And at home, this topic has become absolutely taboo." Mrs. Qiao patted the pillow beside her. "If Old Qiao were at home right now, there's no way I'd dare say any of this to you. Aye, for a long time after that, he made sure not to mention any of his students at home. But recently your name has been coming up a lot, and I can tell that out of all the students he's ever had, you and Sun Pu are the ones he's admired most. At first I considered recommending that you teach the criminology makeup classes, but later I decided that you're still too young. Besides, Sun Pu has been doing an excellent job these past few years, and in his evaluations he's received high marks in all areas. The school has even begun to consider rehiring him to a teaching post. Aye, I don't think even Sun Pu knows about that. On the surface, it might seem like Old Qiao has never been willing to forgive him, but all along he's secretly been doing everything he could to help him. If he hadn't suddenly gone missing, he was going to recommend that the school rehire Sun Pu to begin teaching next semester..."

Fang Mu was no longer paying attention to what she was saying. He knew there was someone he needed to talk to immediately.

27 THE GREAT KNIGHT OF HULAN

"What did you just say?" cried Tai Wei, leaping up with a start from Fang Mu's bed. "The guy that works in the library? The one in the glasses?"

Fang Mu nodded.

"So this is why Old Zhao was transferred. No wonder the guy flies into a rage at the first mention of criminal profiling." Tai Wei frowned. "But he's such a gentle-looking guy. I guess you really can't judge a book by its cover."

"I never said he was definitely the killer. It's just that according to our analysis," Fang Mu said, "the killer was most likely someone who excelled at criminal profiling. And from the looks of things, the only people on campus who fit that description are me, Professor Qiao, and now Sun Pu."

"Then what should we do? At this point, it doesn't seem like we have any evidence to prove it was him."

Fang Mu thought for a moment. "We both saw the killer, and you even chased him for a little while. So what do you think? Does Sun Pu fit the bill?"

After racking his brain, Tai Wei said, "Their heights are about the same. But that night the killer was wearing a long, hooded windbreaker and the light was very dim. I can't be certain it was the same guy."

Feeling a little disappointed, Fang Mu said nothing.

Seeing the kid's expression, Tai Wei quickly changed the topic. "How's your research going on the passage?"

Fang Mu's face grew even gloomier and he just shook his head.

"You think the passage might have something to do with Professor Qiao's disappearance? I had an idea about this," Tai Wei said. "So the passage was torn out of a school textbook, right, and Professor Qiao's occupation just happens to be teaching. You think it could be hinting that the seventh victim is going to be a teacher?"

"Most likely not." Fang Mu thought for a moment. "When the passage was found, Professor Qiao hadn't yet gone missing. I don't think the killer was expecting Professor Qiao to come visit him, so the seventh victim will probably be someone else."

"So is there nothing we can do then?" cried Tai Wei impatiently.

"That's not true either. Tai Wei, you are an excellent investigator, so right now you need to look into everything having to do with Sun Pu. If he really is the killer, and if Professor Qiao is still alive…" Fang Mu paused and raised his voice, doing his best to appear unaffected by what he was saying, "…then Sun Pu must have hidden him somewhere. If you keep tabs on Sun Pu's whereabouts, perhaps you'll be able locate Professor Qiao."

"All right, I'll go make the necessary preparations." Tai Wei stood up, and then suddenly slammed his fist down on the desk. "No matter if the target is Professor Qiao or anyone else, we won't let him succeed this time!"

He strode to the doorway, but just as he opened the door, he abruptly turned around and said, "Kid, you'd better be pretty careful yourself."

Fang Mu glanced at his backpack which he'd tossed on the bed. The military dagger was still inside. He looked up at Tai Wei and nodded.

The nightmares arrived on schedule.

The shadowy, headless figures crowded quietly around Fang Mu's bed.

Without a word, they watched as Fang Mu struggled desperately, and yet couldn't move at all.

Even though he didn't open his eyes, Fang Mu sensed that amid these dead specters, there were a few new members.

Qu Weiqiang, Wang Qian, Tang Yu'e, Jin Qiao, Xin Tingting, Thomas Gill, Meng Fanzhe, Dong Guizhi, Zhang Yao…

All of you…

A hand pressed against his shoulder.

"Actually, you and I are the same."

Suddenly, Fang Mu could move his neck.

He swung his head around.

Sun Pu was smiling at him.

Over the past few days, that face had appeared in Fang Mu's mind more than any other image. Fang Mu was already more familiar with it than with his own face.

The look in his eyes when he reached a crucial point in class. The way the corners of his mouth curled when he was smiling, or his eyebrows knitted when he was thinking deeply about something. The faint twinkle in his eyes whenever he glanced at Fang Mu.

At this moment, the owner of that face was standing at the lectern and enjoying the worshipful looks of the students sitting before him.

"All right, that's all the new material for today," Sun Pu said, placing the chalk back on the blackboard and then clapping off his hands. "But we still have fifteen minutes until class is over, so let's play a little game."

The students, who a moment before had been packing up to leave, now returned their attention to Sun Pu.

"I have here several questions from an intelligence test. Supposedly, the American F.B.I. gave this test to several dozen psychologically aberrant criminals and their answers were all identical, proving that, mentally, they really were different than the average person. Now listen to these questions, and perhaps we'll find that there's a potential criminal genius sitting among us right now."

Excitement went through the students, as if they all felt that being psychologically aberrant would be really cool.

"First question," Sun Pu began. "One evening, an engineer who had once been stationed at a South Pole research station to set up the solar panel array was eating the meat his wife had fixed him for dinner. Thinking that the flavor was very unusual, he asked her what kind of meat it was. 'It's penguin,' she replied. Hearing this, the engineer's face fell, and he stabbed himself in the throat with his fork."

The students all gasped.

Sun Pu continued. "My question for you is: Why?"

So this is what he was talking about, thought Fang Mu.

One year ago, Fang Mu had happened across these same questions, and out of curiosity, had tried to answer them. There had been seven in total, and he had gotten five right. As a result, the test determined that he had a strong tendency toward psychological aberration.

The other students, however, had never seen these questions before. They soon began calling out theories, and the classroom grew noisy. But when no one was able to get the question right, Sun Pu finally revealed the answer: The engineer had once been stranded, and one of his colleagues was killed. Afterwards, he and several others had been forced to eat what he was told was penguin meat so that they could survive until the rescue party showed up. When he tried the actual penguin meat that his wife gave him, he realized that what he had eaten before was actually the flesh of his dead colleague.

Hearing this, several of the students made squeamish faces, like they wanted to vomit, but most were already waiting excitedly for the next question.

Sun Pu continued the test.

Question Two: A man who had been suffering from a chronic ailment looked everywhere for a doctor who could help him. Finally he found a hospital where he was completely cured. But on the train back home, he suddenly began to cry hysterically, injured several other passengers in his frenzy, and then broke the window and leapt out of the train. As a result, he fell beneath the wheels and was crushed to pieces. Why?

As the students enthusiastically discussed the question, Sun Pu walked leisurely around the classroom, his hands behind his back, stopping every now and then to shake his head at a student's answer.

Finally one of the students answered correctly: the man's chronic ailment was that he had gone blind. After being cured, the man believed that he had permanently regained his sight, but then when the train went through a tunnel, the darkness made him think that he had gone blind again, and in his disappointment he leapt from the train and committed suicide.

"Very well done," said Sun Pu, clapping his hands. "Ten points onto your final grade!"

This development made all the students as excited. As the kid who got it right sat there blushing, his classmates all looked at him, some with admiration and some with envy, while everyone waited anxiously for the next question.

Question Three: A man and his female friend were strolling beside a river when the woman lost her footing and fell in. Although she struggled to stay afloat, she quickly went under. Panicked, the man immediately jumped in, but he was unable to save her. Several years later, while walking past the scene of her drowning, the man saw an old-timer fishing on the riverbank. When the man saw that the fish the old-timer had caught were completely clean and free of seaweed, he asked him why they didn't have any seaweed on them. The old-timer replied that there was no seaweed in this river. Hearing this, the man threw himself in the river without another word, committing suicide. Why?

The answer: When the man had jumped into the river to save the girl, he had grabbed onto something that felt like water seaweed, and so hadn't pulled it up. But hearing the old-timer's answer, the man had finally realized that in fact what he grabbed wasn't seaweed, but his female friend's hair.

No one got it right.

Question Four: A man was found dead headfirst in the desert. Pieces of luggage of various sizes were scattered around him. In his hand was half of a match. How did he die?

The answer: The plane this man had been riding on had malfunctioned, forcing everyone to parachute off; however, it was discovered that there was one parachute too few. So everyone decided to draw lots, with the person who picked the short match being forced to jump without a parachute. This man had been unlucky enough to draw the short match.

No one got it right.

Question Five: An older sister and younger sister attend their mother's funeral. While there, the younger sister sees an extremely handsome young man, and instantly falls in love. Unfortunately, this man is nowhere to be found once the funeral is over. A few days later, the younger sister stabs the older sister to death with a knife in the kitchen. Why?

The answer: The younger sister loves the young man, and desperately wants to see him again. But because she knows that she can only see him at a funeral, she decides to create one.

A female student answered this one correctly.

Question Six: A circus troupe has two dwarves, one of whom is blind. One day, the director of the troupe tells them that they only need one dwarf. The two dwarves are both extremely dependent on this job for their survival. The next morning, the blind dwarf is found dead from suicide in his room. The room has wooden furniture and the floor is covered with sawdust. Why did the blind dwarf kill himself?

The answer: While the blind dwarf was asleep, the other dwarf snuck into his room and sawed off a portion of the legs of all his furniture. When the blind dwarf woke up and felt his way around his room, he discovered that all his furniture seemed smaller. Believing that he had grown tall overnight, he killed himself in despair.

No one got it right.

As everyone watched Sun Pu, the sky outside grew darker and darker.

"The final question," said Sun Pu as he held a finger to his lips to demand silence from the eager class, "is also perhaps the hardest. So you must do your best to listen and think it through; don't just start calling out answers."

Everyone held their breath and stared at Sun Pu, listening silently as he read aloud the final question.

"There was a man who lived in a small cabin on top of a mountain," read Sun Pu in a low voice. "One night it began to rain very hard. Then all of a sudden, just as the man was about to go to bed..." his voice rose sharply, causing several girls to cry out softly in alarm, "...he heard a knocking at the door. The man opened it and looked out..." Sun Pu stopped and glanced across the silent classroom, "...but there was no one there."

At this point someone laughed.

"The man then closed the door and went to bed. But only a few minutes later, the mysterious knocking started again."

Noticing that several girls had their hands over their mouths to keep from crying out, Fang Mu couldn't help but chuckle.

"Trembling, the man opened the door again, but still no one was there. That night, the knocking sounded again and again, but every time the man opened the door and looked outside, no one was there. The next morning, a corpse was discovered at the foot of the mountain, covered in bruises."

Sun Pu paused for several seconds and looked contentedly at all the terrified faces before him. "My question," he said slowly, "is how did this man die?"

This time the students' response was much more serious than before. They quietly discussed all sorts of possibilities, often arguing passionately among themselves.

Seeming very pleased with his students' behavior, Sun Pu walked slowly between the rows. "You must consider this problem very carefully," he said loudly, "the answer will probably exceed anything you've imagined."

Fang Mu already knew the answer, and he couldn't help but feel that Sun Pu's deliberately mystifying style was a little excessive. Organizing his belongings, he prepared to leave when the bell rang.

Suddenly, he felt a hand on his shoulder. When he looked up, his eyes met Sun Pu's.

Although the man was still smiling, his eyes, hidden behind his glasses, suddenly shot forth a look of immense coldness. It was fierce look, like something from hell, and even the sight of his faint smile was enough to make Fang Mu tremble with fear.

Suddenly Sun Pu's grip on Fang Mu's shoulder tightened. Still smiling, he bent over slightly and whispered in his ear: "This is number seven, the final question. Can you answer it?"

It was as if a clap of thunder had exploded overhead. In an instant, everyone around them seemed to disappear without a trace. In the whole world, all that was left was Fang Mu and the person standing in front of him.

Six questions, nine dead, and a friend who would never be right in the head again.

Bloody memories flashed through Fang Mu's mind at lightning speed. He felt all the blood suddenly rush to his head. He leapt to his feet.

All the students around him were startled and they shot him looks of surprise.

Sun Pu didn't move a muscle, just continued to look into Fang Mu's eyes, the same faint smile on his lips. "Well, are you able to tell me the answer?"

Clenching his teeth, Fang Mu held on tightly to the edge of his desk.

Sun Pu's gaze dropped to his watch. "All right, class is about to end. Now I'll tell you the answer."

The students' attention shifted from Fang Mu's strange behavior back to Sun Pu.

"The answer is: the dead man had climbed up to see the man in the cabin – remember, he lived on top of a mountain – and after he knocked on the door, the man who lived there opened it and accidentally pushed his poor visitor down the mountain."

Several students began to laugh.

"But the unlucky guy wouldn't give up," Sun Pu said, "so again he climbed up to the cabin, and again he was pushed back down."

The laughter grew louder.

"This happened over and over again, until finally the visitor could take no more, and perished."

The whole class erupted with laughter as all the students began to clap.

Amid this noise the bell rang, and Sun Pu waved his hand. "Class dismissed."

The students all quickly rushed out of the classroom. When Fang Mu finally came back to reality, he found himself standing there alone.

The dais was empty. Sun Pu must have already left.

Still, Fang Mu stared hard at the place where he had once stood.

No matter what, I will find the answer to the seventh question!

When he emerged from the Education Building, the sky had already grown dark. Looking up, he watched as a big black cloud swallowed the last bit of blue sky. Although it was still afternoon, the hour already felt late.

It looked like another blizzard was coming.

His mind in turmoil, Fang Mu took a few deep breaths of the dry, cold air. Gradually he began to feel a little better. Realizing that he should probably give Tai Wei a call, he dialed him several times on his cell phone, but the cop never answered. After hesitating for a moment, Fang Mu decided to head back to his dorm.

Sitting on Fang Mu's desk were all the materials relating to the Zhang Yao murder. At the top of the stack was a photocopy of the passage that had been found on her body and underneath it was the book it was from, Legends of the Hulan River.

He picked up the photocopy. By now he was as familiar as could be with the passage, even down to memorizing the locations of all the punctuation marks. But no matter how he approached it, he was unable to locate a single clue to the killer's next crime. He had tried combining the seventh word of every sentence, even the seventh of every paragraph, but the result was a bunch of nonsense, containing not even the most obscure hint of meaning.

It seemed that the clue wasn't going to be found in the passage itself, but rather in its source.

The direct source of the passage was the sixth edition summer reading textbook for fourth-graders published by the People's Education Press. It also rested levelly on the desk, looking completely innocent. Fang Mu had read every passage inside, completed every exercise, and still he hadn't found a single clue.

The indirect source was Legends of the Hulan River itself. Resplendent Sunset came from the first chapter. Legends of the Hulan River was far from a long book, but finding a single clue hidden inside would be more troublesome than any of the other possibilities, so Fang Mu had left it until the end. Now it seemed this was his only hope.

Legends of the Hulan River was written by Xiao Hong, a modern Chinese author. She had been born into a landholding family on June 2, 1911, in

Hulan County, Heilongjiang, and died of an illness on January 22, 1942, in Hong Kong. Legends of the Hulan River was less a novel than a long prose collection of Hong Xian's cherished childhood memories.

Twirling his fountain pen – a gift from Professor Qiao – Fang Mu patiently read through, page after page.

As he searched for clues, he discovered that the word troublesome didn't even begin to describe the difficulty of the task before him.

Based on the previous crimes, the killer should once more be copying the methods of a famous serial killer from history.

But searching through this book – about the lives and customs of people in a small town in northeastern China – for clues to a serial killer's murders was like trying to find secret kung fu techniques in a cookbook. As Fang Mu flipped through the pages, he paid special attention to words like "kill," "hit", and "death", hoping to find some trace of the killer's intentions.

"Another horse drowned in the small lake." He felt this one was unrelated; after all, it was just a horse.

"Horribly embarrassed, the mother grabbed the fire poker from beside the door and struck the child on the shoulder. The child immediately began to cry and ran back into the house." Fire poker? thought Fang Mu. Had something like that ever been used as a murder weapon?

"She stood inside of an enormous vat, screaming and trying to jump out, as if her life were in danger. Three or four people stood around her, scooping hot water from the vat and dumping it on her head. Before long, her face was red from the water; she couldn't struggle anymore and just stood calmly in the vat. She didn't try to jump out again, as if she no longer thought it possible. The vat itself was huge, so that when she stood up only her head poked out." Was the next murder going to take place in a boiler room, or some other place like that?

"Several ghosts of people who had died wrongful deaths lived under that bridge. Whenever it rained, those who crossed the bridge could hear them crying."

Suddenly Fang Mu swept everything in front of him onto the floor.

The papers and books all fell and fluttered to the ground. A bottle of ink was knocked onto his bed, blackening the sheets. A glass cup flew against the wall, shattering with a piercing sound.

Fang Mu tore at his hair, feeling as if his temples were thumping violently.

He couldn't keep doing this.

Professor Qiao's fate was still unknown and the next victim was in great danger. Yet here I am, he thought, guessing at words.

His chest felt painfully constricted, his every organ on fire. All he wanted to do was tear off his clothes, stick his hands into his chest and squeeze, pinch, and twist.

He suddenly stood up and looked out the window. A heavy snow was already beginning to fall.

It was almost midnight and the rooftop was completely empty. This was what Fang Mu wanted.

Already covered with a thick layer of snow, it shined with a bright, cold light. It was a beautiful sight. After hesitating for a long time, he could wait no longer and finally stepped out.

The sound of his feet crunching against the snow was so familiar it made his heart ache.

A slight breeze was blowing and frequently great quantities of snowflakes would float onto his burning face, melting instantly. The water would then drip down his cheeks, turning from cold to warm.

Looking up, he saw a faint light in the formerly pitch-black sky. The snow fell all around him, as far as the eye could see, making only the slightest sound as it floated gracefully into every corner of the world. Was it sighing with sadness at leaving the sky, or rather rejoicing at returning to earth?

The snow gradually covered Fang Mu's body, so lightly that he neither felt its weight nor its cold. He looked back. His footsteps were deep, clearly showing the way he had come.

He looked ahead. Everything was obscured by a boundless curtain of snow. He couldn't make out a thing.

Midnight. Heavy snow. Faint wind.

It swirled around Fang Mu like a spirit, caressing his skin and whispering faintly. The feeling was warm and sincere.

Like his old friends were surrounding him, speaking to him.

All of you, wherever you are, I know that you're looking out for me…

Fang Mu slowly knelt in the snow.

Please give me a little more time.

Please give me a little more help.

Please give me a little more courage.

The dining hall.

Fang Mu was stuffing food in his mouth as he closely read Legends of the Hulan River. He frequently used his pen to mark various parts of the book and now the pages were covered with all kinds of lines and notes. He knew that he would get yelled at when he returned it to the library, but by now he no longer cared.

Someone placed a tray on the table in front of the seat opposite him. Looking up, his eyes met those of Zhao Yonggui's haggard face.

"You're a hardworking guy, huh?" he said mockingly. Still, there was a trace of friendliness in his voice.

Having no desire to talk to him, Fang Mu was about to stand up and leave, but when he thought of how Zhao Yonggui was leading the case, he asked,

"Any progress recently?"

Scooping some rice into his mouth, Zhao Yonggui shook his head tiredly.

Fang Mu said nothing, just buried his face in his food and ate, wanting to get out of there as soon as possible.

Zhao Yonggui, on the other hand, wasn't hurried at all, and he watched Fang Mu as he slowly chewed his food. After a while, he spoke. "Tai Wei came to talk to me a few days ago. He said you have a different opinion about this case."

Fang Mu looked up at him. Zhao Yonggui was frowning and closely watching him, sizing him up.

Fang Mu didn't see a hint of trust in his eyes. Annoyed, he dropped his head and continued wolfing down his food.

Seeing that Fang Mu wasn't going to say a thing, Zhao Yonggui continued. "Do you still think we handled that last case incorrectly?"

Fang Mu said nothing.

"Do you still believe we treated that homicidal maniac unjustly?"

Fang Mu threw his spoon onto his tray with a sharp clatter, causing food to splatter across the table. Several grains of rice stuck Zhao Yonggui's shirt.

Suppressing his anger, Fang Mu did his best to speak in an even tone. "Officer Zhao, if you don't believe me, then there's nothing I can do about that. However, my opinion will not change; Meng Fanzhe was innocent, and the killer is someone else. You have your ideas, and I have my methods – "

"Your methods?" Zhao Yonggui said, breaking in. "Still those same old tricks? Baseless criminal profiles?" He lifted up Legends of the Hulan River with his thumb and forefinger like it was a dirty object. "This is what you're relying on? You think you can catch a killer by reading a novel?"

Fang Mu snatched the book back from him and slammed it onto the table.

"Whether or not you believe me, the clue to the seventh crime is in here!"

"There's a serial killer in Legends of the Hulan River? Ha!" Zhao Yonggui leaned back and laughed loudly at him. His laugh was almost immediately cut short, as if he had suddenly realized something. A slight change of visage came over him.

Fang Mu no longer wanted to say anything else to him. If he did, he was afraid that he'd curse him out. He stuck his pen in his pocket and put the book beneath his armpit, and then grabbed his tray and started to leave. Before he could take two steps, Zhao Yonggui snatched his arm and pulled him back.

"Get the hell off of me!" he yelled at the officer, no longer able to control himself.

But just as the words left his mouth, he was shocked to discover that Zhao Yonggui now seemed a completely different person than he had been only moments before. He was frowning deeply, a look of astonishment on his face, as if he was thinking about something that he didn't dare believe.

"Sit!" He pointed at the chair opposite, his tone of voice making it clear that Fang Mu had no choice in the matter. At the same time, he pulled Legends of the Hulan River from Fang Mu's arm and began scrutinizing it.

Fang Mu sat down.

"Hulan River...Hulan River..." Zhao Yonggui muttered himself, his frown deepening. "Just now you said this book had something to do with a serial killer?"

Puzzled by the officer's behavior, Fang Mu couldn't help but nod.

For several seconds Zhao Yonggui appeared lost in thought. Then with what seemed a great deal of determination, he looked up and asked, "Have you ever heard of the Great Knight of Hulan?"

"The Great Knight of Hulan? Never heard of him. Why?" Fang Mu asked impatiently. "Who was he?"

"This was back in the eighties, in Hulan County, Heilongjiang. He was a fierce bandit who committed a number of terrible murder cases."

"Then why do I feel like I've never heard of him before?"

"Of course you've never heard of him, because at the time they were never able to crack the case, so they sealed away all information about it. Only us old-timers know about this one."

"So what kind of crimes did the Great Knight of Hulan commit exactly? And why is he called the great knight?"

"Great Knight? That was just the title he gave himself," Zhao Yonggui said. "The guy was a savage criminal, nothing at all like a great knight. Because he was dissatisfied with the social system that was in place back then, he shot a number of people to death. There was also a common characteristic to many of his crimes: he made a point of specifically attacking the police..."

Before Zhao Yonggui had even finished speaking, he saw Fang Mu begin frantically searching his pockets. Not finding what he needed, Fang Mu's hand shot out to the officer.

"Your cell phone, now!"

Startled, Zhao Yonggui unconsciously pulled out his phone.

Fang Mu practically tore it out of his hands, and then punched in a number as fast as he could.

Several seconds later, a faint voice from the phone relayed: "The phone you are dialing is powered off."

Swearing under his breath, Fang Mu redialed the number. He got the same message. He tossed the phone back to Zhao Yonggui. "We need to go find Tai Wei now!"

He leapt to his feet and ran out of the dining hall.

Fang Mu ran as fast as he could to the northeastern end of campus.

He needed to find Tai Wei immediately.

The next victim was none other than him!

It had been nearly two days since Tai Wei had last come to see him. That wasn't like him. Having focused all his energy on decoding Legends of the Hulan River, Fang Mu hadn't even realized what was happening.

And the fact that Tai Wei's phone had been off the whole time gave Fang Mu a faintly ominous feeling.

Please don't let anything have happened, please!

The road seemed unbearably long. Luckily he could already see the old KMT bunker. Fifty feet past that was a low fence marking the edge of the campus. Once he climbed over it, he could grab a cab in the small street beyond and take it to the PSB headquarters.

As he ran past the colossal concrete structure, it seemed to be silently gazing around at the lonely corner of campus.

Fang Mu's steps suddenly slowed.

He stared blankly at the section of bunker that rose above ground.

Seven?

As if drawn, Fang Mu walked slowly forward.

When he reached the entrance he saw that the bunker's rust-covered doors were unlocked. The iron chain that usually fastened them shut was nowhere to be seen.

He walked cautiously up to the doors, grabbed the rusty handle, and pushed hard.

The doors were old and would only open wide enough for one person to fit through. Cold, moldy air blew against Fang Mu's face. Inside it was pitch-black. He could only make out the space just beyond the entrance.

Taking a deep breath, he walked inside.

28 HELL

Thanks to the sunlight filtering through the doorway, Fang Mu could see that an approximately 30-step-long cement stairway descended before him. He carefully began walking down one step at a time, but before long, the way was completely engulfed in darkness. When he looked back, he could only make out the thinnest ray of light coming from the doorway. After hesitating for several seconds, he gritted his teeth and carefully lowered one foot down until it reached the next stair. Continuing on this way for over a minute, he finally reached a section of flat cement.

His surroundings were pitch-black and terrifyingly silent. He stood in place for several seconds and did his best to look around, but in every direction it was too dark to even see his own fingers.

The darkness seemed to have a mass of its own, and as layer upon layer of it wrapped around him, Fang Mu quickly sensed its weight. His body felt heavier and heavier and his legs started to go limp.

Whether from fear or the cold air inside the bunker, Fang Mu's whole body began to tremble. He could even hear his teeth start to chatter. Suddenly, he remembered that he had his lighter in his pocket and he hurriedly pulled it out.

He flipped open the lid, flicked the wheel, and a small bright flame appeared in his hand.

No longer surrounded by darkness, Fang Mu discovered that he was standing in a large hall, roughly 360-square-feet in size.

The room was rectangular, made entirely of concrete, and empty except for some old desks stacked in the corners. A section of the wall directly in front of Fang Mu seemed a little different than the dark gray concrete around it. In the flickering light of the flame, it appeared to be a door.

The little flame actually made Fang Mu feel a lot warmer, and his body stopped shaking so violently. Pulling out his dagger, he took a deep breath and ventured forward.

It really was a door, or rather a pair of rust-covered doors shut together. Putting his hand on the crude, ice-cold door handle, he could tell it was free of dust. Someone had come that way recently.

Giving it a try, Fang Mu pulled hard on the door. It opened with an ear-piercing creak.

An even stronger odor of mold burst forth, choking him until he could barely breathe. He stood in place, holding up the thin flame of the lighter and surveying what was in front of him.

He seemed to be standing at one end of a long corridor. Suddenly he felt overcome by a nearly uncontrollable panic and his hand holding the lighter began to shake.

In the light of the flickering flame, the walls of the corridor appeared to sway. Feeling himself go lightheaded, Fang Mu quickly grabbed onto the door to steady himself.

His hand gripped the rough handle of the dagger in his palm, a contact that gradually calmed him. Composing himself, he did his best not to look at the pitch-black far end of the corridor and used the lighter to survey his surroundings.

Doors made of iron bars stood open several feet ahead of him, one on either side of the hallway. Rooms approximately 60-square-feet in size lay beyond them. Fang Mu could vaguely make out the shapes of dilapidated chairs and desks stacked inside.

A section of the arch above the door to the right had faded slightly. Looking closer, he saw that it was a heavily stained image of the KMT flag, below which was written a nearly illegible "1".

Fang Mu looked at the door on the right. The same symbol was on the arch, only this time the number "2" was written below it.

He understood. These were prison cells.

Unless he was wrong, Tai Wei should be in the fourth cell on the right.

Cell 7.

The thought of this made Fang Mu grow anxious. Raising the already burning-hot lighter, he walked slowly forward.

The floor beneath his feet was no longer cement, and as he walked, the gravel wedged in the soles of his shoes ground piercingly against its surface. It sounded like metal on metal. Looking down, he could vaguely see that he was standing atop a grate-work iron walkway.

He figured it was probably designed so that the guards at the time could monitor both floors at once.

Fang Mu continued with these thoughts as he walked forward, staring at prison cell number three. He drew closer and closer, no longer stopping. Suddenly he felt the ground change beneath his feet. Just as he realized that he had probably stepped on a section of rotting wooden floorboards, his whole body abruptly fell through.

With an enormous crash, Fang Mu and the boards he had been standing on dropped heavily to the bottom floor of the bunker. He landed abruptly. He'd fallen hard, and for several seconds his chest hurt so much he couldn't breathe. After writhing in pain on the cement floor for some time, he finally forced himself to breathe out, and then a moment later he began to cough violently.

With difficulty he managed to stop coughing. He sat up, still gasping for air. The fall had knocked his glasses off and dust was in his eyes. Fiercely rubbing his eyes with one hand, he grasped about blindly with the other for his glasses. All wasn't lost; he quickly grabbed hold of his dagger.

Holding it, he felt a little more at ease. Soon he found his lighter as well.

Flicking on the lighter, Fang Mu shined it overhead. Approximately nine feet above him was a large rectangular hole, from which descended a metal ladder.

It had once been used for people to travel from floor to floor. Originally, there had likely been a removable metal lid, which had disappeared by the time the bunker was discovered by the CCP. Fearing that someone might accidentally fall through, several boards had been placed over the opening. Over time, the damp atmosphere had rotted the boards, making them weak.

Fang Mu stretched his arms and legs, deciding he had not been badly hurt. He looked around.

He was in the water dungeon. He found he was standing atop a cement platform before an enormous cement pool at least six feet deep. The pool was completely empty except for a number of iron rings that Fang Mu could faintly make out attached to the pool walls. He knew they had probably been used to shackle prisoners back when the place was still in operation.

He could see another pool farther ahead. He walked slowly toward it along the platform, guided by the faint light of the flame. Gradually the outline of the second pool began to sharpen.

Suddenly something at the bottom of the pool took shape. Fang Mu carefully stepped closer.

Amid the darkness, the object looked like some kind of box. Tightening his grip on the knife, he cautiously walked closer. When he was standing directly opposite it, he extended his hand holding the lighter as far as it would go, simultaneously straining to see what it was below.

His breath caught in his throat, and his heartbeat started to race as the object took definition.

It was an iron cage. And someone was sprawled inside. He tried to compose himself. Shakily he yelled, "Hello?"

In the vastness of the water dungeon, the sound was infinitely amplified. Bouncing off the walls, it echoed back at him with terrifying clarity. But the person in the cage didn't move at all.

Who was he?

And was he still alive? These questions ran through Fang Mu's mind as he used his lighter to illuminate his surroundings. The flame didn't reveal any stairs leading into the pool. After hesitating for a moment, he squatted down and shined the bottom of the pool. He gritted his teeth and leapt inside. He landed with an awkward thud.

The pool was deeper than he had imagined and his legs shook with pain. He decided it best not to walk immediately over, so he squatted down and listened for any sounds of movement, at the same time quickly illuminating his surroundings with the lighter. Once he was certain that the place was empty, he slowly stood up, gripped his dagger, and carefully advanced on the cage. He had been right. Someone was lying inside.

In the faint light of the lighter flame, he couldn't be certain whether it was a man or a woman. Straining to see the person more clearly, he cautiously approached.

Was it Tai Wei? It didn't seem like it. This person was a little shorter, a little heavier.

Who was it? As he drew closer to the cage, the person's outline became more defined.

It was a man, curled on his side, with his back to Fang Mu. Something about his gray sweater looked very familiar…

The flickering flame shone on the man's gray hair.

Fang Mu's eyes went wide as he hoped against hope.

Throwing caution to the wind, he ran to the other side of the cage and squatted down. He held the lighter flame up to the man's face.

It was Professor Qiao.

For a moment, Fang Mu didn't know whether he was startled or relieved, disheartened or enraged. Kneeling down, he shook the cage as hard as he could. "Professor Qiao!" he yelled. "Professor Qiao!"

His hair disheveled and face so thin he no longer looked like himself, Professor Qiao rocked back and forth in time with Fang Mu's movements. His tightly shut eyes never opened.

Was he dead?

No, please no!

Fang Mu reached inside the cage and placed his fingers beneath Professor Qiao's nose. Fortunately, he was still breathing, if faintly.

Pocketing his knife, Fang Mu grabbed onto the cage with one hand, while using the other to press his thumb against Professor Qiao's philtrum, digging in as hard as he could, hoping to apply the proper pressure. *(Translator's note: The philtrum is the indented spot between a person's mouth and nose. In traditional Chinese medicine, it is considered a very important acupressure point.)*

"Wake up, Professor Qiao, wake up…"

After what seemed to Fang Mu to be an agonizingly long time, Professor Qiao's hand moved slightly and a faint sound emerged from his lips.

Overjoyed, Fang Mu hurried to support Professor Qiao's head and then struggled to raise him to a sitting position.

Coughing, Professor Qiao leaned weakly against the bars of the cage.

After the coughing fit ended, he gasped for breath. "Water…water…" he mumbled, once more closing his eyes.

Water? Where can I find water around here? Agitated, Fang Mu looked around. In the corner of the cage he spied a bottle of water. He hurriedly reached in and grabbed it. He sighed with relief; there was still about half left. After twisting off the cap, he supported Professor Qiao's upper body with one arm while he used the other hand to raise the bottle to Professor Qiao's lips.

Once he had gulped down several mouthfuls of water, Professor Qiao's breathing relaxed slightly, and his eyes slowly opened.

Professor Qiao's eyes, which had once been bright with keen intelligence, were now dazed and glassy. He slowly turned them to look at Fang Mu. After staring at him dully for several seconds, he finally recognized him.

"It's you?"

"It's me, Professor Qiao, it's Fang Mu." He quickly asked, "How did you end up here, sir?"

Professor Qiao shook his head, his lips curling into a bitter smile.

"Aye, don't ask." He sighed. "I'm old...an old fool. I thought I could convince him to turn himself in. I thought he was still the same obedient, diligent student from all those years ago."

"You mean Sun Pu, right?"

"Oh? So you know then?" Professor Qiao was momentarily stunned. Then he laughed faintly. "I really was right about you."

"Save your energy, Professor Qiao. I'm going to get you out of here!" Helping him to lean against the bars, Fang Mu stood and looked the cage over more thoroughly.

With Professor Qiao inside, the cage had to weigh well over 200 pounds. Moving it would be extremely difficult, not to mention getting it out of the pool and up onto the first floor. His only chance was to open the lock, get Professor Qiao out, and then decide on his next step.

After locating the lock, Fang Mu weighed it in his hand. The thing was solid. Pulling out his knife, he inserted the point into the keyhole and fiddled with it lightly. It wasn't going to work. Not only would this not open the lock, it would likely break the knife as well.

He raised his lighter and looked around. The place was empty; there was nothing around that could be used to get the lock open.

After thinking for a moment, Fang Mu remembered the prison cells full of chairs and desks on the first floor. There had to be an iron bar or something along those lines inside one of them. Squatting back down in front of Professor Qiao, he said, "Wait one moment, sir. I'm going to go find something to get this cage open."

But before the words had even left his mouth, he heard something rumble overhead.

A beam of light shot down, illuminating Fang Mu's face.

Dizzy from the light, Fang Mu quickly shielded his eyes with his hand and looked up.

There was a square opening in the ceiling overhead. Through it shone a flashlight beam.

Someone else was in the bunker.

Even though his vision was blurry from the light, Fang Mu could still vaguely make out that it was a man.

"Who are you?"

Fang Mu's heart began to beat fast. Was it the police?

The man didn't answer, just chuckled darkly.

In an instant, an ice-cold feeling gripped Fang Mu's heart. He knew exactly who it was.

Before he could think anything further, something else appeared in the man's hand and then a terrible-smelling liquid came pouring down.

Although Fang Mu dodged back instinctively, one of his sleeves was still soaked with the stuff. But Professor Qiao had nowhere to hide and was drenched all over.

Fang Mu sniffed his sleeve. A chill ran through his body.

It was gasoline.

The man above disappeared, leaving only the square opening. A thin beam of light shed down from it, as if it were a single eye, watching them with evil intent.

For a moment Fang Mu was scared stiff. Then he scrambled toward the cage."Professor Qiao…"

"Stay back!" said Professor Qiao sternly.

Fang Mu stood where he was, not daring to move, not daring to flick on his lighter.

Amid the darkness, he stared stiffly at the cage only a few steps away. He could faintly see that Professor Qiao was slowly sitting up, his eyes alive, as if he were pondering some difficult problem.

After several seconds, Professor Qiao spoke. "Fang Mu," he said, knocking against the bars of the cage. "You once saw someone burned to death, correct?"

Taken aback, Fang Mu couldn't help but respond. "Yes."

Professor Qiao snorted. "So that's what this is," he muttered to himself. "No wonder he kept me alive this whole time." His voice rose. "Fang Mu, will you listen to me?"

"Yes."

"Good. Sun Pu is probably going to return very soon. Now don't go anywhere and listen to me." Professor Qiao's voice slowed. "Previously I once criticized you very harshly for helping the police to solve a crime. Do you remember?"

"Yes, I remember."

"I'm old, so old that I didn't dare let my best student put himself to the test, fearing that I would make the same mistake twice." Professor Qiao paused for a moment. "I admit that I was mistaken. You and Sun Pu are different. Therefore you must make it out of here alive. No matter what, you need to stop him."

"Professor Qiao…"

"Are you listening?" Professor Qiao barked in a stronger tone.

"I'm listening," Fang Mu said, forcing the words out through growing despair.

"Good, you're a good kid." Professor Qiao seemed to have used up all his energy and his voice grew softer and softer. "Now go. Get out of here as fast as you can."

Tears filled Fang Mu's eyes as he realized that this would be the last time he would ever speak to Professor Qiao. He took two steps back, watching through blurry vision as the professor slumped against the bars of the cage.

He ran forward and knelt beside the cage. "Professor Qiao, Professor Qiao…" The tears burned a hot steam down Fang Mu's face. "I can't let you stay here alone…"

"You really won't listen," said Professor Qiao, his voice unusually gentle. "Are you crying? It seems you're not as outstanding as I thought."

A rough, bony hand stroked Fang Mu's face in the dark.

"There's nothing scary about death," Professor Qiao said softly. "What's scary is living without a soul. Sun Pu is a soulless person. That's the biggest difference between you and him. Now go and do what you have to do, using your own methods." A burst of evil laughter echoed from overhead.

Fang Mu looked up. The dark figure was once more looking down through the opening.

He brought his hand up, light coming with the movement. He was holding a mass of burning paper.

"No!" Before the words had even left Fang Mu's mouth, the flaming mass had already dropped from the man's hand.

Fang Mu watched wide-eyed as the paper floated closer down to them, twirling, burning, frequently giving off sparks that spun in the air like a beautiful dance of death.

An enormous force suddenly pushed hard into his chest, knocking him back nearly six feet.

In that instant the flaming mass fell through the bars of the cage.

The flaming paper ignited into a ball of fire, roaring flaming light into the previously pitch-black water dungeon.

There was a brief cry from Professor Qiao and then nothing more. He twisted amid the raging flames, his hands tightly gripping the bars of the cage, his whole body shaking.

Fang Mu watched from where he had fallen, watching open-mouthed as Professor Qiao struggled amid the flames.

A scorched odor filled the air...that old familiar scent.

The scent of death.

Suddenly, everything around Fang Mu disappeared. The water dungeon, the cage, Professor Qiao, all of it vanished without a trace...

He was standing in a flaming hallway.

The doors on either side of him were ablaze. He could see the burnt and twisted bodies of Fourth Brother and Wang Jian lying in Room 352.

Where am I?

Someone slowly stood up against the wall. It was Sun Mei. She no longer looked human. She opened her arms. Bones were sticking out. The strips of clothing still covering her bloody flesh smoked and fell to the floor, piece by piece.

"Don't kill anyone else…"

Sun Mei rocked back and forth as she walked slowly toward Fang Mu.

"Don't kill anyone else…"

Why did you have to bring me back?

Why?

Hold me, said an unknown voice. It doesn't matter if you're Sun Mei or Wu Han, I just need to feel the warmth.

Even if it's the feeling of death.

All these years, all this death. I'm already too tired.

Please let me give up.

"Are you listening?" That stern voice. He knew it was Professor Qiao.

"Ahh!" An earth-shattering cry burst from Fang Mu's chest.

With it, everything in front of his eyes disappeared.

Once more he was back in the ice-cold water dungeon. The flame inside the cage was already much smaller. Only a portion of Professor Qiao's body was still burning.

Fang Mu struggled to sit up. He stared silently at the flaming cage before him.

Goodbye, professor.

Fang Mu's tears were already gone. He would not cry again. He pulled the knife from his pocket and tossed away the burdensome sheath. He no longer felt cold at all.

From the light of the flames, he could see the opening above through which he'd fallen. It wasn't far away. The cold-looking ladder stood there silently.

Fang Mu hurried to it. He quickly climbed the rust-covered rungs and looked at the black corridor overhead.

Get up there, he said to himself.

Even if hell is waiting for you.

A few seconds later, Fang Mu once more reached the first floor corridor.

The flames from the water dungeon below lit up the previously dark hallway. Without hesitating, he hurried toward the far end of the corridor.

Cell 3… Cell 5…

Past Cell 5, the corridor came to an end. In front of him was an iron door.

Was Cell 7 on the other side?

Grabbing the door handle, he pulled with all his strength.

The door rumbled open and Fang Mu's eyes were once more met with darkness.

Flicking on his lighter, he discovered that he seemed to have reached the end of the bunker.

Before him stood a cement wall, with a door to either side of it. Unlike the barred doors on the previous cells, these were made of solid iron. The floor was also no longer a wrought-iron see-through walkway, but was made of cement, with a three-square-foot removable iron lid at its center. Beside it sat a plastic barrel. A small amount of red liquid was still inside.

Fang Mu's hands trembled slightly. This was where the gasoline had come from.

Composing himself, he raised his lighter and looked at the number on the door to the right.

7. Just as he'd thought.

He walked over and stood before door number seven for several seconds. At last, he took a deep breath and pushed it open.

The space before him was suddenly filled with bright light. Having grown accustomed to the darkness, Fang Mu couldn't help but shield his eyes.

"Welcome!"

The voice was icy and coming from somewhere in front of him.

Dropping his hand, Fang Mu looked toward the sound of the voice.

Smiling thinly, Sun Pu leaned against the opposite wall, aiming a pistol in Fang Mu's direction.

"You've reached the core of the bunker, Cell Seven." He nodded at something to the side. "The torture room."

Beside him stood a large iron cross on which Tai Wei was bound, hands and legs. Yellow tape covered his mouth. He was staring at Fang Mu, struggling desperately. Although he tried to speak, his words were unintelligible.

"What's wrong? Do you want to say hi to your friend?" Sun Pu laughed darkly. "Or are you begging him to save you?"

He made a show of sighing sorrowfully. "But I'm afraid that our hero won't even be able to protect himself. What do you say to that, shidi?" His attention turned from Tai Wei to Fang Mu. "How did you like my present just now? It was nice, wasn't it?"

Fang Mu stared at him without expression. After a few seconds, he calmly looked away and sized up the room.

Cell 7 was the same size as the other cells, but it was filled with a number of strange iron racks and chairs. There were two ventilation openings in the cement ceiling, allowing the sun to shine through. This was why the room was so bright.

After looking the room over, Fang Mu turned his attention back to Sun Pu. "Not bad," he said. "You planned this all the way from one to seven. It must have taken a lot of thought."

Seeing that Fang Mu appeared to be neither angry nor frightened, Sun Pu seemed a little puzzled. As he looked at Fang Mu, whose behavior was more like that of a curious tourist, his smile started to come a little forced. "That's right," he said. "I just hoped that after all my hard work you wouldn't let me down."

Fang Mu actually smiled. "Is that so? Then what did you hope I'd do?"

Sun Pu's smile disappeared at once. "What did I hope you'd do?" He cocked the pistol. "Why don't you tell me?"

Struggling violently, Tai Wei bellowed something from behind the tape. His wrists had already begun to bleed from the strain.

Fang Mu glanced over at him, still smiling. "Die?" He laughed. "You're not the first person who's wanted to kill me." He paused. "And I'm afraid you won't be the last."

"Oh?" Sun Pu made an exaggerated show of surprise. "Who do you think is going to come save you?" He stomped his foot. "That old piece of shit down there?"

Raising his arm, he pointed the gun barrel at Fang Mu. "The facts have shown that you're nothing more than an overconfident, conceited little fool."

"Really?" Fang Mu stared at the muzzle of the gun. "Is that why you wanted to kill me?" His eyes moved from the gun to Sun Pu's face. "You're jealous of me," he said softly, "isn't that right, shixiong?"

Sun Pu immediately paled.

"Ever since you killed Qu Weiqiang, I've understood what kind of person you are. To cut off a goalie's hands is to deprive him of his power. You're jealous of my intellect, aren't you?"

"Shut up!"

Seeming not to hear, Fang Mu continued unabated. "It started at that assembly, didn't it? When you saw me invited to the stage like a hero while you, just an insignificant librarian, could do nothing but huddle in the corner and watch, lying to yourself that those honors belonged to you!"

"Shut up!"

Again Tai Wei cried out unintelligibly. Looking at him, Fang Mu saw the pleading, worried look that filled his eyes, clearly begging Fang Mu to stop talking.

"So you schemed and schemed, wanting to compete against me one on one." Fang Mu gritted his teeth and slowly stepped backward. "You killed one person after another, all to prove that I was not as good of a criminal profiler as you. But did you really win? Do you really not have nightmares when you sleep at night? Are you still able to make love to your girlfriend? Or did Thomas Gill already turn you…?" Fang Mu smirked, and then his voice abruptly turned serious. "Well? Am I right, shixiong?"

Sun Pu's face suddenly twitched and he pulled the trigger.

Fang Mu instantly dove to the side. At nearly the same moment, he heard the gunshot. A bullet flew past his cheek and smashed into the door of Cell 8.

With no time to think, Fang Mu spun around and sprinted out of the room, pushed open the iron door, and burst into the corridor.

Another bullet cracked from the gun and whizzed into the door.

With his heart nearly bursting from his chest, Fang Mu ran down the corridor and ducked into Cell 5. Panting, he leaned against the wall and tried to catch his breath.

Hurried steps sounded from the corridor outside. Just as they passed the door to his cell, they stopped.

Holding his breath, Fang Mu listened closely.

Sun Pu stood there, breathing heavily. After a few seconds, he laughed. "You made me lose control, shidi." He paused. "Truly disgraceful, no? A shixiong should always be better at keeping his cool than his shidi."

Two gunshots rang out.

Fang Mu quickly calculated; at most Sun Pu had only five bullets left.

Sun Pu knew this, too. The darkness was the best cover he could hope for. Standing in the inky hallway, he didn't dare act rashly. Raising the gun, he listened for movement.

"Where are you, shidi?" he yelled. "Don't hide like a little rat!"

As the echo from his voice slowly vanished, Sun Pu held his breath and listened closely, but no sounds emerged from the darkness.

He laughed wickedly. "Speaking of rats," he said, cautiously stepping forward, "did you like the ones I left for you at Meng Fanzhe's house?"

Squinting, he took stock of his surroundings. "I was originally going to use them to help Meng Fanzhe overcome his fear; I never expected that I would actually end up using them on his mother. You are the reason she died, shidi." His tone brimmed with derision. "If you hadn't been speaking on the phone so loudly in the library hallway, you would have been able to find that letter and catch me a long time ago." He laughed. "Then Zhang Yao and Professor Qiao would still be alive, no?"

At once Fang Mu felt all the blood rush to his head. In that instant, he wanted more than anything to rush into the corridor and stab Sun Pu to death.

Seeming to hear Fang Mu's quickening breath, Sun Pu did his utmost to figure out what direction that minute sound was coming from.

"Angry? Then come out here. Let's see if you're able to avenge their deaths."

Hearing this actually made Fang Mu calm down. Forcing himself to breathe more slowly, he leaned against the wall and didn't move.

Sun Pu listened again. Unable to determine Fang Mu's position, he continued his taunting. "Do you still remember Meng Fanzhe?" He feigned a sorrowful sigh. "What an unlucky kid. You know, I actually liked him a lot, and really did try to help him. It was such a shame that you and Tai

Wei had to give me such a scare that night." He paused. "That's right, I have to admit it, you scared me. I was a little panicked, so what could I do but sacrifice the kid? But you have to acknowledge that it was an effective trick. Meng Fanzhe always was such an obedient kid." He chuckled. "Do you admire me, shidi?"

Fang Mu slowly crouched down and, very gently, felt around with his hand. He soon touched something that felt like the broken leg of a desk.

"When did you guess it was me?" Sun Pu asked, inching forward. "When I began teaching Professor Qiao's class?" He laughed easily. "I knew that was a bit of a risk, but the teacher's lectern is just too enticing for me. Can you understand that?" He took a few steps and stopped, then did so again, all the while paying close attention to the noises around him.

Fang Mu gently pulled on the desk leg. Realizing that it wasn't heavy at all, he quietly picked it up and then stepped cautiously to the cell entrance.

One, two, three...

Fang Mu suddenly burst out of the cell, hurling the desk leg in the direction of the iron door. He immediately slipped into Cell 6.

By the time Sun Pu heard the noise it was already too late. The desk leg smashed forcefully into his nose, the stunning pain making his vision swim. Protecting his face with one hand, he took a few steps back and fired two shots.

Those twin shots rang out.

In the light of the muzzle flash, Sun Pu discovered that the corridor was empty.

Shamed into anger, he rushed forward. Swiftly realizing this unwise, he hurriedly squatted down.

His nose burned and his eyes stung. Something hot was trickling out of his nostrils and down his face. When he wiped it away, his hand came away sticky and sickly sweet.

"Well done..." Sun Pu said, restraining his anger. He forced a smile.

"You're cleverer than I thought, shidi." Spitting out a mouthful of blood, he continued. "You made me bleed, kid. Lucky for you I'm not Ma Kai, otherwise I'd suck all the blood out of your body!"

Startled, Fang Mu couldn't help but say, "Ma Kai?"

The sound gave away his position.

Realizing immediately that Fang Mu was up ahead in Cell 6, Sun Pu gripped his pistol and cautiously drew closer.

"Surprised? That's right; Ma Kai was once my patient, just like Meng Fanzhe. He was ripe for research, but sadly he didn't trust me and ran off after only a few sessions. Later," Sun Pu said, pressing himself against the wall and slowly feeling for the doorway, "when I heard someone was going around killing people and sucking their blood, I knew it had to be him. Do you know what a pleasant surprise that was? I thought that I had finally found an opportunity to prove myself again. I never expected that you would get there first…" He finally felt what seemed to be the doorway. He could faintly hear Fang Mu breathing rapidly inside.

He was on the other side of the wall, right beside the doorway.

"That should make you understand how much I hate you!" Sun Pu burst through the door and spun to the right. At the same instant he aimed and fired at the space just beside the doorway.

The gunshot echoed into the space ahead.

As the bullet flashed from the end of the gun, Sun Pu saw that the direction he had fired in was empty.

Before he could react, Fang Mu leapt from his crouched position at the foot of the wall. He smashed headlong into Sun Pu's chest.

Sun Pu squeezed the trigger and two more bullets burst from the end of the gun. He lost his balance, falling backwards to the floor.

The collision left Fang Mu dizzy as well. Feeling his legs go weak, he fell heavily to the floor.

Across from him, Sun Pu squeezed the trigger again, but the gun clicked emptily.

Relief flooded Fang Mu.

Now you've got no more bullets.

Holding his blade, Fang Mu slowly stood up, pulling out the lighter and flicking it on.

With a small whiff, a little flame appeared in his hand. Despite its size, it clearly illuminated their surroundings.

Sun Pu sat on the ground a few feet away. His face was shining with sweat and he was madly searching for something on his body.

Gripping the knife, Fang Mu walked closer and closer.

Sun Pu tried to scoot back, mumbling, "Don't…don't…"

Seeing the fear and despair in his eyes, Fang Mu felt a burst of retribution.

"Are you scared?" He slowed his steps. "Did the people you killed ever ask you for mercy? Did they?"

"I'm begging you…don't kill me…please…" Sun Pu's voice sounded like he was crying and his eyes seemed to fill with tears.

But in a flash, that penitent look was replaced with a cunning smirk. He suddenly stopped moving backwards. With one hand, he popped the empty magazine out of the gun and snapped another new clip in with the other.

Fang Mu froze. He had more bullets!

He instinctively hurled the lighter at Sun Pu and then turned and ran.

In the blink of an eye, Sun Pu had loaded the ammunition, cocked the gun, and fired two shots in Fang Mu's retreating direction.

Fang Mu felt the bullets whistle past him and slam against the iron bars of the cell across the hallway. Another shot roared from behind him and the bullet smashed into the floor beside his foot.

Fang Mu sprinted to the iron door at the far entrance of the corridor and pushed it as hard as he could, but it wouldn't budge. He felt the door. An iron lock had been placed over the handle.

Behind him another gunshot cracked out. Another bullet struck the door beside him, sending up sparks.

Diving out of the way, Fang Mu scrambled into Cell 1. Having seen Fang Mu escape into Cell 1, Sun Pu slowly stood up and felt the floor around his feet until he found the lighter. He walked down the corridor.

When he reached the entrance to Cell 1, he flicked on the lighter.

One side of the room was stacked with old, broken-down desks and chairs. The other side was empty.

Sun Pu chuckled, unable to contain his satisfaction. "Tai Wei had an extra clip on him. You didn't know?"

Fang Mu was lying behind the desks and chairs, his heart filled with fear and hatred.

Damn, I was too careless.

"You want to try again, shidi?" Sun Pu asked, sounding as if he thought victory was already assured. "Will you still not admit that you've lost?"

Fang Mu's knife hand began to tremble. His opponent still had three bullets and he knew where Fang Mu was hiding. His death was just a matter of time.

Is this how it's going to end?

"Are you really going to be this stubborn?" Sun Pu sighed dramatically. "You're just like that old fool, you know that?"

Professor Qiao…

"Do what you have to do, using your own methods."

"That's right, I am like Professor Qiao," Fang Mu said, slowly and carefully climbing to his feet. He pressed himself against the wall in the narrow space between it and the desks. "But do you know what the difference is between us and you?"

"Oh?" Sun Pu sounded a little surprised. "What difference is that?"

"You really are an excellent psychological profiler," Fang Mu said, keeping an eye on the light in the doorway. "But you're soulless. Therefore you lack the sense of duty and respect that your profession demands. Everything you've done has been for yourself alone. We, on the other hand, are willing to sacrifice our own lives to protect those of others."

At that moment, Fang Mu finally understood why Professor Qiao had made no sound when he died in the flames.

Killing him had been Sun Pu's final attempt to send Fang Mu into a psychological breakdown. He knew that flames, the scent of burning flesh, and the anguished cries of pain would awaken Fang Mu's most devastating memories. But Professor Qiao knew this as well. Therefore, he had kept quiet, even as he was being burned alive, because he wanted to lessen the psychological impact on Fang Mu.

"Shut up! You're talking nonsense!" Sun Pu's voice trembled as he stepped inside the room.

Fang Mu carefully shifted his body.

"Do you know why Professor Qiao despised you and favored me?"

"You're just an idiotic bungler!" Sun Pu yelled, his voice a little hoarse from the strain. "I'm ten thousand times stronger than you, a million times!"

Fang Mu slowly slid toward the space between all the desks and chairs.

Gradually he drew closer and closer to the doorway.

"In fact," Fang Mu said, "you're just an arrogant man who doesn't know a thing; a pitiful wretch whose only chance to save face was to torture a confession out of the wrong man!"

"Shut up!" It was the last wrong thing to say for Sun Pu, driving him past any logic. He charged wildly into the room, firing in Fang Mu's direction.

Fang Mu smashed his whole body against the enormous pile of desks and chairs, toppling them forward with a crashing roar. Standing beneath them, Sun Pu only had time to scream in surprise before they showered down on him.

Fang Mu also fell forward, landing on an upside down desk. Ignoring the sharp pain in his calf, he scrambled over to where Sun Pu had fallen.

Sun Pu had just thrown one of the desks off and was groping desperately for the fallen gun.

Fang Mu grabbed a chair and smashed it over Sun Pu's head.

The force of the blow broke the chair to pieces and opened a huge cut in Sun Pu's head. The gash immediately gushed blood.

Kneeling on Sun Pu's chest, Fang Mu brought his dagger to Sun Pu's throat with lightning speed. "Move again and I'll slice you open!"

Sun Pu opened his mouth, and then his head fell to the side and he lay still.

Picking up the pistol, Fang Mu looked at the suddenly comatose Sun Pu. He held the gun to his face.

Fang Mu's chest rapidly rose and fell and his teeth chattered as he struggled within himself, glaring down at the man responsible for so much death, his finger wanting to squeeze the trigger. After a few seconds, he slowly lowered the gun. He bent over, grabbed Sun Pu's collar, and with difficulty, dragged him out of Cell 1.

The way back felt unimaginably long. Now that he had lost consciousness, Sun Pu's body was incredibly heavy. By the time Fang Mu managed to drag him back into Cell 7, he was beyond exhausted.

Tai Wei hung limply from the cross, his eyes half-closed and his wrists bloody and torn. Hearing the sound of movement, he looked up. When he saw Fang Mu walk into the room, covered in filth and dragging the blood-covered Sun Pu behind him, his face registered first surprise and then absolute triumph. With newfound strength, he bellowed something and struggled against his shackles.

After dragging and dropping Sun Pu to the middle of the room, Fang Mu stood upright and panted for breath. He walked over and ripped the tape from Tai Wei's mouth.

Ignoring the pain caused by the tape tearing from his lips, Tai Wei immediately asked, "What happened? Is he dead?"

"Not yet," said Fang Mu weakly. He knelt and used his knife to cut the rope around Tai Wei's feet. When he was done, he forced himself to stand up and looked at Tai Wei's chained, bloody wrists. "Where's the key?"

"It's probably on his body. Go and check."

Fang Mu nodded and walked shakily over to Sun Pu. Kneeling beside him, he went through his pockets.

He could feel that the key was inside the breast pocket of Sun Pu's jacket, but the zipper was broken from the fight and wouldn't budge. Pulling out his knife, Fang Mu prepared to cut it open.

Suddenly, the motionless Sun Pu began to laugh.

Startled, Fang Mu leapt to his feet, grabbed the pistol and aimed it at him.

His face covered in blood and filth, Sun Pu opened his swollen eyes a crack and looked at Fang Mu and Tai Wei. The more he laughed, the more pleased with himself he seemed to become.

The sound of his hoarse laughter reverberated in the empty room, growing so loud that it was impossible to endure.

"Stop laughing!" Fang Mu's hands shook slightly as he held the pistol. He felt like Sun Pu's laughter was beating against his own heart. "I'm telling you – stop laughing!"

"You…you really think you've beaten me?" Sun Pu said, coughing as he laughed.

"Pah!" Tai Wei spat on the floor, looking as if there was nothing he wanted to do more than rush over and kick Sun Pu in the face. "You still won't admit it's over? The only thing left for you is to wait for your own execution!"

"My execution?" Sun Pu suddenly stopped laughing and made a strange face. "I've got a mental disorder! I'm a madman! You really think they're gonna execute me?"

Fang Mu's heart fell. No one knew the finer points of mental illness better than Sun Pu. If he really did try to play mad, he just might be able to get away with it.

Fang Mu turned and looked at Tai Wei. He was also staring dumbstruck at Sun Pu, as if he had never expected the guy would try to play this card.

"Stop dreaming!" yelled Tai Wei. "You think the medical experts at the courthouse are all idiots?" His voice was firm, but it was obvious that he lacked confidence in the words.

Ignoring him, Sun Pu prattled on to himself, sounding just like a madman. "After receiving unjust treatment and with no way to shake his despondent mood, a sensitive criminologist finally lost his mind and made a big mistake. Ha!" An exuberant look on his face, he continued. "Well, you two, what do you think?"

His face pale, Fang Mu stared at Sun Pu.

"You're both welcome to come visit me at the mental institution," Sun Pu said, sounding just as insane. "I'll buy you something to eat! What would you like? How about barbecue? What do you say, shidi?" Propping his head up with his arm, he gave Fang Mu a big smile. "Barbecue, mm..." He chuckled. "I just love that smell…"

With a roar, Fang Mu dove on Sun Pu and pinned him to the floor.

Tossing the knife aside, he clamped his hand over Sun Pu's mouth and pressed the barrel of the gun against his forehead.

Tears fell from Fang Mu's eyes as his whole body trembled with rage.

Jin Qiao, curled up inside the packing box…

Meng Fanzhe, with no hope of being saved…

Professor Qiao, dying in silence…

You can't let him get away…

You can't!

Fang Mu cocked the pistol. This action seemed to excite Sun Pu and he began to yell, his words muffled behind Fang Mu's hand.

"Do it…. Come on… Kill me…"

The muscles in Fang Mu's face twitched as he stared at Sun Pu. The look in the guy's eyes seemed to be taunting him on… It would be so easy…

Just one light pull of the trigger…

And this demon would be sent straight to hell…

"Don't shoot, Fang Mu!" Tai Wei shouted. "That's what he wants you to do! Don't fall for it!"

Fang Mu's body shook. He placed his finger firmly against the trigger.

A shot rang out.

And then another.

Tai Wei sadly looked away. It was over. Fang Mu had gotten his payback. But the price was too high. Suddenly he heard a sharp sound. A moment later something seemed to roll beneath his feet.

He looked down. It was a spent bullet shell.

He quickly looked up.

Sun Pu's head was still whole. His eyes were tightly shut and he seemed to be holding his breath, his face red from the effort.

Less than two inches above the top of his head, two shallow holes had been chipped into the cement.

Fang Mu was still in the same position, his arms outstretched and holding the gun. Smoke rose from the barrel. The clip was empty.

After a long moment, he tore open Sun Pu's pocket and grabbed the keys. Sun Pu finally exhaled.

Looking at Sun Pu's startled face, Fang Mu smirked and stood up. He slowly and clearly said, "Is that how you wanted to die? It won't be that easy. You'll have to wait for the execution ground."

He pulled Professor Qiao's fountain pen from his pocket and waved it in front of Sun Pu's face. "You think this is just an ordinary pen?"

He turned around and walked over to Tai Wei.

Tai Wei sighed with relief. He was about to praise Fang Mu, when he saw the student do something very odd. With one hand, Fang Mu reached inside his collar and seemed to pull something out.

Sun Pu lay where he was on the floor for a few seconds, staring up at the ceiling. Suddenly his eyes went wide.

He struggled to his feet; one of his hands brushed against Fang Mu's knife.

With a surge, he seemed suddenly imbued with supernatural strength. Leaping forward, he grabbed hold of the blade and sprinted toward Fang Mu.

Tai Wei saw the attack coming. He felt his heart seize up. Just as he was about to warn Fang Mu, he was dumbstruck by the look on the student's face.

Fang Mu was gazing casually at Tai Wei, a faint smile playing across his lips.

That's right, it seemed to say. I know exactly what Sun Pu is doing behind my back. And I also know that he has my knife in his hand.

Calmly, in a controlled manner, Fang Mu tore the bullet from his necklace and snapped it in the pistol chamber. He gently cocked the gun. With a click, the hammer fell back into place.

He even had time to raise an eyebrow at Tai Wei.

You still remember this bullet? his look seemed to ask.

He turned and raised the gun. Suddenly the figure before Fang Mu wasn't merely Sun Pu; it was simultaneously – impossibly – Wu Han and Sun Pu, seemingly to merge, both raising the same knife and facing Fang Mu.

It doesn't matter who you are. This case is closed. Fang Mu pulled the trigger.

In an instant a small hole appeared in Sun Pu's forehead and his head snapped back, absorbing the blast. A stream of blood and bone burst from the back of his skull as the bullet exited.

He fell back onto the floor.

Ding. A brass shell struck lightly against the floor. Tai Wei's mouth was wide open, and not until the sound of the gunshot slowly disappeared from Cell 7 did it finally close.

Fang Mu slowly placed the gun on the floor, feeling as if the last bit of strength had been pulled out of him. For a moment he looked at Sun Pu's body where it twitched on the floor.

Then he turned, unlocked Tai Wei's shackles, and helped him off the cross. The cop's whole body was stiff.

Doing his best to avoid Tai Wei's puzzled, fearful eyes, Fang Mu said quietly: "Come on; let's get out of here."

EPILOGUE

At the Jiangbin City police lockup, Fang Mu slept peacefully for several nights. He didn't dream at all.

As he had requested, Tai Wei arranged it so that he could have his own cell. All of his meals were takeout, and each morning he was given the day's newspaper and a pack of expensive Zhonghua cigarettes.

When he didn't feel like doing anything else, Fang Mu would lie on his iron bed and look out the window, silently watching the clouds pass and day turn to night.

Occasionally Fang Mu would think of those who had passed, the things that had happened. But now he was much more at peace and it seemed like it would be difficult for anything to shake him.

So this is all that it feels like to have killed someone.

A few days later, officers from the PSB discovered an abundance of evidence in Sun Pu's home proving that he had committed all the murders. Someone was then sent to Jiangbin City University to inform them of the situation, and Meng Fanzhe's name was officially cleared. At the same time, it was determined that Fang Mu had acted in self-defense and the case was closed. Tai Wei's testimony had been the critical factor.

Fang Mu's only regret was that he had been unable to attend Professor

Qiao's memorial service.

It was Tai Wei who came to let Fang Mu out of his cell.

The day was clear and bright. As Fang Mu walked out of the detention house, the sun was shining overhead. He bathed in its warmth, his whole body pleasantly tingling. Like many of those on the street around him, he couldn't help but raise his arms and stretch.

When they reached the jeep, Tai Wei gave Fang Mu his belongings, including the fountain pen. Fang Mu looked the pen over for a long time, and then placed it carefully in his breast pocket.

Tai Wei watched this and then suddenly asked: "You did all that on purpose, right?" He pointed at the pen. "That's just a regular pen."

Fang Mu didn't respond. He knew that Tai Wei hadn't mentioned what happened with the pen when he testified.

Seeing that Fang Mu wasn't going to answer, Tai Wei didn't ask anything else, just silently started the jeep.

When they reached the school gates later, something suddenly occurred to Tai Wei.

"Oh, that's right." He searched in his pockets as the jeep sat at the school entry. "I meant to give this to you, too."

He handed something to Fang Mu. It was the dagger.

Fang Mu didn't immediately take it from him. For a few seconds he just stared at it, not saying a word. Finally he grabbed it.

"I'm gonna head back," he said, his voice low. Then he hopped out of the vehicle.

After he had gone a few steps toward the gates, Tai Wei called out to him.

This guy is always like this, huh? thought Fang Mu.

He turned around.

Frowning, Tai Wei looked into his eyes.

After a long moment, he asked: "You remember how I once recommended that you become a cop?"

"Yeah."

Tai Wei looked down, thinking deeply about something. A few seconds later, he looked back up. In a determined tone, he said, "I take it back."

He drove off.

Fang Mu watched the jeep disappear into the distance. Then he smiled, turned, and walked through the gate.

Today was the last day of finals. Unable to wait any longer, the students who had finished their tests had already packed their stuff into boxes and were heading to the train station. Amid this crowd of homeward-bound students, Fang Mu walked slowly toward Dormitory 5.

When he was back inside Room 304, Fang Mu sat on the bed and looked at all the papers still stacked on the desk. Touching them, he found they were covered with dust.

After sitting in silence for a while, he began to organize his things.

At this point he had finished everything he needed to do. There was no reason to stay here any longer. That afternoon he would go to the graduate student office and apply to switch dorms.

Fang Mu didn't have much stuff, and before long he had packed all of it up. After brushing the dust from his hands, he grabbed his washbasin and towel and then opened the door.

He frowned.

A bunch of people were standing in the hallway, Du Yu among them. They were all looking at Fang Mu as he walked out of the room.

He was stunned.

Du Yu walked over and stood in front of him. He looked at him for several seconds, and then at Room 304.

"You packed your stuff?" he asked, turning back to Fang Mu. "You're leaving here?"

"Yeah," Fang Mu said. Not wanting to have to say anything else, he walked past Du Yu.

"Hey!" Du Yu called from behind him. "What about your promise?"

Fang Mu turned back around. "What?"

Du Yu gave him a cold look. "You promised me that when you found the killer I would be the first to know."

Fang Mu was briefly taken aback. Shaking his head, he smirked and then turned to go.

"You're just gonna leave like this?"

Unable to help himself, Fang Mu was about to say, "What else do you want me to do?" but when he turned around, he saw that Du Yu was smiling at him.

"What if someone else like Sun Pu appears? What are we supposed to do then?" Du Yu, nudged Zou Tuanjie, who was standing beside him. Taking the hint, Zou Tuanjie winked at Fang Mu and then waved the guys around him into Room 304.

Du Yu was still looking at Fang Mu as he had before. "So, you have to stay."

He slowly walked over to Fang Mu as their dorm-mates bustled about around them, moving Fang Mu's stuff back into Room 313.

Du Yu stood in front of Fang Mu for a moment, and then gave him a sudden punch to the shoulder.

"There's some more good news. Liu Jianjun called me today. He's doing a lot better, and says he'll probably be back real soon."

Two months later.

Winter was already almost over. Still wearing a thick cotton coat, Fang Mu walked through Changhong City Teacher's College campus. Before long he was drenched with perspiration.

Liu Jianjun had just sent Fang Mu a text message, telling him happily that he was already able to walk slowly on his own. As Fang Mu smelled the sweet scent of trees budding in the air, his mood felt just as brilliant as the weather.

The ice had already thawed on Jing Lake and Fang Mu could see the water drift back and forth like fine gauze. On the opposite bank where a patch of willow trees had once stood, there was now a small store. Its loudspeaker was playing a familiar song: Boundless as the Sea and Sky.

"I chased you through the wind and rain, I lost you in the mist, the sea and sky will never change, but will we stay the same...? "

Fang Mu found a rock on the bank of the lake and sat down. He thought of how he had looked two years ago, when he had to walk around with a cane. A smile came to his lips.

"In the blink of an eye I lost myself, and the love in my heart grew dim – Who will still love me...? "

He pulled the knife from his pocket and looked it over.

The bottom of the dark-green handle used to be bumpy from having been burnt in the flames. Now the material had already been made smooth and shiny from the caress of his hand.

He unsheathed the blade and its sharp edge glinted in the sunlight. Gently, Fang Mu ran his thumb along the serrated edge, feeling the ridges against his skin.

The knife had already followed two owners, had witnessed too many things. Back when it was gradually put together on some crude assembly line, it probably never expected that it would lead such a full life.

Now it just lay in Fang Mu's hands, happily enjoying its owner's attentions, as if it had already forgotten what a terrifying weapon it had been when held by those two other people.

In the end, a knife was just a knife.

Why must people hold them responsible for so much?

Fang Mu laughed quietly. What does a knife know about responsibility? In the final analysis, only we can take the blame.

He stood up, weighed the knife in his hand, and then suddenly launched it over the lake.

The knife shone in the sunlight as it arced through the air. Then with a plop it dropped beneath the water. A few small ripples drifted out from the spot, but soon the lake was just as placid as before.

Goodbye, Wu Han.

(To be continued)

ABOUT THE AUTHOR

Lei Mi, formerly known as Liu Peng, a teacher of criminal psychology at China Criminal Police University, is well versed in both criminal psychology and forensic science. His career has given him insight into all sorts of crime, perhaps more so than most people learn in a lifetime. Having become known across the internet for psychological thrillers such as his Criminal Minds series, he has attracted countless fans. His major works include The Seven Readers (published as a serial novel from July to September 2006 in Legends from Today and Ancient Times: End of the Month Stories, and won their prize for best suspense story of 2006), Profiler, Skinner's Box, Blade of Silence, and City Lights. Lei Mi currently teaches in Shenyang.

CPSIA information can be obtained at www.ICGtesting.com
Printed in the USA
LVOW07s1949010813

345842LV00016B/326/P